Engine
City

Tor Books by Ken MacLeod

THE FALL REVOLUTION

The Star Fraction
The Stone Canal
The Cassini Division
The Sky Road

THE ENGINES OF LIGHT

Cosmonaut Keep
Dark Light
Engine City

Engine
City

KEN MACLEOD

A TOM DOHERTY ASSOCIATES BOOK
NEW YORK

ENGINE CITY

Copyright © 2003 by Ken MacLeod

This book is printed on acid-free paper.

A Tor Book
Published by Tom Doherty Associates, LLC
175 Fifth Avenue
New York, NY 10010

www.tor.com

Tor® is a registered trademark of Tom Doherty Associates, LLC.

ISBN 0-765-30502-X

First Edition: January 2003

Printed in the United States of America

0 9 8 7 6 5 4 3 2 1

To Carol, with love

ACKNOWLEDGMENTS

Thanks to Carol, Sharon, and Michael, as always; to Andrew Greig for listening about light-years; and to Farah Mendlesohn for reading and commenting on the first draft.

There is no middle path between these two, for a man must either be a free and true commonwealth's man, or a monarchical tyrannical royalist.

Kingly government governs the earth by that cheating art of buying and selling, and thereby becomes a man of contention, his hand is against every man, and every man's hand is against him; and take this government at the best, it is a diseased government, and the very city Babylon, full of confusion.

—Gerard Winstanley, *The Law of Freedom in a Platform* (1651)

Contents

Engine
City

Prologue: States of Mind

·

T HE GOD WHO later became known as the asteroid 10049 Lora, and shortly afterwards as the ESA mining station *Marshal Titov*, was not unusual of its kind. Around the Sun, as with most stars, gods swarm like flies around a sacrifice. Life arises from states of matter. From some of these states of matter arise states of mind.

In the asteroids and cometary bodies the units of life were extremophile nanobacteria. Regulating their ultra-cold molecular processes, the vanishingly tiny temperature differentials, detecting the quantum signature of usable energy—over millions of years, these and other selective advantages drove the development of delicate networks adapted to processing information. Random variations in the effects of their activities on the asteroid's outgassings and on the glacially slow transport of mass within it were selected for whenever they resulted in more stable orbits and fewer collisions. Increasingly complex networks formed. Subjectivity flickered into being on trillions of separate sites within each life-bearing asteroid or cometary mass.

Those within 10049 Lora found themselves in a society of other such minds, exchanging information across light-hours. They had much to learn, and many to learn from. Billions of years of evolutionary fine-tuning had given the cometary and asteroid minds an exquisite sensitivity to the electromagnetic output of each other's internal chemical and physical processes.

Communication, exchange of information and material between cometary clouds, became rumor that ran around the galaxy's outer reaches, which ring like residential suburbs its industrial core where the heavy elements are forged.

Just as minds are built from smaller information exchangers—neurons or bacteria or switches—so from the vast assembly of intercommunicating minds within the asteroid emerged a greater phenomenon, a sum of those minds: a god. It was aware of the smaller minds, of their vast civilizations and long histories. It was also aware of itself and others like itself. Its component minds, in moments of introspection or exaltation, were aware of it. In moments of enlightened contemplation, which could last millennia, the god was aware of a power of which it was a part: the sum of all the gods within the Solar System. That solar god, too, had its peers, but whether they in their turn were part of some greater entity was a subject on which lesser minds could only speculate.

On Earth, evolution worked out differently. On its surface, the multicellular trick took off. Beneath the surface, the extremophile microorganisms that riddled the lithosphere and made up the bulk of the planet's life formed extensive interacting networks which became attuned to the electromagnetic fields of the planet and its atmosphere. Constantly disrupted by processes far more violent than those of the smaller celestial bodies, they attained the level of symbolic thought, but never quite intelligence. Earth's mind—Gaia—was like that of a pre-verbal child or an animal. Its thoughts were dreams, afterimages, abstractions that floated free and illuminated like sheet lightning.

The large squid of the genus *Architeuthys*, which men later called krakens, were the first real intelligences on Earth, and the ones whose outlook on life was closest to that of the gods. They communicated by varying the colored patterns of the chromatophores on their skins. The minute electrical currents thus generated interacted with the electromagnetic flux of the planet and were amplified by it to come to the cometary minds' acutely sensitive attention. Responses tickled back from the sky. As the gods began to make sense of the squids' sensoria—a research project which kept the equivalent of a billion civilizations' worth of scientists happily occupied for several centuries—they modified their own internal models accordingly. The visible spectrum and the visual field burst upon astonished inner eyes. Sight dawned for the gods, and enlightenment for the squid. Megayears of happy and fertile intellectual intercourse followed.

Towards the end of the Cretaceous period, alien ships emerged from nowhere. Their occupants were warm-blooded, eight-limbed, eight-eyed, and furry. Celestial minds were already familiar phenomena to them. They swarmed across the Solar System, cracking memetic and genetic codes as they went. They talked to the gods with their noisy radio systems, gibber, jabber, boasting in technical detail of the lightspeed drive and the antigravity engine. Their discoid skiffs scooted through the skies of all the planets. They flashed banks of lights at the kraken schools. They listened to the collective voice of the Martian biosphere, which in all its long dying never rose above a sad, rusty croak.

They made friends. They found a promising species of small, bipedal, tailless dinosaurs and fiddled with their genes. The new saurs were intelligent and long-lived. The octopods taught the saurs how to fly skiffs. (Gaia took the saurs and skiffs into her dreams, and spun shining images of them in plasma and ball lightning, but nobody noticed back then.) They dangled the prospect of space travel before the kraken. Many of the squids pounced at the chance. The octopods designed ships and skiffs; the saurs built them and flew the skiffs; the krakens embraced the algorithms of interstellar navigation. Long ships, whose pilots swam in huge aquaria, blinked away.

By this time, one thought in the baffled minds of the gods resonated from one side of the Oort cloud to the other: KEEP THE NOISE DOWN! The radiation noise and the endless blether of information were not the worst irritations. Despite all appeals, the octopods persisted in digging on the surfaces of asteroids and comets. They itched like nits. Some saurs and kraken began to see the gods' point of view, but they were unable to convince the octopods. The cometary minds made small, cumulative changes in their orbits, nudging a metallic asteroid onto a trajectory that ended on the octopods' single city and brought the Cretaceous epoch to a cataclysmic close.

The destruction appalled even the gods. The octopods and their allies fled, while the saurs and krakens who remained behind labored to repair the damage done. They still had skiffs and ships. Laden with rescued specimens and genetic material, lightspeed ships traveled to the other side of the galaxy. The saurs selected a volume about two hundred light-years across and seeded scores of terrestrial planets—some hastily and blatantly terraformed—with the makings of new biospheres. Saurs and kraken settled the new planets, originally as ecological engineering teams, later as colonists. Others returned to the Solar System, to bring more species. The traffic was to continue for the next sixty-five million years.

Echoes and rumors of other conflicts circulated around the galaxy. The kraken picked them up from the gods in the newly settled systems and passed them on to the saurs. In those multiple translations, subtleties were lost. Knowledge of the past became tradition, then religion. Gradually, the saurs, in what they came to call the Second Sphere, diverged from those in the Solar System. Meetings between the two branches of the species became mute, and matings sterile.

In the Second Sphere, a quiet and contented civilization was held together by the kraken-navigated starships that plied between its suns. It assimilated new arrivals at intervals of centuries. Some fast, bright mammals increasingly reminded the saurs of the octopods. Lemurs and lorises, apes and monkeys, successive species of hominid; bewildered, furious bands of hunters, tribes of farmers, villages of artisans, caravans of missing merchants, legions of the lost. The saurs' patient answers to their frequently asked questions became the catechism of a rational but zealous creed. Yes, the gods live in the sky. No, they do not listen to prayers. No, they do not tell us what to do. Their first and last commandment is: Do not disturb us.

Slowly, with the help of the saurs and the two other surviving species of hominid, the transplanted humans built a civilization of their own, whose center was a city that never fell.

For the gods in the Solar System, the human civilization of the Second Sphere was a history too recent for them to have heard of. They knew only that the saurs' snatch-squads continued their work with ever-increasing caution as the human population grew. The clutter of images generated by Gaia's excitable response to the saurs' presence provided the perfect cover for their activities. The gods had real aliens to worry about. The starships might bring back news from the Second Sphere a hundred thousand years out of date, but they collected much more recent news in their occasional stops on the way back. From these the gods learned that the octopods were a few tens of light-years away, and heading toward the Solar System.

The god in 10049 Lora had already lived a long life when it and its peers noticed the rising electronic racket from Earth. It volunteered to swing by for a closer look. It absorbed the contents of the Internet in seconds, and then found, microseconds later, that it was already out of date. It was still struggling with the exponential growth when the European Union's cosmonauts arrived. To them, it was a convenient Near-Earth Object, and a possible source of raw materials for further expansion.

The humans had plans for the Solar System, the god discovered—plans that made the past octopod incursion seem like a happy memory. But the coming octopod incursion might be still worse. If the humans could expand into space without the devastatingly profligate use of resources that their crude rocket technology required, an elegant solution could be expected to the presence of both species of vermin.

Bypassing the local saurs, who were quite incapable of dealing with the problem, the god scattered information about the interstellar drive and the gravity skiff across the Earth's datasphere. Several top-secret military projects were already apparently inspired by glimpses of skiff technology, but their sponsors unaccountably failed to take the hint. (In their mutual mental transparency, the celestial minds found the concepts of lies, fiction, and disinformation difficult to grasp.) The minds within 10049 Lora opened communication with the cosmonauts on its surface, where the ESA mining station *Marshal Titov* was giving the god a severe headache.

Having their computers hacked into by a carbonaceous chondrite came as a surprise to the cosmonauts. In the sudden glut of information, they failed to notice the instructions for a radical new technology of space travel until it was almost too late. Politics dictated first that the contact should be secret, then that it should be public. Political and military conflicts resulted in a mutiny on the station. Before the space marines of the European People's Army could arrive to suppress it, the cosmonauts built a lightspeed drive that took the entire station away. They thought they had understood how to navigate it. They had not. It returned to its default setting, and arrived at the Second Sphere.

Before their departure, one of the cosmonauts made sure that the instructions distributed by the god would not be ignored, and could not be hidden. The gods approved. Soon the noisy humans would be somebody else's problem.

I

The Very City Babylon

I

The Advancement of Learning

T HE JUMP IS instantaneous. To a photon, the whole history of the universe may be like this: over in a flash, before it's had time to blink. To a human, it's disorienting. One moment, you're an hour out from the last planet you visited—then, without transition, you're an hour away from the next.

Volkov spent the first of these hours preparing for his arrival, conscious that he would have no time to do so in the second.

My name is Grigory Andreievich Volkov. I am two hundred and forty years old, I was born about a hundred thousand years ago, and as many light-years away: Kharkov, Russian Federation, Earth, in the year 2018. As a young conscript, I fought in the Ural Caspian Oil War. I was with the first troops to enter Marseilles and to bathe their sore feet in the waters of the Mediterranean. In 2040, I became a cosmonaut of the European Union, and three years later made the first human landing on the surface of Venus. In 2046 I volunteered for work on the space station *Marshal Titov*, which in 2049 was renamed the *Bright Star*. It became the first human-controlled starship. In it I traveled to the Second Sphere. For the past two centuries I have lived on Mingulay and Croatan.

This is my first visit to Nova Terra. I hope to bring you . . .

What? The secret of immortality?

Yes. *The secret of immortality.* That would do.

Strictly speaking, what he hoped to bring was the secret of longevity. But he had formed an impression of the way science was conducted on Nova Terra: secular priestcraft, enlightened obscurantism; alchemy, philosophy, scholia. A trickle of inquiry after immortality had exhausted hedge-magic, expanded herbalism, lengthened little but grey beards and the index of the Pharmacopia, and remained respectable. Volkov expected to be introduced to the Academy as a prodigy. Before the shaving-mirror, he polished his speech and rehearsed his Trade Latin.

The suds and stubble swirled away. He slapped a stinging cologne on his cheeks, gave himself an encouraging smile, and stepped out of the cramped washroom. The ship's human quarters were sparse and provisional. In an emergency, or at the owners' convenience, they could be flooded. In normal operation, it was usual to travel in one or other of the skiffs, which at this moment were racked on the vast curving sides of the forward chamber like giant silver platters. The air smelled of paint and seawater; open channels and pools divided the floor, and on the walls enormous transparent pipes contained columns of water that rose or fell, functioning as lifts for the ship's crew. Few humans, and fewer saurs, were about in the chamber. Volkov strolled along a walkway. At its end, a low rail enclosed the pool of the navigator. Eyes the size of beach balls reflected racing bands of color from the navigator's chromatophores and the surrounding instrumentation. Wavelets from the rippling mantle perturbed the water. Lashing tentacles broke the surface as they played over the controls.

Volkov was halfway up the ladder to the skiff in which he had spent most, and intended to spend the rest, of the brief journey, when the lightspeed jump took place. The sensation was so swift and subtle that it did not endanger his step or grasp. He was aware that it had happened, that was all. In a moment of idle curiosity—for he'd never been within sight of a ship's controller at such a moment—he glanced sideways and down, to the watery cockpit twenty-odd meters below.

The navigator floated in the middle of the pool. His body had turned an almost translucent white. Volkov was perturbed, but could think of nothing better to do than scramble faster up the ladder to the skiff.

The door opened and he stepped inside, rejoining his hosts. Esias de Tenebre stood staring at the display panel, as though he could read the racing glyphs that to Volkov meant nothing. Feet well apart, hands in his trouser pockets, his stout and muscular frame bulked further by his heavy sweater, his shock of hair spilling from under his seaman's cap. Though in the rough-duty clothes that merchants traditionally wore on board ship, he had all the stocky and cocky dignity of Holbein's Henry—one who did not kill his wives, all three of whom stood beside him. Lydia, the daughter of Esias and Faustina, lounged on the circular seat around the central engine fairing behind her parents, returning Volkov's appeasing look with sullen lack of interest. Black hair you could swim in, brown eyes you could drown in, golden skin you could bask in. Her oversized sweater and baggy canvas trousers only added to her charm. The other occupant of the vehicle was its pilot, Voronar, who sat leaning forward past Esias.

"What's going on?"

The saur's elliptical eyes spared Volkov a glance, then returned to the display.

"Nothing out of the ordinary," said Voronar. His large head, which lent his slender reptilian body an almost infantile proportion, tipped forward, then nodded. "We are an hour away from Nova Terra."

"Could you possibly show us the view?" said Esias.

"Your pardon," said Voronar.

He palmed the controls, and the entire surrounding wall of the skiff became pseudotransparent, patching data from the ship's external sensors and automatically adjusting brightness and contrast: Nova Sol's glare was turned down, the crescent of Nova Terra muted to a cool blue, its night side enhanced. Scattered clusters of crowded lights pricked the dark like pleiads.

"That's a lot of cities," Volkov said.

Compared with anywhere else he'd seen in the Second Sphere, if not with the Earth he remembered, it was.

"There's only one that matters," said Esias. He did not need to point it out.

Nova Babylonia was the jewel of the Second Sphere. Its millennia-old culture, and its younger but still ancient republican institutions, made it peacefully hegemonic on Nova Terra, and beyond. The temperate zones of Nova Terra's continents were placid parks, where even wildernesses were carefully planned landscape features. All classes of its people were content. Academicians and artists assimilated the latest ideas and styles that trickled in over the millennia from Earth; patricians and politicians debated cordially and congratulated themselves on their fortune in knowing, and avoiding, the home world's terrible mistakes. Merchants traded the rare goods of many worlds. Artisans and laborers enjoyed the advantages of a division of labor far wider than any the human species could have sustained on its own. Emigration was free, but the proportion of emigrants insignificant. The hominidae cheerfully tended and harvested the sources of raw materials, and the saurs and krakens exchanged their advanced products and services for those of human industry and craft. As an older and wiser species, the saurs were consulted to settle disputes, and as a more powerful species, they intervened to prevent any from getting out of hand.

The lights of Nova Babylonia shone just short of the terminator, and somewhat to the north of the halfway point between the pole and the equator. Genea, the continent on whose eastern shore the city stood, sprawled diagonally across the present night side of the planet and southward into the day and the southern hemisphere. Its ragged coastline counterpointed that of the other major continent, Sauria, a couple of thousand kilometers west:

the two looked as though they had been pulled apart and displaced, one northward, the other south. Much of the southern and western part of Sauria was wrapped out of sight around the other side of the planet, at this moment; in the visible part, even at this distance, the rectangular regularity of some of its green patches distinguished manufacturing plant from jungle and plain.

"Do any humans live in Sauria?" Volkov asked.

Esias shrugged. "A few thousand, maybe, at any one time. Short-term contract employees, traders, people involved in travel infrastructure and big-game hunting. Likewise with saurs in Genea—lots of individuals, no real communities, except around the hospitals and health services."

Hospitals and health services, yes, Volkov thought, that could be a problem.

"What about the other hominidae?"

"Ah, that's a more usual distribution, except that they have entire cities of their own." Esias pointed; it wasn't much help. "Gigants here, pithkies there. Forests and mines, even some farming. More of a surprise than the cities, that; it's only developed in the last few centuries. They've always been herding, of course."

As the ship's approach zoomed the view, the city and its surroundings expanded and sharpened. The immediate vicinity and hinterland of the city was a long, triangular promontory, about a thousand kilometers from northwest to southeast and five hundred across at its widest extent. It looked like a smaller and narrower India: an island that had rammed the continent at an angle. Very likely it was—the ice of a spectacular and recent mountain range glittered white across the join. The west coast of this mini subcontinent was separated from the mainland of Genea by a semicircular sea, three hundred kilometers across at its widest, its shore curving to almost meet the end of the promontory just south of the metropolis. From the mountains sprang a dozen or so rivers whose confluence channeled about halfway down to one major river, which flowed into the sea near the tapered tip. The central, and oldest, part of Nova Babylonia was on an island about ten kilometers long that looked wedged in that river's mouth.

The city drifted off center in the view, then swung out of sight entirely as the ship leveled up for its run into the atmosphere. Why the great starships approached on what resembled a long, shallow glide path was unknown, and certainly unnecessary, but it was what they always did. The air reddened around the ship's field and, following another unnecessary and invariable habit, its human passengers returned to their seats.

Volkov leaned on the rail of the open sea-level deck of the starship and gasped morning-cool fresh air. The starship had, to the best of his knowledge, no air-recycling or air-circulating mechanisms whatsoever, and after a couple of hours even its vast volume of air grew slightly but noticeably stale. Around him, unregarded, the ship's unlading went on, bales into boats and sometimes into skiffs. The machinery that he had imported from Mingulay and Croatan—marine engines and diving equipment, mostly—would be a small fraction of the de Tenebres' cargo, and that itself insignificant beside the wares of the ship's real owners and major traders, the krakens. Beneath him, the ship's field pressed down like an invisible, flexible sheet on the waves, flattening them to a waterbed wobble. Under that rippling glassy surface, the krakens from the ship and from the local sea flashed greetings to each other. Off to Volkov's right, behind the bulk of the ship, the sun was just up, its low full beam picking out the city, about a mile away across the water, in rectangles of white glare and long triangles of black shade. Ten thousand years of heaping one stone upon another had stacked the architectures of antiquity to the heights of modernity. A marble Manhattan, massive yet soaring, it looked like something from the mind of a Speer with humanity, or a Stalin with taste. The avenues that slotted the island metropolis from east to west were so broad that Volkov could see the sky on the far side through the one directly opposite him. Bridges, sturdy as ribs, joined both shores to districts that stood, less grand only by contrast, on either bank.

Starships by the score dotted the broad estuary. Skiffs flitted back and forth between the sound and the city like Frisbees in a park. Long-limbed mammals like flying squirrels—this world's equivalent of birds—skimmed the waves and dived for fish and haunted the wakes of fishing boats in raucous flocks. Above the city, airships and gliders drifted, outpaced and dodged by the flashing skiffs. Between the starships, tall junks and clippers tacked in or out of the harbor and both branches of the river, and among them feluccas darted, their sails like the fins of a shoal of sharks. At this distance, the city's dawn din of millions of wheels and feet rose in a discernible and gradually increasing hum.

For a moment the immensity and solidity of the place made Volkov's heart sink. The stone crescendo that rose before his face was like some gigantic ship against whose bow history itself cleaved and fell back to slip along its flanks and leave a wake of churned millennia. And yet ultimately it was only an idea that kept it afloat and forging forward, a thought in millions of all-too-fragile skulls. Let them lose that thought, and in a year, the place would sink. Volkov had set himself the harder task of raising it, and at that, he felt weak.

He heard and smelt Lydia behind him, and turned as she stepped up to the rail. She gazed hungrily at the city, transfixed.

"Gods above," she said, "it's good to see it again." She smiled at him wryly. "And good to see it hasn't changed much." Another, more considering, look at the city. "Except it's higher."

"It's impressive," Volkov allowed.

"And you want to change it."

Volkov jerked a thumb over his shoulder at the work being done behind them. "You're the revolutionaries," he said. "Bring in enough books and ideas, and the city will change itself. All I want to do is make sure it's still there the next time you come back."

He grinned at her, controlling his features. His heart was making him shake inside. "If I believed in your people's ideas of courtship, I would offer it for your hand. I would tell Esias that I could take this city and lay it at your feet."

Lydia, to his surprise, blushed and blinked. "That's what Esias is afraid of," she said.

She stared away, as though weighing the city, and the suggestion.

"Gregor offered more," she added, "and he delivered it, too, but he didn't want me after all. No, I'm not open to that kind of offer. Not after that."

"I see," said Volkov. "I'll just have to fall back on my fine physique and engaging personality."

Lydia laughed. "I can never tell if you're joking or not."

"Neither can I," said Volkov in a gloomy tone.

She punched him lightly. "There you go again."

He turned to her, with a smile to cover his confusion, and even more to cover his calculation. He did not know how he felt, or what if anything his feelings meant. A few weeks earlier, his affair with Lydia's mother, Faustina, had come to a mutually agreeable end. He got on best with women of his own apparent age, or older; preferably married, or otherwise unlikely to form a permanent—and from his point of view, all too temporary—attachment. He wasn't in love with Lydia, or even infatuated with her. He didn't think about her all the time. But whenever he saw her, he felt an electric jolt inside him, and he found it difficult to look away from her. It was embarrassing to find himself stealing glances like some besotted youth, but there it was.

At the other end of the scale, almost balancing that, there was the knowledge that in terms of Nova Babylonian—and Trader—custom, they were potentially good partners. Marriage was a business, affairs an avowed diversion; issue, inheritance, and fortune the only serious matters, over which geneticists and astrologers and matchmakers kept themselves profitably occupied.

In between, at the balance point, he and Lydia had developed a sort of tempestuous friendship, which every so often blew up in clashes in which his values and ideas appeared to her as a jaded cynicism, and her passionately held ethics to him seemed ancient prejudices, immaturely held. At the moment, their relationship was going through one of its calmer patches. He didn't know whether a squall would have been better. More bracing, certainly; but there was no need to bring it on. It would come of itself soon enough.

"Can we at least be friendly, for the moment?"

She smiled back. "You may be sly, Grigory Andreievich, but I do like you. Sometimes."

The first skiff slid out of its slot in the rack and skimmed across the navigation pool and out of one of the ship's side openings. It soared to an altitude of a couple of hundred meters and flew into the city, the other skiffs carrying the rest of the clan and the crew following one by one at intervals of about half a minute. Voronar took his time, evidently enjoying showing off to Volkov the city's towers and his own skill in flying between them. From above, the city looked astonishingly green. Trees lined the streets, and stories rose in steps like terraces, many of which supported grass and gardens: the hanging gardens of Nova Babylonia, a wonder greater than their ancient original. Monkeys scrambled and swung on long vines and branches; goats grazed the lofty lawns and capered up or down external stairways; flying squirrels, their fur bright and various as the feathers of parakeets, flashed across the artificial canyons.

The skiff dipped, making the view tilt alarmingly while the internal gravity remained rock solid. Volkov glimpsed a buttress on which was carved an eagle, wings outspread to ten meters, and beneath it the inscriptions "IX" and "SPQR"; and then, before he could quite grasp the allusive stir of memory, they were past it and sidling in to a tower, down whose fifty-meter lower tier a column of neon spelled out DE TENEBRE. The skiff landed on one of the building's terraces and everyone except the pilot descended the ladder onto soft turf, and the skiff flitted away to make room for the rest of the skein.

"Sliding glass doors," Volkov murmured to Lydia, as they walked toward the entrance. "It's been a long time."

"Oh, so they had them on Earth?"

From the sliding doors emerged a crowd of the clan's retainers and office workers, and—as Volkov learned in the swirl of fast introductions as the new arrivals were ushered inside—members of the home-staying branch, the oldest of whom might remember from childhood someone old enough to have been alive when the ship had departed. Also in the crowd were saurs, for whom the past two centuries were an episode in their lives, and who swiftly renewed old acquaintances among their counterparts in the traveling crew. For all of them, human and saur alike, the return of the ship was a major event and a huge celebration. This floor of the building was evidently the function suite, a vast deck whose open space was only interrupted by support pillars, and on it a thousand or so people were partying. Most of them wore some kind of pleated kimonos, with variations in cloth, cut, texture, and pattern that differentiated the sexes in predictable ways. Others wore loose jackets and trousers, likewise varied.

Volkov circulated, nibbled and sipped, chatted discreetly. Esias's family and the few crew members who knew who Volkov really was had agreed to keep it to themselves and to the saurs, at least until the Academy, the Electorate, the Senate, and the Assembly of Notables had had a chance to consider the situation. He introduced himself as an immigrant marine engineer importing some new technology, which was true as far as it went. A slow circumnavigation of the room took him back to Lydia's orbit.

He gestured at his clothes and hers, then at those of the other revelers. "Doesn't this make you feel a little . . . underdressed for the occasion?"

Lydia brushed her hands on her hips, leaving crumbs on canvas. "Not at all," she said. "Traveling gear is the most prestigious garb at this party, I'll tell you that. If we were to come here in what were our best clothes when we left, we'd look as though we were in some kind of antique costume." She looked around critically. "Mind you, I can see where this sort of silk origami style came from, and I'm quite looking forward to trying it, but there's no way I'd change into it straight off the ship. I'd look as ridiculous as I'd feel."

"I doubt that."

Lydia acknowledged the compliment with a shake of the head. "And how do you feel?"

"Somewhat overwhelmed by all this, to tell you the truth. Not just the occasion, but the city."

"Aha," said Esias, looming into view behind a brandy balloon. "I detect a bad case of cultural cringe. I can see it in your eyes, Volkov. Relax, my friend. We're the hosts here, remember. And from our point of view, we attend such occasions every few months."

"Perhaps at the next one," Volkov murmured, "all the people here will be there."

Esias raised a finger, then winked. "But yes," he said, "an interesting thought . . . I've set some wheels in motion about a hearing from the Academy, by the way. It'll take a day or two, of course. In the meantime, I'll deal with the usual turnaround business, and you . . . ."

"I'll sell machines," said Volkov.

Volkov spent the next few days wandering around the city, sometimes in Lydia's company, sometimes on his own. From street level, the terracing gave an illusion of its being built on a human scale. From the pavement, the nearby towers would seem only a few storeys high, those farther away like cliffs striated with verdant ledges. Awnings and cloisters, courtyards and porticoes, plazas and fountains, and the long shadows of the buildings themselves, made the air on the streets bearable, almost cool. Higher up, breezes did the same work. Access to the upper levels was by lifts, or interior stairs, or by perilous stairways that zigzagged up their outer walls. The whole city ran on a like combination of muscle power and electricity. Less dense than it had looked from the sea, it contained endless pocket parks and gardens, fertilized by draft-animal dung, whose collection and distribution was a business in itself. Hardly a splash of shit ever reached the streets. Processing human waste was another specialization, conducted with such skill and speed that Volkov for a long while did not catch more than a passing whiff of it.

The gardens in the business district were decorative, but elsewhere, their floral fringes enclosed vegetable patches, small rice paddies, beds of herbs, tiny meadows for the goats, guinea pigs, and other minor livestock; the trees of the avenues and parks were harvested for fruit, and even timber. It was not something Lydia or anyone else explained to him, it was something he worked out with pencil and paper: The city was a permaculture, self-sufficient in at least its basic necessities. The cash-crop latifundia of its hinterland brought in money, not food, or at most brought variety to the diet.

Its biggest external source of food was the sea, or rather two seas: the Half Moon Sea and the Eastern Ocean. The feluccas fished the former, and the big oceanworthy junks trawled the latter. Even the harbor was clean enough to sustain a fishery of its own, conducted by hordes of boys and girls who sat along the piers from morning to evening with long bamboo rods. In the dusk they sold basketloads of small fry to the felucca skippers for bait, and sizzled the remainder on roadside griddles long into the night.

Volkov, too, hawked wares around the docks, every day lugging samples of the smaller devices, models, and plans of the larger, around shipping and fishing companies. He knew from decades of experience where to go, usually not to the offices but the sheds, not to the owners or administrators but the engineers, who, once they were sold on a new idea, did his selling for him. He picked up the local vernacular as he went; gradually, his Trade Latin approximated to a sort of Trade Italian, and he made enough deals to reassure him that even if nothing came of his larger plans, he could make a living here. There was a kind of contentment in the work that warred with his ambition.

Guilds, associations, companies, cooperatives, and corporations combined the hustle of private enrichment or survival with the stability of municipal administration and held the city's economic life in what Volkov—used as he was to the less regulated markets of the outer, younger worlds—could only think of as a strangling net. Even the European Union's "feasible and sustainable socialism" had been, to his recollection, much more dynamic. Artels plus electrification, he thought wryly, added up to something that wasn't capitalism and wasn't socialism. Its exact classification puzzled the residually and obdurately Marxist modules of his mind until he arbitrarily consigned it to the conceptual catch-all of "pre-capitalist." From this society, capitalism could emerge, and—with more upheaval and less substantial change—socialism too, but Volkov's fingers still smarted from a previous experiment in detonating a bourgeois revolution.

Identifying a ruling class and state posed no such problem. The upper and usually senior ranks of the various corporate bodies, patricians and patriarchs of the merchant houses, administrators of cooperatives, guildmasters and latifundists, heads of religious orders and philosophical schools, retired courtesans, professors emeritus, and so on and so forth, formed what was blatantly called the Electorate, who just as blatantly elected the Senate and staffed its administration, and that was that. Volkov had no scruples about elites—having been part of one—and was surprised to find himself shocked by the sheer effrontery of the Republic's lack of the forms of democracy. All his experience had been with people who insisted on at least the illusion of popular rule, and it was disquieting to encounter a people who seemed satisfied with the substance of self-government in everyday life while letting high politics and statecraft go on over their heads—as it almost always and everywhere did, of course.

As he walked through mazes of markets and malls, past workshops and mills, glimpsed ranks of pale-faced clerks filing and scribbling and ringing up totals on calculating machines, and marveled at the countless threads of communication—the racing messenger boys' bare feet slapping in echoing stairwells, the cyclists yelling and dodging in the streets, the long sigh of pneumatic tubes and the ring of telephony—Volkov realized that this city could become the hub of a militarily and industrially formidable state without changing a single institution. All it needed was information.

They already had some—news of the arrival of the *Bright Star*, and bits and pieces of the recent knowledge it had brought, had trickled in long before the de Tenebres' ship had set out to bring back as much as possible. And they had the means to disseminate and discuss it—the press here was multiple and full of rude vigor, as were the numerous radio channels. The massive addition to knowledge that had just arrived would set the place intellectually alight. Rumors of it were already setting everyone agog.

The banner of his revolution would be: *Knowledge is power.*

The Academy's interior was cool—its granite blocks retaining, it seemed, a nip of cold from the previous winter—and quiet. Its air carried a tang of wood polish and disinfectant; aeons of application of the former had given the high doors of the Senate Chamber a patina millimeters deep, and ages of the latter had worn centimeters of dip into the sandstone steps.

"Nervous?"

"No," said Volkov, belying it slightly by fingering the knot of his tie. He was wearing a hastily tailored but reasonably accurate copy of his old dress uniform, made after the photograph taken on the day of his investiture as Hero of the European Union (First Class) which he still carried around in his wallet. Esias, in a magnificent fur-trimmed brocade robe at least two centuries out of fashion, looked scarcely less quaint and exotic.

The black iron handle of the double doors was turned from within and the doors swung back, silent on well-oiled hinges. Volkov had assumed they would creak. A lean, elderly servitor in a long black gown bowed through the widening gap, then stepped aside. Volkov hesitated.

"After you," growled Esias. "You're my guest, not a captive specimen."

"I'll try to remember that," Volkov said, and with a nod to the servitor, marched into the Senate Chamber. It was about thirty meters high, illuminated by electric lamps and a roseate skylight. Semicircular tiers of benches rose from the podium to the rear, and on them sat a grave multitude of ancient men, among whom were a modicum of younger but still mature men and a very few women. One long-bearded, long-gowned sage stood by the podium, a hand out in a beckoning gesture. Volkov reminded himself that he was older and probably wiser than anyone else present, and strode over to shake the extended hand, rather to the recipient's surprise.

"My name is Luke Sejanus," the scholar murmured, "president of the Academy of Sciences."

He turned, threw out an arm with a practised flourish, and announced: "My lords, ladies and gentlemen, I present our distinguished visitor, Grigory Andreievich Volkov! Cosmonaut of the European Union, colonel in the European People's Army, Hero of the European Union . . ."

He rolled on through a list Volkov's achievements, including the succession of his business ventures on Mingulay and Croatan, several of which Volkov had thought he had taken to the obscurity of a marked but empty grave in the centuries during which the Cosmonauts had concealed their longevity. He had, however, mentioned them to Esias.

Esias had taken a vacant place at the end of one of the lower rows. Volkov glared at him; Esias smiled back.

Sejanus stepped aside, sat down in the front row, and added his expectant face to a thousand others. Volkov swallowed hard and wished there was a glass of water in front of him. Or vodka.

"Thank you, President Sejanus. My lords, ladies and gentlemen, I am honored to stand before you. What is unusual about my life is not what I have accomplished—though I can look back on it with more satisfaction than regret, thanks be to the gods. What is unusual about my life is . . . its length. I am here to show you how you too can live as long a life, and in health and vigor—even those of you who are already old.

"To show you, not to tell you. I am sorry that I cannot tell you. In the third and fourth decades of my life, I consumed many drugs and medicines that promised to preserve youth. As you can see, one of them, or some combination of them, worked. I do not know which, and because the formulae of these medicines were commercial secrets, I would be unable to reproduce it even if I knew which nostrum was, in fact, the panacea. I and the other Cosmonauts have consulted among ourselves, and we have failed to discover which medicine or medicines we had in common.

"What I can do, however, is this. I can show you the method by which you can independently discover the nostrum—the elixir—for yourselves. This would involve extracting material from my body and analyzing it—finding out what molecules are in my blood, for example, that are not in the blood of others. Possibly one or more of these molecules would provide a clue. Or perhaps you might find something unusual in the structures of my cells—I do not know, but that is what I would expect. At the same time, I can give you a list of the types of molecule which are known to have been used in the various medicines, and the parts of the human cells which these medicines were intended to—and were known to—affect. These could be tested on short-lived animals—rats and mice, let us say—then on monkeys, and finally on human volunteers. Many experiments would be necessary. Their results would have to be scrupulously recorded and carefully examined.

"It might be a long process. It might be costly. But we would have, to encourage us, the priceless knowledge that what we were attempting was possible, that it had been done once, and that it could therefore be done again.

"Thank you."

He bowed, and stood aside as Sejanus returned to the podium.

Esias was nodding and smiling; almost everyone else seemed lost in thought.

"I shall now take questions," said Sejanus, looking as though he had some himself.

A middle-aged man near the front stood up. "Theocritus Gionno," he introduced himself, obviously unnecessarily for most of those present. "Chairman of the Department of Medical Sciences." He preened his robe for a moment. "In recent days, the Trader and Elector Esias de Tenebre has provided us with evidence for Colonel Volkov's remarkable, nay, extraordinary, claim. We have all had an opportunity to acquaint ourselves with it, and we must, I think, admit that it is extraordinary evidence. Documents of undisputed provenance, photographs, fingerprints. . . . Likewise, we and our predecessors have had many years indeed to examine such evidence of the level of scientific knowledge prevalent in the Solar System at the time of the, ah, *Bright Star*'s departure as has trickled in over the past two centuries. We have no reason to doubt the possibility of the treatment of which the Colonel has spoken."

He cupped an elbow in one hand, his chin in the other, and gazed around the auditorium.

"However," he went on, "the method that the Colonel proposes by which we could independently, as he puts it, rediscover the nostrum must surely strike all men—and women!—of science as preposterously cumbersome and, above all, uncertain. This is not how science is done at all! The scientific method is based upon logical reasoning from observation, and from logical analysis of available data. An immense wealth of such data is available to us already. An even greater addition to it has been bestowed on us by the successful expedition of the family de Tenebre, which beyond the memory of the oldest man now living, set forth to bring from distant Mingulay the full fountainhead of that knowledge of which we and our predecessors have long lapped up the veriest drops and trickles. I have every confidence that a few years of careful study and exact reasoning will enable us to deduce the composition of the elixir."

A low hum of approbation greeted this. Others stood up, one by one, and held forth on the power of logic to reason from old facts to new.

"Let us take for example the theory of evolution," one man, depressingly young, said. "Could that have been discovered experimentally? No! A thousand years ago, Alexander Philoctetes stood in this very hall and explained to the Academy how in each generation more are born than can survive, how consequently there is a struggle for existence, and how therefore small variations conducive to survival must necessarily be preserved— and so on, in that masterly deduction of the origin of species with which we are all familiar. If Philoctetes had used this vaunted *experimental* method—fossicking about in quarries, no doubt—he would have found the most misleading results in the fossil record, and come up with some theory of successive creations, or spontaneous generation, or such like."

And more in the same vein. Volkov would have sat with his head in his hands if he'd had anywhere to sit. As it was, he just stood there, feeling his jaw muscles first slacken and then, increasingly, clench.

"Your pardon," he said finally to Sejanus, "but I must speak."

Sejanus bowed him to the rostrum. Volkov gripped it and leaned forward.

"I fully understand," he said, "and deeply appreciate what the sciences of this great city have accomplished by examining and comparing information obtained by your own careful observations and from study of the information won on Earth in the past. You have indeed accomplished great things. But not all, not by any means all, of what anyone can see in this wonderful metropolis was built by such methods. No amount of reasoning, from observation or from first principles, could have built the machines I have seen in the shops, the ships I see on the ocean, the vehicles in your streets, and the crops in your fields. They were designed by the method I suggested, the empirical method, the method of trial and error, of hypothesis and induction as well as—indeed, hand in hand with—deduction. Your mechanics and artisans, your pharmacists and farmers, your fishers and flyers may not be able to tell you the method by which they have so successfully worked, but the fact of that method and its success are surely beyond dispute here. Let us reason and compare, to be sure, when we investigate the discoveries of others. But let us experiment and test when we wish to make new discoveries ourselves."

As he spoke, he glanced from face to face, and here and there he saw agreement, even—and it thrilled him to see it—enlightenment dawn, but these occurrences were few. The overwhelming mood of the assembly was bafflement, even affront. Theocritus Gionno was simmering, and jumped to his feet as soon as Volkov stepped back.

"Of course," said Gionno, "many of us here do appreciate the value, and understand the significance, of what the esteemed Colonel rightly calls the empirical or experimental method. Some here have devoted their lives as scholars to such works of the masters Bacon and Popper as have reached us. The commentaries upon *The Advancement of Learning* alone would fill a not insignificant shelf, and those upon *The Logic of Scientific Discovery* a small library. But there are many deep problems with such a method, and until they are resolved, it is best left to guide, consciously or otherwise as it may be, the crude blundering of mechanics, artisans, and herbalists. Such methods are no doubt good enough for them. The requirements of exact science are considerably more rigorous."

Volkov laughed. He had not intended to, and he saw at once that its effect was bad, but he could not help himself.

"Somewhere in one of the works of science in the de Tenebres' cargo," he said into a shocked silence, "you'll find a quote from a great scientist of Earth, one Poincaré, who said: 'Science advances, funeral by funeral.' I see that its truth is universal, and I bid you good day."

"Well," puffed Esias, having caught up with Volkov in the shade of a cloistered quadrangle, "that did not go down well."

Volkov ran his hand over his brush-cut hair. "No, it did not," he said. "My apologies, my friend. I hope I haven't dragged you down with me. But these scholars, my God! They'd sooner die than think. And they will."

Esias chuckled. "Some of them. Perhaps not all. Let us proceed to the refreshment patio and wait there, in as dignified a fashion as we can muster, and see if there are any exceptions to the rule." He clapped Volkov's shoulder. "The scientific method!"

"I don't want to hear those words again for a week," said Volkov. "But you're right. And I'm parched."

They sat at a table under an awning and gulped one glass and sipped a second glass of what Esias insisted was beer. Volkov knew better than to press the point. He relaxed and watched the students, at the other tables or walking in the quadrangle. Apart from the black bat-sleeved short robes they wore like overalls, they looked on the one hand like younger versions of the Academicians, and on the other like students everywhere, alternately earnest and relaxed. The proportion of female students was a good deal higher than it was among the scholars, though nowhere near parity. What a bloody waste, Volkov thought. Changing that alone would speed up development.

"You know," said Esias, "you may be underestimating the Academy. They are not dullards. They have millennia of experience behind them of teasing out unexpected implications. Your journey here will not be wasted. It may take them time, longer than you might wish, but the knowledge we have brought back will be assimilated and extended."

"All right," Volkov said. "Let the Academy rummage through books if it wants. What I'm more concerned about is the other institutions. Are they as hidebound? Because time is what we don't have. If the aliens turn up before this place has a space defense capability, then the question of longevity is, you might say, academic."

"Ah yes," said Esias. "The aliens." He glanced around. "I think any allusion to that matter is best . . . postponed, until we can put it before the Electorate—in the first instance, the Defense Committee of the Senate."

Volkov smiled. "That's how it was done on Earth. The consequences were not good."

"Oh," said Esias, looking over his shoulder again, "you won't find any of that paranoia here. You'll see."

But Volkov was only half listening; he was gazing away to the shade of the quadrangle, from which a dozen or so black-gowned figures had emerged blinking into the sunlight and were making their way over.

2
===

Hardy Man

L EMURIA BEACH WAS the worst place in the world, and Elizabeth Harkness was happy to be there. She trudged along the shingle shore, her head down and her left shoulder hunched against the knife-edge wind off the sea. Hooded parka, quilted trousers, fur-lined gloves and boots weren't quite enough, especially when she had to push her hood back or take her gloves off. Big smooth pebbles ground against each other, and dried wrack crackled under her soles. Seabats screamed as they wheeled overhead. Behind all the sounds, the white noise of the white water filled her ears. The abandoned whaling station where she and Gregor Cairns had parked the skiff was a couple of kilometers behind her, its rusted boilers tiny at this distance, like some wrecked laboratory apparatus. Gregor had chosen to spend the morning hacking fossils from the foot of the cliffs, the same hundred-meter-high rockface that rose to her right. Elizabeth was intent on finding more recent signs of life. Although the season was what passed for spring in these latitudes, there wasn't much: Seabat roosts whitened the cliffs, and the occasional wind-dried corpse of a failed fledgling would be caught on the windward side of a boulder; on the lee side of boulders, lichens spread out their wrinkled mats of grey and orange; on the lichens, tiny red arthropods scurried like the dots before a bloodshot eye; and here and there a drift of soil sustained a small tough flowering plant, white as the sea's froth.

The sea itself, choppy in the wind off the ice-capped polar ocean a thousand kilometers southward, was a more hospitable abode of life than anything the island could offer. Every seaward glance couldn't but take in, somewhere between the horizon and the shore, the plume of hot breath from a spouting whale. Sea-bats of several species, from the tiny watershears skimming the wavetops to the three-meter-spanning alcatrazi gliding high above, patrolled and plunged to pillage the inexhaustible shoals that thronged the waters below. Every so often, about five hundred meters out from the shore, the black bullet heads of seals or sea-lions or some such seagoing mammal would pop up, peer around in a disconcertingly human manner, then disappear again in a humping curve of back.

Elizabeth worked her way steadily along, scraping rocks, making notes, taking samples and placing them in airtight plastic cases or small, stoppered jars. Even the minute insect or arachnid specimens found their way there, via an arrangement of L-shaped glass tube and long rubber suction tube and rubber bung with holes through it for both, which, in all its centuries of scientific use, had never been given a more scientific name than "put-er." The biota of Mingulay, like that of all the other Earthlike planets of the Second Sphere, shared a common terrestrial ancestry but had, over megayears, diverged in unique and interesting ways. Not that the ancient arthropod or other invertebrate lineages showed much sign of it—she could identify most of the ones she picked up, right down to the species level, from memory of the standard manuals reprinted from originals published millennia ago on Earth. Mingulay's own geology and biology had been left for several centuries in something of a mess. The planet's earliest human settlers had barely sorted out a few recognizably successive epochs—Pelagic, Noachic, Nevisian, Corpachian, Strontian—and one or two bold philosophers had just begun to postulate a theory of evolution when the last starship from Earth had arrived with the disheartening news that while the scientists were in principle right, the planet they were standing on had indeed undergone a succession of creations and catastrophes and was in all likelihood the bodged work of gods.

After forgetting time for a while, Elizabeth glanced at her watch and at the sun, decided it was time to rest and to turn back, and selected a large boulder to shelter behind. The pebbles were dry this far up the beach. She swung her pack off and sat down and pulled out a thermos flask of coffee. Just as she was unscrewing the cup, she noticed some whitened thing sticking partly out of the ground, a few meters up the beach where the pebbles ran out into thin sand below the cliffs.

Curiosity got the better of her tiredness. She wedged the flask among the stones and stood up, a little stiffly—forty years of life, twenty of them spent in varied gravities, were beginning to tell on her knee joints—and stalked over, tugging off a glove, fumbling in her jacket pocket for the sturdy clasp knife she used for her rough fieldwork's probing and digging. She hunkered down on the sand and peered at the half-covered thing: a fossil in formation, sinking into sand that would one day be sandstone. At first she thought it was the washed-up exoskeleton of a brittle-star or a long-legged crab: There was a handsbreadth roundish central bit with jointed appendages coming off it. She could see three evenly spaced cup-shaped depressions, each with a tiny central hole, in the exposed part of the main bit, and below these concavities other holes, and below these holes a triangular artic-ulation of delicate, roughly rectangular plates, and along the in-ner edge of each plate a row of something whiter than the rest of it.

Teeth. Jaws. Eye sockets. The cascade of successive recog-nitions sent a shock of adrenaline through her body. She walked back to take a trowel from her pack, returned and began to dig around it, very carefully. When it was all uncovered, she stood up and took a long look at it. It had eight appendages in all, each about forty centimeters long, with ball-and-socket joints proximally, medially, and distally. On the distal joints were what looked like miniature versions of the whole skeleton—buds, or eight-fingered hands. The central part was at the top something like a skull, curving inward beneath the jaws; the lower part, joined to the upper by a stubby central rod, and to which the appendages were attached on each side in rows of four, was something like a pelvis. The three sockets she'd initially seen had five others like them further around the circumference, all evenly spaced, and the triple-jaw arrangement was repeated, sans teeth, on the opposite side.

Already it was so unlike any invertebrate she'd ever seen that it was making her shake. It was making her almost sick, actually: It was much too like the remains of hideously conjoined quadruplet infant monkeys to be easy on the eye. What clinched it for her was the presence of shriveled but recognizable tendons on the outside of the joints, still holding them together, and in the parts which had been covered, the clinging fragments of leathery, fuzzy skin. Unless she was misinterpreting it completely, what she was looking at was an internal skeleton, not the external skeleton of an invertebrate, not even one unknown to science. It looked like a vertebrate—hell, if that fuzz was hair, like a *mammal*—that had evolved from some invertebrate without losing its radial symmetry. Either she'd stumbled upon some bizarre malformation, or a new phylum, or an organism that had no terrestrial ancestors at all. She could imagine its possible ancestors. She did not have to imagine, because she'd already seen pictures of its probable descendants. Or, if this was a juvenile, its adults.

Still staring down at it, Elizabeth reached inside her jacket for her radio to call Gregor. Just as she was about to thumb the dial, she heard behind her the sound of heavy footsteps crunching up the beach. Startled, but not scared—someone might have landed silently from a boat or skiff while she was preoccupied—she turned around, and came face-to-face with her second unknown species of the morning.

At first, as before, Elizabeth's perception tried to make sense of what she saw in terms of what she knew. The figure stood about two and a half meters tall, and about twenty meters away from her. It could have been a fat gigant in a black wetsuit. But the staring eyes and opening mouth and snorting nostrils were set in the same shining hair-covered skin as the rest of it. The rest of him. He had long hands and feet, and his neck sloped smoothly to his shoulders, but otherwise his proportions and features were human. She realized that he could be one of the marine mammals she'd noticed earlier.

He said something, in a deep, barking voice, but evidently speech. He spread his broad hands wide, palms forward, and then walked towards her, staring with apparent curiosity all the while, and repeating his utterances. Elizabeth backed away. He stepped over the boulder she'd thought to shelter behind, and paused to look down at her gear, with a long sniffling snort. Then he strode forward again, to stop before the small excavation she'd made. The cliff face was pressing into her back. She could feel the revolver in her thigh pocket knocking her leg as her knees quivered.

He squatted down and poked a long finger at the strange bones, stirring them gently. Then he stood up and looked straight at her. He pointed at the bones, then pointed to the sky, then looked up and slowly brought his arm around and down until it was pointing at an angle to the ground. He dropped his arm to his side, raised it and pointed at her, waved his arm about, and made a loud grunt.

The only sound she could make in response was what came from her teeth chattering. He cocked his head, turning a small ear to her, then faced her directly. He rocked his head from side to side, shrugged, turned and walked back down the beach and, without breaking step, into the water until he was waist-deep, and stooped forward and was suddenly gone with barely a splash.

Elizabeth's thumb at last engaged the knurl of the dial, her fingers found the switch. Finding the right channel was easy; there was no other traffic here.

"Gregor—"

"Are you all right?"

Deep breath. "Yeah, I'm fine. But I think you'd better come over here quickly. I've . . . found something interesting."

"Okay. Be right over. Signing off."

Hands shaking, Elizabeth opened the flask and poured herself some coffee, as if to return to her interrupted action, and therefore to her previous equilibrium. She kept looking out to sea—where the round black heads bobbed up as before—and over to her left, to the whaling station. She'd taken only a few sips and slurps of coffee when she saw the skiff rise from behind the tumbledown wooden buildings and the ochre boilers to skim along the beach towards her, its course so steady that it seemed to enlarge rather than approach. The lens-shaped, fifteen-meter-wide craft halted a few meters away and hovered. Its three landing legs telescoped out, their bases grinding into the pebbles as the field was powered down and its weight came back. The hatch on the underside opened, the stair ladder extended, and Gregor descended. He ran over to her and caught her in his arms.

"I'm all right," she insisted.

"You look like you've had a shock."

"Um," she said, pushing him away gently. "One at a time." She showed him the thing she'd dug up. Gregor glanced at her, whistled, drew a long breath in through his teeth, and squatted down and poked at the bones with his forefinger, just as the other primate had done. He stayed looking for a minute, then stood up.

"You know," he said, "we're going to have to find a better name for these than 'the monkey-spider things.' "

She laughed, some tension going out of her as her identification was validated.

"I thought it might be a relative," she said. "As close to them as a monkey or maybe a lemur is to us."

"That or a juvenile," Gregor said. "We'll have to look again at the records."

Elizabeth nodded. "And look again at the island."

"Oh, gods, yes." Gregor frowned. "This isn't what shook you up."

"No," agreed Elizabeth. "What shook me up was that I met a—"

She hesitated, knowing that as discoverer she had the privilege of naming, and that the name would matter, the popular name perhaps more than the scientific.

"A selkie," she decided.

"What?"

She pointed seaward. "Those, out there. They're not seals. They're aquatic hominids. Probably closer to us than the gigants or the pithkies. Same genus as us, I'll bet." She found herself giggling. "Just like Alister Hardy speculated long ago—you know, the aquatic ape hypothesis? We could call them *homo hardiensis*: Hardy Man."

She told him about her encounter.

"You know what's weird about that?" she concluded. "It was like he *recognized* it."

"It's not so much weird as inevitable," Gregor said. He looked down at the bones, then out to sea. "Even if that thing wasn't here, we'd still be thinking *aliens* as soon as we saw the selkies. Because they sure as hell haven't been here long. The last whalers were here ten years ago."

"Are you sure they couldn't have been unnoticed earlier? The Southern Ocean's big enough."

"Yeah, but its islands aren't. And if they're any kind of viable population, they must use islands to breed, if nothing else. I suppose it's just possible that sailors and whalers misidentified them all this time, but I doubt it. Nah, they must be recent arrivals. And that raises the question of who brought them here. I seriously doubt it was the saurs."

Elizabeth knocked on the underside of the skiff. "Assuming they didn't come here themselves."

"There is that," Gregor conceded. He was gazing intently out at the bobbing dots. "You know, not to get too excited or anything, I think we may soon be able to ask them."

Elizabeth realized that they were now only about two hundred meters out. She counted twelve of them.

"Should we get into the skiff?" she asked.

"Just keep our pistols easy to reach." Gregor clicked open the flap on his thigh pocket, and Elizabeth did likewise. They waited silently.

After a couple of minutes the selkies were standing waist-deep in the water and wading ashore. They were all adults, seven males and five females. The females had large breasts, and long hair on their heads. As they stepped out of the water, they were wringing out their hair and twisting it to hang forward over one shoulder. The water seemed to slide off their bodies; they didn't look wet for more than a moment. They paused at the strand and spread their empty hands.

Elizabeth, then Gregor, mirrored the gesture.

The selkies advanced up the beach to about ten meters away, then stood in a semicircle and looked at the two intruders. Elizabeth recognized the one she'd seen earlier. Their height was intimidating. On an impulse, Elizabeth sat down on her heels. The selkies did the same, taking care to keep their hands open, palms upward.

"Body language looks reassuring," muttered Gregor.

"Uh-huh. I just wonder if a smile means the same."

"Try it without baring our teeth."

Elizabeth stretched her lips and crinkled her eyes. The selkies responded with broad grins. Their teeth were not much larger than human teeth, in proportion to their body size. They just looked larger, white in their black, hairy faces. So Elizabeth told herself.

"Hallo," said Gregor, raising his right hand slowly. The selkies responded with a brief, barking phrase and raised their hands also, but hesitantly, as though the gesture was unfamiliar. Everyone relaxed a little. Three or four of them had, as though absently, begun grooming each other and themselves, scratching and snatching and popping things caught between thumb and forefinger into their mouths. It was disconcertingly apelike. But their expressions remained intent, curious, patient.

The one she'd already met stood up. He looked at Elizabeth and opened his eyes wider—no, he was raising his eyebrows. Elizabeth nodded. He walked forward and past them and laid his hand on the rim of the skiff. Then he patted it and made a happy-sounding chuckle, a deep, liquid note, bassy and warm. Elizabeth wondered if he recognized, in the rough pitting of its metal, and in its general appearance of being a copy made from too many generations of copies, that it was a skiff built by humans and not by saurs. The selkie strolled around it, ducking under to examine the hatch, then went over and looked again at the bones, and called back to his fellows. After standing there scratching his head, he turned and strolled back to the group. They began a quiet and orderly sounding conversation, pointing now at Gregor and Elizabeth, now at the skiff. When everyone had spoken—Elizabeth was watching and listening carefully, and she noticed—he came forward again and squatted on the shingle a couple of meters in front of them. Elizabeth could smell the fish on his breath. He leaned an elbow on his knee and held his chin in one hand for a moment, then rubbed a finger along his lips, then nodded as though to himself. He looked about among the stones at his feet, selected one, and picked up another at random. He held the first stone in the palm of one hand and brought the other down sharply on it, splitting it. He held out the two pieces. They contained a fossil of a coiled shell, an ammonite. He raised his eyebrows and grunted on a rising note.

"Yes," said Elizabeth, nodding.

The selkie tapped the fossil with a blunt, ridged fingernail. Then he pointed over to the bones; at the skiff; at the sky; then away at an angle as he had done earlier; pointed at himself, and finally waved his finger back over his shoulder at the others. He settled back, buttocks on heels, elbows on knees, waved a hand to include Gregor and Elizabeth, and repeated the interrogative grunt.

"Translation," Elizabeth said, turning to Gregor. " 'The spidery things carried us in skiffs long ago. Where do you come from?' Agreed?"

"Yup," said Gregor. "But maybe there's more to it than that. What's with that pointing at the ground?"

Elizabeth shrugged. "I don't know. Maybe there's more of the things buried over there?"

"Hey, that's a thought. We can check it later. What do we tell him? And how?"

"Same way as he told us."

Elizabeth stood up and walked over to the bones. Gregor watched her with a slightly worried look. She beckoned to the selkie, who came over but stayed a few meters distant. She pointed down at the alien skeleton, then at herself, then moved her head from side to side. The selkie tipped his head back a couple of times. She hoped this was a nod.

Elizabeth reached for the trowel, still lying there undisturbed, and sketched in the sand a spidery shape. Indicating it, and the bones, elicited another backward jerk of the head. She smoothed over the disturbed sand and drew a semicircle joined to a V to make a crude outline of a saur's head. Four curved strokes outlined the almond-shaped eyes, a slash the slit mouth. She pointed to the saur face, then to the skiff.

The selkie stared at her. He made what she'd taken as the interrogative sound, but this time with a sort of strain in his voice—the human equivalent would have been *"Huh*?!" He squatted beside her and held out a hand for the trowel. She gave it to him; he grasped it confidently as though holding a paintbrush and rapidly added a rendering of a saur's spindly body beneath the head. Beside it, he drew with equal speed and economy an ellipse with three legs, then put down the trowel and looked at her.

"Yes," she said firmly, nodding backwards.

The selkie's mouth and eyes widened. He stood slowly, as though weary, and walked back to the others. They conferred in a huddle. Some of them made downward slapping gestures that puzzled Elizabeth for a moment, until she realized that in water it would have been deliberate splashing at the surface, perhaps as a warning. Then they all jumped to their feet and fled into the sea; but the bold one was the last, and he looked back over his shoulder as he ran.

After marking the spot and photographing it they finished the excavation, laid the small skeleton carefully in a plastic tray, and into another tray they shoveled the sand in which it had been buried and which contained myriad tiny rods that might be small bones or internal parts or otherwise related to it; or perhaps just the spines of sea urchins; in any case, part of the puzzle. They lifted the two trays into the skiff, along with clinking racks of tubes containing the other specimens Elizabeth had collected. By comparison with the apparently alien skeleton, these specimens seemed trivial, but in the long run nothing was trivial in science. Not wishing to hang around where the selkies had been, as much to avoid further alarming them as out of uncertainty about how dangerous the alarmed selkies might be, they took the skiff back to the whaling station and parked it well up the beach. Over a hasty midday ration, they discussed what to do next.

"The first thing we have to do," said Gregor, "is take another look inland."

Elizabeth waved a half-chewed chewy bar at the cliffs. "We've already looked. There's nothing but sea-bats and insects."

"We weren't looking for *that*. What we need to know is whether it's just some waif or part of a breeding population."

"Okay," said Elizabeth. "I'll fly. You look."

The skiff was human-adapted, but its control panel still assumed four-fingered hands: that configuration was buried so deep in the manufacturing-control program that it was impossible to change without a radical redesign of the craft. Elizabeth sat on the padded seat in front of a section of the circular shelf under the encircling viewscreen, a section that contained a few dials and gauges and a pair of shallow, hand-shaped but four-fingered depressions. She rested her fingers in the hollows, her thumbs to the sides, and consciously relaxed for a moment. Control was intuitive, something you had to ease yourself into, dependent on chords of varying pressures rather than any one-to-one correspondence. She let her fingers do the flying, and the craft lifted.

The view tilted from side to side as her initial tremors of hesitation transmitted themselves to the drive, then steadied as the machine rose above the top of the cliff. Higher, and the jumbled landscape of Lemuria Beach opened before them. The island was about a hundred kilometers east to west, and fifty north to south. Behind the tilted sedimentary strata of the southern cliffs were ragged strips of rock alternating with long bands of rough grass, which, after a few kilometers, gave way to a more recent mixture of volcanic rock and tuff, basalt flows, sulphurous geysers, and bogs of lime-green algae, interrupted by snow-covered remnant plateaus and outcrops of the sedimentary rock and lumpy intrusions of even older metamorphic and basal layers.

"Let's follow the clifftop grasslands first," said Gregor.

Elizabeth leaned down on her left hand, spinning the skiff to that side. She pressed her fingertips down and the skiff moved forward, rocked back the heels of both hands and it rose. They settled on a cruising altitude of thirty meters. Gregor paced around the circular space between the viewscreen and the central engine fairing, gazing out with binoculars. Every so often he'd spot something and Elizabeth would bring the craft down, tip it on edge or even right over, so that they could look at the ground just inches above their heads. But the bones always turned out to be of sea-bats, and the momentary excitement of finding in a grassy bank a huge warren of burrows was dimmed somewhat by the discovery, which at any other time would have made their day, that they were the work of a peculiar flightless bird which they provisionally dubbed the "mole penguin."

"I'm amazed the whalers didn't hunt them to extinction," said Elizabeth.

"Probably taste disgusting."

She looked at him sidelong. "And your point would be?"

They laughed and took themselves aloft.

The volcanic badlands were, not to their surprise, an even less thriving habitat for land animals. They chipped some interesting mats of yellow, stinking extremophile bacteria and netted a few specimens of a small spider that skittered across the algae-clogged pools, but that was it. They returned to the whaling station as the short day ended. The wind had dropped, and the sea was calm, smooth on the surface of its ceaseless swells. Elizabeth and Gregor stowed their less fragile specimens, marked and tagged for later collection, in the whaling station. In the long twilight they built a fire from the whitened timbers of a ruined boat and cooked over it their first hot meal of the day. They lingered, huddling closer together against the cold, as the embers faded with the light and the stars came down to the horizon. The southern hemisphere constellations were so unfamiliar they didn't have names. Repairing this omission and identifying the two stars, among the many visible that they'd visited themselves, was keeping them idly occupied when they heard heavy footsteps crunching up the beach.

"Behind the fire," Gregor said quietly.

They scrambled to their feet and backed off, one to each side, and peered toward the shoreline. The footsteps became quieter as they moved from the shingle to the sand, then stopped. Elizabeth could dimly make out a selkie silhouetted against the starlit sea. He spread his hands wide and stepped forward into the dim circle of light from the fire. One arm was raised, shielding his eyes from the glow as he peered over his thick forearm at them. It was the bold one they'd met before.

He began to speak, his deep voice loud above the surf but quiet in itself. There was something in it of frustration, perhaps sorrow, but nothing of anger or fear. He spoke for about two minutes, then trailed off and ended with a gurgling laugh. Then he hunkered down, spread his hands, and looked at them across the fire, his eyes having apparently adapted to the light. Elizabeth stepped over beside Gregor, put a hand on his shoulder, and he joined her in squatting down. She faced the selkie, spread her hands, and leaned forward earnestly.

"What you are saying," she said, her voice speaking to the selkie but her words for Gregor's benefit, "is that you are speaking, and therefore you are a rational being, and that you want us to recognize you as such, and that you find our lack of a common language as frustrating as we do. Well, I understand and agree with that. In fact, I think that for all your nakedness and living in the wild, you arc not a savage, a hunter-gatherer, although that may be how you live now. I think you're basically as civilized as we are, and as aware of the nature of the universe. You can draw, you've seen a skiff before, you've met aliens. Am I right?"

Gregor nodded. The selkie responded with another minute or so of speech, looking down a little, as though in abstraction. When he'd finished, he looked up, and his teeth flashed in the embers' glow. He reached for a stick from the fire, motioned to them and began to draw in the sand. They joined him and watched as he slashed in the sand the glyphs of skiff and spidery alien—ten lines, little more. He pointed at himself, waved a hand out to sea, and then raised a hand, palm forward: Wait. He rose and tramped into the dark, beckoning them after him. When they were all out of the circle of light, a few tens of meters along the beach, he held out an arm stiff with a pointing finger. It started at the angle to the ground he'd pointed at before, then swung smoothly up and around, until it was aimed at a bright red star about halfway up the sky to the east. They joined him in sighting along their arms at the star. Just to make sure they were looking at the right one, he poked a finger in the sand and dotted out the pattern of the stars around it, completing the picture with the one he'd pointed at, jabbing his finger in deep, then pointing again. He pointed at his chest again, then at the sea, then at the star again. Elizabeth and Gregor nodded vigorously. The selkie's lips peeled back from his teeth in a grin that would have been frightening had they just encountered him.

He laid a hand first on Gregor's shoulder, then on Elizabeth's—it was like being a child again, looking up at him—and said something, then walked away into the waves.

"You know what I just figured out?" Gregor said, as the selkie's back vanished.

"What?"

"The way he was pointing downward earlier, and at the start just there? He was pointing to where the star was in the morning, when it was below the horizon."

She stared at him. "Could you do that?"

Gregor had been a navigator for twenty years. He had a more direct and practical knowledge of the sky than most astronomers. He thought about it for a moment and shook his head.

"Which means," said Elizabeth, "that I may have been wrong about the selkies. They're not as smart as we are. They're smarter."

A storm blew up later that night. Gregor and Elizabeth had already stowed some of their kit in the whaling station's gloomy rooms, but they decided to spend the night in the skiff. With its field on it was less moveable than a rock. Its encircling viewscreen picked up enough light from outside to give them a clear view, even with the interior lights on. They sat exhausted, gazing outward. It was like watching black-and-white television—white the surf, black the waves—but interesting.

"Wonder how the selkies are doing," Elizabeth said.

"They can ride it out," said Gregor. "Like seals."

"But they're not like seals. They're not that aquatic. I can imagine them huddled on a beach somewhere. Poor things."

"They look tough." He grinned. " 'Hardy Man,' all right."

Elizabeth saw Gregor's gaze drift back to the plastic tray in which they'd placed the anomalous octopod's bones. Of all the specimens they'd collected, this was the one they could least afford to lose. They had not cared to examine it further with the crude instruments—scalpels, tweezers, pliers, hammers—

that were on hand. They hardly dared to think about it. Not thinking about it was making them dizzy.

"This is big," he said. "This is evidence, the first solid evidence we've had of the aliens for a start, and it looks like evidence that they've settled the selkies here. Or that they're still doing it."

Elizabeth smiled wryly. "The long-awaited invasion?"

"Something like that." Gregor sighed. "Whatever. We have to report back." He reached sideways and clasped her right hand, intertwining their fingers. "The journey's over."

"Yeah," she said. "It's the next journey I'm worried about."

It had been a good journey, almost a holiday. It could even have been the beginning of a retirement, or the resumption of their true careers after a long interruption. They'd always promised themselves that someday they would pay their home planet, Mingulay, the attention of a *Beagle* voyage. Marine biology had been, for both of them, their first love. When they'd both been twenty years younger, eighty-odd years ago, Gregor had found in the structures of the cephalopod brain the key to his family's generations-long Great Work—to reverse-engineer the control program of the lightspeed drive, hitherto monopolized by the kraken navigators who plied the fixed trading routes of the Second Sphere. Implementing the program on the ancient onboard computers of the *Bright Star*, the ship in which Gregor's ancestors had been hurled across the galaxy to humanity's second home, had taken Gregor and Elizabeth across the four light-years to Croatan and, a month or two later, the four light-years back.

The lightspeed jumps were subjectively instantaneous. While they'd been away, people had grown up or aged or died. That first experience of skipping forward in time had been a jolt. As the Cairns clan's starship fleet had expanded and new planetary systems were laboriously added to the navigation programs, their journeys' reach had extended, and that first jolt had been followed by many more. Already, the oldest members of Elizabeth's family, who'd had decades yet to live when her starfaring had started, were long dead. Her parents were barely recognizable centenarians. Her children—at least they had kept pace, because they'd traveled with her. Elizabeth was already beginning to feel that disconnection with common humanity, and that identification with her traveling-companions, that was so patent in the long-established merchant families who for millennia had traveled in the krakens' ships, slipping through centuries in months.

—And she thought for a moment of Lydia de Tenebre, still young in the momentary eternity of her century-long journey to Nova Terra, and she blinked that thought away—

It had seemed their task was done. It was no longer necessary for Gregor, the First Navigator, to go on each newly charted course; or for Elizabeth, the Senior Science Officer, to accompany him. They had been able to get away, to leave the pioneering to others, and to return to exploring their own underpopulated and diverse world. And even, for once, to leave the children at home. Weeks, then months, of wandering the planet's oceans and islands in the skiff had not tired them, nor ceased to bring them new discoveries each day. This day's discoveries would end all that.

3

RTFM

M ATT CAIRNS, OUTWARD bound from Rawliston on Croatan
to Kyohvic on Mingulay, mooches about among a few
hundred other milling passengers. There's not much to do. The
ship is just a more or less airtight box with an interstellar drive,
inadequate seating, and a few refreshment stalls. There isn't even
a window. After the lightspeed jump, Matt has become so bored
that he finds himself reading the orientation leaflet for newbie
passengers. It's available in various languages and in a variety
of formats, including one entirely in pictures. The one he selects
has a little boxed note at the foot in tiny print:

> Literate, largely prescientific (suitable for sailors, traders,
> shamans, etc. Not recommended for clergy of desert mono-
> theisms.)

Long ago, he had written the first draft of it himself. His
private title for it was: *GREETINGS, IGNORANT SAVAGES!*:

Welcome to the Bright Star Cultures

> This may be your first journey in a starship navigated by human
> beings. Please take a few moments to read this document, which
> should help you to understand your journey, and your destination.
> It explains how we on the English-speaking planets of Croatan

and Mingulay explain the worlds in which we live. Your own explanation may well differ from the one given here. We respect your opinion as much as you respect ours.

When you look up at the sky at night, you see a broad, bright band of stars overhead, which is sometimes called the Milky Way or the Foamy Wake. What you are looking at is the edge of an immense disk of stars—a galaxy. There are many galaxies in the universe, the nearest of which you may know as the Little Cloud or That Fuzzy Dot There.

The Foamy Wake galaxy contains a hundred thousand thousand thousand stars. The stars are suns like the one you know, but very far away. The worlds on which we live travel around these suns. (See "Copernican Hypothesis, Evidence in Favor of.") They are so far away that the distances between them are measured in light-years. This refers to the distance that light travels in one year. Light travels three hundred thousand thousand thousand strides in one heartbeat. We are at present traveling at the speed of light between two stars—when we arrive, very soon, the sun will be different from the one which shone above us when we left. There is no need to be alarmed by this.

We live in a very small region of the galaxy, which we call the Second Sphere. It is a spherical volume of space that contains several hundred stars. Many of them are the suns of worlds like the one on which you were born. The Second Sphere is about two hundred light-years across. We call it the Second Sphere because it is not the place where human beings first came from. Human beings came from a world which we call Earth, a hundred thousand light-years away, on the other side of the Foamy Wake. So do all the other people, animals, and plants that you will find on the worlds of the Second Sphere. (See "Evolution, Theory of.") When you go from one world to another, you may find that the animals and plants are different from those on your own world. There is no need to be alarmed by this. In your pack you will find a separate leaflet that will tell you which animals and plants at your destination are dangerous.

64

As well as human beings and the kinds of people who resemble human beings—the tall hairy people and the small hairy people—there are two other kinds of people in the Second Sphere. These are the small grey people, whom we call the saurs, and the very large people with tentacles, whom we call the krakens. You may know the saurs mainly as the pilots of the small round aircraft we see in our skies, and the krakens as the navigators of the great starships that you have seen in the sky or on the sea. The trade routes followed by their starships are what define the limits of the Second Sphere, at about one hundred light-years in all directions from Nova Babylonia, its oldest human civilization, though not its oldest settlement. The krakens and the saurs have lived in the Second Sphere for much longer than human beings.

You will have been told that there are much greater minds in the spaces between the worlds—the minds that some people call the gods, and others call the powers above. This is true. The gods live in very small worlds, like the ones which we sometimes see in the sky as comets. There are many, many such gods around all the suns that we know about, including the sun of Earth. The gods are minds whose bodies are made up from many very small animals that can endure severe cold and heat. They are similar in some ways to the many small animals which we cannot see but which exist all around us. There is no need to be alarmed by this. (See "Disease, Germ Theory of" elsewhere in this information pack. If you already understand this, see "Extremophile Nanobacteria" and "Emergent Phenomena.")

There is much we do not understand about the gods. One thing we do know is that for a very long time they have arranged for saurs who live near Earth to transport people, animals, and plants to the worlds of the Second Sphere. These have always arrived in starships with saurs from the Solar System on board, and have been met by saurs from the Second Sphere, who in turn transported them to the nearest world. This is how the worlds of the Second Sphere came to be populated. The saurs, of course, came from Earth a very long time ago.

The planet we call Croatan was settled in this way more than seven hundred years ago, in the Seasonally Adjusted Year of Our Lord (SAYOL) 1600 (see "Calendar, Croatan") by people from North America. Its daughter colony, Mingulay, was established two hundred and fifty years later by the followers of a heretical prophetess (see "Taine, Joanna").

Almost three hundred years ago, in SAYOL 2051, a starship from Earth arrived near Mingulay. It was a starship built by human beings, and it was called the *Bright Star*. It was left to travel in the sky around Mingulay when the several hundred people on board were met by saurs and taken to the main city of Mingulay, Kyohvic, where they settled. They were different in three important ways from other people who had arrived from Earth.

First, they had traveled into the space outside their world by themselves. These Cosmonauts, as they were called, had encountered a god in one of the very small worlds we have mentioned earlier, and it had communicated with them. It gave them copies of instructions on how to build the engines which enable us to travel at the speed of light, and the other engines to fly in the air like the saurs do. Unfortunately, it had not told them how to navigate, and when they used the engine they found themselves in the Second Sphere, with no idea of how they had got there or where it was. Their descendants, over several generations, had to work out how to navigate for themselves, and succeeded about ninety years ago. The Cosmonaut families went on to build ships such as the one you are now traveling in. The *Bright Star* also contained much new knowledge, discovered on Earth, which we are still learning. That is why we call ourselves the Bright Star Cultures.

This brings us to the second important way in which the Cosmonauts differ from most human beings. Many of them had taken medicines that enabled them to live for many hundreds of years, just like the saurs do. Unfortunately, neither they nor the saurs understood how this had happened, and we are still trying to find out. Many of the original Cosmonauts from the *Bright Star* are still alive today, and some of them are trying to help. They would be very happy if everyone could live as long as they do.

Thirdly, the Cosmonauts were the last people to arrive here from Earth. As of this date (SAYOL 2338) we know of no other arrivals from outside the Second Sphere. It is very possible that people on Earth, or the saurs near Earth, have come into conflict with another star-traveling species, which we call the aliens. It is possible that Earth has been destroyed. There is no need to be alarmed by this. If you have, now or in the future, any knowledge of creatures resembling furry spiders and about the size of a large dog, please inform the nearest militia officer or starship crew member as soon as possible.

And now, a word about the militia. We in the Bright Star Cultures believe that, in general, people should be free to do whatever is compatible with the freedom of others. Here and below, "person," "people," and "human" refer to members of all intelligent species. Some religious, sexual, and other practices of which you disapprove may be permitted by law. Some of your own practices, which you believe to be righteous, may be prohibited by law. For your comfort and safety, it is important that you do not make mistakes in this area. Please study the following carefully:

Permitted practices of which you may disapprove:

All forms of sexual relations between people over the age of
    puberty.
All forms of attire (other than uniforms worn for purposes of
    deception) or lack of attire in all public places except places
    of worship or public ceremony.
All modes of address to people of any rank.
All modes of worship not involving prohibited practices.
All forms of artistic expression, including descriptions and
    depictions (but not commission or incitement) of prohibited
    practices.
Self-medication, including for ennui.
Suicide.
Reading books in public.

Writing in the margins of books.

Abortion.

Keeping and carrying weapons.

Prohibited practices (with or without consent) of which you may approve:

Human sacrifice.

Entertainments of lethal combat.

Sexual relations with people below the age of puberty.

Sexual relations with beasts.

Slavery.

Inflation.

Infanticide.

Piracy.

Cattle-raiding.

Dueling.

Nonmedical surgery on people below the age of puberty, including but not limited to: scarification, infibulation, circumcision.

Animal sacrifice grossly incompatible with the codes of kosher and halal.

Interference with public or private practices not on the list of prohibited practices.

Public exhortation of prohibited practices or heinous crimes, except in the public reading of scriptures revealed before the date of the passage of this law (SAYOL 2226) or in the performance of traditional rites.

Unauthorized possession of nuclear-explosive devices.

Theomancy.

Heinous Crimes:

Murder.

Rape.

Kidnapping.

Trafficking in slaves.

Torture.

Poisoning.

Maiming.

Nonmedical vaginal or anal penetration of a person below the age of puberty.

Prevention by force or fraud of any accepted passenger or crew member from embarking or disembarking from a starship.

Causing a nuclear explosion within a habitable atmosphere.

Theicide.

Anyone convicted of a heinous crime may be sentenced to death by public stoning. There is no need to be alarmed by this. The maximum sentence is seldom applied, and when it is, it is usually commuted to death by firing squad.

Have a safe journey, and enjoy your stay.

And *whee!* Back in Kyohvic—"Misty Harbor," as the helpful stab-in-the-dark translation says in squiggly italics on the sky-port sign, dittoed below in the barred neon of chi-chi Ogham— Matt Cairns shoulders his duffel bag and heads through the concourse for the shuttle train to town. Foam earpieces tab his throat. The contract brokers will already be yammering after him, but he's not ready yet to come online. He needs a break and doubts his skills are obsolete, for all that his want of trying is everywhere evident in shimmering monitors and remote eyes and the infrared flicker of robot scuttlebutt. In the sixty rack-renting days of his contract on Croatan, this place has jumped forward eight years, and seen more change than in the previous sixteen: Matt knows the pattern, he can clock the curve, he's lived through this shit before; they're running up the steepening slope to the lip of Singularity like there's no tomorrow, and if the gods have their eye on the ball as usual, there won't be. Cue cannon ball: Somewhere out there in the long orbits, a shot is being lined up in the godgames of Newtonian pool. Or the spidery aliens will irrupt into the system, and Darwinian dice will roll.

Outside the low, flat-roofed concourse, he pauses to inhale the autumn late-afternoon wind off the sea, its salt tang muffled by the faint freshwater scent of the fog in the sound, and the sharper notes of acetone and alcohol derivatives. The skyport's on a plateau above the town, its traffic everything from buzzing microlites and zippy little skiffs through new lifting-body aerodynes to the great clunky contraptions of human-built starships like the one he's just stepped off. The town has spread up the valleys like a lichen, sprouted towers like sporula—tall, thin hundred-meter spikes of gene-hacked cellulose offshoot. The factory fringe is a fast merge of that sort of biotech or wet nano stuff with the rougher, more rugged carapaces of steel and aluminum, concrete and glass. It reminds him of the Edinburgh he left, centuries ago in his life, millennia ago in real time. The harbor's busier than ever, the tall masts bearing computer-optimized wind panels rather than sails, the steamships wispy and clean rather than smoky.

Out beyond the surface vessels, a Nova Babylonian starship— a quarter-mile of iron zeppelin, its hull running with rainbow colors—is poised above the water as though impossibly halted in the last few meters of a long fall. On the headland that shelters one side of the harbor like a shielding arm, the Cosmonauts' keep still stands, its prehuman megalithic proportions as unyielding to the eye as ever.

The crowd of merchants and migrants and refugee sectaries off the starship funnels, thickening, to the station entrance and packs the carriages. Matt straphangs through the electric downslope glide, his knees' grip holding the big duffel upright. His reflexes haven't quite adjusted to the fractional difference in the gravity, but he's used to this transition; hell, he's done free fall often enough, he's bounded across the rusty desert of Raphael in a clumsy pressure suit, he's earned his honorary title of Cosmonaut. Others, the first-timers, are thin-lipped and whey-faced, lurching with each sway of the train. The cheap housing slides past the windows, then the University's crag-built complex, sprawling and soaring like everything else here, then the older, richer streets of the town center and shorefront.

Matt detrains at the esplanade terminus and hesitates. He has never quite gotten used to being feted by his descendants. The Cairns are now the richest of the Cosmonaut clans, thanks to their monopoly of interstellar navigation that they're exploiting as blatantly as the old merchants ever did their long-cut deal with the krakens. He has nowhere to sleep for the night, nobody apart from the brokers expecting him home, and the merchants off the Nova Babylonian ship will be at the castle, probably being entertained royally. A good party to gatecrash. On the other hand . . .

Nah. He's not up for it. He needs to find his feet first. The terminus is new since eight years ago, a cavernous glass shed full of hurrying people—the three major hominid species, and saurs—and cluttered with concession stands: coffee, flowers, snacks, drugs. Announcements are murmured from cunningly focused speakers, and displayed in midair holograms that don't quite work. The female gigant at the coffee stall has had all her hair dyed blonde and curled. Matt tries not to laugh at the thought of this car-wash-scale coiffure, smiles politely and takes his cup—thin plastic, but insulating—to a round enamel table.

"Mr. Cairns?"

He starts, almost splashing the coffee, and sets it down with both hands around it and glares into the smile of the young woman swinging into the seat opposite, slinging down a bag. She has a camera behind her ear like a pen, and a mike on a parallel spoke against her cheek. Her hair, eyelids, and lips are a sort of frosted gold. Behind all that she actually looks quite good. She's wearing black leather trousers and a black T-shirt with a broad rectangular panel of multicolored abstract tapestry on the front.

"Susan Harkness," she says, sticking out a hand which Matt clasps as briefly as politeness permits.

"I don't do interviews."

"I'm not a journalist," she says, fussing momentarily with the recording gear at the side of her head. "Well, I am, but I'm here on family business."

(He detects the increment of the local accent's change since he's been away: *fah-armlie*.)

"You're family?"

"Daughter of Elizabeth Harkness and Gregor Cairns."

"Ah." Matt relaxes and relents, smiling. "So I'm your ancestor."

"Yes," she says, looking at him with the unabashed curiosity of a human child seeing its first gigant. "It's hard to believe."

"In a good light, you can see the scars," Matt says.

"You've had cosmetic surgery?" She sounds disappointed. (*Suhdge'*ry.)

"Just two-hundred-fifty-odd years of shaving cuts." He shrugs. "And fights, of course."

"Of course." She tips her head sideways a little and smiles. Matt realizes she's putting up a good show; she's intensely nervous about him, or about something.

"So," he says, over the rim of the cup, "what family business? And how did you find me?"

She waves a hand. "Oh, I knew you had to pass through here. Mam—" She winces at herself—"Elizabeth and Gregor sent me."

Matt doesn't have to ask how she recognized him. Hanging in the castle is his ancient portrait in oils. There've been more recent photos, too, since he came out of hiding. Decades old, but not out of date.

"How are they?"

"They're well. They're just recently back from an expedition."

"Space?"

"No, sea. That *Beagle* tour they've been threatening as long as I can remember."

"Longer than that," says Matt. "Well, I'm glad they finally made it."

"They had to cut it short and come home in a hurry."

"Why?"

Her eyes widen. "Haven't you seen the papers?"

He shakes his head, thinking, *Don't tell me they've reinvented war while I've been away . . .*

Susan runs her thumbnail across the top of her bag. It opens in a way he can't quite see and she pulls out a bundle of news-flyers, hours old and already tattered. Matt spreads them out to see that they're all downmarket—their money pages cover the lottery rather than the stock exchange—and their front sides all have articles and headlines and photos of odd phenomena: a flattened whorl in a wheatfield, a waterspout, the face of a worried-looking man in dungarees, and something that might have been a thrown ashtray. There's a sketch of two grim-faced men in the Puritan-style suits affected by scoffers, the clergy of the local irreligion, captioned: "Sinister visitors—Heresiarchy denies knowledge."

"*This* rubbish?" Matt says.

"It's true," says Susan. She leans forward, voice dropping. "That's what Elizabeth and Gregor found out. The aliens are here. We're being invaded."

Matt sighs, clasps his hands at the back of his head and tilts back the flimsy chair. He's been expecting this for decades, ever since the expedition to the gods, but it still pisses him off. Through the glass roof he can see a couple of silvery lens-shaped skiffs scooting overhead. A couple of tables away, two small grey-skinned figures with large bald heads and big black eyes are canoodling over a shared bloodshake. The blonde person who'd served him at the stall has just shuffled through a spilled sticky drink and is leaving forty-centimeter-long footprints. There's a good chance that several of the commuters striding past had an ancestor on the *Mary* fucking *Celeste*. Three hours ago by his body clock, he was four light-years away. And it was early morning. He's a hundred thousand light-years from Earth and he's hundreds of years old and he feels every meter and minute of it.

"Aliens," he says, looking up again. "Unidentified flying objects. Crop circles. Men in black. This is *too* fucking *much*."

He swings forward, his gaze still focused on the middle distance, and he has a sudden hallucination that he can see right through Susan's T-shirt to a glowing green hologram of her naked torso. He blinks as the chair settles, and it's gone, there's just that pattern of colorful stitchery. He looks away and back, covertly, then meets her eyes. She's smiling.

"Stereogram," she says. "Computer-generated. You just let your eyes go—"

"I know," says Matt. "That's the most indecent garment I've ever seen."

"You haven't seen the skirts."

Matt stares at her face as though it too were a stereogram, and something clicks into focus. He knows she's attractive but he isn't attracted to her. To attribute this to the incest taboo would be absurd—intellectually, there's nothing to it, she's generations removed from him, and emotionally there is no way that inhibition would have had a chance to lock on—it depends on childhood imprinting of siblinghood, as far as he knows. It must be something else. He has the body and brain and appearance of a man in his early twenties, but mentally, inside, he is just too old. That must be it: Susan is too young for him. She's sucking a strand of her frosted fair hair, and tiny fragments of her matching lipstick are clogging the tips. As though realizing what she's doing, she flicks it away.

"Anyway," she says, "Elizabeth and Gregor want to see you."

"Up at the castle?"

"No. Too busy up there. For the merchants, this place is becoming a bit of a culture shock. Along the shore, at the marine biology lab." She stands. "We can walk." She sees his duffel, and his look. "Or take a tram."

The laboratories are single-storey blocks with wide windows, and walls whose pebbledash and roughcast have fallen off in great flakes here and there and mostly been patched up, so that over the years they've acquired a mottled texture like a lichen-covered boulder. The place is old and important enough to have its own tram stop, Aquarium. Inside, there's an atmosphere of barely controlled frenzy: knots of people in white coats arguing in low or raised voices, technicians wheeling equipment down corridors with the urgency of hospital porters in Accident and Emergency. Susan leads Matt through it all. Anyone who gives her a puzzled look or starts to ask her business is tugged back at the elbow by someone else.

At the end of a long corridor with shore-facing windows along one side, she marches into a room with rows of wide white-topped lab benches, aquaria and sinks and display cabinets around the sides, charts and diagrams papering the walls and a broad whiteboard at the far end, in front of which a woman is standing tapping a long pointer at multicolored scribbles and talking to the score of people sitting or standing around. It's her voice Matt recognizes first, just before she recognizes him and interrupts herself.

"Matt!" She walks toward him, arms opening.

"Elizabeth, it's good to see you. Salasso, Gregor . . . wow."

Of his old companions, only the saur Salasso is unchanged, his small thin lips stretched in what for a human would have been a wide grin, his long arms poking far beyond the cuffs of his standard and therefore ill-fitting lab coat. Elizabeth and Gregor have aged fifteen years since Matt last saw them, fifty years ago. As usual it's a jolt but he can hardly see it as a deterioration. Elizabeth's broad, angular features have tightened more than they've sagged, and her walk has gained poise. Her hair is better styled than he remembers and still black, though not (Matt bitch-ily notes, as she air-kisses beside his cheek) at the roots. She's wearing a sharp, elegant grey trouser suit that looks like, and may even be, a uniform. Gregor's handshake is harder, his thin face looks more worn, and his swept-back hair (which, like his face, distantly echoes Matt's own) grows grey-flecked, and from farther back on his head; his clothes are as casual as ever. Salasso's long hands grasp Matt's shoulders, briefly. Matt smiles down into the huge eyes, black as though all pupil, and wonders if the saur can feel the faint reflexive shudder induced, against all reason, by his friendly touch. If he does, he gives no sign, and is probably wise enough to realize it's just a reflex, not a reflection.

Elizabeth turns back to the gaggle of scientists.

"Take five—take ten," she says. "We'll bring Matt up to speed and get back in ten minutes."

They disperse, some into huddles around the room, others outside. As they depart, Matt sees a table previously obscured by their backs. There are bones on a black plastic sheet, tweezers around them like sated steel piranhas. Matt finds himself drawn toward the array like an abductee to a skiff.

"Jeez H," he says, so close that his breath moves dust. It's the Holy Grail, right there before his eyes: physical evidence. He's seen pictures; by the gods, he has seen pictures, but until this moment he has never seen real hard evidence of multicellular life of extraterrestrial origin.

"That's what we've all been thinking," says Gregor dryly as Matt straightens, still fascinated, still tracing out in his mind how the thing hangs together. Gregor and Elizabeth take about one minute to recount their encounter with the selkies and their discoveries at Lemuria Beach.

"You're all sure?" says Matt, suddenly struck with a doubt. "You don't think it could be just a new terrestrial phylum, I dunno, some kind of Burgess Shale survivor—"

He keeps to himself his momentary hallucinogenic vision of a pre-Cambrian civilization, which had gone off into space and returned to Earth at the end of the Cretaceous, just in time to meet the ancestors of the saurs, tweak their genes and set *them* off on their travels after the gods' wrath hit Chicxulub. . . .

"No, because that's not all we have," says Gregor. "It gets worse."

And he's pointing to an elaborately sealed vivarium on a bench over at the side. Sand and a puddle and a clump of algae. Something moving. This time, Matt has to force himself close enough to look. He finds he has mild arachnophobia, rather to his surprise. Probably picked it up in a dodgy lodging house years ago. Well, the only way to overcome a phobia is to face its stimulus and extinguish the response. . . .

Considered objectively, it's quite beautiful. Like a golden-furred tarantula, with tiny splayed hands at the ends of seven of its eight legs Tiny eight-fingered hands, each a minature of itself, as becomes evident when it skitters up the glass and walks upside down across the underside of the clamped-down glass slab on top. Matt gropes for a hand lens, peers through it as the animal repeats the manoeuvre. The brief flickering glimpse leaves no doubt. At the end of each appendage's eight fingers there are other tinier appendages, eight of them, and these fingers' fingerlets are what open out to grasp the microscopic frictions of the pane.

"Holy shit," says Matt. "A natural bush robot."

"A what?" asks Elizabeth.

"Kind of like the fabricators off the ship," says Matt, "but free-moving. Manipulators on the manipulators, right down to the molecular level. Early idea, never got built because the fine motor controls get hellishly complicated. But with a natural one, the lower levels could run on reflex, like digestion or something. Maybe it doesn't go that far down, but it goes a hell of a long way."

He looks again at the thing in the tank, and notices a much smaller specimen running around. "Please don't tell me the top-level hands are *buds* . . ."

Elizabeth, Salasso, and Gregor look at each other, and at him.

"That's exactly what they are," says Gregor. 'We picked up a few small ones, which we thought were spiders, on Lemuria Beach. It was only after we came back that we noticed they were still alive.'

"What do they eat?"

"Anything organic," says Salasso. "Their initial sustenance was the ether in the killing jar. Then each other. This is the survivor, and its first offspring."

"Did I see it wrong," asks Matt, "or does it have two mouths?"

"It has," says Elizabeth. "One for eating, one on the opposite side of its head for breathing."

People are coming back. This is a discussion that assimilates interruptions and swirls on. Elizabeth returns to the whiteboard. Matt moves in to perch on the edge of a table; Susan Harkness hangs back, it seems shyly until Matt notices that she is discreetly recording. Fair enough: This is history. No, it's worse, it's evolution . . .

Elizabeth wipes the board and begins scrawling anew. A circle, a tangent, a couple of dots.

"We've identified the star that the selkie pointed out," she says "It's on the edge of the known Second Sphere—actually just over a hundred light-years from Nova Sol—but definitely off the trade routes and about four light-years from here. So assuming we interpreted the selkie correctly, it seems a plausible enough place of immediate origin. Gregor, over to you."

Gregor takes her place at the board. "I've done a first-cut analysis," he says, waving a sheaf of papers. "Because it's so close to us, we already have a solid body of knowledge built up from navigating around the neighborhood, which should enable us to plot a jump within weeks. If we want to go there, that is."

"Why should we want to go there?" someone asks.

Gregor shrugs. "Scientific curiosity?"

Polite laughter.

"Okay," Gregor goes on, "but seriously . . . it looks very much as if these octopods, or whatever we want to call them, have been here in the past few years. Which raises the question of how they got in and out undetected—we've had the skies pretty well covered for decades. I was with Matt here just before and after he went off on the expedition seventy-odd years ago to contact the gods near Croatan, from which most of our admittedly scrappy information about the aliens—the octopods—is derived. I've had a long time to think about its implications. One of them is that we are dealing here with the actual inventors of the lightspeed drive and the gravity skiff, and the species that—"

He glances at Salasso, and at the two or three other saurs in the audience, as though he's about to mention something indelicate.

"—genetically uplifted the ancestors of the saurs, and culturally—at least—uplifted the kraken. We are used to thinking of these species as wise and ancient, which indeed they are, but the octopods are *their* 'Elder Race.' I don't think we should underestimate their abilities, which may include making a lightspeed jump to a point arbitrarily close to a planetary surface; various stealth technologies, et cetera." Expansive handwave. "We can only place the limits of their capabilities as within the laws of physics which, come to think of it, we don't know either. So maybe the stuff we're seeing in the more, ah, uninhibited newsflyers is not entirely out of the question."

In the ensuing hubbub Gregor looks at Matt, rather helplessly. Matt jumps to his feet and strides to the front.

"This is all completely bizarre," he says. He waits for the nods, then goes on. "That's what makes it believable. I know what a planet undergoing alien intervention looks like, because I was born on one! And I can tell you, this is all horribly familiar. Most of what you read about it is rubbish, hysteria, hoaxes, but if you dig deeper you'll find a hard core of cases that remain unexplained. Not that I'm recommending you dig deeper."

"Why not?" Gregor asks, looking baffled. "If we could only clear out some of the clutter   "

"Waste of time," says Matt. "You'll get bogged down. The phenomena are elusive, that's part of what they are, it's definitive, it's how I can recognize the situation." A thought strikes him. "Just when did you and Elizabeth come back from Lemuria Beach?"

Gregor hesitates. "Couple of weeks ago," he says.

"Let me guess," says Matt. "You've been back since, right? With lots of skiffs skimming the sea, lots of people scouring the bogs and moors."

"That's right," says Gregor. He shifts uncomfortably. "And, well, the fact is—"

"The selkies and the octopods are nowhere to be found?"

Everybody stares at him.

"How did you know?"

Matt grins evilly at Gregor, then swings his gaze around the room. "Like I said, it's a feature. Believe me, folks, better minds than ours have been destroyed trying to make sense of this sort of thing. We're dealing with the unknown, with something irreducibly strange."

"That's a counsel of despair," says one of the scientists.

"No, it isn't," says Matt. "It's to recognize that we can never make sense of it while part of the picture—perhaps most of it— is inaccessible. So I concur with Gregor's suggestion—if we have the slightest reason to think we know where these things are coming from, let's go there and invade *them*. Make *them* watch the skies for a change."

"Were you serious about that?" Elizabeth asked. She'd found herself, not entirely to her delight, walking alongside Matt while her husband and Salasso had got into some deep conversation and her daughter walked behind them recording it. They were on their way along the esplanade from the lab to find somewhere to have dinner and catch up.

"About what?"

"Going there. Invading the aliens."

"Oh, yeah, sure. I'd sign up for it tomorrow. Fuck, I'd go on my own." He cast her a conniving glance. "Just lend me a ship?"

"Not a chance," she said cheerfully. "I wouldn't trust you with a ship even if we could spare one. Which we can't. So that would mean going on a proper expedition, armed no doubt, on what might turn out to be an eight-year-long wild-goose chase."

"That's looking on the bright side," said Matt. "We could blunder into something that would start a war with the aliens."

"Or the war—or whatever—might start while we're away."

Matt grunted and shook his head. "I don't think that's how

these things work. This *probing*"—he laughed, nervously she thought—"and assorted anomalous phenomena could go on for at least another century. That's about how long I give us, at our current rate of development, before the gods decide we're getting too big for our boots. And if they do something before that, putting a few light-years between us and it, sounds like a good start."

"Not much help in the long run." She shot a bleak look at Matt. "But then again, what is?"

"Oh, it's all unutterably fucking depressing," said Matt, not sounding depressed at all. "It's like biological pest control—the species introduced to keep down the pest becomes a pest itself, and we're it. Or the aliens are. Whether the gods are setting us or them up as the vermin this time around is as irrelevant to us as it is to them. If we make peace with the aliens the gods can line up something else to come out of nowhere and clobber us both."

"It makes me wonder," she said, "if Volkov wasn't right after all."

4

The Modern Prince

THEY LOOKED, VOLKOV thought, like samurai. The seven men and five women of the Senate's Defense Committee all wore identical black-silk kimonos, very plain, without any of the elab orate folds and pleats of the current mode. The men's hair was cropped, the women's coiled and stacked; their ceremonial swords, too, were in the ancient Roman style, stubby *gladii* in scabbards stuck behind broad sashes. None of them seemed over forty which, after the Academy, was a relief. They sat around a long table, the head of which faced a tall window. The room was on the top floor of the building Volkov had noticed close to the de Tenebres', a neo-brutalist tower surmounted by a sculpture of an eagle and chiseled Latin letters. It was the headquarters of the city's lightly armed militia, and of its external defense force—a smaller but more formidable army—which together were known for some reason as "the Ninth." Like most such forces in the Second Sphere, its main enemies were bandits and pirates. It hadn't been in an external war for several centuries, and the total number of losses in that war were memorialized in the entrance lobby on a far from grandiose plinth. The more frequent, but still rare, civil wars in the city's history were not commemorated at all.

Their lesson, however, had not been forgotten: the Ninth's civilian political oversight was close, and literal. The Committee met weekly, here on the top floor.

Volkov and Esias sat side by side at the foot of the table, cast at a disadvantage by the strong light from the window—a position in which, no doubt, many officials and officers had sat. As the Committee members shuffled papers and sipped water and talked amongst themselves as they prepared to begin, Volkov reached inside his dress-uniform jacket and found two old pairs of sunglasses. He passed the Ray-Bans to Esias and slipped on the ESA-issue reflective-lensed Leica Polaroids. Then he settled back and faced the now much more observable Committee in greater comfort to himself and, he hoped, less to them.

Carus Jin-Ming, at the head of the table, unfolded his hands from inside his sleeves, lifted his briefing papers and tapped the edges of the stack into place. He nodded at Volkov.

"Begin," he said.

"Chairman Carus, my lords, ladies and gentlemen," said Volkov, "thank you. In the documents before you, you will have read how the *Bright Star* came to Mingulay, and how two centuries later it traveled to Croatan and back. What you will not have read, because it is too sensitive an item to entrust to paper as yet, is what was done with that ship while it was in Croatan's system of worlds. News of what happened there will no doubt arrive, in secondhand and distorted form, over the next months—the ship of the family Rodriguez is, I understand, due to arrive here in a matter of weeks. From that and other ships the news will spread uncontrollably, like a flash flood through the streets. It is vital that the people's representatives should have a full and accurate account in advance of popular rumor.

"That account I can give you, firsthand. I and some others took the ship to the Croatan system's asteroid belt, and communicated with the gods within two of the asteroids. From them we learned that ships of another intelligent species will soon arrive in the Second Sphere. How soon, we do not know. It could be today, it could be a century or more from now. We do know that the gods expect our species—the children of Man, and the saurs—to come into conflict with those aliens. And, I regret to say, the gods look favorably on such conflicts, because they pro-

84

vide an apt nemesis to any human or other hubris. I have seen evidence of terrible mutual destruction in the deep past, between saurs and the aliens. As you must know, for such a conflict we are all ill-prepared. I have some suggestions as to what preparations we should make. Whether you wish to attend to my suggestions is of course a matter for yourselves."

Carus stilled the ensuing commotion with a sharp glance.

"I must say that this is a surprise, Colonel Volkov," he said. "From the background papers which you and the Trader de Tenebre have provided, I expected a discussion on possible implications for our security, as well as for our prosperity, from the Mingulayans' apparent recent mastery of interstellar navigation. The discussion of an alien invasion is something for which I am as ill-prepared as, you say, we all are for its eventuality. However, let us proceed. The first thought that comes to my mind is that we have no reason to trust the gods, as is well known." He glanced around, smiling frostily. "Within educated circles, that is." A small, nervous titter ran around the table, like an escaped mouse. "The second thought that comes, nay, springs to mind is that if your information is correct, the first people we should lay it before are the saurs. They are our friends, our benefactors, our protectors, and they have space travel. They have communion with the krakens, and the krakens have communion with the gods. Any emergency from the heavens is their province, and any help we can give, I am sure we will be as ready to offer as they to ask."

Volkov refrained from speaking, preferring to let someone else bring up the objection. As he'd expected, someone did.

"My lord Chairman," said one of the women—Julia de Zama, according to the crib of the seating plan that Esias had surreptitiously doodled—"in the background paper it has been pointed out that some, perhaps most, of the saurs on Mingulay and Croatan were less than happy with human-controlled space travel. They believe that it draws unwelcome attention from the gods, and they may be right. We, in any case, do not have space vehicles of our own. Suppose, then, that we hand this problem to the saurs. What can they do? We have seen the saurs project the fields of their skiffs to use as battering rams, and we have seen them fire plasma rifles. And that, my lord Chairman, is the sum total of human knowledge of saur military prowess after ten thousand years."

She looked directly at Volkov. "Perhaps the Colonel has seen evidence of other weapons in this communication from the gods?"

Volkov shook his head. "No, my lady, my lord Chairman, I have not. The space-going species seem capable of inflicting terrible destruction on each other, but that has more to do with the vulnerability of their habitats and the availability of kinetic energy in the form of metallic asteroids and so forth than any advanced weaponry. I've seen visual displays of conflicts which appear to have occurred intermittently over millions of years, and certainly no nuclear or particle-beam weapons were deployed in them. I suspect that the gods disapprove of their use, particularly in space, and take measures to prevent it. Not that they stopped anyone on Earth from developing them. The empire which I once had the honor to serve, the European Union, had much more destructive capacity at its disposal than anything I have seen evidence of since."

Carus drew a breath through his teeth. "Well, Colonel Volkov, while that may give us as children of Man a certain perverse satisfaction, it doesn't really help us, now does it? We are all well aware of the kind of weapons that were developed on Earth in the century and a half before your departure. Thanks to the saurs, we have never needed them, or anything remotely like them. The saurs have no need of such weapons, and given their well-known reluctance to provoke the gods, are unlikely to wish to develop them, or to help us to do so."

"You have grasped the essence of the problem, my Lord Chairman," said Volkov: "If we are to defend ourselves against the aliens, we must do so with the cooperation of the saurs or without it. We must develop space rockets and nuclear weapons of our own."

Then he sat back to wait for the explosion, and the fallout.

・   ・   ・

"You are a devil," said Esias as, for the second time in three days, he caught up with the departing Volkov, minutes after the Cosmonaut had stormed out. "You are like the Shaitan of the monotheists, a sower of discord."

"Am I, indeed?" Volkov snarled. "Then I am glad of it."

He realized he'd been stalking along, legs and arms stiff, fists clenched. He stopped and willed himself to relax. The midday sun bore down mercilessly on the deep, wide street. The crowd that flowed along the busy sidewalk spared him curious glances, steering clear. Flying squirrels, in all sizes from mouse to monkey, combining the ubiquity of urban pigeons with the arrogance of urban rats, chittered and gnawed wherever he looked. Rickshaws and cycles whirred, electric-tractored vehicles whined, heavily built horses whinnied. The glare—white off statuary, multicolored off mosaic—hurt him through the sunglasses. Esias seemed genuinely disturbed, sweat oozing from his creased brow, his armpits staining his blue pajamas. In the merchant's borrowed glasses Volkov saw his own reflection, his hair gone spiky and his eyes masked and his suit and shirt rumpled.

His hand loomed in the reflection as he reached for Esias's shoulder. "I'm sorry," he said. "I . . . lost command of myself. Let's do what we did before, and take a beer in the shade."

Esias, mollified but still looking worried, followed him through the glass doorway of the nearest beer parlor. Office workers from the commercial quarter filled it with lunchtime clatter and smoke. Some stared at Volkov's curious garb, and flinched from the blank flash of his shades. He bought two beers and escorted Esias to a corner at the back. After he removed the sunglasses, the world seemed brighter; after a few sips of beer, brighter still.

Esias was giving him a look that said *what do you have to say for yourself?* Oddly, for all his longevity, Volkov felt for a moment the younger man; a distant memory of his father's frown at some wastrelly act stirred uncomfortably, deep in his mind.

"When I was a student," Volkov said, winging it, "I had to

attend lectures in what was called the philosophy of practice. It was a bore, and a chore, but a requirement. Unlike most of my cohorts, I paid attention, and got top marks. Strange to relate, that may have been crucial to my career. One of the things I recall from that class was the line we were given on the Epicurean and Stoic philosophers: While the Epicurean philosophy was materialist, and therefore in principle progressive, it had no notion of internal conflict or inner dynamism—no dialectic, as the cant went—and was therefore in practice passive. And indeed, politically it did recommend disengagement—"Live unknown," as the man said. It had no answer to the idealist but even more fatalistic philosophy of Stoicism, which duly conquered the best minds of the time. All of this of course was related to the lack of progressive forces in the slave-based ancient economy, or so the story went."

He leaned forward, relishing Esias's puzzled suspicion. "What none of this prepared me for, but which it should have, was to see the effect of the ancient philosophies' having a further two thousand years in which to stew in their own juice. You have no slaves here, but you have the saur manufacturing plant, and the saurs' friendly advice. You have no barbarians, and few Christians, and fewer Jews. Now they had dialectic all right, they had enough contradictions built into their theology to keep them busy forever. And, yes, one of them was Shaitan. You need a Shaitan here. Because without that, you get the kind of crap I heard from the Defense Committee—'If there is nothing we can do, it is as well to do nothing.' Look at how people on Croatan reacted to our warning about the aliens! Not much Stoicism and Epicureanism there! None of this waiting with folded hands!"

"Not all of us are waiting with folded hands," said a cool voice.

Volkov turned and Esias looked up, startled, to see Julia de Zama and another Committee member, Peter Ennius, standing with drinks. Both of them had taken the minority argument, though very subtly, in the meeting. Esias jumped up and bowed.

"May we join you?" asked de Zama.

"Of course, of course," said Volkov, standing and shifting a chair for her. She swept forward and lowered herself into it with a smile, set down her glass and took a moment to straighten her kimono. She was tall and thin, her features fine and firm, her piled hair fashionably hennaed, her eyebrows fair under token penciled arcs. About mid-thirties, Volkov guessed, though the combination of saur medicine and local cosmetics made it hard to tell. Peter Ennius seemed a bit older—a short, thin man whose erect posture and black kimono made him look heavier and taller until he sat down. The musculature of his shoulders and forearms was real and impressive enough. An old soldier, Volkov guessed.

"How did you know we were here?" asked Volkov.

"We had you followed," said Ennius. "Discreetly."

"This is hardly discreet," said Esias.

Julia de Zama sipped a lemon-colored liquid from a twisted-stemmed glass.

"Oh, we don't want it to be discreet," she said. "Let people nudge and stare, let news of our meeting you get back to dear Jin-Ming, hot-foot." She waved a dismissive hand, wide sleeve flapping, as though sending messengers on their way.

"I take it," said Esias to Volkov, "that you have inadvertently drawn the attention of some ongoing intrigue." He smiled at the Senators. "That should certainly save him some time. Good day, my lady, my lord. You will no doubt have much to discuss, but as for me, I'm a businessman, and business is pressing."

With that he drained his glass and left, in no hurry not to be seen leaving.

"A wise move," said Ennius, gazing after him.

"He is not as conservative as you may think," said Volkov. "But you have Senatorial immunity, do you not?"

"We do," said de Zama in a lazy voice. "But our intrigue, so-called, is no secret. We are members of a most respectable association, with support in the Senate, the Academy, and the Ninth, as well as on the Exchange and in the streets of the city. Its aim is the same as its name: It is called the Modern Society. We are, you might say, an open conspiracy."

She paused, as though the phrase were some kind of pass-word. Volkov vaguely recognized it, then the allusion clicked into place. A happy thought struck him.

"You are familiar, I take it, with the history of the Roman general, Fabius Cunctator?"

"Of course," said Julia de Zama. Peter Ennius nodded, grin-ning broadly.

"Very good," said Volkov. "Perhaps, then, you are Fabians?"

"Yes," said Ennius. "Just as Wells was."

Volkov felt relieved that he'd got the connection right. It was about all he knew about Wells—another piece of trivia remem-bered from his philosophy classes. Other than that, the name of Wells conjured nothing for him but a vague image of heat rays and tentacles. Where did that come from? Ah, yes, *The War of the Worlds*. And there was something else, another title that had been mentioned in the lecture on the history of socialism. . . .

He raised his half-empty glass. "To the war of the worlds," he said. "And the modern utopia!"

Julia de Zama was inspecting him with a sardonic but admir-ing eye. She clinked her glass on his.

"To the new Machiavelli," she said.

Lydia twirled, sending the pleats from the waist at the back of her chrysanthemum-print kimono-like robe flaring out, then tot-tered and grabbed the nearest pillar. She pushed away from it, recovering her balance and holding out her arms, the sunray-pleated sleeves opening like fans. She walked as though on a tightrope across the grass of the roof terrace to the table where Esias sat under a fixed umbrella with a jug of iced fruit juice and a stack of newspapers.

"The platform shoes take some getting used to," she admitted, taking a seat.

So that was why she looked so tall.

"But the main thing I like about this," she went on, "is that it's office wear. Isn't it beautiful?"

"Very pretty," said Esias. "Gorgeous, in fact."

Lydia poured herself a drink and pouted around the straw. "You don't sound too enthusiastic."

Esias rocked his seat back and waved a hand. "No, no, nothing to do with you. You're lovely. I'm a bit disgruntled, that's all. Our friend Volkov is up to his old tricks."

Lydia blushed, as well she might. Esias still simmered with disapproval over her involvement with Volkov's intrigues on Croatan, a few jumps and a few months behind them, and he still harbored a deep suspicion that the Cosmonaut's intentions toward his daughter were honorable. If they were having an affair, it was none of his business, any more than it had been when Volkov and Faustina had been going at it like rabbits. But if Volkov were to make a proposal, and Lydia were to accept, then he would find it difficult—in fact, outright embarrassing—to refuse it. And then he would lose his number seven daughter forever, unless—forlorn hope—Volkov's project of remixing the elixir came to fruition in something less than a lifetime.

But Lydia's reply showed she'd kept her composure. "Trying to assemble a coalition of progressive forces, is he?"

Esias groaned. The smatter of ugly jargon Lydia had picked up from the incorrigible ancient Communist was not the least of his bad influences.

"It's worse," he said. "He seems to have found one."

He told her about the morning's meetings. "This Modern Society"—he flicked at the stack of newspapers—"seems to be quite influential. It's all talk, because the guilds and workshops are as conservative here as they are anywhere else—they'll gladly seize on new machines, but not on great disruptions to their methods of work. Grand ideas about giant assembly lines don't really appeal to them. But they have the most confused and exaggerated ideas about Earth, about the great independent achievements of mankind back in the Solar System, all based on the snippets that dribbled in from the ships that came back before we did. Heaven knows what's going to happen when Volkov speaks to the Senate—they've already summoned him, and everyone knows it. There's not a chance of that session's being held *in camera,* and not a chance of his being discreet. The whole place is primed for Volkov to detonate."

Lydia gazed out over the upper tiers of the city shimmering in the heat haze, then back at her father.

"I'm not so sure about that," she said. "It's not like Croatan was, with all that social discontent in Rawliston and their funny religions and unstable political system. This city's pretty good at assimilating new ideas without changing very much. There've been times in the past few days when I've felt we've been away for two weeks, not two hundred years."

"That's just the trouble," said Esias. "Volkov can completely revolutionize Nova Babylonia—Nova Terra, come to that—without a revolution. The Academy and the Defense Committee have been skeptical of his plans. No doubt the Senate will be, too. But in each case, there was a minority whom he managed to fascinate. And that minority can take it to the populace. Once the ideas get out that people can be as long-lived as saurs, and that they can get into space without the saurs, and that there is a threat from space that the saurs can't help us meet, then—well, frankly, I'm glad we'll be out of here in a couple of months."

"So am I," said Lydia. She twiddled ice in the bottom of her glass. "And back in a couple of centuries, by which time the dust should have settled."

Interesting, Esias thought, that she still didn't take the prospect of an alien incursion seriously. Perhaps that instinctive skepticism would prove Volkov's undoing in the long run. On the other hand, there was something else she wasn't taking seriously, and it was a good deal more important and closer to hand.

"Ah," said Esias. "It won't be the usual round trip this time. We could be back in one century, or even less."

Lydia frowned her puzzlement. "What do you mean?"

"Ninety-six years have passed since we left Croatan. Fifty or so more will have passed before we are halfway back. Time enough, I think, for the Cosmonaut clans of Mingulay to build more starships, to extend their operations, to expand their range. Even allowing for a long time to calculate the navigation for each new jump, I should not be at all surprised to find that they have expanded far enough to meet us somewhere *en route*. And if they do"—he rubbed his hands—"here is the beauty of the deal I made with the Cairns family: They will have wares from the outer worlds that we can exchange for our Nova Babylonian commodities right then and there. We can then transfer to another merchant vessel on its return trip—for a suitable consideration, no doubt, but that shouldn't be a problem, we can cut them in on the deal—and return to Nova Terra much sooner than expected, thus stealing a march on our competitors."

"Oh," said Lydia, "very good!" She thought about it for a moment. "And what if they haven't?"

Esias shrugged. "Then we're no worse off. We return in two hundred years as usual and, as you say, the dust should have settled by then." He smiled wryly. "Assuming the aliens haven't invaded, that is."

"What do you think of . . . all that?"

"Consider the probabilities," Esias said. "The Second Sphere has existed for thousands of years, to our certain knowledge. For millions, according to the saurs, and I believe them. Earth has existed on the other side of the Foamy Wake for even longer, according to the books in the *Bright Star*'s libraries, and I believe them, too. In all that time, there has been no evidence of any other space-traveling species than the saurs. In fact, the only scraps of evidence that *Earth* has been visited turn out to have been because of the activities of saurs, and the saurs originated on Earth. The god in the Solar System with which the crew of the *Bright Star* were originally in contact gave them no hint of any other space-going species."

"It didn't tell them about the saurs, either," said Lydia.

"That's a point," Esias conceded, "but it doesn't affect the argument I find most persuasive in my own mind, which is—given how long the situation has remained as I've said, how likely is it that a huge change in it should coincide with our brief lives? The chances are at least thousands to one against, I should say."

Lydia pondered this. "I suspect there's a fallacy in that argument somewhere, but I can't put my finger on it."

"Hah!" said Esias. "It's true, unlikely events happen, and that argument can't rule them out—merely show that unlikely is what they are. But at an intuitive level, some such reasoning must account for my subjective lack of panic about Volkov's, ah, 'monkey-spiders.' And everybody else's, I shouldn't wonder. Including yours, respected Number-seven daughter."

Lydia let her eyes almost close. "You have something in mind for me to do," she said.

"Yes," Esias said, sitting up. "Show lots of enthusiastic interest in what Volkov is up to." He raised his eyebrows. "If, that is, you can still stand his company?"

"Oh, yes," said Lydia. "I can that."

Peter Ennius had left. Julia de Zama tracked his departure with a cynical eye.

"Off to make a report," she said.

"You mean—"

"Of course. There's always somebody, isn't there?"

Volkov agreed that there was always somebody. "A useful man to have on the inside," he said.

"Exactly," said Julia. She waved a hand, and fresh drinks were placed in front of them.

"So," she said, "it's just us."

"Indeed," said Volkov. He chinked his glass against hers. "Long life!"

She repeated the toast. "You know," she said, "that's a much more interesting prospect than alien invasion."

"I know," said Volkov. "I intend to make much of it."

"A good idea, but not exactly what I had in mind. I have a strong personal interest in it myself."

"You're a bit young to concern yourself with that."

She gave him a severe look. "You need not flatter me."

Volkov raised his eyebrows. "No flattery was intended, but"—

he smiled—"if you say so, I must take your word against the evidence of my eyes."

She flushed slightly. "The light is kind, if you are not."

He smiled again, over the rim of his glass. "I expect progress in that area within, oh, ten years, even if half the Academy has to die of old age first."

"Progress," said Julia. "If you only knew how hard it is to find someone who understands the meaning of progress."

Mother of God, he thought, if you only knew.

"Tell me about the Modern Society," he said.

Lydia joined them, without pretense that it wasn't deliberate, about halfway through the afternoon.

"I've been looking over some of the Modern Society's ideas in the papers," she explained, after introductions.

"Your father sent you," said Volkov.

Several empty beer glasses had accumulated on the table; Lydia knew him better than to assume this meant he was drunk. Julia de Zama, on the other hand, looked as if her self-control was less secure. She was sitting back in a louche manner, one arm draped along the back of the seat behind Volkov, and she was giving Lydia a fiercely territorial stare.

"Of course he did," Lydia said, primly arranging her skirts. "He's interested in what you're doing. But that doesn't mean I'm not interested in it myself. This is my city you're messing with."

On reflection, she could have put it better than that. But there was something about Volkov that had always impelled her to be blunt. He seemed to like it. Julia de Zama didn't. She leaned, or maybe (Lydia thought uncharitably) swayed forward and aimed a forefinger.

"It's not your city," she said. "The presumption that it is is half our problem. You people—the Traders—bring changes with every ship, and blithely depart before they take effect, yet always expect the city to be much the same when they return."

Lydia could see the justice of this—it was after all what she herself had said earlier, but expressed in a hostile tone.

"That's not a problem," she said. "It's a solution. We give the city stability without stagnation, progress without destruction."

"No you don't," said de Zama. "You give it muddle and waste and cross-purposes, and evade both consequence and responsibility. And I'll tell you something else. We don't need you. We don't need the Traders, and we don't need the saurs. If we were to rely on our own resources, we should astonish ourselves."

"I'm sure you would," said Lydia. "But how would you do it, exactly? How would you cut the city loose from all the attachments of trade with other stars and other species? How would you manage affairs without saur mediation? Tell me. Go ahead, I'm all ears. Astonish *me*."

And recklessly, passionately, eloquently, Julia de Zama did. She seemed even to astonish Volkov, who for once was acting the part of moderation. Lydia listened and watched the Cosmonaut and the Senator, their voices and eyes and hands, and realized something more astonishing than the Modern Society's ambitions: Volkov and de Zama were falling in love.

Lydia felt nothing but relief.

Volkov had never before in all his long life seen a saur shudder. When Voronar, the saur pilot and translator from the ship, had finished talking, Volkov saw seven saurs shudder at once. Deleneth, the apparent speaker for the group, turned her head slowly to Volkov, and the other heads turned in unison, like caged lizards watching a fly on the other side of a glass pane.

"You *talked*," she said, "to the *gods*?"

Evidently Voronar had given an accurate account. The saurs all understood Trade Latin and other human languages—their linguistic facility was something Volkov admired without being impressed with, vaguely relating it to the imitative knack of birds—but for serious matters they preferred the subtler nuances of their own speech. This meeting was the most important of any he'd attended so far; more so even than the Senate hearing tomorrow. Its calling had been on shorter notice and had been more imperative. He could finesse anything that happened with the Senate, there or afterward. This group of representatives of the saurs resident in Nova Babylonia could not be blindsided.

"Yes, we did," said Volkov, trying not to shift in his seat. The tiny room was built for saur comfort, not human. A back room of a saur dive near the harbor, its lighting was dim, its furniture was made of something like cork and was so small his knees were higher than his waist, and it all stank of hemp and fish. He was the only human present, and the only person who might just possibly be on his side in any contretemps was Voronar, assuming that saur's loyalty to his employers overrode his solidarity with his kind, something on which Volkov was not counting and hoped not to find out.

"We know that the gods are angry with the saurs," said one of the seven who sat facing him and Voronar in a long row like a bench of inquisitors. "If the gods you spoke to made you mistrust the saurs, perhaps that is another expression of their anger. Perhaps they wish to turn the hominidae against us, to punish us."

Voronar hissed some acid comment, then turned to Volkov. "You explain."

"I know this is difficult for you to accept," said Volkov. "I tell you honestly, and you can compare what I say with what Voronar has just said without my understanding—the gods are not angry with the saurs. Some of the saurs on the outer worlds have come to agree with that, but—and again you can see I am being frank with you—most have not. The saur Salasso who first told them that, and who went with us to inquire of the gods, was in my own presence almost hurled to his death from a great height."

A susurrus of hissing consultation followed. Volkov was surprised at the reaction until he remembered that the saur method of hunting, megayears established and ingrained, was to stampede herds of herbivorous dinosaurs off cliffs. To be thrown from a height must be the most disgraceful and terrible death that could be inflicted on a saur.

The saurs all looked at him again in silence.

"I do not mistrust the saurs," Volkov said into the silence. "I would like to work together with the saurs of Nova Terra and other worlds to prepare for the arrival of the monkey-spider aliens. If we are to set up defenses in space, it would obviously be preferable to have the use of gravity skiffs. The god in the Solar System who spoke to us long ago gave humans the instructions for building skiffs and lightspeed ships, and the humans, and some saurs, on Mingulay and Croatan are working together to build them. After some years—I do not know how many—these humans will be here, and humans here will have the skiffs and ships in any case. But by then, the monkey-spiders may have arrived, and made war on us all. So why not work together now?"

"I can tell you why not," said Deleneth. "The gods do not mind that we travel between the worlds on which we live. But they do mind, very much, if we venture into the gods' domain. There was a time long ago when the saurs did that, and the gods showed their anger and struck at them."

Volkov knew that this was true. He had seen the ancient ruins on Croatan's moon himself.

"That is so," he said. "But the defenses that I recommend we build in space would also be defenses against the gods' wrath."

The saurs facing him swayed slightly back in their seats. Three of them went so far as to claw at their sleeves. Even Voronar sat rigid and still. At last Deleneth spoke.

"Very few will help you with that," she said. "If you persist, if you persuade the humans to follow this this course, very few saurs will work with humans at all. We cannot fight against you, because that too would anger the gods, but we can withdraw from you. We can leave your cities, and the ships in which you travel. What the kraken will do we do not know, but we can guess."

Volkov sighed and laid his hands on his knees, palms up. "You will do what you must, and so will I, and so will those I persuade."

"There is nothing further to discuss," said Deleneth. She and the other six rose and withdrew, and after waiting a couple of minutes to let them get out of the building, Volkov did the same. Voronar stayed with him and walked out beside him.

The narrow street was dark. Volkov walked down it and across a broad esplanade and leaned on the rail. Voronar solemnly propped his chin on the same railing and they looked out across the harbor, bright with the lights of ships and starships.

"That did not go well," said Voronar.

"I'm getting used to hearing that," said Volkov. "I'm also getting used to having a small minority agreeing with my proposal."

"In this instance it appears that I am that minority," said Voronar. "Though I cannot help you much, for I intend to travel again with the de Tenebres."

"Good for you."

"Yes," said Voronar. "I think Deleneth was mistaken about the saurs who travel on the ships, and the skiff pilots generally. We are more openminded than the saurs who stay on the worlds."

Volkov smiled. The skiff pilots he'd known back on Mingulay were indeed, by saur standards, rakish.

"Do you think," Voronar went on, "that the humans here can get along without the help of saurs?"

Volkov had thought about this. Apart from space travel and the products of the manufacturing plant—all of which could be replaced, or done without at a pinch—the main saur contribution to human well-being was in their unobtrusive medical help. From the first, as far as he knew, the saurs had patiently explained the germ theory of disease and its consequences, and something like the Malthusian principle of population and its consequences. The saurs supplied contraceptives. They supplied some kind of life-extension treatments, so that the normal healthy human lifespan was about a hundred and twenty years.

Nothing for the genetic causes of aging, which—he presumed—had been synergistically and serendipitously found on Earth in the treatment, whatever it was, that had worked on him. Surgery they taught, tissue regeneration they applied, though not for trivial cases. They moved fast to contain and cure the epidemics that inevitably got shuttled around the Second Sphere by starships.

"It'll be tough," he said.

The news broke the following day. Lydia was working in one of the offices midway up the building—a quite pleasant office, open-plan and open to a terrace, and, unlike most offices she'd worked in—including this one at the time of her previous landfall—full of workers in comfortable and colorful clothes. It clattered with telegraphy and teleprinters, most of which were connected with the big calculating machines down in the basement. The work itself was laborious, but interesting, as she and her siblings and cousins coordinated what they knew of the cargo with what the locals knew of the markets. At exactly an hour before noon everyone stopped. The machines fell silent, and radio receivers were switched on. Lydia couldn't be sure, but she thought the sounds from outside of traffic and general mechanical background hum diminished at the same time, as all across the city people stopped work to listen to the news.

It was a direct feed from the microphones in the Senate's council chamber, and the channel was always on whenever the Senate was in session. No commentary was permitted. The citizens of the Republic might not all have the right to elect the Senators, but they had the right to the raw data of what was said in their name.

Esias de Tenebre had just been called before the assembly, and began his address with a concise account of his family's commission to go to Mingulay and bring back as much new information as possible. So far, so familiar. He held forth briefly on the wealth of information from the twenty-first-century Solar System and its significance. Then he moved on to the surprises:

the Cosmonauts' longevity, and their first steps toward mastery of the lightspeed drive. This was news to most of the people around Lydia, though perhaps not to most of the Senate, who were sure to have heard rumors. The room rustled with whispers and silk, and Lydia thought she heard, through the open windows, the sound of the whole city drawing in its breath.

After a brief word of thanks from the Senate's chair, the floor was given to Volkov.

Lydia could hardly pay attention to what he said. She knew it all already, knew exactly what he would say and how he would say it. Instead she watched the office workers, saw how their mouths opened and their hands crept into their sleeves to clutch their elbows as they listened to his insidious message and insinuating voice. When he had finished, the newsfeed fell silent. After thirty seconds a brief, nervous announcement followed. For only the second time in the past seven hundred years, the Senate had gone into closed session.

Lydia walked out to the terrace, wanting to shut her ears to the angry or fearful voices that filled the room, but found no respite. From the terrace, she could hear a sound she had never heard before, the clamor of a city of millions arguing with itself, like the buzz of an upturned hive.

5

Tidal Race

A NOTHER BEACH, ANOTHER world.
Elizabeth walked along purple-tinged sand, the skiff keeping pace a few meters behind her. The skiff's pilot, Delavar, was an old acquaintance on whose loyalty and reflexes she was more than ready to rely. Somewhere behind the navy sky the Cairns ships hung in gravity-defying non-orbit, in any emergency a screaming red-hot minute away. The air was thick and stank of iodine. A few tens of meters to her left, the last exhausted ripples of breakers whose surf broke hundreds of meters farther away hissed into the sand. The tide was far out and on the turn. Giant oystercatchers the size of moas stalked the shallows, stabbing the sand with beaks like swords. Kilometers to her right, a row of cliffs defined the horizon. This beach was huge, visible from space as a white crescent like a life-size drawing of a small moon. They'd called it Atlantis Flats. The red sun loomed high in the sky, far bigger than any sun she'd ever stood beneath, but utterly dwarfed by the ringed gas giant that, gibbous, filled an eighth of the sky above the sea. It looked as though it were floating on the ocean beyond the horizon, the colors of its bands and the dark of its nightside segment and a long, wavy ink-black line from its razor-thin ring bleeding into the water.

Just half a kilometer ahead of her, the city of the selkies rose from the beach and the sea, straddling the mouth of a broad river. Built on stone pillars and wooden pilings resting on the bedrock beneath the sand and silt, and rising about twenty meters above them, the city extended to about a hundred meters beyond the low-water mark and spread for nearly three kilometers along the shore. Intricate inlays of shell fragments embedded in its wood-and-stone buildings shone in the sunlight and glittered in the reflected light from the sea. A haze of smoke and steam hung over it, constantly replenished by the funnels and flues of an industry which, going by the expedition's earlier discreet aerial surveys, processed wood, fish, algae, and kelp. It resembled thousands of such settlements dotted along the coasts of the planet's continents and islands; it was twice the size of the next largest. Inland from the coastal villages and towns unpaved roads linked quarries and logging sites. Other than that, all traffic and communication seemed to be by sea or river: small sailing vessels, long canoes, signaling by smoke and flag and mother-of-pearl mirror flash. No aerial traffic had been detected, not even skiffs.

Beneath the pillars in front of her, a sail snapped up and began to move swiftly across the sand toward her. She stopped, and the skiff did likewise.

"Wait here?" asked Delavar, through the beads on her ears.

"Yes," she whispered back, through the bead on her throat.

Their communications, like the visual display of the scene, were being relayed to the fleet.

After a couple of minutes the sail-powered vehicle—a three-wheeled, low-slung frame of wood and wicker—tacked and slewed to a halt not far away. Two selkies vaulted out; another remained on board, one hand on the rope connected to the boom of the sail, the other resting casually on three spears.

The two selkies on the sand walked forward, empty hands spread. Elizabeth reflected the gesture with even greater polite hypocrisy. One walked ahead of the other, and stopped a couple of his long steps away. His looming face peered down at her. She tried to smile.

"Welcome," said the selkie, startling her immeasurably. "We have been expecting you."

Elizabeth stepped back, staring. It was the selkie from Lemurai Beach.

"You may remember me, from another shore," continued the selkie. "I think I recognize you."

"How do you speak our language?" Elizabeth asked. "And how did you get here?"

The selkie scratched his midriff absently. "Those of us who were on that shore returned to this one, on a ship of the eight-armed ones. The same taught some of us your speech."

Once again Elizabeth revised upward her opinion of selkie intelligence. "And how did they know it? We have not spoken with them."

"They listen and watch," said the selkie. He scratched again, and put a fingertip between smacking lips. "They listen and watch us now."

Reflexively, Elizabeth looked behind her, then, more rationally, upward. The zenith was empty. The selkie's deep chuckle welled up.

"They are near, but not there. They wish to know if they can come here safely."

"We will not attack them," said Elizabeth.

Delavar made a sort of strangled noise that set up feedback in her earbeads. She silently willed him to shut up.

"Very well," said the selkie. He looked up, as though belying his earlier statement, and said something in another language. Then he turned again to Elizabeth.

"My name is Khaphthash," he said.

"Mine is Elizabeth."

For a moment, its syllables sounded just as strange in her ears.

Khaphthash smiled, tipping his head back, and looked to one side. "They are coming," he said.

Elizabeth looked in the same direction and saw, as it seemed far out to sea, a tiny silver disk rapidly approach. A few meters away, a small elliptical patch of shadow as swiftly enlarged on the sand. She blinked and shook her head, and saw that the disk was not above the sea, but tiny and above the sand in just the right place to cast the shadow, but it was at the same time unquestionably far away and approaching—no, it was really small and becoming bigger and bigger. The sand beneath it began to move, the grains arcing in precise trajectories quite unlike sand being blown about: She could look down and see it flowing around her boots. A wide circle with a complex internal pattern formed as the disk approached, or enlarged. The perspectives kept shifting until it was suddenly there in front of her, its three legs extending and settling on the beach in the exact position of three internal sworls in the sand circle. The mode of arrival was deeply unsettling and uncanny to witness.

"Did you *see* that?" she whispered to Delavar.

"An incident of high strangeness," said Matt's voice in her ear.

"That was an emergence from a lightspeed jump," said Delavar. "I have never before seen it done in a skiff, or so close to a planet."

"Yep," muttered Elizabeth, "three meters is close to a planet all right. . . ."

Still, that explanation made the arrival, if not comprehensible, at least rational. The skiff's hull was perfectly reflective, a huge lens of what looked like the surface of a liquid in its smoothness, like mercury. In a moment, a hatch opened and a ladder extended. An octopodal alien skittered down it and across the sand to her. As it approached she heard Delavar making small, distressed noises.

"Are you all right?" she whispered.

"I will be," said Delavar. "I am experiencing fear that I know to be irrational. This is new to me."

Elizabeth was experiencing no fear at all, which at some level of her consciousness she thought disturbing. The alien's golden fur was astonishingly beautiful—she had to resist an impulse to stroke it—and it gave off a pleasant, musky fragrance: laced with soothing pheromones, she guessed. The tips of its limbs, as it walked, were compressed to hard, sharp points that left deep, small indentations in the sand. As it stepped closer she saw that the fur was irridescent, and was almost certainly not simply hair but some kind of optical fiber. Every follicle must be light-sensitive, for that to make any kind of functional sense. She tried to imagine the sensorium of a mind that could use so much input, a flow of information orders of magnitude greater than even the all-around vision provided by the eight eyes, and failed.

Its breathing-mouth—a triangle of overlapping lips, with jaws but without teeth—was on the side facing her. The alien raised its two front limbs and waved them. The palm-buds expanded, opening to the tips of the tips of the tips, like a ring of dandelion clocks, then contracted back to eight-fingered hands that it moved together, the fingertips touching and rhythmically tapping each other in a curiously human, almost effete gesture. It stood about a meter and a half tall, its head-thorax somewhat larger than a human head, and more domed than that of the specimens Elizabeth had seen so far.

Thinking to reduce any possible intimidation from her greater height, Elizabeth moved to squat. Instantly the octopod whirled around, presenting its eating-mouth, open in a flash of teeth. Startled, Elizabeth fell back on her butt, hands scrabbling the sand. The selkie, Khaphthash, reached over a hand and helped her back to her feet as the octopod returned to its former position.

The breathing-mouth opened and the alien spoke, in a curiously high-pitched and breathless voice, like a very old person with emphysema.

"My apologies. Please do not do that. The posture triggers a fighting reflex."

"My apologies," Elizabeth replied, mentally kicking herself. It seemed too banal to be the first words spoken to an extraterrestrial. "We are pleased to meet you at last."

"And we you," said the alien. "As you can deduce from my grasp of your language, we have been observing your planet for some time."

"We had suspected that," said Elizabeth. "We have come here to learn of your intentions."

"Very good," said the alien. It swung its head as though looking around, a surely unnecessary thing for it to do, and therefore likely meant as a reassuring imitation of the human. "Let us repair to the city, where we can discuss these matters in more comfortable surroundings."

It scuttled back off to its skiff, which led the way at a slow pace along the beach. The selkies wheeled their odd contraption along.

"Who is piloting your skiff?" asked Khaphthash.

"A saur named Delavar."

"Your people were taken to your world by saurs?"

"Yes," said Elizabeth.

"Our people have old tales of encounters with saurs," said the selkie. "They are not pleasant."

"Would there be trouble if Delavar came out of the skiff?"

"Trouble?" The seal-man looked sidelong and down at her, his small chin disappearing into the blubber of his neck. "No, not hostility. There would be surprise. It might be a good surprise, for our people. And they have to meet sometime. Why not now?"

"What do you think, Delavar?"

"I am consulting with the fleet," Delavar murmured back.

"Go for it," says Matt, before anyone can object.

Gregor glares at him, Salasso casts him a heavy-lidded look of reproof, Susan Harkness busies herself with the recording apparatus, and the Cairns' flagship skipper, Zachary Gould, pointedly looks away out of the viewscreen. Matt doesn't care: He's the First Contact Convener, and he decides this sort of stuff, even if Elizabeth did pull rank—and, to be fair, her prior experience with the selkies—to be the one on the ground. Anyway, he's on a roll, in a mental state that his distant but still vivid memories associate with amphetamine-fueled all-night coding sessions, and which he is sensible enough at some level to recognize as dangerous, but seductively productive.

The ship he's on is, like its four companions, shaped like the fuselage of a rather boxy aircraft, maybe a World War Two bomber or something like that (Matt is vague about aviation history) made from thick steel and armor-plated glass and about fifty meters long by four high and ten across, except for the skiff-docking bay, which is at the stern and is eighteen meters across. The ship is called the *Return Visit*. The others are called *Explorer*, *Investigator*, *Translator*, and *Experimenter*. Matt's suggested names (*Rectal Probe*, *Up Yours*, *Probably Venus*, *Strange Light*, *No Defence Significance*, et cetera) were all rejected at the committee stage.

It's taken years to get here. Two years and a few months, which to Matt's edgy impatience felt longer. Partly it's been a whole lot of tedious politicking, within the Cairns clan, with the other Cosmonaut Families, with the Heresiarchy and with the city-state governments, starting with Kyohvic and working down. Negotiating with the heretical minority of saurs who agree with Salasso and are working in space with the humans has been a whole 'nother kettle of fish, and by the gods Matt knows by now what a kettle of fish actually is, having consumed many of them in the negotiations. Running on the rolling logs of a public discussion of a real alien presence and alien invasion threat, a discussion conducted amid the waterspouts, crop circles, cattle mutilations, sea serpents, and general flying crockery of mass hallucination and hysteria—has had Matt for the first time in his life devoutly if guiltily wishing he could engineer a good old-fashioned government cover-up, not that there's a government on Mingulay or Croatan that could cover its own ass if you handed it a Blue Book.

On top of that there's been the hard technical graft, from the sort of thing he's been making a living at for the past few decades—porting applications from ancient wet and dry nanotech salvaged from the old *Bright Star* across to a renascent technology where debugging really does mean cleaning the moths off the valves—to top-level project management of the teams building closed-system life-support from old spec and first principles. Because of the short journey times neither the established space-going species nor the upstart humans have any experience in the field, or even much in the way of theory. Even convincing folk that breathable air and potable water, not to mention an unopposed landing, at the other end is not the way to bet when you're making a four-light-year jump into an unexplored system has been a wearing, because essentially political, struggle.

Anyway, it's done, and they have carbon scrubbers and distillation kits and filter beds and hydroponics and some icky gunk from the saur manufacturing plant that, allegedly, manufactures plants. They even have space suits. The five ships of the fleet, each with a complement of twenty or so variously warm bodies, human and saur, have primitive ship-to-ship and space-to-ground missiles, none of which would have impressed a moderately competent pyrotechnician of the Ming Dynasty, and a piratical arsenal of firearms and plasma rifles, which would. If the explorers have to convince anyone that their intentions are peaceful and their armaments defensive, it shouldn't be hard. Nevertheless, this is the biggest collective effort ever mounted by the Bright Star Cultures. The human two-thirds of the crews are— apart from Gregor, Elizabeth, himself, and a few other old and unaging Cosmonauts—young and adventurous types who can stand the thought of dying and the even more daunting thought of finding everyone they knew a minimum of eight years older when they get back. And if they are daunted, well, pay reckoned by time elapsed rather than time lived is a big inducement, as it has hitherto been in the Cairns commercial fleet.

One of these young adventurers is Susan Harkness, the Cairns' youngest daughter, who has wangled her way as recorder onto this dangerous expedition by threatening to do something more dangerous if she isn't. Over the past couple of years Matt has stopped seeing her as too young, and she has stopped seeing him as too old, and they have had an intermittent and relaxed relationship, to her parents' fury and disgust.

Right now she's seeing things from her mother's point of view; but only, Matt hopes, literally.

Close up, the selkies' city looked more than ever like an enormous pier. Its stone pillars and wooden piles were crusted with barnacles and limpets, tufted with green algae, draped with wrack. All of the buildings that she could see looked, on this closer inspection, more like scaffolding. There was little in the way of walls or roofs, and few structures seemed entirely enclosed. Elizabeth supposed that the selkies did not set much store by shelter. Much of the wood was rotten, or bored by shipworm. The stonework was pitted and slimed; even above the tidemark it looked thoroughly weathered. Deep in the structure's dim underside great wheels turned, presumably mills driven by the river; when the tide was coming in, they would revolve in the opposite direction, to just as powerful effect. On this Earth-sized moon of a gas giant with a red giant sun, the tides were swift and fierce.

Crowds of selkies sat or stood on the internal planks and platforms of the structure, or waist-deep in the water beneath, gazing at her. Scattered among them, octopods swung or scampered with the liquid grace of gibbons. Here and there in the city the silvery disks of skiffs glinted; there seemed to be no passages wide enough for them to enter or leave by, and Elizabeth puzzled about that for a moment until she suddenly realized that they could have emerged from lightspeed jumps in situ, right there. No wonder there were no skiffs in the sky!

The two skiffs beside her stopped as the selkies hooked their sailing vehicle to the end of a long rope, which began to be winched up. The two pilots emerged at the same moment and walked together to the foot of a winding wooden stair. A clamor boomed through the piers as the watching selkies craned their necks and shouted, hooted, drummed on the timbers or smacked

the water. It was like the din of an enormous kennel. After re-
coiling for a moment, Elizabeth walked forward and ascended
the stair. Khaphthash and his companions brought up the rear.
Gradually the noise died down. Above the smells of wrack and
sea Elizabeth caught whiffs of the octopods' soothing scent, and
wondered if it was this that calmed the selkies.

The steps were soggy and slippery, but fortunately wide
enough to accommodate the great slapping feet of the selkies.
Its handrails were too high for her, but all the more reassuring
for that. As she climbed higher Elizabeth noticed the abrupt
change at the high-tide mark, where the encrustations of barnacles gave place to the new, artificial encrustation of colorful
shell fragments, and the wood was no longer rotten but
smoothed, and treated with some tarry or oily substance. But the
signs of age and weathering persisted: the wood was often white,
almost papery to the touch, and the stonework crusty with lichen,
soft with moss; some of the shells were faded or crumbling.

At length the octopod stepped off the stair onto a long platform with a broad, low table in the middle. The place stank of
fish—no, of their bones and of shells, which had been tossed in
a loose-woven wicker basket in one corner. Large clamshells,
evidently dishes or drinking vessels, marked positions around
the table. The selkies, so advanced in other simple technologies,
seemed not to have invented pottery. The octopod skittered to
the far side of the table; Delawar and Elizabeth hesitated for a
moment, then joined the selkies in reclining beside it. As she
lay on her side, propped on one elbow, Elizabeth could see numerous eyes—octopod and selkie—peering down from the dim
vaults above and around. She could feel through the floor a constant vibration, which came to her ears as a hum overlaid by
rhythmic thuds, as the tide-powered wheels sped up on the incoming race.

Khaphthash gave a long, loud sigh. "It is good that you are
here," he said. "I wish we could offer you hospitality. But our
food might not be palatable for you. We do not treat it with fire,
as you do."

Delavar's head bobbed as he looked sideways at the selkie. "My species enjoys fish. Perhaps we shall trade for it, in the future."

"The future, yes," said the octopod, its wheezy voice sounding impatient. "That is what we must discuss."

"We have some questions about the past," said Delavar.

Elizabeth had found herself surreally wondering if all that kept the selkies from venturing farther inland was their ignorance of kippering. The reedy tremble in Delavar's voice shocked her out of it. She looked closely at the saur, and saw the small tremor in his hands just before he noticed it himself and locked his fingers together and pressed the edges of his palms against the edge of the table. By saur standards, this all indicated a serious loss of sangfroid. The unease, the prickling of the hairs, that some humans experienced in the presence of the saurs must be vastly multiplied for a saur meeting an octopod. To humans, saurs were an enigmatic, vastly more ancient, and vastly superior species that had haunted the human habitat and imagination, glimpsed in the shadow and in the corner of the eye, since the Ice Ages. The saurs had not even that dubious tradition to buffer their encounter with a species older and wiser still, and more intimately involved in their origin. For them, to meet the octopods was to meet their makers.

The octopod waved a limb. "We know little of the past," it said. "The past is eaten and assimilated. We do not share the interest of all your kinds, in"—it made a poking, stirring motion of its bunched fingertips—"what remains. We prefer to reach for the new fruit, the fresh fish, the bright strange molecules."

"It is possible to learn from the past," said Elizabeth.

The octopod fixed her with its multiple gaze. "It is not. We have observed your kind for some time, and the saur's kind for longer. We see no evidence of this learning of which you speak."

"Very well then," said Elizabeth. "Let us speak of the present and the future."

The octopod's fiber-optic fur moved as though a wind passed over it. Its fingers flowered to thistledown.

"That is good," it said. It placed fingertips together, cat's-cradling a sphere, then expanded the sketched ball like a child's construction toy. "We are part of a wave-front of our kind that is passing through what you call"—the ball shrank, solidified—"your sphere. Some of it is already deep within your sphere, other parts—such as ourselves—are still outside, but we will soon be within."

Elizabeth winced at the cacophony as Gregor, Matt, and others shouted simultaneously. She snapped her fingers by one ear to tune them out for a minute.

"Do you intend to settle on our planets?"

The octopod fanned two of its hands. "Only the unoccupied portions. There is no need for conflict. Your kinds do not make full use of the biospheres."

Elizabeth stared at the alien—for the first time seeing it as alien.

"You must be aware," she said, "that our populations are increasing, and expanding into what you call the unoccupied portions. That could result in conflict in the future."

"Khaphthash's people are of your people," said the octopod. "They too increase, but they do not come into conflict with us. You share your planets with the other hominidae, with the saurs and with the great squid, and you do not fight. What is one species more? By developing the unused parts of your planets we could offer you much to exchange, as do the species which are there already. We are aware that the world-minds may wish us to fight, to diminish our numbers. We wish to avoid this by becoming that of you as we are that of Khaphthash's people."

"I'm sorry," said Elizabeth. "I don't understand that . . . last thing you said."

"We and Khaphthash's people wish to join the Bright Star Cultures."

Elizabeth and Delavar have returned. With them around the table are Gregor, Matt, Salasso. Zachary Gould, the captain, is chairing. Susan sits to one side, running her cameras and scribbling notes. The room is spartan and terrifying. It smells vaguely of food. Along two walls it has windows, but only an occasional rolling glimpse of the planet below, or a longer and less reassuring look at the gas giant above, make them anything but black mirrors.

The discussion has been going on for some time.

"It's very straightforward," Matt says. "They're telling us"— he shifts to the breathy register of the octopods—" 'Resistance is useless. You will assimilate us.' "

The sough of ventilation and the creak of bulkheads are for a moment loud.

"I'll give you the first," says Elizabeth. "I'm not so sure about the second."

"My view is the opposite of Elizabeth's," says Salasso. "The human capacity for both resistance and assimilation is considerable. The choice is genuine."

"It strikes me," says Gregor, "that both alternatives may be pursued. Our friend Volkov set out to persuade Nova Babylonia to prepare for resistance, after he failed to persuade us. We know he is very persuasive, especially when he doesn't have another Cosmonaut running interference."

Matt smiles in acknowledgment.

"Well, that's all right," he says. "Volkov may have the whole Nova Solar System bristling with nukes and death rays and gods know what by the time the Bright Star Cultures—with or without the octopods—spread to it. If in the meantime things have turned out badly between us and the octopods, well, tough shit for us, but we'll get some posthumous revenge. And if not, if we're walking along holding their eight hands, there'll be nothing to fight about. As the one Elizabeth and Delavar spoke to said, they'll be just another species in the Second Sphere."

"There are times," says Elizabeth, ostentatiously making sure Susan is getting this and not just recording it, "when I don't know whether to be more shocked at Matt's cynicism or his naivety. I'm not interested in posthumous revenge, thank you very much! I am interested in the safety and happiness of our own people." She glances at the saurs. "Of all our peoples. So much for the cynicism. What is naive is Matt's remark that if all goes as the octopods say they hope, there'll be nothing to fight about. Suppose Volkov succeeds, and Nova Terra is all geared up to fight an octopod invasion. Two things can happen. One is that some of the octopod travelers who *haven't* been in contact with us—and we know there are other parts of the migration en route right now—emerge from the jump and blunder straight into Volkov's defenses, which they have no reason to expect. The other is that we—the Bright Star Cultures, now including the octopods—spread there, jump by jump, just as our traders are spreading now.

"We make our final jump into the Nova Sol system, evade the defenses because we're expecting them, and tell the Nova Terrans the good news: the long-feared aliens are now a part of our rich tapestry! They don't want to take over the worlds, oh no! They just want to settle the underdeveloped parts of our biospheres! Do you have any *idea* how that will look, to the kind of paranoid militarist culture that Volkov will have built? Of course you do, Matt, you are not a complete fool."

Zachary Gould coughs politely. "The Science Officer will please address her remarks to—"

"Sorry, Zack," says Elizabeth. She stops glaring at Matt and looks around at the others. "They'll have spent decades preparing for an octopod invasion—perhaps already, as they see it, fought one off—and when we turn up, we will look to them like collaborators with the aliens. The octopod invasion will be *us*."

"This is indeed a problem," says the orange-furred emissary of the octopods.

It's here with two others, one black and the other multicolored. Their arrival, though prearranged, has been unnerving. The sight of an alien skiff emerging from a lightspeed jump right inside the *Return Visit*'s temporarily empty docking bay without the airlock's having to be opened has given everyone on board a vivid impression of just how advanced the aliens are.

The three aliens are huddled at one end of the messroom, which has been used as a conference room. They cling to the edge of the table or the backs of chairs with some of their hands, and with others keep touching each other's hands, and with yet others gesticulate. They keep changing position unpredictably and startlingly. Matt has no doubt that it's only their calming pheromones that are keeping most of the people who are in the room, and especially the saurs, from climbing a few chairs or walls themselves.

"Fortunately," says the black one, "we have a possible solution. We do not have the jump coordinates for any of the stars in the Second Sphere, other than the one you have come from and the one at the center." It makes some agitated movements of three limbs. "The former, we have only recently calculated ourselves. The latter, we have as an item of legacy information. It is very common knowledge among us. Consequently we can jump from here to your Mingulay, and also from here to your Nova Terra. We suggest that most of us and you go to Mingulay, and some of us and you go directly to Nova Terra."

"What good would that do?" asks Elizabeth. "Your other travelers will have already arrived by the time the Nova Terra expedition arrives."

"That is true," says the orange-furred one. "They will very probably be dead. That is unfortunate but cannot be helped. However, the expedition we propose would be armed, and cautious."

"Ah," says Matt, leaning forward. "You have weapons?"

"No," says the alien. "Some plasma rifles." It sketches a shrug with several of its shoulders. "But you have."

Matt tries not to laugh. He can see the others doing the same.

"I don't know that we'd get many volunteers for going straight to Nova Terra," says Zack, manfully keeping a straight face. "That's a two-hundred-something-year round trip. Most of the crews are expecting to go home and still see their folks, and even the few as don't haven't signed up for jumping forward a couple of lifetimes."

"I'd go," says Matt immediately. He glances at the two saurs. They both nod slowly: The two saurs have a lover in common, Bishlayan, but long partings are something they are used to.

"Maybe some of the other Cosmonauts, as well," he adds.

"Not much of a crew," says Zack, still making as if he takes the proposition seriously.

The aliens' hands are busy with mutual blurry touch. They do that a lot, Matt has noticed, and he has a good idea why; it's direct exchange of molecular-coded information—memories, perhaps even genes. Social intercourse, or sexual—with their mode of reproduction, perhaps there is no difference.

The rainbow-hued octopod flourishes a blossoming fuzzy hand, and inhales. "Please explain to us the problem about the crews going home."

They explain.

"Ah," wheezes the orange octopod. "We have a possible solution to that problem. Any of your people can live as long as the saurs and the Cosmonauts. Would this help?"

Elizabeth sat in the cockpit (or on the bridge—the terminology hadn't quite been settled yet) of the *Return Visit* and scanned the viewscreens, which were much more useful than the windows. They showed three of the other ships, surrounded by a small cloud of the beautiful smooth skiffs of the octopods (or Multipliers, to use their own troubling term for themselves). A hundred kilometers away the *Investigator* hung in a lower orbit, moving slowly ahead of the other group. Around it were five Multiplier skiffs, apparently keeping pace. How the jump coordinates for the Nova Sol system had been transferred from the Multipliers' drive to the *Investigator*'s she didn't know; it had kept Matt, Gregor, and two of the octopods busy for several days.

In a few minutes the *Investigator* and its tiny convoy would be making a lightspeed jump of a hundred and three years, taking them to one year out from Nova Sol. "Defuse the situation, or defang the defenses," Matt had said. "Hell, if Volkov is still alive I might even be able to *persuade* him."

Even with most of the armaments from the other ships transferred to its arsenal, it still seemed pathetically inadequate for the task. On the other hand, it was hard to see how anything would be adequate, short of a massive military mission, which neither the humans nor the Multipliers were willing or yet able to mount. The ship had a crew of eight humans and two saurs, Salasso and Delavar. She did not underestimate the courage of any of them, but she would miss the saurs most.

The radio crackled. "*Investigator* to the fleet. Jumping in two minutes."

"Gods be with you," said Zack.

"Hopefully not." It was Matt's voice. "But thanks, Zack, I know what you mean."

Gregor shifted in his seat, glancing around the screens. "I hope Susan's getting all this—where is she, by the way?"

"Over on the *Explorer*," said Elizabeth.

At that moment Susan's voice came over the radio. "Uh, Gregor, Elizabeth, I'm sorry, I just couldn't miss this chance, and I knew you wouldn't—"

Elizabeth felt as if she'd fallen through ice. *"Where are you?"* She already knew; the voice had come on the open channel to the *Investigator*.

"Jumping in one minute," said Matt.

"Abort the jump!" Gregor shouted.

"You know I can't do that," said Matt's voice, maddeningly calm.

"This has nothing to do with Matt," said Susan. "I'm sorry, I love you, but I want to go."

Elizabeth unclenched her teeth and grasped Gregor's hand. "We both love you, Susan," she managed to say. "And we'll see you again. You can be sure of that, darling."

She took another deep breath and spoke slowly, weighing and meaning every word: "Matt, we're going to take the Multipliers' offer. We're going to live for a very long time, and we're coming after you, and when we get you, we're going to fucking kill you."

"Good luck," said Matt, as though he hadn't heard.

"Good-bye," said Susan.

"Okay, people," said Matt. "Let's jump."

6

Bright Star Cultures

NOVAKKAD, THE PRINCIPAL city of a planet fifty light-years from Nova Babylonia, had always been a strange place. More than anywhere else Lydia had visited along her family's trade route, it had struck her as not just different but foreign. Its people were either much darker or much paler than the standard Second Sphere swarthy melange. They wore tall hats of fur in winter and shallow wide-brimmed cones of straw on their heads in summer. Their priests investigated the nature of fire with crude spectroscopes; their philosophers worshiped geometry. Their accents were thick and various, and their dialect of Trade Latin had a way of mutating unpredictably. Claiming that their city was older than Nova Babylonia, they implausibly attributed certain gigantic prehuman and prehominid ruins in its vicinity to their ancestors. Their own buildings were peculiar, tall wedges with sharply sloped roofs curving to ornate overhanging scoops of eave, like tents of brick and tile. In other ways too the city had the aspect of an encampment, clustered along the shore of a freshwater lake the size of an inland sea at the edge of an endless plain on whose grass the Novakkadians raised vast herds of horses and cattle. On the far side of the lake the glaciers of a jagged mountain range replenished its deep cold waters, within which fish shoaled by the million, some growing to lengths of ten meters and weights of three tons. Hardwoods from the lower slopes of the far mountains were harvested by the gigants and floated across the lake in such quantities that from the sky they looked like mats.

Strange and foreign, but more so this time.

Lydia walked, in native high boots and quilted clothes, through the chill streets and alleys of the autumn market. The air smelled of horse shit and fish roe, with tangs of woodsmoke and unfamiliar polymers. Crowds of several species of people and herds of beasts swirled in slow crosscurrents from one end of the market to the other, like a demonstration of the theory of price. Stalls filled the sidewalks, banners hung across them advertising their wares—new sharp stuff, glittery and colorful and strange; machines that talked and sang, clothes whose fabric and work seemed worth ten times the asking price, ceramic knives that sliced through meat like fruit and bone like gristle, calculators with little glass screens and unfeasible capacities, radios small and cheap enough to hang on key rings and that blatted forth songs whose words were hard to make out but whose tinny tunes made your feet tap and fingers snap along. Medicines were offered soberly by respectable-looking stall-holders with huge companies behind them—the same names and seals cropped up again and again—whose small print offered things that only witches dared promise anywhere else. The local fishing trade had been taken over, completely it seemed, by a new kind of gigant—tall heavy people with black sleek hair all over them and big mournful eyes. These were far from the strangest newcomers here.

Saurs for a start, saurs like none she'd ever seen, all the prickly dignity of their species dropped like an old cloak as they hustled and schemed, haggled and yelled, and accompanied by swarms of their offspring, some so young they still had their hatchling yellow feathers, others toddling along, tiny under their big and heavy heads, the older ones scooting about and screaming or whistling signals between and among their gangs.

The human traders were dark-skinned men in pajamas and turbans, or women wrapped around in long, broad single strips of silk. Their ships stood outside of town. She could see dozens of them, beyond where the streets ran out into stalls and pens, parked on long jointed legs that went with their shape, which was something like enormous flies: faceted panes of glass at the double cockpit front, stubby swept-back delta wings along the top of the tubby, segmented fuselage. The huge insectile machines sank a little in the trampled mire, their gravity fields evidently switched off. Large and many though they were, though, they couldn't account for all the goods she'd seen in the market, let alone the stuff in the city's downtown shops. And there were no new factories. Where did the goods come from?

Where did the traders come from?

"Chandrakhar," one of them told her. Gold-canine grin, jerk of thumb over shoulder. "Couple light-years back." Nod down at the stall. "Mingulayan opticals, lady? Best price in town, you see for yourself."

"Thanks, maybe later." She wandered off. Chandrakhar? Never heard of it. It wasn't on the trade route, close though it might be. This was a whole new culture that had been in the Second Sphere for gods knew how long, which the kraken ships from Nova Terra had never visited. And they spoke English with the broad Mingulayan accent.

But that wasn't the strangest thing, no, not at all.

"What are . . . they?" she asked a saur who sat behind a stall covered with shiny disks the size of sequins. You put them in machines. He wore headphones covered with yellow fur, from which the rocking music trickled irritatingly. He read her lips, followed her glance.

"Oh, they're Multis," he said. "Short for Multipliers. It's what they call themselves." He leaned across the stall, disengaged a blaring phone from his ear, and spoke behind his hand in a low voice. "They're *aliens*, you know."

He rocked back, small shoulders shaking, lips stretched, the big ellipses of his eyes narrowed to slits. He found something funny, but Lydia didn't see it. She knew they were aliens, and they certainly did multiply. The strange thing was that nobody here seemed to mind, or notice. The eight-limbed furry folk scampered and swung, overhead and underfoot everywhere, common as monkeys in a ruined jungle temple, and as unregarded. Except when they ran stalls themselves.

She stopped in front of one, and the Multi perched on two hands at the far side of the table made little model spaceships in bottles from wood and chips of stone. It held one model in front of it, like a template, and with its other five hands it made more, like magic: one moment there would be a fistful of wood and gravel, then something at the ends of the arms would blur and hum, and a minute later the hands would open on a beautiful little object, like an insect in its perfection as much as its shape. And on it would go to the next.

The thing was, it was making them *inside* the bottles.

Other miracles went on elsewhere. At the busiest stalls of the Multis, people were being cured—or more precisely, mended. People shuffled up and strode off; were carried up, and walked away. Lydia distinctly saw a man walk up with one healthy eye and leave with two. It was like the miracle stories of the gospels of the Jesus of the Christians, and it was happening in plain sight and without fuss. The patients were delighted and grateful, but not surprised, not wondering and glorifying the gods.

Lydia stepped around a corner and into an open space where cattle awaiting slaughter inside a fenced corral regarded her suspiciously. She powered up her ship-to-shore radio and raised Voronar. The ship was thousands of kilometers away, over the ocean where the kraken refreshed themselves and did their own deals, but the skiffs were parked along the lakeside quays and warehouses with the cargo for hominid and saur customers.

"Where are you?" the saur asked.

"Behind the market," she said. "I'm seeing things you wouldn't believe."

"I do not doubt it," came the dry reply. "The question your father wishes me to ask, however, is—are you safe?"

"Yes, I'm fine. Why doesn't he ask me himself?"

"He is in a meeting and can only communicate by buzz codes," said Voronar. "I shall reassure him. The city Elders are plying him with something he refers to as horse piss, but he retains his sobriety admirably."

"Good," said Lydia. "I'll endeavor to do the same with my sanity." She smiled at an anxious crackle. "That was a joke, Voronar."

She signed off and walked on through the ragged fringe of the market, toward the alien—no, that wasn't what was strange—toward the *human* ships.

"You're not fucking local," the boy told her, after a few minutes of ostensibly idle chat. "You're a goddam Nova Babylonian babe, you are."

His teeth were as perfect as his language was foul: Mingulayan English with Croatan swear words, blasphemous and obscene. He lounged on the lower steps of the ship's ladder, torn between pride in the responsibility of guarding the ship—a revolver that looked too big for his hands was stuck in his belt—and boredom at having to stay there. Blue-black straight hair flopped over his eyes.

" 'A goddam Nova Babylonian babe,' " Lydia repeated, grinning. "You certainly give good lines. You should keep notes of them, to use after your balls drop."

The crudity put him at his ease. He leaned back against the treads in a way that would have been uncomfortable but for his bulky fur jacket.

"What are you snooping around after, anyway?" The question came out curious, not suspicious.

Lydia shrugged. "Just checking things out," she said. "We only came in today, and we're not sure how things are. Bit of a change since two hundred years ago."

The boy laughed. "Changed a fucking hell of a lot in four, I can tell you that."

"Oh?"

"We were one of the first ships in here," he said. "Four years ago." He wiped a hand over his eyes, as though tired. "Fucking last week, it feels like. Nah, maybe a month. Me Da and Ma, they made a real fast turnaround back on Chandrakhar, loading up new gear. And even then, shit . . ."

He paused. "I didn't ought to be telling you this."

"We're not your competition," said Lydia. "But let me guess. By the time you got here, you were just ahead of the game. All the stuff that was new when you loaded it on Chandrakhar was already being made locally here."

He gave her a look of grudging respect. "Damn near right," he said. "We're ahead on a few lines, but some things you can't even give away. The only thing that'll pull this jaunt into the black is passengers." He sounded as though in his eleven or so years he'd learned all the weight of a merchant's risks. "Fucking Multis," he added, with startling venom; then, more reflectively: "Clever little monkeys, though."

"What have the Multis got to do with it?"

He looked at her as if she had asked where babies came from. "They multiply," he said, "*things*. They make stuff. They make. Fucking. Everything."

Esias felt the tickle of the radio's buzz against his ankle and counted. Three dashes. Lydia was safe. That was some reassurance but, as he sat naked on a wooden bench in a hot-room with three men, a woman, and an eight-armed, eight-eyed green ball of fur that persistently felt him up, he could have done with more. The radio was in a puddle of towel at his feet and he suspected the heat or humidity would soon short it out. He took a squig of the glutinous local drink from the vacuum flask his hosts had provided. Its chill and its high alcohol content were all that it had to recommend it. The Novakkadians called it khiss. Their listing of its ingredients had started with fermented mare's milk and stopped, at Esias's urgent request, when it reached dinosaur-egg yolk. You could live on it indefinitely, they'd told him. There were worse things than death, he'd not told them.

The Elders were the biggest local business people, as well as hereditary chiefs of the herding clans. Esias recognized their names from their ancestors, with many generations of whom he had dealt: Viln, Vladimiro, Sargonsson, Elanom. They were all old but in good shape, and had matted hair to their waists. There was something troubling about their hair, but Esias couldn't see what it was. The lights were dim and when the room wasn't full of herb-scented steam his eyes stung with salty sweat.

It was customary for the Elders to meet the Traders here in the Traders' Lodge, the lakeside house set aside for starship merchants and their crews. It was likewise normal for them to do their preliminary deals in the hot-room over a melting ice slab spread with fish roe and other delicacies and accompanied by flasks of khiss. For them to get through the preliminaries so quickly, and to have virtually agreed to his opening price, was not normal at all. Usually the haggling and the drinking continued to the point where the following day's hangover would be compounded by his regret at not having been more sober for the handshake.

The presence of the Multiplier was disturbing, but in an oddly abstract way. It should have bothered him more than it did. This was one of the octopod alien invaders that Volkov had warned about, and it was in here and thousands of its like were out there, and somehow he was not alarmed by it. It skittered about the room, its multiple manipulators touching faces and heads and skin. Esias found its feathery, tickling touch all the more uncomfortable for its being physically pleasant, warming and relaxing the muscles like a brief massage. The Elders ignored it, apart from moving slightly and with visible enjoyment—again as though being massaged—when it touched them. It had said nothing, though it was, he understood, both articulate and intelligent. The Elders had not introduced it, explaining that the aliens did not have names in the form of sounds. Their names were written in molecules, and if he were more familiar with it he would recognize the distinctive odor that spelled out its chemical signature.

The woman, Sargonsson, stood up and stepped over to the ice block. She picked up a sliver of roe on a shell and sat down beside Esias, who moved a little to make room for her. Despite her weathered and lined face, and the slightly bandy legs that a life in the saddle had left her, she was a fine figure of a woman, shapely and lithe, gleaming with steam and sweat. She smiled politely and scooped up roe on the back of a fingernail and licked it with the tip of her tongue.

"We are almost done," she said. "Your cargo will fetch a good price."

"If it is as we agreed," said Esias. The phrase was formal, just short of a handshake.

"We have another deal we can make with you," said Sargonsson, settling back into the corner. "The goods we have exchanged so far are the same as you and our fathers' fathers' fathers have traded. The hardwoods and the fresh roe, the strong herbs and the fine brasswork. Likewise with you."

Sargonsson glanced around, to nods from the others and a small flailing of hands from the alien. As she did so Esias noticed what had troubled him about her hair. The length of it between her ear and her butt was a salt-and-pepper grey; the first few centimeters of more recent growth out from her scalp were a pure glossy brown. Her head was crawling with lice.

Esias scratched his own scalp. Turning back, the woman saw his reflex and smiled. He lowered his hand, embarrassed.

"They don't itch," she said.

She put a finger to her temple and one of the creatures crawled onto her fingernail, which she held out for inspection. Perched there was not a louse but a spider—no, a tiny version of the alien. It scuttled up her arm and disappeared again into her hair.

"Ah," said Esias with false heartiness, "so that's why they're called Multipliers!"

"It is not," said Sargonsson. Again she glanced around; again they nodded. The alien climbed onto the bench opposite and crouched there. The mouth on the side that faced Esias had no teeth. Vladimiro threw another ladle of water over the coals. The alien's breathing was loud.

"They are called Multipliers because they can make copies of things. Of almost anything, given the right materials. They can certainly make copies of your Nova Babylonian manufactures. Your way of trading is obsolete. We in the Bright Star Cultures do not need to have merchant clans who live on the ships. We can make short journeys of a few years, because we set our own courses. That is how the Bright Star Cultures have spread from Mingulay to Novakkad, without anyone's having to travel more than a small part of the distance, or knowing how to navigate the jump."

"Yes, yes," said Esias. "I expected that, and I've made plans for—"

"Because of that," the woman continued relentlessly, "we need the long life, the very long life like the saurs. The Multipliers gave the saurs long life long ago, and they have given the same to us." She smiled. "Or so they say. We have no way of knowing, yet. But I will say I feel better than I did four years ago."

She wiggled her shoulders. Esias stared at her, for the first time shaken out of his detached acceptance.

"This is astounding news!"

Sargonsson turned her shoulder rotations into a shrug. "They offer us more than that," she said. "They have given us immortality."

Esias took a gulp of cold slime that burned in his throat on the way down and glowed in his belly.

"That is impossible," he said. "Not even the gods are immortal."

Sargonsson held out a hand to the alien. "Tell him," she said.

"In your body," it wheezed, "there are patterns of information that have instructed the building and instruct the working of your body. Some of them are older than the gods, older than the light from the visible stars. Some of my memories are older still. I remember seeing with four of my eyes the galaxy you call the Foamy Wake, and with my other four eyes the one that you call Andromeda. Yet never have I traveled between them. I remember scuttling through the grass by the lake outside, also. I am four years old."

It hopped down from the bench. "We can make you live long, by changing the instructions of your body. To do that, we must read them. By reading them we read your memories, and they can be shared among us, and will be among some of us until our line dies, as are those of the Novakkadians. In that sense we can offer you immortality."

Esias jumped as the radio on the floor buzzed against his skin, once, long. It signaled an urgent call back to the skiffs. He could hear a commotion and running feet in the rest of the house. It did not seem to matter.

"How can you read us?" he asked.

"That is simple," sighed the Multiplier. It raised two of its hands. Fuzz formed around the fingertips.

"The smallest of the smallest of us are too small for you to see. They are small enough for you to breathe in like smoke. They can travel through your body and read you."

"Travel—through—my—body?"

"You hardly notice it," said Sargonsson. "It's like a slight fever for a day or two, nothing more. And then any that have grown larger crawl out of your ears and nostrils and . . ."

Esias was shaking as hard as the insistently buzzing radio. The Multiplier flicked its hands. Esias stared as a cloud of green motes, some like dandelion seeds, some like pollen, wafted through the steamy air toward him.

He jumped up and ran to the door, bashed it open and rushed along the rickety wooden jetty and dived into the lake. The shock cleared his head instantly. What had passed in the hot-room seemed like a dream. He swam down through the clear cold water until it filled his sinuses, his mouth, his ears. He shot to the surface gasping and spitting and swam at a racing crawl, plunging and surfacing again and again, until a skiff appeared above him. The ladder came down, and he snatched it and hauled himself up and inside. The hatch closed behind him. He floundered for a moment, then stood up, dripping. His wife Claudia, two of his daughters, several nephews, and a saur pilot stared at him.

"What happened to you?" Claudia asked.

Esias shook his head. "Later," he said. His gaze swept the wraparound viewscreen. The skiff was rising fast, Novakkad tilted and dwindling below, an echelon of skiffs behind them. He padded across the corky floor and around the engine fairing to stand behind the saur. "What's going on?"

"The ship is leaving," said the saur. "We will rendevous in the atmosphere above the ocean."

"Why?"

For a ship to make an unscheduled departure was unprecedented. The pilot shook his head, not turning from the screen and the incomprehensible display below it. "The kraken decided, minutes ago. There has been no time."

"Have we got everyone?" Esias asked.

"Safely lifted," said Claudia. "Everyone in the lodge has checked in."

"And Lydia?"

"Lydia?"

"She was out in the town on a mission—"

Claudia paled instantly. "What were you thinking—" She shook her head. "We must turn back!"

"Yes, yes, turn back!" urged Esias.

"If we do, we shall not make the rendevous," said the pilot.

Esias clenched his fists at his sides. "We can catch another." He knew the other merchants' schedules to the hour. "The Delibes will be here in seventeen days."

The pilot glanced from the clear sky in front to the crowded display on the control board. He read something in its complex glyphs.

"Ah," he said. He turned to Esias. "Do you *wish* to join the Bright Star Cultures?"

Claudia looked bemused and distraught.

It would not be so bad, Esias thought frantically. People were not subsumed. They had free will. The Multipliers were friendly. Lydia was his number seven daughter. The spiders crawled on the scalp and their tiny offspring swam through the blood and the brain, and crawled out. His shudder was involuntary even as he opened his mouth to speak.

"You may," said the pilot. "I do not."

Esias stood still, shivering and unseeing. The skiff flew on.

Three comets lit the sky. Out here in the fields, the lights from the market and the town made the silhouettes of the parked ships stark and monstrous. It was dark enough to see the jagged outline of the mountains against the stars, and the comets' converging tails, a chevron pointed at the sunken sun. Novakkad had no moon, and only solar tides stirred its ocean. In the Second Sphere, this made it a backwater.

Dim reddish lights moved here and there in the broad meadow, barely raising a whinny from the resting horses. The lights came on only for a moment, illuminating complex wheel-mounted arrangements of brass and wood, with long tubes poking up like antiaircraft guns. Around these astrolabes the ships' navigators fussed and muttered, plotting the positions of nearby stars. Now and again a green glow from the screen of a hand-held calculator would light up an intent face from below.

Lydia wandered quietly among them, unregarded. Once or twice she heard a low cry of "Hey, Multi! Give us a hand!" and saw a Multi scurry over and poke a limb into a piece of machinery. Other than that they took no part in the observations or calculations. They could make and adjust things, but they did not seem to know everything already, the way the saurs and the krakens knew, or gave the impression that they knew.

Lydia had given a lot of thought to the aliens in the hours since she had been stranded. If nothing else it served to distract her from her plight while she wandered around, looking and thinking. She had heard the evacuation call but no response to her frantic queries had cut through the babble on the radio, so she had no idea why the clan had fled. The only message she had picked up was a crackly, apologetic, anguished good-bye from her father, who told her that the krakens were taking the ship back to Nova Terra and could brook no delay. No explanation was given, and she had no time to ask. It must be something urgent and fearful for them to leave her behind, but she could see nothing so fearful in the city. It was amazing how quickly one got used to the aliens. There was something soothing about their scent, and their variously colored fur and constant activity and curiosity had a charm that evaporated any associations with spiders. What humans toiled for in factories and saurs spun in the manufacturing plant, the Multipliers made for fun, if they could be so persuaded. Which, she had gathered, was not always easy. Their jittery attention span made humans seem like saurs.

She made her way back to the market and bought with the last few local coins in her pocket a fast meal of beef in a spicy sauce parceled in some kind of thin bread and munched it as she walked back to the lodge. It was a big stone building with a sharp-pointed wooden roof. She flicked on all the lights she could find and wandered through the rooms, disconsolate. Everywhere were the strewn signs of hasty evacuation. The skiffs' landing-feet had left deep prints in the soggy lawn. The hot-room, its door swinging open, was cold and stank of warm seafood and spilt khiss. Her father's clothes lay folded outside. She did not touch them, and started clearing the decayed repast and sluicing the room with a wall-mounted hose.

Gradually this displacement activity calmed her. She felt let down rather than abandoned. The next ship was due in just over a fortnight. There was always money in the lodge if you knew where to look. She worked her way through the house, tidying things away. The servants would not be in until just before the Delibes arrived, just as they had been in the previous day, before the de Tenebres. Her ramble ended in the room where her own luggage lay on a freshly made-up bed. At the top of the case lay the Nova Babylonian robe she had neatly folded, in her own hopeful yesterday. She would wash, put it on, go downstairs and put out some of the lights, make herself a drink and go to bed. Why not?

She was sitting at an empty table in the big dining hall, sipping a long voka, when she found herself feeling more cheerful than even the bath and the drink could account for. At the same time she had a feeling she was being watched. She turned to the corridor. A green-furred Multiplier came clicking along the flagstones, into the room. It hopped onto the end of the table, hands spread, and padded along the tabletop, then clambered onto the seat opposite her.

"Do not be alarmed," it said.

She wasn't.

Lydia stood alone at the end of the long pier at Novakkad docks, the one reserved for the star merchants. Her suitcase rested beside her, she had her traveling clothes on, and she had a watch in one hand and a radio in the other. High nimbus made the sky silvery and hard to look at. When she glanced back at the watch, it was hard to read, but she kept looking, from the watch to the sky, from the sky to the watch. At last, and right on time, she saw the dark speck, high above, far away up the lake.

She stuck the watch in her pocket and picked up the suitcase and walked to the top of the ladder. The man in the dory looked up at her.

"Now," she said, handing the case down.

The passenger was meant to sit facing the steersman, but she crouched the other way. The electric engine whined and the boat pulled out from the pier. The Delibes' starship was now a solid black, now a wavery worm in the heat haze. She waited until she was sure it was within range and switched on the radio, preset to the hailing sequence.

"Lydia de Tenebre to the Delibes ship, come in please."

There was a long pause, filled with static. The ship was low now, about a kilometer away. The place where Lydia expected it to set down was a few hundred meters ahead of her.

"Ship to de Tenebre, receiving you. What do you want?" The voice sounded irritated and puzzled. A radio operator was always on standby on an approach, and almost never had anything to do.

"De Tenebre to ship. I would like to come on board as soon as possible."

"Huh? Sorry, I mean, yes, that's not a problem, but why? Are you in some—"

More static.

"Ship to de Tenebre. Sorry, I've just had a message. There's an emergency, I don't know what it is. The kraken want to *pull out!*" The voice rose in an indignant, alarmed, disbelieving squawk.

Now the ship stood just two hundred meters in front of her, a stationary, impossible object, half a mile of streamlined cylinder glowing with Novakkadian symbols and words, the water bending beneath its shimmering fields.

"I know that," said Lydia, with a calm she didn't feel. She had half-expected something like this. "You're safe enough though, you can wait a few minutes to take me on board."

"Hold on a minute."

At the same moment as the radio at the other end clicked off, the boat's engine died. Lydia whirled.

"What's the problem?"

The doryman smiled placatingly and waved ahead. "I can't go on—look."

Lydia looked foward again and saw what she had missed in her attention to the ship. Between the boat and the ship the pointed front end of an enormous mat of logs floated on some fast current, filling the space like an entering wedge. The tugboat that had been riding herd on it had evidently cast loose on sight of the incoming starship and was now speeding away on a diagonal course at, as the phrase had it, a rate of knots.

"Can't we get around it?"

It was a stupid question. "No," said the doryman.

The angled leading edge of the mat was coming closer; the doryman was loyally holding their relative position with small bursts of power to the motor. The side of the mat would pass just in front of the bow.

The radio crackled. "Ship to de Tenebre. The saurs say the

kraken agree to hold our position for ten minutes or so. Come on board as soon as you can."

"Can you send out a skiff?"

She overheard some background consultation, indistinct but loud.

"No, sorry." The voice sounded genuinely apologetic. "The saurs are . . . well, they're a bit paranoid, between you and me. I've never seen them . . . like this."

"Okay, thanks, I'll do what I can," said Lydia. "Hold the door."

She put the radio away and looked over her shoulder at the doryman. "How long will this thing take to pass?"

He shaded his eyes and looked up the lake. "Half an hour, maybe more."

"Burning hell."

Lydia half-stood, gazing at the logs that drifted by a couple of meters in front of her. The mat was held together by cables around the outermost logs; within that kilometers-long loop the logs were (another phrase literalizing before her eyes) log-jammed, wallowing and bumping like a school of whales in a bay. The trunks were huge, up to fifty meters long and two or three meters on the bole. As she stood there, her balance sharpened by her long familiarity with small boats, Lydia suddenly saw the logs as the backs of a galloping herd of wild horses, and an image of leaping from back to back (the neighing, the dust, the roar of a thousand hooves) was real behind her eyes.

She motioned the boat forward and the steersman, perhaps not understanding, complied. The nearest log was a meter and a half away. Lydia picked up her case and put one foot on the prow.

"No!" yelled the doryman.

Lydia jumped—it was hardly more than a step, but the boat moved backward behind her—onto the wet rough bark. Then she sprang to the next, and the next, dancing across the rolling logs (the bucking backs), from one to the next before each had time to roll further (to notice), with her case (her frantically-held pack of food) a burden but at the same time a help in keeping her balance.

Halfway to the ship, she slipped. She crashed forward, the arm with the case thrown over the top of the log. Her side thumped hard against the bark, her legs in very cold water to the knee. There was no pain but the breath was knocked out of her. She saw the crushing logs converge (the pounding hooves trample) and her whole body convulsed in one complex movement she could never have intended, and she was astraddle the log and then standing, running along its back to regain her balance, and then she leaped sideways.

A minute later her last leap took her through the open deck door of the ship, where her heel skidded on slopped water and she fell hard and slid four meters on her arse and banged up against a bulkhead. Everything hurt. She sat and stared at her grazed palms and cried.

The deck door shut behind her like a snapping clam.

Saurs glared at her, then turned away. The human clan members looked at her with compassion and amazement. A kid helped her to her feet.

"How did you *do* that?"

She looked at her hands. The grazes were already fading. Bits of dirt and bark, expelled from under her skin, flaked away. She dusted her palms and smiled.

"Just luck."

The Delibes were kind; they took her to the senior family's skiff and helped her into dry clothing and gave her hot drinks, even though they were themselves in upheaval over their landing's being aborted. The krakens had set a course back to Nova Terra. The Delibes' route only intersected the de Tenebres' at some points, of which Novakkad was one; they had left Nova Terra a few weeks before the de Tenebres had arrived, so they knew nothing of Volkov and his dire warnings and wild projects, and little of the historically recent arrivals on Mingulay. Lydia spent the hour before the lightspeed jump filling them in. But they were more interested in the Multipliers, and the Bright Star Cultures.

"This is bad for us," said Anthony Delibes, the clan patriarch. "It is a new sphere, intersecting the Second Sphere and supplanting all our routes. The saurs and the kraken are terrified. They seem too shocked even to talk. But—"

He hesitated, stroking his beard. "In itself it does not seem bad. It is not the invasion and war that your Volkov feared."

Lydia nodded eagerly. "I feared much worse myself. But what I've seen on Novakkad is very different from what I expected. The species we know already are mingling much more than before, and the two new species are just"—she spread her hands—"accepted."

She did not tell them all she knew. She could remember touching a carbon atom, and how its springy, slippery feel matched the sight of its wavelength in the spectrum of a supernova; the dissolution of death, and the wild joy of jaws closing on a deer's throat; flying with wings, and swimming with fins. These and myriad other fragmentary memories, random thoughts, equations solved and principles understood, floated in her mind as disparate bright shards, which someday and with untold effort she might assemble to a mirror, and see in it a new self.

Until she saw that new self, she could talk about none of this. She felt restless, and excused herself to take a walk around the ship. She was at the navigator's pool at the moment of the light-speed jump.

The navigator had recoiled to the side of the pool. Gouts of sepia blackened the water. This was not the normal response to a jump. Within a couple of seconds, alarms sounded. The saurs and humans of the ship's complement rushed to evidently prearranged posts. Lydia scrambled to the nearest skiff. Only the pilot was in it.

"What's happening?"

"I do not know," the pilot said. "We are definitely at our

destination, but Nova Terra bears . . . an unfamiliar aspect. And we have been hailed, perhaps even challenged. The kraken are disturbed."

"Indeed they are," Lydia said. "Which suggest that we should be terrified."

The saur himself was trembling slightly. "I am awaiting instructions," he said. "I am ready to die."

Lydia regretted her flippant tone. "Shall we look outside?"

The pilot palmed the controls. Lydia scanned the familiar landmasses of Nova Terra.

"Look at Nova Babylonia!" she said. "The air's filthy!"

"Yes," said the saur, as though something more important had been missed.

Lydia felt an odd sensation on the back of her neck. She turned and saw a huge shape glide—as it seemed—above them, then come to a halt in front of them.

"It is we who are moving," explained the saur. "The other craft is in Trojan orbit."

"How far away is it?" Lydia asked.

"About a kilometer."

The scale of the thing snapped into focus. Toroidal, rotating about a stationary hub, bristling with antennae and what Lydia guessed were armaments, and accompanied by a dozen or so small vessels with long jointed legs.

"Gods above," she said. "It's bigger than we are."

"Orbital fort," said the pilot. "Keeping station on the jump destination."

Lydia had not known that jump destinations were at Trojan points.

One of the small craft burned off a brief boost and scooted toward the starship, closing the gap in seconds. Its retro-flare almost overloaded the screen's brightness controls. As Lydia blinked away afterimages she saw its rockets make a few smaller nudges. It vanished below her line of sight, apparently docking. The saur fingered a control and the view cut instantly to the side

of the starship, on which the craft resembled a small spider clinging to a large pipe. The docking bays, Lydia noticed with interest, were compatible.

"We have been boarded," said the saur. His tone carried a
faint note of melancholy.

"Can you switch to an internal view?"

He shook his head. "I have no access to the ship's internal
sensors."

"No," Lydia said patiently. Saurian thought ran more deeply
than the human, and therefore in deeper ruts. "But you do have
access to the skiff's external—"

"Ah."

In a moment a band of the skiff's hull had become as glass.
On the wall across from the skiff, beside the equivalent rack of
skiffs, a stairway zigzagged to the interior deck near the navigator's pool. Three space-suited figures trooped down it, heavy-
duty plasma rifles at the ready. As they turned on a landing, their
open helmets revealed human faces.

The pilot stared at them and turned to Lydia, and she could
see by his expression that he had never seen and barely imagined
their like. Their clumsy suits were of obvious human manufacture, their rocket maneuvers were perfect; their fort resembled
one of the space stations Volkov had told her about, the kind the
Germans had imagined and the Americans never built, perhaps
because by the 1950s the Americans already understood that
deep space would never be theirs. They'd abandoned it, too hastily, to the Russians, not realizing that it didn't belong to the
skiffs' little grey pilots either. Knowing nothing of this, the Russians were the first to meet the galaxy's real masters. The Nova
Terrans in the past century had founded a human space presence
more formidable than anything even the Russians had attempted,
and they had done so in a full knowledge of its possible consequences. Lydia had to admire them for that. She was afraid of
them, but she admired them, and she took a certain malicious
joy in the saur's discomfiture at this unexpected display of human capability.

"What are they?" the saur asked.

"Cosmonauts," Lydia said.

It turned out they called themselves astronauts.

Lydia returned to the deck and found the senior Delibes had gathered there ahead of her. Anthony, his pugnacious jaw thrust forward, was making an effort to be polite.

"Naturally," Lydia heard him say, "I share your concern for the security of the Republic. I assure you that nothing and nobody on this ship could compromise it. You have my word. I am a Member of the Electorate!"

"So'm I," said the cosmonaut who stood in the apex of the group. He gestured at the other two, a pace behind his shoulders. "So're we all."

"Ah!" The merchant smiled and relaxed. He held out his hand. "Welcome aboard, fellow citizens. Anthony Delibes, at your service, officers."

"Thank you, citizen." The cosmonaut returned the handshake, then jerked a thumb at his chest. "Astronaut Sarn't Claudius Abenke; Astronauts Alexander Obikwe and Titus Adams. Space Defense Force of the Democratic Republic of New Babylon."

"Oh, shit," said Lydia, unable to stop herself.

The astronauts glowered at her; the Delibes turned, startled.

"You have a problem with that, citizen?" said Abenke.

"Volkov," said Lydia.

The astronauts all looked uncomfortable. Abenke composed his features to a steadfast frown.

"Volkov is dead."

7

The Modern Regime

EVERY DAY WAS the same. Reveille, canteen breakfast, assignment. For most of the steadily growing number of inmates—a thousand or so, increasing by scores every day as new ships came in—the assignment was to light work, or recreation. For Lydia it was to interrogation. Torture had been abolished.

One interrogator sat on the other side of the table, the second over to her side, just at the edge of sight. Every so often they would change places.

"What do you know of the aliens' plans for invasion?"

"Nothing."

"What happened to you on Novakkad?"

"I've already told you."

"Tell us again."

Sometimes there was a different tack. "What was your assignment from Volkov?"

"There was no assignment."

"What were your relations with Volkov?"

"I've already told you."

"Tell us again."

The detention center was on an island in the Half Moon Sea, within sight of the city. Concrete blockhouses, barbed wire, a jagged shore and hungry currents—nobody tried to leave. Every day a few dozen people were released and loaded on a boat to the city. Grim rumors circulated about what happened to them, but nobody thought in their hearts that they were fed to the whales. Every day a few score more people arrived. The starships from which they had been taken would remain for a few days in the harbor, and then depart.

Lydia was certain that her own clan had been detained and released. She was not at all certain that she would be. Every night she went down to the fence and gazed across the kilometers of water to the lights of the city. It was winter, and dark came early, and cold. There were far more lights than before, and they reached higher into the sky, but they were almost always veiled in murk. Overhead passed aircraft like she had never seen before, with bright lights at the wingtips and along the sides, and engines that roared. Surface vessels almost half the size of starships arrived, sitting low in the water, and left a day or two later riding high. Lydia was told that they delivered petroleum. It could be distilled and burned; hence the murk. She had seen this done on Croatan, but she had never thought that Nova Terra needed terraforming.

On clear nights, though, she could still see the stars. They now seemed forever beyond her reach. She could also see the moons, and the tiny new moons, the orbital forts and communications satellites in stately steady array. Beyond them, she could see the comets. Five in the one sky.

She talked to people in the evenings. Their stories were similar to her own, though none admitted, any more than she did, to having been changed by the aliens. Most of them had, like the Delibes, not encountered the aliens at all. Their kraken navigators had recoiled from the planets on which they landed, all of them fifty light-years or more away. Nobody had any idea what had happened here on Nova Terra.

After a month her interrogators either became convinced of her innocence or bored with her intransigence. They turned her over to the center's administrative office, who returned her suitcase and gave her ten thousand thalers. In Nova Babylonia this would have been a year's pay for a skilled worker. In New Babylon it was a month's. Lydia assumed this meant the standard of living had risen twelvefold in her absence. Every note and coin bore on its obverse the profile of Volkov, and on every one that image was defaced.

She climbed the ladder off the boat and found Esias waiting for her on the quay. They hugged each other and then stepped back. Other reunions went on noisily around them.

"How did you know to expect me?"

"I've been coming here every day."

"Oh."

They looked at each other warily.

"Are you all right?" Esias asked.

"How do you mean?"

"You don't suspect yourself of going mad?"

"Not at all," said Lydia. "Do you?"

Esias sighed. "No."

"Well then."

"Yes."

Esias insisted on carrying her suitcase. "Let's walk for a bit," he said. "See the sights." He grinned. "Welcome to New Babylon, by the way." He waved his free hand to encompass the banks of lights stacked in front of them in the gathering dusk. "And the glories of the Modern Regime!"

They walked from the docks to the Avenue of the Kings, on which the de Tenebre building had once stood. At the foot of the avenue, where Gilgamesh II had once stood in granite, rose a taller and grander statue in concrete. It showed a smiling and handsome young man in a spacesuit, helmet under one arm, and a crushed octopod under one foot.

"When did this happen?"

"About thirty years after we left. The aliens came and New Babylon was ready for them. The battle was brief."

"I'll bet," said Lydia.

"They've just started calling that "the first invasion." What we left behind on Novakkad is the second. And they'll be ready for it, too."

The street name had been changed to Astronaut Avenue. Heavy metal vehicles filled it from end to end. Trucks and buses, mostly, which somehow despite all their noise and stink labored to carry or pull their loads. Bicycles wove perilously between them. The people who filled the pavements were drably dressed; even their better suits were modeled on work clothes: plain jacket, trousers, shirt. All the color had been leeched from the street and concentrated in tubes of neon, spelling out advertisements and assertions. The faces of some of the older people looked stretched and pitted, like copper beaten until it broke.

"Smallpox epidemic," said Esias. "It's a solved problem now."

The new buildings were higher and their sides more likely to be vertical. In other places new towers had been built on top of the existing buildings, extending them upward to double their original impressive enough height. What had been white marble was now black. The terraces had survived, but the gardens had not. Flying squirrels were few, and their variety diminished. Here and there the old cheerful erotic and ecstatic statuary clung on, like lovers and mystics hiding in corners, but most of the statues were heroic and earnest. Among them, on this corner and that traffic island, were occasional plinths empty except for jagged fragments of the feet or the boots. Lydia did not need to guess whose name they bore.

"What happened here?" she said. "What happened to Volkov?"

"He changed things less than you might think," Esias said. "The Senate and the Assembly, the guilds and associations—all these are still here. The main reform was that everybody became a Member of the Electorate. Many of the new Electors, and some of the old, joined the Modern Society. It became like the Party he used to talk about so proudly and so cynically. They harnessed everything to the space defense effort. They taxed everything that moved. They had the defenses built just in time. They destroyed the alien ships. And then they kept building more defenses. They had wars with neighboring provinces, and when these wars were being lost, Volkov was shot by his own security detail. The wars were lost anyway, the provinces broke away, but the space defense forces continued to be strengthened. We're told there's more freedom now. Reform. Liberalization. If this is freedom I'm glad we missed the tyranny."

"Yes," said Lydia. "But I'm sorry we missed Volkov. In his pride, in his power. A third Gilgamesh, one who really did find the secret of life."

"Except that he never did find it. It was in his body, but his scientists could never read it."

Lydia glanced sideways sharply at her father, but she could not read him.

The de Tenebre building was long gone, replaced by a concrete-and-glass tower. The headquarters of the Ninth still stood. Black-uniformed guards strutted and turned on its long steps. Close by was a much taller building, so tall in fact that Lydia had not registered it as a building, though she had seen its aircraft warning lights often enough from the island. It was like a wall of black glass, and was built with a twist, so that its top floor was at about thirty degrees to its lower. Set well back from the street, it overshadowed a plaza with fountains and lights. No name was indicated.

"Space Authority," said Esias. "It's supposed to represent the shape of a lightspeed engine." He smiled, relishing some well-worn joke. "It would have been more impressive if they'd actually built one."

Lydia shivered. She had seen a lightspeed engine. Its shape was nothing like this, but the architecture had indeed captured something of the spirit of that extraordinary machine: the feeling it had given her . . . of being watched.

"What did the saurs and the krakens think of all this?"

"They went away," said Esias. "Most of them. They are still going away, as ships come in and go. Of our ship, only Voronar has stayed." He smiled. "He calls himself a Salassoist."

"Where do they go?"

Esias shrugged, huddling deeper in his coat against a chill breeze off the wall of black glass. "Who knows?" he said.

" 'They all go up the line,' " she said, quoting an old and sinister space chantey.

"Perhaps." He caught her hand. "That reminds me. A truly great accomplishment which you are about to see."

He took her to the underground railway station, and they went up the line.

I'll die here, Lydia thought. All that had brought this on was that water had overlapped the welts of her shoes. It was not even as if they were good shoes. But the oil would do them no further good.

Oil on water. It was an indelible mark of industrialization. Lydia gazed gloomily at the puddle's rainbow hues and heaved another plastic sack of rubbish into the overflowing skip. Turning about, she made way for the invincibly cheerful Esias, who was lugging another sack. They did not exchange words or glances. As she picked her way to the foot of the block's outside stairwell Lydia heard her father's simian grunt as he disposed of his load, the brisk brush of his palms as he turned away, the squelch of his footsteps as he trudged back. Lydia hurried up the iron steps, looking up all the while. Behind her, Esias climbed more slowly, puffing and panting. At the landings Lydia could see the sky, blue after the rain, crisscrossed with contrails whose chalky scrawls marked another score on the progress chart.

Their flats were halfway up, on the eleventh level. Lydia stopped a few steps along the concrete balcony and leaned bare, dusty forearms on its black-painted iron rail. The adjacent block faced her across a ten-meter gulf. A line of washing, small garments that someone had neglected to take in from the recent shower, dripped and swayed. Music leaked from a hundred radios, up and down the shaft. A cleaning robot clambered, trailing hoses and cables, squirting and sudsing, sponging and rinsing. Here and there it had missed a window, and left behind a washed rectangle of wall.

Lydia heard Esias ascending the last flight. She straightened, turned away and strolled to the open door of the new flat. About half the clan had taken up residence along this balcony; the rest were scattered in ones and twos around the city's housing projects. New Babylon did not acknowledge polygamy; fortunately it recognized Claudia and Faustina as a couple in their own right. Their flat was between the one that had been kept for Lydia and the one rented in the names of Esias and Phoebe.

She still mourned Volkov. That must be why getting her socks wet made her miserable. Perhaps when she was as old as her father she would be as good a stoic. She had not loved the Cosmonaut but she had liked him and been fascinated with him, and over the past few eventful months of subjective time his capacity to change history had drawn her reluctant, even hostile respect. He had seemed as invincible as he was immortal, and now he was defeated and dead. And yet the regime perversely insisted on reminding people of him, every time money changed hands. Not all the coins and notes, surely, could have been in circulation at the time of his fall. Some of them at least must have been printed or minted since, and officially defaced. Unless people did that to new currency as soon as it was issued, as some kind of gesture of continuing hate. She wasn't sure which possibility was the more depressing to contemplate.

The flat was almost clear now of the rubbish from its recent refurbishment. The municipal authority workers had replaced some old walls and fittings with new ones, but had not cleared out the rubble. That was a job left for the new tenants. There was a kind of justice to it, a first few drops of sweat equity. Lydia picked up a brush and pushed some more brick and tile into a heap, then shoveled it into a sack. Esias came into the room and joined in.

While gathering up the last bits, he cut his hand on a piece of broken tile. He had always been careless about gloves. He hopped up and down, cursing. The cut was nasty and deep, blood was dripping everywhere. Lydia ran to the dusty new sink in the kitchen and ran cold water on a clean cloth. She caught his wrist and wiped the dirt and blood from his palm. The split skin sealed itself up as she watched, leaving nothing but a white line from which specks of dirt rose to the surface. She brushed a finger against the grubby flecks and looked at the palm again. The cut had left no trace.

Esias stared back at her. "It doesn't hurt any the less," he said.

"I know," she said.

"Perhaps we should not say any more."

She nodded. They lugged the last two sacks of rubbish down to the skip.

The clan had trade in their bones. They adapted to the new situation, and worked around the new restrictions, which to the rest of the city were the new relaxations: the post-Volkov reforms. Esias and his wives opened a stall at the docks. Lydia's cousins and siblings took up jobs or hustles; the distinction was obscure, as were the details.

Lydia applied and, to her surprise, was accepted, for a clerical job at the core of the Regime: the Space Authority. The twisted megalith of the building did not intimidate her. For her first day at work, she wore the best garment she had, her dress from old Nova Babylonia, and was amused to find in the days that followed that this was considered a gesture of defiance, but one for which—from sheer embarrassment—nobody in authority could reprove her or forbid. Other young women working on the statistical machines or the typewriters began to turn up in copies made from the artificial silk sold in the markets.

One day a message popped out of the pneumatic tube on her desk. She opened it expecting another report for her to abstract, and found it a summons to meet the President.

The President's office was in the top floor of the headquarters of the Ninth. Lydia's roll of paper took her past three sets of heavily armed guards to the reserved lift entrance on the ground floor. Inside it was a small burnished room, all carpet and mirror. The lift was so fast that Lydia felt the blood drain from her head, like it sometimes had on a ship when the field fluctuated.

The doors opened on more guards, and a metal detector, through which Lydia passed without a buzz or a challenge. The whole floor was open-plan, thickly carpeted. People bowed over rank upon rank of polished desks, scribbling and marking, ticking and signing in silence. Huge bouquets of fresh flowers stood in as many vases as there were desks. The fragrance was thick and the hush was thicker. Lydia was reminded of a crematorium.

A functionary in the strange archaic uniform of the breed—a suit of trousers, jacket, shirt, and necktie—looked at Lydia, peered at her summons, and guided her silently to a door at the back of the bureaucratic mausoleum. There was nothing special about the door. He opened it and bowed her in, then withdrew.

The room was an office. It had a tall high window behind the desk, stacked bookshelves around the walls, and doors that opened off to what a quick glance confirmed were living quarters. Tall vases of flowers filled this room with color and scent, even more overpowering than in the great antechamber.

Behind the big desk sat the most aged woman Lydia had ever seen. She seemed to have shrunk and shriveled within the black-silk kimono that swathed her. Her cheeks were sunken, her skin yellow, her teeth brown and long. The hand on the pommel of her ceremonial sword, and the hand on the open book on the desk, looked like some contraptions of thin leather and thick wire. This was not the swift dissolution that overtook people toward the end of their twelfth decade. This was something preserved, pushed through, carried forward beyond that by some desperate will, and doubtless by some corrupted application of saur or human medicine.

"Ah," breathed the President. She drooled slightly, and wiped her chin on her cuff. "Lydia de Tenebre. Thank you for coming." The eyes flashed, some life and humor shining through the yellowed sclera. "You may not think you had a choice, but you had. So I thank you. Sit down."

"Thank you, Madame President."

"I have been eager to see you since I heard of your return," the President went on. She leaned forward; Lydia caught a whiff of her terrible breath, and understood why there were so many flowers about. "Unfortunately it takes time for information to reach me, and even when it has, I have much to do."

Not much by the look of things, Lydia thought, but she nodded politely.

"It was your clan who brought us Volkov," said the President, closing her eyes. "Ah, how he charmed us all! We called him the Engineer. It was not like politics, you understand. It was like religion—no, it was like a mania, a bubble on the market, and we were all speculators. And when we had stopped believing, it was too late for us to turn back. He made us believe by force."

Another sigh, another stench. It was not from her mouth that this was coming—the teeth were dark but clean, the tongue was pink. It was coming from her lungs and her bowels.

"And years after we had stopped believing, and all feared to admit it to each other, the aliens came. They ran into the orbital defenses that Volkov had lashed us to build. They ran into them, smack! Their ships burst in the hellish light of the particle beams! Their outposts vaporized in the hellish heat of the nuclear bursts!"

Back and forth she swayed as she told the story, in a singsong voice like a crone of the pithkies reciting a tribal lay.

"Oh, how we all loved him again! Our Cosmonauts came back from the battles with his name on their lips! We built more forts and ships and waited for the next invasion. We built more rockets and waited for the gods to send down rocks in their wrath. We waited, and waited."

Her eyes snapped open. Her voice resumed a conversational cadence.

"They never came. And after a while, after a few more years, we stopped believing that they would ever come. Not for another million years, anyway. We grumbled at the taxes and the conscriptions and prescriptions. But that was not why I had him killed."

As the President's face had become more animated with her discourse, Lydia had gradually built up from glimpses an image of the face it once had been, and what now dawned on her was an awful recognition.

"Volkov not only promised us victory over the invaders. He promised us the long life, the long life like the saurs. Oh, the research, the institutes, the papers, the arguments. The labor of men and saurs, all of it sincere, all of it well-meant, some of it horrific, none of it successful. And for that failure to extend our lives and youth, I took his own."

Her gaze was distant, yet to Lydia it seemed like needles aimed at her eyes. The preternaturally old President sighed.

"He disappointed me," said Julia de Zama. "Severely."

2

The Human as Alien

8

New Earth (Political)

THE WINDOW WAS tiny and the glass was thick. Susan Harkness pressed her forehead against it, gasping, heart pounding, and stared out until all she could see was the stars. She imagined she stood in a field on a very dark night, looking up at the constellations. The Musketeer was there, and the jeweled pleiad of the Thrown Net, and the Hind. She imagined a cool breeze in her face, and that the sough of the ventilation was its sigh. Gradually her breathing eased, the bands around her chest loosened.

She had expected a price for her reckless light-century leap into the dark: regret, sorrow, homesickness. Fear. She had thought them all worth paying, for the chance of life at this intensity, and of being present at moments that could not but become history. She had not expected claustrophobia. It had sneaked up on her from behind. She felt betrayed by her own mind. They had spent two days lurking in the system's Oort cloud. It was absurd, but the thought of that cloud was actually making her sense of confinement worse, even though all it meant was a high probability that there was a piece of cometary matter within a few million kilometers.

Rolling in orbit around the selkies' world had been different. The beauty and variety of that terrestrial planet from space, and the alien fascination of its gas-giant primary and its red-giant sun, had made living in the narrow ships feel anything but confinement. One's attention was always turned to the outside. The skiffs had flitted from ship to ship, and she'd always been able to wangle a ride, always with a good reason: interviewing crew members, documenting discoveries. The only sense of confinement she had felt was the suffocating presence of her parents. That they were enlightened and meant well she knew, but they couldn't help casting long shadows. Anywhere in the Bright Star Cultures, she would always be the First Navigator's daughter, the Science Officer's girl. On cold reflection it seemed mad to move a hundred and three light-years to get away from her parents, but analyzing the moment of impulse that had made her do it revealed no other explanation. She felt obscurely insulted that her mother had automatically blamed it on Matt, as though Susan had no will of her own. She was certainly not besotted with Matt, nor he with her, though she suspected that without the ulterior motive of their irregular attachment he would never have connived at her escape, or escapade. In that sense he could be blamed, but she knew that if she ever blamed him she would never forgive herself.

She stepped back from the porthole and groped for the light switch. The cabin she shared with Ramona Garcia, a Cosmonaut mathematician slightly more ancient than Matt, seemed tinier than ever. She ducked out of it into the corridor before that thought could close in again.

The corridor was wider than the room. She could stretch out her arms and not touch the sides. But with the lights on, the windows showed nothing. She walked up to the cockpit. The viewscreens and windows in there gave the illusion of space, or would have done if the cabin hadn't been crammed with people: Matt, Salasso, and Delavar, the old Cosmonauts Mikhail Telesnikov and Ramona (who gave her a quick friendly smile), the Mingulayan captain Phil Johnson, and first mate Ann Derige, both of whom were an embarrassing year or two younger than she was and acted like they were about ten years older; and two of the Multis, the orange one and the blue one.

The Multipliers had spent the first day spinning a thirty-meter dish aerial and a complex receiving apparatus from a kilogram of scrap steel and some random bits of junk, and had detected a very faint microwave beam that swept across them every Nova Terran day. Just before her panic attack, Susan had heard an announcement that they'd extracted some information from it.

They were all staring at a rectangular patch on the viewscreen above the fore window. All except Matt looked delighted. Nobody told her what it was, and it took her a moment to recognize it as a map, a Mercator projection of Nova Terra. Maps in the Second Sphere were physical. The only imaginary lines on them were trade routes. This city, they told you, was linked with that. The map on the viewscreen was covered with imaginary lines separating patches of different colors, none of which looked as if they had anything to do with geography.

"What is that?" she asked.

"It's the first piece of information we've managed to crunch out of the microwave beam," said Ramona. "It's a world map, the logo of the official television station, New Babylon News. Presumably the beam's a daily news update aimed at deep-space missions. Almost certainly military missions, because it's encrypted. Matt doesn't know if it's worth the effort to crack—any news will be a year out of date anyway."

"I know it's a map, but—"

"What you're looking at," said Matt, "is the most obscene and disgusting thing I've seen for centuries. It's a map of the world that happens to be a rectangular sheet of chauvinist shit. Every one of those barbarously, artificially carved-up fragments of the world is tagged with a little rectangle of its own, a bloody badge of shame—a flag! They've got *nationalism* down there. If they had a virulent strain of bubonic plague instead, I'd be happy for them. I'm still red in the face from explaining all this to the Multipliers."

He was indeed red in the face, but he'd been looking flushed for the past day or so, and occasionally shivery. He'd brushed aside any enquiries. Just a cold or something. It hadn't spread.

The Multipliers quivered slightly, perhaps embarrassed themselves. Matt simmered down a little.

"The good thing, though," said Telesnikov, "is that we aren't picking up any deep-space radar beams. I expect there'll be some close in, but they're unlikely to be probing out farther than the asteroid belt."

"Nova Sol has an asteroid belt?" Matt asked.

"You don't know the system?" Telesnikov sounded incredulous.

Matt shrugged. "All the descriptions I ever saw of it were Ptolemaic. Couldn't get my head around the epicycles."

Ramona snorted. The saurs looked slightly abashed. Their species had not thought it necessary to inform the Nova Babylonians about the heliocentric hypothesis, knowledge of which had in the past few centuries spread inward from Croatan to shatter the most horrendously complicated arrangement of crystal spheres ever devised.

"All right," said Telesnikov. "Here it is in Copernican. Working in from here, and not counting contentious lumps of rock and ice which might be stray gods . . . we've got two gas giants, Juno and Zeus, about oh point seven and one point six Jupiter masses respectively. Both have a spectacular array of moons and rings—it's a fair bet these are garrisoned, if we assume Volkov has succeeded. Which we must, on the basis that pleasant surprises are not to be counted on. Next there's the asteroid belt, which is much richer than the Solar System's, probably the richest in the Second Sphere. There's nothing in the equivalent of Mars orbit, like our Raphael back home—probably never formed, hence the extent of the asteroid belt. Then there's Nova Terra itself, with its two satellites, Ea and Selene, each about two-thirds the size of Luna and resulting in diabolically complex tides. Finally, you have one which is kind of like a big Mercury or a close-orbit airless Venus, a thoroughly nasty ball of hot rock with a high albedo. Named Lucifer, aptly enough.

"Now, if I were applying the doctrine of system defense which I learned in Moscow Cosmotech—"

"You learned *Solar System defense?*" Matt interrupted.

"Asteroid detection and deflection was the practical side," said Telesnikov. He scratched the back of his neck. "The matter of repelling alien invasions was, ah, the speculative part. Anyway, I'm sure Volkov studied the same classified texts. The basics are the gas-giant moons, the asteroid belt—minimum of three armed and fortified mini-observatories cum missile or particle-beam stations, evenly spaced around it so you essentially have the inner system triangulated—and finally the home planet's moon—moons, in this case—and low orbit. All likewise fortified, and with harder armor and hotter weapons the closer in you are. Anything that gets through all of that is a matter for air and ground defense. Or disaster recovery."

"What about any inner planets?" Susan asked. "Didn't Volkov go to Venus?"

"He did," said Telesnikov. "But that was just a stunt. We never considered fortifying Venus! The great majority—I think historically, all—impact events come from the other direction, from outside Earth's orbit. As for intelligent threats—well, there was one theoretical case, a slingshot approach round the sun and out to Earth on the daylight side. Obviously a very smart manoeuvre if you could pull it off—observation would be difficult, interception an absolute nightmare. But that would come in so fast that frankly your lunar and low-orbit defenses would have a much better chance of catching it."

"Hmm," said Matt, tipping back the gimballed chair he'd appropriated and looking as if he wanted to light a cigarette, "it sounds like the dark side of Lucifer would be a good place to lurk. We could jump straight into its shadow cone and stay there—safe from Nova-Solar radiation, and within easy listening distance of Nova Terra."

"Provided it's not in opposition at the moment—I mean, when we get there."

The blue Multiplier jumped to the window and spread itself against it, like an expanding snowflake. Then it shrank its extensions back into its limbs and hopped back to its previous perch.

"It shall not," it said. "If we were to jump now we would encounter Lucifer at thirty-eight degrees from Nova Terra."

"Thank you," said Matt dryly. "The next thing we need to know is whether Volkov got any cooperation from the saurs, and therefore whether or not he has lightspeeders and skiffs." He looked hopefully at the alien. "I don't suppose you can tell us that?"

"Our skiffs have instruments for detecting other space-bending quantum manifold devices in operation," it said. "They can only be used when the skiff is in operation, which of course leaves them open to such detection themselves."

Everybody turned to look at the saurs.

"Ours do not have such devices," said Delavar.

"How do you avoid collisions?" asked the Multiplier.

"They just don't happen," said Delavar. "It's a question of skilled piloting."

"It is because of something called the Exclusion Principle," said Salasso stiffly.

"Ah," sighed the Multiplier, as though inhaling in order to say something, and then fell silent.

"Okay," said Matt, in a tone of heavy patience, "and have your skiffs detected any other ships or skiffs in the system?"

The two Multipliers touched hands, conferring.

"One starship arrived two days ago," said the orange Multiplier. "Another left yesterday. Some minor and local skiff activity accompanied them. That is all."

"How about rocket exhausts?" asked Ann Derige.

"We have no instruments to detect them," said the orange Multiplier. "Though doubtless," it added in a hopeful tone, waving its limbs excitedly, "such instruments could be improvised."

"Very difficult anyway," said Telesnikov. "Fusion torches and such apart, and even they'd be almost invisible at this distance."

"We seem to have arrived at a negative conclusion," said Delavar. "The deep-space communication suggests a deep-space presence, the absence of evidence of antigravity or nuclear drives suggests that this has been accomplished with conventional rockets. This is more or less what we would have anticipated, if we had done any anticipating."

Was this a dig at Matt? If it was, he laughed it off.

A day later, they jumped a year.

The dark side of Lucifer. Susan liked the idea; she knew that the Lightbearer was a dark power in some perverse mythologies. The interstellar flotilla, the *Investigator* and its five companions, hung in starlight a few hundred meters above the planet's cracked surface. This was lower than many of its mountains; their chances of detection equivalently small—

"We've been pinged," said Ann.

The two Multipliers pounced toward their apparatus. Their hands scrabbled over it and each other. Outside, the dish aerial moved, tracking.

"There appears to be a small artificial satellite in polar orbit."

"We can improvise a control system to send one of your missiles toward it."

"Within two of its orbits."

Phil Johnson looked over at Matt. It was Phil who gave orders to the crew, but it had been well established that it was Matt who was leading this expedition.

"Go for that?"

Matt rubbed his nose. "No," he said. "I have a better idea."

He turned to the Multipliers. "Could you ask one of the skiffs outside to go after the satellite, catch it, and reinsert it in equatorial orbit?"

Even he could hardly have expected the speed with which his suggestion was carried out. The orange Multiplier tapped at the apparatus. Within seconds one of the skiffs riding alongside disappeared. Two minutes later, it was back.

"We have picked up and redirected the satellite. It was approximately one meter in diameter."

"Fucking sputnik," said Matt. 'Now let's shift a thousand or so kilometers out of the way.'

"Why?" asked Johnson.

"We've been spotted by what is probably a scientific satellite mapping Lucifer," Matt said. "Within about one minute, the information will reach Nova Terra. If it's a purely scientific probe, the likely result is that it won't be processed for months. If it's not, if it's part of their space-defense network, we could be burned by a particle beam in about five or six minutes. So let's move."

They moved. It wasn't a lightspeed jump, just a very fast move. The landscape below didn't look any different.

"Right," said Matt, "now we set up a jump to Nova Terra. Make it somewhere on the surface with plenty of cover and far away from any settled areas. Ann, could you patch up that map again?"

Matt peered at the map for a moment, then pointed at a zigzag line marking the northern border of the Republic of New Babylon. "There," he said. "In the forests just north of the mountains, on the north side of the border. It looks pretty well uninhabited."

Everybody just stared at him.

"I was wrong about Lucifer," he said. "It's not a safe place to lurk. The safest place I can think of is Nova Terra itself. If you're watching for invaders from space, where's the last place you'd look?"

"They'll have spy satellites," Telesnikov pointed out. "They'll see *something*."

"Yup," said Matt. "I'm counting on it. I'm also guessing that the spy satellites are not likely to be those of"—he peered again at the map—"the Free Duchy of Illyria, and that it and New Babylon are not exactly friends."

"And if you're wrong?" said Phil.

Matt shrugged. "If I'm wrong, we'll move somewhere else."

Salasso stood up. "I am afraid," he said, "that that is not an adequate answer. I think I see what you are trying to do, Matt, and I very much look forward to finding out how the Nova Terran news media cover—or cover up—the anomalous event of a satellite suddenly orbiting at ninety degrees to its previous orbit. I agree entirely that Nova Terra is the best place to lurk, now that we have found that even Lucifer is under observation. However, I strongly suggest that we make our base somewhere much less accessible and much less noticeable than a border region, however wild it may appear."

He pointed to the map. "You will notice," he went on, "that the lines depicting political divisions are only present on one continent, Genea, the one inhabited mainly by the hominidae." He tapped a long finger on the other one. "The one inhabited mainly by saurs is still marked simply as Sauria."

It was something so obvious that none of them had noticed it. Every planet in their experience had at least an island continent reserved for saurs, and they had taken this one's for granted.

"I don't think blundering into a saur city or manufacturing plant is going to make us any less conspicuous," said Matt.

"Indeed not," said Salasso. "But as the Multipliers have told us, there are no skiffs operational except around the occasional starship, presumably in the harbor of New Babylon. That suggests strongly to me that there are no, or very few, saurs present on the planet. If for any reason we are detected there, what could be more natural than for our skiffs to be taken for those of returning or remaining saurs? Also, Sauria includes extensive areas of rainforest, mountain ranges, temperate forest, ruined cities. One in particular has ruins more than adequate to conceal our entire expedition."

"How do you know all this?" asked Susan.

The saur gave her his almost undetectable smile. "I remember it well," he said.

At that moment, Susan noticed Matt looking at his watch. A moment later, a bright flare filled the windows on one side, and the viewscreens went into an unstable cycle of failed adjustments. Several alarms went off. It was as though the ship had drifted out of the shadow cone into the savage sunlight; except it was the wrong window, and the light was fading, not increasing.

Matt looked from his watch to the window. "Plasma-cannon strike," he said. "Vaporized the ground just below where we were a few minutes ago. From lunar orbit, by my reckoning— shit, they must have something big up there, one hefty mother-fucker of a death ray projector. Let's jump."

They jumped.

Rhododendrons and flying squirrels in a big square of blue. Susan staggered away from the foot of the *Investigator*'s stair ladder, mistiming her steps in the subtly different gravity, then found her feet and ran to the door of the hangar-sized megalithic structure within which the ship and the ships were parked. They'd come out of the lightspeed jump a thousand meters up and a few thousand meters away—the Multiplier navigators, and Salasso's memory, were that precise. Strangely, the flying squirrels avoided the structure, which might have seemed a suitable roost; Susan noticed as she ran that the floor was thick with dirt, but clear of any animal droppings.

Out in the open she stopped, and breathed deeply. She was ecstatic with relief. Only now that she was out of the ship could she realize how confined she had felt inside it; how tightly she had screwed a lid down on that feeling of confinement. The air was colder than she had expected, and better than she had hoped. It carried a sweet-sour smell of vegetation. She was facing northward, the mid-morning sun high to her right. Ahead of her was an area of ground covered with short grass and rhododendron overgrowth, riotous with rotten flowers. After about a hundred meters, the ground dropped away sharply to a rainforest valley many kilometers across, on the far side of which a range of mountains raised jagged white teeth to the sky. The cacophony of whoops and the symphony of chirps from the various species and sizes of flying squirrel, and the buzz and hum of insects, were the only sounds, and they were enough.

She turned to look back at the great door, fifty meters in width and height, whose lintel cast the black shadow from which the others were emerging. The two saurs first, and the other eight humans, and a dozen Multipliers. The aliens, to her surprise, suddenly rushed past everyone else, past her, and leapt onto the tops of the rhododendron bushes and then away down the slope into the trees, chasing the startled flying squirrels into flapping, screaming flocks.

"Are you all right?" Matt asked.

"Zeus! Wow! Am I all right!"

Nobody else seemed to be having quite the same reaction. They all stepped out into the glaring sunlight cautiously, sniffing the air like prey animals; turned around at once to check the sky and the skyline; the saurs wandered off to examine the side of the entrance. Matt stood beside her and looked about with more enthusiasm than the others, but without abandon.

"Plasma rifles," he said.

His high temperature seemed to have run its course; Susan noticed that she couldn't see the tracery of subcutaneous scar tissue he'd ruefully pointed out when they'd first met. It must be something about the light.

"What?"

"We should keep them handy. There are dinosaurs on Sauria." He laughed harshly. "Perhaps that's what's kept it from being colonized by humans. 'Here be dragons.' "

"Assuming it *has* kept it," said Telesnikov, coming up. "I can see a scramble for this continent as soon as the rival nation-states on the other one work themselves up to it."

"Yeah," said Matt vaguely. "The falling rate of profit, and all that."

"I hope not," said Susan. "Wow, it's beautiful!"

Matt's attention snapped back to her. "You're very high," he said.

"It's, um, just good to be off the ship," she said. "Uh, cabin fever, you know?"

"Oh, shit," said Matt. "*Now* I get it. You suffer from—"

"*Don't* fucking say it!"

The two Cosmonauts laughed unsympathetically.

"Just as well you didn't get the tests we went through—"

"You mean, the pipes we went—"

She grabbed his arm hard enough to hurt. "Don't. Fucking. Say it."

Matt gave her a warmer look. "All right," he said. "Sorry. Christ, I've been worried about you. You haven't cracked a smile since we jumped from Planet Selkie." Then he ruined it all by adding: "Thought you were missing your parents or having PMS or something."

She shrugged away from him. He looked at her helplessly for a moment, then turned away and called and beckoned everyone together.

"We have a couple of things to talk about," he said. "Let's get the first one out of the way while our friends are away enjoying themselves. Have any of you here taken up the Multipliers' offer?"

They all shook their heads. Including the saurs, Susan noticed, as if the question might be relevant to them. Maybe it was.

"I didn't know they could just do it, like, any time," said Obadiah Hynde, the rocketeer. "Didn't know we had the option, see."

"Well, we do," said Matt. "They don't need machines. It's like . . . an infection. They give it to you. I took it, when we were lurking out in the cometary cloud."

"How could you do something so crazy and irresponsible?" said Ramona. "Oh, what am I saying? I am talking to Matt after all. Well, Matt, tell us what it is like."

"That's the trouble," said Matt. "I don't know if I can, because one part of it didn't take. The orange Multiplier, the one who tried, said it was 'like biting fruit and finding stone.' They read your genes, then tweak them. I think that's what they do. They could read mine but they couldn't alter them, because they've been altered already by the process—whatever it was—that gave us longevity. But apart from that . . . yeah, I can tell you what it's like. It's like having an infection that doesn't make you ill, then an infestation that doesn't itch, and after that you remember things that never happened to you. That's the most disturbing thing about it, I'll give you that. But it's not delusional . . . I remember them happening, but I don't think they happened to me. I can remember doing things, without thinking that I did them."

"What kind of things?" asked Ramona.

"Budding," said Matt. "Seeing my hand break off and run away, and wishing it well. Sharing knowledge, knowledge of the world and knowledge of how my body was built. The pleasure of that." He laughed. "Our friends have more fun than we know. And now I know more. Strange things. So anyway—is anyone else willing to try it?"

"So you're telling us," said Ramona, "that the Multis can give us the long life. Except for those who already have it. For the rest of us, it's hardly an issue—I don't think there's one of us here who is over twenty-five, am I right? And besides that, they mess with your head. So what's the advantage in taking the risk?"

"Its one big advantage," said Matt, "apart from the long life, is that you do not fall sick, and that most injuries self-repair very fast. I do have that."

"How," asked Telesnikov, "if they could not alter your genes?"

"That part of it has nothing to do with genes," said Matt. "It has to do with . . . some of the very small offspring of the Multipliers continuing to live inside you."

"You stay infected?" Ramona Gracia took a couple of steps away from him. "No thanks."

Matt shrugged and spread his hands. "I see I haven't sold anyone on this. Well, you can all watch and see if I turn into something strange."

("You're there already," Ramona muttered.)

"The next thing we need to discuss is what we are doing. We didn't have any detailed plan before we came here, because we didn't know what we'd find. In a sense, we still don't. We know they have separate states, and that at least one of them, most likely Nova—New Babylon, as it calls itself now—has some pretty heavy space defense. Now I don't know about you, but I don't fancy our chances going up against that kind of hardware with our fireworks. I've considered stunts like, you know, jumping a skiff or even the *Investigator*, right inside one of the orbital forts, but, well, I'd rather not rely on dumb luck or brute force. So." He brushed imaginary dust off his palms. "Anyone got any bright ideas?"

"I had the impression," said Ann, "that Salasso thought you already had one."

"Well, kind of," said Matt evasively, "but I want to hear other suggestions first."

"I have one," said Ramona. "Let's brew up some goddam coffee and have something to fucking eat."

Susan had never before heard Ramona speak coarsely. The mathematician met her surprised look with a sullen flush.

"He has that effect," she said.

After the gunners and rocketeers had come back from the ship's galley with hot coffee and cold rations, people began to feel less fractious. One light-year lightspeed jump, one crack at turning a mapping satellite into a blatant anomalous phenomenon, a near miss from a plasma bolt, and another lightspeed jump to ruins so old there were fossils younger—all made for a tense morning.

"The first thing we should do," said Ramona, "is watch some television. Not as easy as it sounds—I doubt if even satellite broadcasting covers this continent."

"There's always radio," said Susan. She remembered that she had a radio in her pocket. "Hey! Wait a minute."

She switched the radio on and spun the dial slowly. Most of the stations played music. The scales were unfamiliar, the lyrics mostly in languages that had drifted from Trade Latin or never started from it, but the music was a reassurance of the planet's humanity. Other channels carried news or discussion—without context it was difficult to make sense of it, but context could be built up. One wavelength was pure bedlam: a welter of voices and sounds, fragmentary phrases, strange noises. It wasn't that she was picking up lots of stations at once; the more precisely she tuned it the weirder it got.

"Well," said Matt, "the radio is something to work on. Susan, could you look after that and try to compile a picture?"

"Sure."

"Okay. Anyone else?"

"I haven't finished," said Ramona. "I've been doing some back-of-the-envelope calculations. We have jumped from the selkies' world to here, more or less in the shortest possible time. It appears that the normal trade routes have been severely disrupted, if the number of starships in this system at any given moment is one or less! The obvious explanation is that our people are supplanting the kraken-saur-Trader partnership. Assuming that the Multipliers have indeed been assimilated to the Bright Star Cultures, and that they are spreading from star to star with only a small delay to build more ships and navigate the next jump, they cannot be far behind us. We have at the very most a few years, at the very least a few months, before the first Bright Star Culture ships arrive. In that time—short at best—we have to arrange matters so that they are not blasted out of the skies. We have one lightly armed starship, one human-built skiff with antigravity only, and five jump-capable Multiplier skiffs. The other side have an extensive space defense capability, built to all appearances with rocket technology. Evidently they have been unable or unwilling to persuade or coerce the other species into sharing antigravity and lightspeed tech."

She waved a hand at the dark interior of the enormous building. "All our advantage, such as it is, is right here. What we have to decide is how to use it."

"Exactly," said Mikhail Telesnikov. He stood up, incongruously gesturing with an empty coffee mug. "We have two basic options. One, and the most economical, is to make a direct approach to whoever is in power in New Babylon—presumably Volkov or his successors—and convince them that there is nothing to fear or fight. Considering that there are obviously no Multipliers here, and that some were on their way, it seems evident that the New Babylonians have already *won* such a fight and are unlikely to be persuaded that it was all a terrible mistake. I still say it should be our first option. The second—which the failure of the first might foreclose, so it's not the second in time—is to approach one or more of the rival powers, who are more likely to be convinced, and who must surely fear the power of New Babylon. It is at least possible that they would agree to a military strike against New Babylon, if they have the military capacity and the hope of winning. If they have the former, we can provide the latter."

"I don't see how we could," said Hynde. "Each of our missiles could take out a spy-sat. At close range. Maybe. That's about all we could do, and it don't sound like enough."

"I was thinking more," said Telesnikov, "that if the other powers have nuclear weapons, or even decent-sized conventional bombs, we could deliver them to the space battle stations very fast and unstoppably by lightspeed jump, then jump back out of the way."

"Problem with that," said Matt. "Do we want to destroy New Babylon's space defenses? If the gods get angry, we might shortly need them ourselves."

Susan jumped up. "We don't need to put bombs on them!" she said. "We can put troops on them!"

"You can't get many troops in a skiff," one of the gunners said.

She glared at him. "I know *that*," she said. "But you're thinking of one trip. Think lots. Every Multiplier skiff can zap back and forth lots of times—say it can carry six soldiers at a time, it could shift dozens in minutes, just pour them in. And at different places in the battle station, too."

Telesnikov was looking at her as though seeing her for the first time. "That's a very good point," he said.

By the time the Multipliers swarmed back from their cavort in the forest, the rest of the expedition was ready to explain their contingency plans. The Multipliers listened to Matt's enthusiastic outline and announced that they would not hear more of it. They squatted around the circle of humans like so many miserable balls of fur, twitching slightly and occasionally stroking each other's hands. At length Matt walked over to the orange Multiplier. Susan followed, discreetly recording.

"Do you have an ethical objection to taking life?" Matt asked.

The alien wrapped its limbs around its body and rolled away. After a tense minute it uncoiled and reached out to the nearest of its fellows. That one, magenta-furred, eventually stood up shakily and tottered into the center of the circle, near to the remains of lunch. It inspected spilled coffee grounds and bread crumbs and reconstructed a shrimp from a sliver of paste. The shrimp twitched and scrabbled, dying in the air. The Multiplier observed it with apparent curiosity, then ate it.

Then Mr. Magenta (a naming convention that Susan hit upon at that moment, and thereafter spread) waved a limb in a circle above itself and fixed, it seemed, its all-around gaze on everyone simultaneously.

"We are distressed," it announced, "by your plans. They are inelegant. We were under the impression from our reading of the Matt Cairns that you all understood how to survey a planet and neutralize its defenses. You have had such beautiful examples. Why do you not follow them?"

"What examples?" Matt asked.

"You are the Matt Cairns," said the alien. "You know. Please educate the others, and then we will be happy to make your invasion a wonder and delight for the ages, and give our descendants memories to warm them while they watch the stars turn to iron."

By the time Matt was five minutes into explaining his contingency plan he was beginning to scare people.

"Do you know how many Multiplier skiffs were in our system in the years before we left? Two! And you know what they did to us! They had us thinking we were under constant surveillance!

Thinking we were about to be invaded! For every real incident there were ten unreal incidents! We made them up ourselves! That's what we have to do here! Make them doubt their concept of reality! Guerrilla ontology!"

He glared around like a lone gladiator facing a hostile colosseum.

"Fuck with their heads!" he shouted. *"Fuck with their heads!"*

That night Susan sat outside on a block around the side of the big building. The block was thirty meters long and five on a side. She had scrambled up the tough creeper that overgrew it. The air was cold and the sky was black. Fog lay over the forested valley, lit by the two small moons, both waxing gibbous, their surfaces so cratered that their terminators were visibly serrated even to the naked eye. Six comets were visible, low in the sky. She had never seen so much as one comet before. The Foamy Wake blazed a trail across the zenith. Every so often a meteor flared, and now and again what appeared to be a star would move steadily across the sky. These, she guessed, must be artificial satellites, like the spaceship yards that orbited around Mingulay.

After a while Salasso joined her. "That is a frightening sky," he said. "The gods' anger is written on it. Fortunately my anger is greater."

"You don't know what anger is," Susan said. "What Matt has, now that's anger."

"I am angry with the gods," said Salasso. "Matt is only angry with the saurs."

"I thought he liked you."

"He does," said Salasso. "It is not personal. All of the old Cosmonauts are like that."

"Ah!" Susan had a sudden insight. "It's because of what the saurs were doing back in the Solar System. All that stuff about Greys and flying saucers, it must have been like a bad dream."

"No," said Salasso. "At the time when Matt and the others lived on Earth, almost all of that was decades in the past. I have

174

studied the literature, if you can call it that, and I found no reported sightings, abductions, or anything untoward for many years. The old stories were not taken seriously except by students of popular delusion, and the deluded, and a very few stubborn investigators."

"Oh! So it was the shock of finding that something they had dismissed was partly true after all—"

"Again, I fear not," said Salasso. "They had no emotional investment in its dismissal. It was not a live issue, either way."

Susan looked at the saur sitting beside her, gazing out over the valley in the double moonlight. His small shoulders were slumped, and his large head hung heavy.

"So why—"

Salasso turned to her. "Do you have your recording devices with you? Of course you do, I am telling you this because it is something I wish to be known after I . . . after all this is over. When the Bright Star Cultures come here, and find a welcome, I want this to be known. Not before. Will you promise me this?"

Susan clamped her hands on her quivering knees. "Yes," she said. She fumbled, setting her apparatus, then turned to face the saur as though interviewing him.

"When the *Bright Star* arrived in orbit near Mingulay, three hundred—no, it is now four hundred—years ago, we were shocked and frightened. The crew claimed to have navigated here, and though we soon realized they were lying, that did little to allay our fears. We had no reason to think there might not be more ships. We knew that the Cosmonauts had received the instructions for the drive directly from a god. This suggested to us that the gods in the Solar System had lost patience with the saurs, and perhaps that the gods here had too.

"The saurs discovered how to manipulate genetic material many millions of years ago. With that discovery we built the manufacturing plant. This was an industry that did not disturb the planets, or displease the gods. With that knowledge we have been able to screen all the new arrivals from Earth, and to prevent the spread of diseases. We explained this to the Cosmonauts, and they agreed to be examined. They told us freely that they had taken life-extending drugs, and we soon found out why some of these drugs had worked. They modified a gene which is common to many species, including ours. In their case it was only somatic, not heritable, but it was still alarming. The effect of human longevity on the stability we had so carefully cultivated would be immensely disruptive—as indeed it is proving now, if Ramona is right, and I think she is.

"The effect of the knowledge in the ship's computer libraries, and the machinery it had to replicate the computers and disseminate the knowledge, would have been even more disruptive. At the same time it was not in our nature to deny or destroy that knowledge. So we later allowed the computer libraries to be transcribed to the manufacturing plant, and subsequently printed in books—a necessarily slow process, which made assimilating the knowledge the work of centuries, still incomplete. But we did not allow the Cosmonauts further access to their ship, and only allowed them to take from it such machinery and computers as they could carry.

"Before we even allowed them off the ship, we took one further precaution. We took them one by one and subjected them to a second medical examination. It was traumatic and intrusive, and not merely physically. We did everything to them that they had jokingly told us saurs were supposed to do." He looked away, then looked back. "We terrified the living shit out of them."

Susan's mouth was dry, her eyes wet. "Why are you telling me this, now?"

"Because I feel bad about it. And because as more and more people take up the Multipliers' offer, these memories will be shared and passed around like diseases. It is important that people are able to make sense of these frightening fragments of memory."

"You mean," she said, "that they don't find themselves fearing and hating the saurs for no reason they can understand."

"That too, yes."

"I don't know what to say," she said.

"Nor do I," said Salasso. He made a cutting gesture. She switched off her apparatus.

"Well, hell," she said, "I think you've made up for it since, Salasso."

"I wish you had recorded that," said Salasso.

"I will say it again."

They sat in silence for a while.

He took out his pipe. "Would you share a smoke?"

"Yes," she said.

The hemp knocked Salasso into a twenty-minute trance, and left Susan to gaze at the Foamy Wake and imagine the Solar System on the far side of it, and wonder what had befallen the saurs and humans there.

Salasso came to himself with a start. In silence the woman and the saur, one after the other, descended the precarious ladder of creeper.

"What is this building, anyway?" she asked, as they headed back.

"Before the saurs learned how to make the manufacturing plant," said Salasso, scuffing through the leaves beside her, "they constructed such buildings. This one, I believe, they used as a place to park their skiffs."

Susan glanced back at the megalith, one of many strewn around, evidently surplus to the requirements of the gargantuan structure, which was built from blocks of similar or greater size.

"And they used the skiffs to lift the blocks up here, and move them into position?"

"Oh, no," said Salasso. "That is physically impossible. They built enormous ramps of close-packed earth, and made ropes of the creeper vines, and tens of thousands of saurs dragged the blocks up." He spread his long hands and shrugged his small shoulders. "But when you tell people that, they don't believe you."

177

In stealth mode the skiff was visible only to the insane, the users of psychoactive chemicals, the very young, and dogs. To anyone else it was something that could be glimpsed, perhaps as an unfeasibly large meniscus of water, but not directly seen. It was certainly invisible to the sober agents of national defense, security, and law enforcement.

It had been highly visible earlier, during the day, when its sonic boom was breaking windows and its radar trace was scrambling jet fighters right across Genea. Over the New Babylon subcontinent it had appeared as a fleet above a small town in the Massif, making lightspeed jumps back and forth between five separate points so quickly that it was seen as five separate ships. It had been even more visible late in the afternoon, when it had loomed over the brows of nearby low hills like an early rising Lucifer and confronted and confounded a number of isolated farm laborers and one latifundia chairman. The skiff's occupants knew he was a latifundia chairman because they had followed him back to the biggest house in the village. He had kept looking back over his shoulder, unable to see the now stealth-mode skiff, but obviously feeling that he was being watched. His dog had dashed past him and barked at something outside the gate for a quarter of an hour.

Now it was barking again. Matt and Susan gave the dog a wide berth and walked up the short drive, their footsteps crunching in gravel. All the lights in the house were on. Under the lamp by the porch Matt gave Susan a critical look.

"Straighten your tie," he said.

She and Matt were identically dressed in black suits, white shirts, black ties, and black hats.

"I've always wanted to do this," Matt confided as he knocked on the door.

The latifundia chairman peered around it, holding a shotgun just in view. His expression went from suspicion to terror the moment he saw them.

"Good evening," Matt said, raising his hat. "There is no need to be alarmed. We're from the government."

9

The Hanging Libraries

THE MAN CAME into Gaius's office without knocking. Before Gaius could get up the stranger heeled the door shut behind him and sat down in the seat on the other side of the desk. He left his hat on. The plume fluttered slightly in the draft from the open window. None of this was good.

Gaius nodded at him, then at the door. "The sign says 'Gonatus Aerospace,'" he said. "Not 'Walk right it.'"

Ginger ringlets and a neat pointed beard, blue eyes behind eyelids like the slits in a shield. "My name's Attulus," he said, as though it wasn't. "Pleased to meet you, too."

He reached through one of the slashes in his blue padded jacket and withdrew a rolled piece of paper tied with a thin red ribbon. It made a hollow sound as it hit the desk.

"Read it."

The Ducal seal was enough, but Gaius read it anyway.

"The Department's number is in the book," the agent said. "Feel free."

"My export licenses are in that filing cabinet," Gaius said. "Feel free."

Attulus retrieved his commission and disappeared it. "That's not what this is about," he said. He pinched the bridge of his nose and gave his head a small shake, blinked and looked up. "We have reason to suspect that you, Ingenior Gonatus, are a loyal subject. Or a patriotic citizen, if you prefer."

So they knew about that. But of course they knew about that.

"I've done my service," Gaius said. "I understand that cancels out any youthful indiscretions."

"It does," Attulus said. "But—" He scratched his moustache. "There's another bargain, which applies to businessmen who make a habit of trading with the other side."

Again Gaius indicated the filing cabinet. "It's called an export license," he said. "On the other side, it's called a bribe. Either way, my accounts are in balance."

"Oh, but they're not, Ingenior. You owe your country a little more than a fee and a docket."

Gaius shrugged. "I've filed a report with the Department after every trip."

"Indeed you have, and I've read them. Observant, informative, complete. Quite useful, as these things go."

"Thank you."

"But, as I say, not enough. Not if you wish to continue trading."

"Continue trading with the other side?"

"Continue trading."

That, thought Gaius, is the trouble with the invisible hand. It leaves you wide open to the invisible fist.

"No need for that," he said. "Look, if you want me to spy for you, I'll do it gladly."

"That's what I like," Attulus said. "An enthusiastic volunteer. Sadly rare in the business community. And I didn't even have to ask."

And that was how it began.

Gaius Gonatus ran up a steep grassy bank and ducked through a rusted barrier to step onto the abandoned motorway. He walked onto the central lane and strolled up the intersection ramp for another hundred meters, until he was on the flyover. At its brow he looked around, remembered that the left-hand side afforded the better view—the other was cluttered by the small town and the striding pylons of the monorail—and crossed over to stand a pace or two back from the crumbled concrete of the parapet. It was at places like this that he felt most strongly the power and presence of the goddess. She alone had known how to call forth this mighty work, an overthrust of concrete implacable as rock. She alone had known to let it die, leaving it a twined green ribbon like the raffia knot on a wreath. Though the fancy pleased him, it struck him as too morbid, for the goddess had found a new use for the obsolete structure. Confined by the roadside crash barriers, flocks of sheep grazed along all the lanes, which formed strips of meadow through the forest and moorland. In the morning sun the smell of drying sheep droppings was faint above the smell of the grass and the trees. Far away a dog barked and a ewe bleated. At a further distance a sheep farmer's autogyro buzzed, quieter than a bee.

Where Gaius stood was above the tops of the tallest pines, and he gazed out across twenty miles of forested plain and foothill to the mountain range on the western horizon. Their tops, as on most days, were covered by clouds. Somewhere up there, on most days, small bands of people would be making their way through those clouds, on the high passes. The frozen faces of those who had failed in the same passage would grin at them from the side of the road. Tomorrow, Gaius thought, he would look down on those clouds, and not even see the mountains.

The sound of another autogyro rose to the south. Gaius turned, squinting against the sun. A nearby flock of sheep scattered as the small craft sank toward the long green strip. It touched down and bumped along to halt a few yards from him, its prop feathering, its rotor beating in slower and slower cycles. The pilot dismounted and strode over, pulling off goggles and leather helmet and running his finger through the bushy hair thus released. He was a slim, small man in his mid-twenties with red hair and a neatly trimmed beard. His flying-jacket was incongruous over his blue and distinctly urban suit; likewise the canvas satchel and the shiny, thin-soled shoes, already sheep-shat.

"Good morning, Attulus," said Gaius.

Attulus glowered. "Do you realize how inconvenient this is? And the cost to the Department?"

Gaius glanced over at the tiny flying machine and raised his eyebrows. "Lose it in the paperclip budget, why don't you?"

"Hah!" snorted Attulus. "Why don't you meet me in a café back in town?"

Gaius shrugged. "I like to keep our dealings out in the open."

Attulus snorted again. "All right," he said. "We don't have much time. At least *I* don't."

He lifted the satchel's flap and pulled out a thin sheaf of paper. Gaius folded it lengthways in half and stuck it in his inside jacket pocket, without looking.

"Don't take them with you," said Attulus, as though it didn't need saying but he had to say it anyway. "They give the background of a man we want you to see. He looks like a good prospect for your sales pitch, but he isn't. However, meeting him and stringing out the realization that he's a seat warmer and buck passer should give you the chance to talk to the person we really want you to meet, one of his assistants who do the actual work, who might turn out to be a useful business contact, but that's up to you. Full background on her, too. Her name is Lydia de Tenebre."

"Let me guess," said Gaius. "Old merchant family—"

"Fallen on hard times and working in the Space Authority. Yes. Also a malcontent, and part of a group."

"How long has she been back?"

"Ten years. Her previous landfall was a hundred years earlier, our time."

Gaius felt a chill. "She remembers old New Babylon."

"Nova Babylonia, yes, she does indeed. Which is more than most of the malcontents can claim. It carries a certain cachet, in these circles."

"How does she keep her job?"

Attulus grinned. "Competence counts. She has business skills the Modern Regime spent fifty years forgetting and another fifty trying to reinvent from first principles."

"Or pretending to," said Gaius. "They pirate our management textbooks, you know."

"The Department makes sure they pirate the right ones."

Gaius chuckled, under the misapprehension that Attulus was sharing a joke, then frowned. "Does she have access to any of their technical secrets?"

"Nothing like," said Attulus. "Her security clearance is two ticks above zilch, which is why she's stuck where she is."

Gaius took a deep breath. "So what," he said, "do you want me to talk to her about?"

Attulus stared away at the mountains for a moment, then asked abruptly: "Do you follow the litter press?"

"In an idle moment . . . the sports and television pages. The rest, well, I just look at the pictures."

"Look at them carefully, next time you get the chance."

"There's a connection?"

"If you don't see it," Attulus said, "then we'll have made a mistake, but apart from that, no harm will have been done. And . if you do see it"—he smiled—"you'll let nothing stop you. You'll *want* to find out, and you'll *want* to tell us."

"You seem very sure of that."

"You'll do it," said Atullus, "or die trying."

He walked, then flew, swiftly away.

Gaius stared after the departing autogyro for a few minutes, until the dot was lost in the dazzle. Then he made his way back down the bank. He recognized rocks, now sinking into the grass, and trees, now reaching higher above it, that he'd used as handholds and footholds in boyhood scrambles. How well he had known that bank, known every tussock and hollow where a ball could come to rest or an ankle could twist. That intimate acquaintance and depth of detail had made it seem huge, even in his memory, and when he revisited it in dreams. How small it seemed now.

.   .   .

Gaius paid the visit to his mother that was the excuse for his trip, and took the monorail back to the city. He arrived at his office an hour before it was supposed to shut. He decided to call it a day. He put the phone on tape, locked up, and told Phyliss, the receptionist downstairs, to deflect any incoming calls until after the weekend. She looked up from her novel.

"You're going away for ten days after the weekend."

"So I am," Gaius said. He dropped the key on her desk. "Water my plant?"

"Of course, Gaius."

"Thanks. See you when I get back, then."

She waited for a beat. "You've forgotten something."

Gaius turned back, to see her holding out his airline tickets.

"As soon as I can afford a secretary . . ." he said, taking them. He almost meant it.

"You'll hire someone else," she said. "And you'll still rely on me. Happens all the time."

"Have a good weekend," he said.

Outside, the street was at the muggy end of autumn. Gaius slung his linen jacket over his shoulder and walked to the café on the corner. Inside, it was air-conditioned, which made it better than his office. In the old days it had *been* his office, and he sometimes regretted his move up in the world. Not that Gonatus Aerospace was much of a company. One office, one man, a lot of import-export deals. It looked like the sort of company a spy would set up as a front.

Gaius took a chilled coffee and cloves to a window table, scooping up abandoned newspapers as he went. Ten separate titles, all equally bad. Two glasses later he was cool, jumpy, and none the wiser. A dead kraken had washed up on a beach. The Duke's third son had a new boyfriend. The established cults had quarreled over their share of the god-tax. A forester claimed to have seen a gravity skiff. Scientists said the saurs had not come back. Cloud people had rioted in an overcrowded holding camp.

Defense and electronics shares were up. His fingers were black with cheap ink.

He remembered what Attulus had said, just after Gaius had mentioned looking at the pictures. This time he ignored the text and looked at the pictures. The news and publicity pictures were less interesting than the erotica. Some of the sexual positions looked as though they might be spelling out some kind of message, but he put that down to fatigue. His, not theirs. The only photograph all of the papers had in common was one taken by the forester, of something that might have been a thrown ashtray. He stared at it for a while, letting the grainy dots blur together. Under this crude enhancement it looked almost realistic.

It was a connection of a sort. A merchant's daughter and a gravity skiff. Gaius had seen gravity skiffs, but only over the harbor of New Babylon, and then not for long. No one had seen a gravity skiff anywhere else in the past hundred years. If this was what Attulus had hoped would turn him into a fervent seeker after state secrets, it was a disappointment. All he felt was a tiny itch of curiosity.

There is this about that kind of a tiny itch, he thought. You do have to scratch.

Next he looked over the document Attulus had given him. It was a New Babylon Board of Trade handout. Not exactly deep background. David Daul sounded like a typical Modern Regime lower middle cadre. Son of a latifundia chairman. Farm school, military service, university, Society school, Space Agency. His current post was in technology procurement. He looked handsome in a spoiled way. Plenty of healthy sports, all with a military angle: skiing, martial arts, rifle shooting, hang gliding. He seemed exactly the man to approach with a sales pitch. Gaius almost regretted having not heard of him sooner.

The picture of Lydia de Tenebre had been taken at a long distance. She looked quite pretty. According to the briefing, she was about thirty years old. He'd have to allow for that. He scanned the background briefing, which was thin. Family large and conservative; former Traders usually were. No known political involvement, low profile, but she hung out with known malcontent artists and activists, and liked to mouth off about the good old days and the bad new ones. That was allowed. The Republic was a police state, but not totalitarian. You could think what you liked, and even say it. You just couldn't print or broadcast it. It saved the state a lot of trouble. Mere tolerance made that sort of dissidence inconsequential.

It was the rest of Lydia de Tenebre's background that was unusual. When he'd finished reading he could feel the hairs stand up on the back of his neck. The tiny itch of curiosity had become poison ivy.

He put the documents back in his briefcase, binned the papers, paid his tab, and left.

A bell chimed and Gaius refastened his seatbelt. Around him people stubbed out cigarettes. Uncollected litter rattled down the cabin floor as the airliner's nose dipped. Gaius pressed his temple to the small ellipse of window and peered out. Within seconds the uniform white of the cloud broke into racing strands, and the land came into view below. First a brown and green checkerboard of logged or growing forest; then, as the aircraft passed over the foothills and above the long undulations of the Massif, the similarly uniform rectangles of collective latifundia, gridded with irrigation trenches, dotted with villages built on a uniform circular plan. After a while the Massif dropped away to the coastal plain. Here the farms were much larger, the fields many hectares of wheat and barley, and each village the hub of a wider and more natural-looking small town.

As the airliner banked to sideslip into its steep final descent—New Babylon Airlines was officially part of the air force, and all its pilots were jet-fighter veterans—Gaius glimpsed in some of the fields a regular series of elaborate whorls, as though the crops had been flattened by a tornado as precise as a drill. Some strange folk art or public display, he guessed, as the circles slipped out of sight. Perhaps it had something to do with lithomancy, a fad or cult in New Babylon—a row of lithomancy pylons stood on a nearby hill. Lithomancy had been another of the Modern Regime's failures, a crackpot scheme of Volkov's to contact the mind that he had supposed inhabited the lithosphere, much as the gods inhabited the asteroids and comets. If there was a mind in the world it was mad. Gaius himself regarded the whole thing as an artefact of radio noise, spillover and echo from the communications networks.

He'd never tired of seeing the city from the air in the last moments of the flight. The river divided around the island, stapled to each shore by numerous bridges. The industrial and residential suburbs on either bank rose smoothly like lower slopes around the peak formed by the island. The buildings on the island itself looked like columnar basalt, a stepped ascent for giants. Built over ten millennia, further built upon and blackened by one century's industry. The tallest of the towers was the most recent. The Space Agency building was like an obsidian monolith that had been half-twisted while still hot. It was a bravura display of architectural skill, and an homage to the supposed shape of a lightspeed engine. It would have been more impressive if they'd actually built a lightspeed engine.

The city slid away under the wing and there was nothing but water below. The unmistakable shapes of oil tankers made him realize the aircraft was higher up than he'd thought—no matter how many times he'd seen New Babylon from the air, its scale didn't register. Another sharp bank and they were heading straight for the city at a fast-dropping height, over a lonely starship lost in the harbor's traffic, skimming masts, then above the long, projecting concrete finger of the airfield, and one wheel hit, then two, then with a jarring shudder the third, and they were down. He'd had more comfortable landings on carrier decks.

Gaius hauled his bag and briefcase from the overhead locker and joined the shuffling queue to the front. Half the passengers had lit up as soon as the seatbelt lights had gone off. After that landing, he couldn't blame them.

In the customs hall the officer thumbed through his passport as if it was subversive literature. With its gaudy variety of visa stamps, maybe it was. Gaius gave him more reactionary propaganda in body language.

"Point of departure?" the officer asked.

"Junopolis, Free Duchy of Illyria." *I would like to shout this in your streets.*

"Purpose of visit?"

"Business." *Who would come here for pleasure?*

"Duration of stay?"

"Ten days." *Too long.*

"Place of residence?"

"The Foreigners' Hotel, Messana District." *Where else?*

Lick, thumb, stamp. "Enjoy your stay."

"Thank you." *This is not your fault.*

At the Change Money, Gaius handed over a bag of Illyrian silver, and got in return a bale of paper and a fistful of nickel. Every note from the million up and every coin down to the hundred had been defaced—the paper with a pen, the base metal with a knife. The scribbles and scratches obscured the face of Volkov. Why the Regime had not simply replaced their worthless currency after the Great Engineer's fall Gaius had never discovered. Perhaps it was for the same reason that they'd left the plinths of his statues standing.

Gaius stuffed it all in his wallet—his actual business would be conducted in hard money—and headed for the underground station. He had hand luggage only. The case of samples would go direct to the hotel. Nothing would be missing, but everything would have been taken out, shaken, turned over. And, no doubt, photographed for the Bureau of Technology Procurement, where it would do them no good whatsoever.

Public transport was one of the things that New Babylon did well. The stations were vaults of white tile. The trains had carriages of polished steel and seats of pale wood. Everything about it was good, and modern, and cool, except the passengers. Their clothes didn't quite fit, their skins were missing a vitamin, their bodies wanted to be somewhere else, and their minds didn't know where it was. Gaius sat with his briefcase on his knees and his bag between them, and stared straight ahead like everybody else. The intersections afforded other opportunities, in the long curving corridors of bright tile. Before he'd made two transfers he'd had three offers for his shirt. It wasn't a good shirt.

By the time he'd walked the hundred meters from Messana East to the Foreigners' Hotel, the shirt might as well have been flannel. After the hours in air-conditioning his pores opened to the street like storm drains. His shadow looked cut off at the knees. The traffic was a slow snarl of underpowered trucks and clanging bikes. The sidewalks were crowded but quiet. Everybody was hurrying to some place they didn't want to go. One person in fifty was a cop, and one in a hundred wore a cop's uniform. The hotel was at the top of a small rise. At the step Gaius paused and looked back, down the whole length of Astronaut Avenue, a smooth sweep from the five-story tenements and office blocks around him to the black canyon of the expensive end, and the blue slot of sky and sea, and the dark speck of the starship.

If the concierge remembered him from six months earlier she gave no indication of it. She took his passport and money and gave him a key for Room 503. The lift was out of order and the stair carpet was frayed, but for the air conditioning Gaius could forgive anything. He dropped his baggage on the bed just to hear the springs creak and opened a window. The room was non-smoking, but not its most recent occupant. Gaius showered in a rusty trickle, dried on scratchy nylon, changed into a lighter shirt and thin trousers, and sat down on the bed. There was a table with a mirror and a phone, and no chair. The boy who brought up coffee stammered when Gaius tipped him ten million. This was their good stuff, their best foot forward.

Gaius carried the phone over to the bed and worked down his list of contacts, setting up appointments. Some were previous clients, others new possibilities. All of them were departments of, or suppliers for, the Space Agency. Under the post-Volkov economic reforms, they were supposed to compete with each other. In practice they bought each other off. Under the Ten-Year Plans the Trusts' executives had competed fiercely, hitting each other with purges in the official system and hijackings and armed robberies in the unofficial system. Corruption was a step back toward civilization.

He put David Daul in about a third of the way down the list. The cadre was out but the woman who took the call made an appointment for the day after tomorrow. Gaius hoped the voice on the phone was that of Lydia de Tenebre, because it was a voice he wanted to hear again.

The thought kept him going for the rest of the afternoon and the rest of the list. By the end of it he had the next ten days blocked in. Most of the trusts had offices on Astronaut Avenue, and the Departments were of course in the Space Agency building. The few actual factories he had managed to arrange to visit were all close to the underground stations. His sample case arrived. Everything was there but in the wrong compartments.

He ate out in a local shop-front restaurant, another product of the economic reforms. There was a law about how many chairs it could have, so like most of the customers he ate standing up. Then he decided to go out and have a good time, so he went to the nearest public library.

The following day he made only one sale, but it was of one of his own inventions, a solid-state switching mechanism that would replace half a ton of diodes. It made the day a net plus but the trek around the offices left him drained. After dinner he just collapsed onto the bed and slept, and woke early and sticky. At this time in the morning the shower had enough heat and pressure to be refreshing. The underground railway journey undid all that, but Gaius still felt good as he strode in to the Space Agency building.

The guards were edgier than he'd expected. They ran his briefcase and samples through the scanner five times, patted him down thrice. He sweated calmly through it all, gazing at the murals around the reception area. Blow-up photos of rocket launches, orbital forts, plasma cannon, smiling astronauts. A blank space on the wall where once, he guessed, there had been a portrait of Volkov. The lift was shabby and its attendant had a pistol on his hip.

"Floor Twenty-seven, please." He showed his pass, dated and time-stamped under laminate.

The cage door rattled closed, the lift doors thudded. Gaius smiled at the attendant, who looked right back through him.

"Floor Twenty-seven." The attendant refused a tip, then took it in a deftly upturned palm as soon as his back was turned to the camera.

Daul's office door bore his name and the legend "Small Parts Procurement." Gaius let his smile at that carry over. The office was fairly large, with about a dozen people at small desks and one man at a large one in a glassed alcove at the back with a window. The rest of the walls were covered with trade advertisements and Agency or Regime posters. Typewriters and calculators clattered. It was a busy place; hardly anyone looked up as he came in. Most of the workers were in the modern suits favored by the Regime, a couple of the women wore old-fashioned wrap robes. With a jolt, he recognized one of them as the woman he'd come to meet. She seemed younger than he'd expected. The picture had done her less than justice. She didn't look up.

Gauis walked through to the alcove and tapped. David Daul, looking slightly older and grainier than his picture, nodded him in. They shook hands.

"Good morning, Citizen—" Daul broke of to correct himself, smiling—"*Mr.* Gonatus. Make yourself comfortable."

"Good morning, Citizen Daul. Thank you."

As he pulled a swivel chair into position, Gaius took the opportunity to glance over Daul's desk surface. It was cluttered with technical drawings and critical-path diagrams and work schedules, along with the predictable empty coffee mugs, full ashtrays, and chewed pencils, a pen holder, a small intricate mechanical calculator, and a slide rule. Daul rang out for coffee, which a brisk young man brought in; offered cigarettes.

"I've been looking forward to seeing you," Daul said, preliminaries over. "Frankly, getting decent kit on time out of some of the bastards I have to deal with is a pain in the arse. If the foreigners can give me better, on schedule and under budget, bring 'em on, I say." He cocked a grin at Gaius. "And don't think I'm giving too much away at the start. There are other foreign salesmen on our case, and not just Illyrian."

"Don't I know it," said Gaius. "However, I think you'll find us competitive."

"Great! Let's have a look at what you've got."

As Gaius worked through his well-researched and well-rehearsed pitch, Daul hit him with a succession of searching questions, not just on the technical side—which he'd expected—but costs and delivery dates, quality control, penalty clauses, and possibilities of undercutting or overperforming documented competing bids. Gaius found himself liking the man, and rapidly revising the assessment he'd been given by Attulus. In different circumstances, Gaius thought, Daul might have been the salesman, and he the bureaucrat.

Eventually they straightened their backs from leaning over the same diagram and looked at each other with a laugh that covered a certain mutual embarrassment—they'd been discussing a design problem as though they were on the same team.

"Well," said Daul, "I think I can make you an offer. Can't shake hands on it yet, I'm afraid—some paperwork has to be passed upstairs, forms in triplicate, you know the sort of thing. Call me back tomorrow and I can let you know if you've hit the mark."

Was this the buck-passing he'd been warned about, or was it genuinely a busy and competent man doing his best in a bureaucracy? Gaius couldn't be sure. Either way, Daul's swift proceeding was leaving him without the chance to meet Lydia de Tenebre. He tried to think fast.

"Excellent," he said. "I wish everyone I have to deal with were as prompt." He glanced at his watch. "You know, you've just cleared hours off my schedule—given me a bit of free time this evening. I'd quite like to wander around with someone who knows the city, maybe take in a beer and a meal."

Daul raised a hand. "Sorry, I can't help you there—strict rules about favors and all that. Kind of you to offer, though. Cuts both ways too, dammit, or I'd show you a good time myself."

"Oh, not at all, maybe another time." He feigned disappointment and let his gaze drift to the window. "Quite fascinating, the buildings that remain from the old city. Bit of a hobby of mine, to be honest."

"Ah," said Daul, "you're an old city man?" He punched his palm. "Of course, of course—you Illyrians. Bloody reactionaries to a man, eh? Well, you're in luck there, I know someone who isn't a buyer, so no rules bent, and who'll be delighted to tell you all about it, if she's free."

He poked his head around the door of the alcove. "Lydia? A moment please."

A young woman in an old-fashioned robe walked in. Gaius smiled, shook hands, and tried not to stare as Daul introduced him and explained his request.

"I'd be delighted," said Lydia. Her voice sounded even better than it had on the phone. "Where shall we meet?"

Gaius suddenly realized that he didn't know any good places. Well, maybe one. Call that two.

"What about the Library of Earth?" he said.

Lydia's smile was more than polite, it was complicit.

"Perfect," she said. "Seven after noon."

You could forget nuclear-power stations, orbital forts, plasma cannon, space rockets, interplanetary ballistic missiles, the public health service, education, irrigation, sanitation, the collectivization of the latifundia and the electrification of the proletariat. The greatest achievement of the Modern Regime was its libraries. Downtown stood two gigantic marble edifices: the Library of Earth, and next door to it, the Library of New Earth. The latter was by far the older. Its earliest texts were on clay tiles, in cuneiform. You could buy plastic replicas of them in the foyer. The former came originally from a machine smaller than a single book. You could buy plastic replicas of it too, as paperweights. A cosmonaut's pocket computer, it had the 2045 Library of Congress as a standard feature. It also had the libraries of the Vatican, the Kremlin, and the Academy of Sciences of Beijing. These were not standard. The manufacturer's marketing department had added them as a sales gimmick. The cosmonaut was Volkov. By the time he'd arrived on New Earth the computer was dead metal, a sentimental souvenir; but in the early years of his life on Mingulay the saurs had reproduced these millions of stored books on paper in their manufacturing plant; and via the merchant families, at least a million of them had reached New Earth.

Copies of books from both collections circulated endlessly through the system of public libraries. It was the one source of information in New Babylon that had never been censored. The Modern Regime allowed anyone to read books whose writing would have got them hanged. In its early years, it kept the old scholars of the Academy happily occupied in compiling a digest of human knowledge, the endlessly fascinating and dubiously reliable *Encyclopaedia Babylonica*. Gaius had a cheap, Illyrian-pirated edition of its thirty volumes on a shelf back home.

Lydia turned up a few minutes late with six thick books under her arm. She'd changed her antique robe for an aggressive outfit of leather jacket and trousers, rips and zips, but she still astonished his eyes.

"Sorry I'm late," she said. "The books slowed me down. Do you mind if we go in?"

"Not at all, this is one of my favorite places here."

She looked hard at him as they emerged from the revolving doors. "Surprised I haven't seen you before."

Gaius laughed. "I don't exactly come here often."

"Oh, I know, but—"

The library's vast hush silenced her.

She returned her books. He read their titles, side-on: *Capital* (three volumes); *Theories of Surplus Value* (two volumes); *The Accumulation of Capital* (one volume). He was impressed that she studied business methods in her spare time.

They went out. The street seemed loud, though it was far too quiet.

"I love the library," she said, "but you can't talk. And you don't need me to show you around it. So—where would you like to go?"

To bed with you, he thought. Actually, no. Anywhere would do.

"Are there still beer parlors in the old business district?"

"Yes," she said. "They're not as good as they were, of course. Bureaucrats don't drink like businessmen. At least not in public."

She ran down the steps and swung into an easy pace, as though not caring if he walked beside her or not.

"The bars around here are bugged," she said. "The staff are cops. So let's get this over out here. You're a spy, right?"

"What makes you think that?"

"Common sense and long experience. Any foreign business-men who aren't spies are too stupid to be recruited, and you're not stupid."

"You're jumping to conclusions."

"You're not denying it."

He couldn't say anything to that.

"Let's get one thing clear," she went on. "I have my own opinions, but I'm a loyal citizen. More to the point, I'm a loyal employee. I like David Daul. If you're looking for some inside track on your sale or you're into industrial espionage, forget it."

"I'm not interested in any of that."

"Aha!" She stopped dead, throwing him a couple of steps forward. He turned back to face her.

"So what *are* you interested in?"

"You," he said, more forcefully than he'd meant. "I've been asked to contact you. That's all."

She started walking again, making him catch up. If she wanted them to look like lovers quarreling she was doing a good job of it.

"There must be some context," she said. "The name of the Free Duchy isn't enough to make me go weak at the knees. What do you want?"

"There is a context," he said. "Well, two."

"Uh-huh. Tell me the first one."

"Skiffs."

She broke her stride, recovered.

"There's the harbor." She pointed. "Go down and ask a saur, if you can find one."

"I'm talking about unidentified skiffs."

"Fuck off."

"What?"

"You heard me. Don't try to jerk me around. If you want to know about the Bright Star Cultures you can ask me right out. You don't need to pretend they're here."

"I don't know if they're here or not. All I know is that unidentified skiffs are being reported in our litter press."

She turned on him a look of withering scorn. "Oh, *that*."

"I share your contempt for it," he said.

"Glad to hear it. What was the other context?"

"I was given to understand," Gaius said cautiously, "that you are known as a malcontent."

Lydia stopped again. When he'd turned back he saw her smiling, for the first time since the library. It had felt like a long time.

"Oh boy," she said, "have they ever sent you after the wrong girl."

"You're not a malcontent?"

"I am, just not the way you think." Her smile became a baring of teeth. "I'm a Volkovist."

They were standing outside a beer parlor. Gaius felt dizzy and slightly sick. He indicated the door.

"Shall we?" he said.

"I know somewhere better. Safer, anyway."

She led him down to the end of Astronaut Avenue and sharply right along the waterfront to an area where the lights were orange and the buildings were long and low, warehouses and offices long since turned to other purposes. Outside one of them, a beer parlor by the sign if nothing else, Lydia paused, then crossed the road to look across the quay and the water to the starship. By the time Gaius had caught up with her, she was looking up, at an orange sky through which a handful of stars were visible.

"I miss the stars," she said. "I miss traveling to them, but I miss seeing them even more. I'm a pantheist. Pollution is persecution."

"I'm an agorist," said Gaius. "Planning is sacrilege."

She gave him a tight smile. "Let's see you spend some money," she said.

They went back across the street to the drinking dive.

The bar had too much dust, smoke, verdegris. The roof beams were low and bare, with bare electrical bulbs hanging from them. The tables had benches that might have been recovered from a demolished temple. The clientele, thin at this time, looked unrespectable. The beer was still good.

"You knew Volkov," Gaius said "Is that safe to talk about?"

"Yes, and yes." She raised her glass. "To the Republic."

He moved a jug of water and lifted his glass above it. "The Republic."

He'd seen malcontents do this. On the other side of the Half Moon Sea, and not a dozen kilometers from where they sat, was the Republic of Lapithia—another breakaway province, of impressive size but largely desert, its coastal fishing devasted by New Babylon's industrial runoff. They exported mainly nurses, sailors, and mercenaries; imported exiles who sat in seafront bars and plotted till they died of drink.

She smiled. "Very good. The strait is patrolled. You have to go a long way up the coast to get past them, and by that point it's actually quicker and safer to go over the mountains."

"Cloud people."

"Yes. It's not illegal to emigrate, you know. Even the patrols are mainly to stop smuggling and raiding."

"So why do people—"

"Because your precious Duchy doesn't give visas. They'll take a trickle of cloud people, oh yes. Legal immigration would be too much to handle, and wouldn't supply sob stories for your litter press."

"It's a sore point," Gaius conceded. "You were saying about Volkov?"

Lydia shrugged. "I went to bed with him a few times. He was all right." She smiled. "Experienced."

Gaius felt himself go red in the face. "That's not what I was asking about."

"What is there to say? You must have read about him and my family. We met him on Mingulay, we brought him here, we went away and came back. He was dead. We found what he had left."

"Yes," said Gaius. "The greatest city in the known universe, turned into this heap of shit."

"It's a heap of shit all right," Lydia said. "But what he built was worth it."

"You can't truly believe that," said Gaius. "He fought off the aliens, I'll give you that."

"You don't need to," said Lydia. "The aliens aren't a threat anyway. I should know."

"I know you encountered them," said Gaius. "And the people who had been corrupted by them."

"Yes, and none of that is a threat. The Bright Star Cultures are out there, and coming closer, and no doubt when they do arrive the SDF will fight them off. Or maybe not." She chopped with her hand. "None of that matters."

"So what does? If you don't like the Modern Regime and you don't fear the aliens, what did Volkov do that was so great?"

"He gave us back our pride," she said. "He showed us we could be a great people, that we didn't need to limit ourselves to what the saurs would accept. All but a few of them cringe before the gods. Volkov said we can go out to space ourselves, face and fight the aliens, and deflect anything the gods care to throw at us. The saurs went away, they stopped sharing their skiffs and the krakens stopped sharing their ships. New Babylon built rockets. For the first time in ten thousand years, people stopped traveling to the stars—but for the first time, they actually visited the planets of this system. The saurs stopped healing us, and thousands upon thousands died in plagues. Maybe millions on the planet as a whole. The Modern Regime built hospitals, invented medicines, expanded health services to fill the gap. We lost the trade with the saurs, and everything they produced in their manufacturing plant. The Modern Regime built factories. The provinces broke away under the burden of Volkov's space defense taxes—and what are they now? They're nations, like yours, independent centers of development, with the capacity— if not yet the will—to build rockets of their own. You have no idea, Mr. Gonatus, no idea at all how much of a triumph it is for Volkov that I'm sitting here talking to you—gods above, an Illyrian, uh, businessman, of all things! Without Volkov Illyria would still be a sleepy agricultural province, with nothing to sell but sheep, and a dozy patrician on the Senate of Nova Babylonia, who left every hard problem to his saur scribe!"

"We had to fight New Babylon to *get* independence!"

"Exactly," said Lydia. "And my friends here"—she waved vaguely at the now-growing crowd in the bar, a rabble of types who looked like artists or musicians or criminals—"who talk about the glories of old Nova Babylonia are right—I remember it, and I loved it too. But we can't go back to it, and we shouldn't want to. The Modern Regime will fall someday. Madame President will die, the gerontocratic camarilla around her will fall out with each other and with the security forces, the Society will split, and the crowd will pour through the gap. Competent people, like my boss, will move to the top floor. The crowd will pull down all that remains of Volkov's memorials, they'll demolish the bloody *plinths*. A century later, two centuries, it doesn't matter, their grandchildren will erect a modest statue of Volkov, the Engineer, maybe at the bottom of Astronaut Avenue, and nobody will think it strange."

Gaius covered his confusion by buying another couple of drinks. Somebody had started playing a zither. Others, even more misguidedly, were singing. Gaius was grateful that the malcontent musical ethos eschewed electrical amplification. He returned and set down the drinks and slid himself into the high-backed bench beside Lydia, who was sitting on a stool at the head of the table with her back to the wall. The matter of Volkov, he'd decided, was best dropped. He was not sure whether Lydia had been corrupted by adaptation to the Regime, or had acquired an inhumanly long view of history from her earlier life as an interstellar traveler. He leaned forward a little and spoke in a low voice.

"Your ideas deserve a better discussion," he said. "What concerns me at the moment is that the managers of my business back in Illyria clearly believe the unidentified skiff sightings are real, and that you know something which might explain them."

Lydia looked down into her drink. Her lips compressed, her fingers pressed on her temples.

"I can't begin to hope," she said, "that the ships have got through. Unless . . . oh, I remember now. We're such good navigators. Better than the kraken. Better than Gregor."

Gaius stared at her. "Who's 'we'? Who's Gregor?"

Her eyes were glazed. She wasn't really looking at him. Then she blinked and recovered. "Gregor Cairns," she said. "You know, the Mingulayan navigator."

Gaius had heard of the Mingulayan navigator. News of what went on in the Mingulayan-dominated sector of the Sphere—the Bright Star Cultures, as its inhabitants called it—had arrived in approximate reverse order over the past few years. Gregor Cairns had also been referred to in the information that had arrived more than a century earlier, with Volkov himself. That

Lydia had had some acquaintance with him was briefly alluded to in Gaius's briefing.

"I know about Gregor," he said. "You haven't said who 'we' are."

"I'll show you," she said.

She took a dinky pen knife from her pocket and opened it, and very deliberately made a small cut in the tip of her ring finger (which bore no rings). She squeezed out a drop of blood and let it fall on the table.

"What are you doing?"

Lydia pointed at the red drop. "Watch," she said.

High Strangeness Incidents

"T HIS WON'T HURT," said Mr. Magenta.

He puffed some spores over Susan. She inhaled them and immediately went into a spasm of coughing and sneezing.

"That is good," said Mr. Magenta. "It drives the small offspring into your sinuses."

Susan found herself breathing more calmly. She stepped away from the side of the hangar and looked around at the others, who stood at a safe distance.

"My mother said she was going to do it."

Even to her, it didn't sound like a good reason.

"And it hasn't harmed Matt."

"Hah!" said Ramona Garcia. "How could anyone tell?"

In truth there was a sort of fatalism to Susan's decision. Her own curiosity, if nothing else, would sooner or later drive her to it. The Multipliers would not force their infection on anyone, but sooner or later almost everyone was going to accept it. She might as well get there first.

It still didn't sound like a good reason.

The guerrilla ontology campaign, as Matt persisted in calling it, was into its second week. A sort of routine had become established. The *Investigator*, concealed in the hangar, remained the base camp and headquarters. The Multiplier skiffs were used to conduct operations. Apart from piloting the skiffs, the Multis foraged. They followed the saurs' advice about which fruits and seeds were nutritious and which were not, but they also—more or less at whim—synthesized new foods. They could make beef from a pile of grass, a process that as Matt pointed out was also regularly accomplished by cows, but that still seemed like a miracle.

The skiffs' missions varied from spectacular or subtle displays of their presence, to stealth missions for the sole purpose of information gathering. The latter sometimes shaded illicitly into shopping expeditions—not even the Multis could assure a supply of coffee and tobacco reliable enough for those addicted to them.

Gradually a picture of the world had been built up, from talking to people—whether in Matt's MIB stunts or more discreet contacts—and from books and newspapers, and from radio. The discovery that Volkov was dead—had been killed in a palace coup by his own security detail on the orders of his lover, the President—had left the Cosmonauts who'd known him shaken but, Susan thought, not altogether surprised. It didn't fundamentally alter the big picture.

Working inward:

The closest contact with the Bright Star Cultures had been from about fifty light-years away. These contacts reported an evidently stable and productive relationship between the Multipliers and at least the saurs and the hominidae. The most recently arrived information, ironically, came from farther away, as merchant ships jumped straight from the emerging Cultures on the home planets, Mingulay and Croatan, to Nova Babylonia, arriving shortly after others who had jumped fifty-odd years later but from fifty-odd light-years closer.

The Bright Star Culture wavefront was, of course, only intersecting the Second Sphere from one side. Traffic in the other sides of the great volume was becoming just as disrupted, as the majority of saurs and krakens broke off cooperation with New Babylon, or recoiled from the news of the new alien-human alliance. To an ever-increasing extent, New Earth—and, it would seem, all the other planets—were becoming isolated from interstellar trade.

The fortifications of the Nova Solar System were almost entirely the work of the Republic of New Babylon, and were much as Telesnikov had projected—his only mistake had been to assume that they extended to the gas-giant moons. There were three forts, as he'd supposed, in the asteroid belt, and orbital forts in the cislunar region to meet incoming starships. All of this cost money and resources, and some of the costs were met by the former provinces—when you have system defense, as the Cosmonauts pointed out, it wasn't that difficult to persuade other powers to contribute to the system defense budget. This was the cynical bottom line—there was genuine widespread support in the other states for the common defense, and although the supposed Multiplier invasion was fading from living memory, the suspicion of what was going on in the Bright Star Cultures was renewed with every panicking starship that arrived. The Cosmonauts, however, remained convinced that some of the other powers were approachable.

The Republic of New Babylon had expanded from its initial position as a hegemonic city-state to become a nation-state of the entire subcontinent. Its nearest neighbors, Illyria and Lapithia, were implacably hostile—Illyria as a richer power, Lapithia as a poorer. Beyond them lay a checkerboard of small states, really no more than the olden cities with their hinterlands, each with its own unique proportion of hominid species and its own fiercely local patriotism, somewhat mitigated by their economic union and defensive alliance as the grandly named Genean League. The diplomacy of the other powers consisted largely of manoeuvres designed to split the League or play its members off against each other. There was a sort of logarithmic relationship between the states—New Babylon outweighed Illyria and Lapithia together, and these three major powers about balanced the League as a whole, if not in wealth and firepower then in population and difficulty of conquest. The hominid population of Genea had increased from about a hundred million to about five hundred million in the last century.

This increase was more than balanced by a far steeper decline in the population of Sauria. If any saurs remained they hadn't been spotted by the Multis' stealth-mode overflights, which had returned with pictures and descriptions of invading jungle and of manufacturing plant gone to seed. A small fraction of this decline was attributable to the departure of those saurs who were willing to cooperate with the Modern Regime. The rest had fled to the stars.

Some few were left, though none had been seen—small bands that must be living in the forests, the only evidence of their presence some recently slaughtered dinosaurs, clearly deliberate forest fires, and traces of strange rituals—tree trunks piled into conical pyramids, dinosaur skulls mounted on hilltop poles like some magical early warning system. What this signified, the saurs with the expedition were unable or unwilling to divulge, and reluctant to discuss.

Susan felt the fever coming on her. She took a couple of tablets to bring down her temperature, and carried the bottle of water with which she had washed them down with her out of the hangar. The sun cast long shadows among the enigmatic ruins. Pushing through underbrush, jumping over long cables of creeper, she made her way to a part of the abandoned city that might once have been a public square. She sat down on one of the long, low steps that beveled the square's perimeter and sipped some more water. The blood moved in her veins like trickling sand.

As the sun set, the colors around her first became more vivid, the purple shadows seeming to have neon behind them, the greens and yellows of the foliage glossy like the skins of frogs; then they faded out to a silvery monochrome. The moons, now waning, became visible and as bright as the sun, though looking at them did not hurt. One by one, as if somewhere switches were being flicked, the planets and the brightest stars blinked on, then the steady procession of the satellites, and with a rush that made her gasp, the bright path of the Foamy Wake.

She leaned back against the steps behind her, the little steps of the saurs, so incongruous with the gigantism of the rest of their architecture, and gazed up at the crowded sky. After a while, one of the stars became a light that shone brighter and brighter until it was visibly growing bigger and then—in a sudden shocking shift of perspective and involvement—coming closer. Susan sat forward, and tried to stand, but her knees betrayed her. They would not, could not lock. She sat back heavily. The moving blood was a roar now, a rhythmic pulse that at first she mistook for the sound of her breathing, then realized that, slow as it was, her breath was slower still.

The light became the familiar lens shape of a skiff, picked out in the small lights at its top and bottom and around its rim. A few tens of meters above her it went into falling-leaf motion, and settled on the square in front of her on its tripod of landing legs. By this time the lights had disappeared, or been incorporated into the general glow of its surface. It was definitely a saur skiff—it didn't have the roughness of the ones humans built, nor yet the liquid-mercury gloss of the Multipliers' craft.

This was confirmed when the hatch opened, the ladder extended, and a saur descended. The way he walked across the overgrown ancient flagstones toward her was peculiar, as though he wasn't quite touching the ground—no, it was as though he was walking on a moon with a much lower gravity, rising too high and drifting down. But she only had seconds in which to form that impression, because by then he'd stopped and was standing about three meters away from her.

"Who are you?" he said in English.

The accent was Mingulayan, like Salasso's.

"Susan Cairns Harkness," she said.

"Why are you here?"

"We're here to stop a war," she said.

"That's good," he said.

The saur rose slightly off the ground and returned to the craft without further movement, like an image shrinking in a zoom lens. The hatch closed behind him, still looking straight at her; then all the gear retracted and the skiff rose into the sky—again, more like an image shrinking than something actually moving away. Within a minute it was once more an indistinguishable light among the stars.

She heard a footstep behind her and jumped up, stumbling and struggling to keep her balance as she went down the steps five at a time. Down in the square she stopped and whirled around.

A saur stood at the top of the steps, regarding her.

"It's all right, Susan," he said, in English with a Mingulayan accent, but she recognized the voice.

"Oh, Salasso!"

She bounded up the steps as fast as she'd fled down them and hugged the saur, holding his head to her midriff.

Then, slightly embarrassed, she released him and stepped back.

"Did you *see* that?" she cried.

"I saw a light through the trees," said Salasso.

The following morning she had a bad sunburn on her face and the backs of her hands. The Multipliers told her this was not a symptom of the infection. Neither were hallucinations. Their skiff-detecting instruments had detected nothing, and nobody but Salasso had seen any light. Susan dragged Matt to the square and pointed triumphantly to three indentations in the crushed vegetation. He was unusually quiet on the way back.

"For the next three days," Matt announced, "we're not going to make any manifestations. No daylight disks, no crop circles, no funny lights in the sky, no MIB. We've got to plan some trips, but all in stealth mode, and any EVA has to pass for local. In fact EVAs are going to be our main activity. We need to find out, on the streets, what effect we've been having."

Susan sat and shivered. She'd been tempted to give the early morning planning meeting in the hangar doorway a miss. The pain in her skin was easing off, the red was fading. She hadn't slept well, and she couldn't even remember the dreams which had woken her, except one, which was of being tiny and being stepped on. She could remember the tread pattern on the sole of a descending boot.

"I have another suggestion," said Ann Derige. "If we're going to do stealth surveys, why not sneak up on some of the space installations?"

"Because we don't want to," said Matt, over a murmur of enthusiasm for Derige's idea—the gunners and rocketeers were getting impatient. "We don't want to give the slightest impression that we're interested in the space installations."

"We won't, if the stealth tech works," said Ann.

Mr. Orange waved a limb. "If I may," it said. "The stealth technology works against radar observation, and visual in most circumstances. It is not invisible to modes of detection outside the electromagnetic spectrum."

"Such as what? Telepathy? Smell?"

"Smell, yes, in the sense of ionized particles. Telepathy we know nothing about. More to the point, there are instruments for detecting minute variations in gravitational fields, instruments well within the capacity of this civilization's technology, and useful in space. The gravitational anomalies caused by the near presence of a skiff in stealth mode are more than minute."

"I'll take your word for it," said Ann, who clearly didn't.

"All right," said Matt, after they'd thrashed out a schedule for visiting various towns, timed for just before the dawn crept over the western continent. "Volunteers?"

Everyone stuck up a hand, or several.

"No saurs on EVA," said Matt dryly. "And nobody who's just taken the Multiplier treatment. Sorry, Susan."

"Didn't stop *you* making decisions," Ramona muttered.

Matt heard. "It was all right for me," he said. "I used to do drugs."

You get used to the weirdest things, Susan thought, as one by one the five Multiplier skiffs vanished from the hangar, leaving the *Investigator* alone in the middle, and her with Mr. Sort-of-Rainbow, Obadiah Hynde the rocketeer, Salasso, and Delavar.

"Drawn the short straw," said Obadiah, a cheerful young man with black hair and big hands. He peered at her over the flare as he lit a cigarette, a habit Susan was glad not to have. "Are you all right?"

"Yeah," said Susan. "I feel kind of weird. Light-headed."

"That is because of the very small offspring moving among your neurons," said Mr. Sort-of-Rainbow.

"Thanks," Susan glared. "That image is just what I need to calm me down."

"That was my intention," said the Multi, and scuttled off out to forage.

Obadiah looked down at the detritus of breakfast. "Might as well clean up," he said. "Give the old ship a good going over while I'm at it."

"We have decided," said Delavar, "to spend the day studying the information retrieved earlier."

Susan looked around. "I'm sorry," she said. "I'm just not up to anything right now. I'll just go and sit in the door."

"That is strongly recommended," said Salasso.

Susan dragged a log from the area in front of the hangar to the side of the entrance and sat down on it, leaning against the wall. She closed her eyes and watched the catherine wheels and rockets for a while. Then she opened her eyes and looked at the incredible intricacy of the lichens on the log, and contemplated the molecular machinery of the leaves on the trees. The insects moving about in the grass communicated by throwing little molecular machines at each other. She could almost understand what they were saying. She closed her eyes again. The sheer amount of information in front of her was too much to take in. She had to think about it.

When she opened her eyes again an inordinate amount of time had passed. The sun was a little higher in the sky. Mr. Sort-of-Rainbow emerged from the trees, jeweled with droplets of water, each of which refracted the light and reproduced the colors of his fur. He strolled up to her on four legs, the other four forming a mesh in which he held a great variety of fruit.

"Are you well?" he asked.

"Yes," she said. "All is well. God," she giggled helplessly, "is in *everything*."

"Yes," said the Multiplier. "Did you not know?"

Oh gods but this was a drag. People had come back, skiffs emerging inside the hangar as usual, and everybody was scurrying about and jabbering and ignoring her and she was tired like she had been working hard all day bloody hell she had been working hard all day she had gathered all this information and nobody was fucking interested and she had bloody spiders crawling out of her nostrils and nobody wanted to look at her and she just wanted to *die*. She heaved herself to her feet and trudged to the *Investigator* and climbed the ladder and crawled to her bunk and went out like a burnt filament.

"Good morning," said Matt, crouched over the electric heater and a coffeepot. "Welcome back."

Susan felt all bouncy and clean as though she had just had a shower, although she hadn't. Even her clothes felt clean, although she had slept in them.

"Oh, yeah, thanks." The previous day was a blur, but she distinctly remembered going away. "Everyone went away yesterday, didn't they?" She paused, puzzled. "Where did I go?"

He handed her a coffee. "Off on a little trip of your own."

Everything came crashing back. "Oh, God," she said.

"Well, quite," said Matt. "That was some sermon you gave us."

Susan felt like putting her head in her hands. "But it's still true," she said. She looked out through the wide doorway at the early morning landscape. Through the fog over the valley the sun was a red, coppery circle somewhat like a penny, and . . .

"Look at the *sun!*" she said.

"Yup," said Matt. " 'A great multitude of the heavenly host crying, "Glory, glory, glory to the Lord God Almighty." ' Well, something like that. You'll get used to it."

"It doesn't go away?"

"I'm afraid not," said Matt. "I understand it has something to do with an irreversibly increased awareness of the information density of reality. According to the Multis, anyway. Think about it. Your brain has been walked over by beasties that can *feel atoms.*"

Susan snapped out of a contemplation of the steam rising from her cup. She examined the skin on her arms. "Speaking of beasties—where are they?"

"Crawled out of your bodily orifices, cleaned up your skin and clothes, and gone trooping back to Mr. Magenta."

"How embarrassing."

"Speaking of embarrassment . . ." said Matt. Elsewhere in the cavernous hangar, people were beginning to stir. "I think it might be best if we agree not to talk about, um . . ."

"All that infinity in a grain of sand shit?"

Matt grinned. "It's good to find someone whose mind is cruder than mine."

She smiled conspiratorially back, then very deliberately turned her attention to other things.

"Do you think I'm ready to go out on reconnaissance today?"

"Yeah," said Matt. "Just don't let your mouth hang open, and you'll pass for normal."

The inside of the Multiplier skiff was remarkably like the inside of every other skiff Susan had been in. She and Telesnikov sat side by side on the circular bench around the central engine fairing, and Mr. Blue squatted on a stool in front of the control panel. It was only when the Multiplier turned on the viewscreen that a major difference, or refinement, became apparent. The hull was all viewscreen. It was like sitting in midair. Susan grabbed the edge of the seat and smiled self-consciously at Telesnikov.

The view changed—the inside of the hangar was instantly replaced with dark-blue sky above and a wide stretch of Genea below. She looked down between her feet and saw greens and browns and the white of clouds, the fractal line of the coast, the semicircle of Half Moon Sea. After her first intake of breath her second emotion was a pang of nostalgia for Mingulay—she'd seen her home planet from space many times, on the way to or from her family's orbital factories where the saurs brought the exotic components—black hole atoms, unusual stable elements with atomic weights in the hundreds—for the engines and drives.

Instantly the view changed again. They sat a couple of hundred meters above the surface—they didn't want to leave crop circles—then descended to hover above damp grass in a field by a metaled road. A hundred or so meters away were low slope-roofed houses, which if Mr. Blue had got it right were on the edge of Junopolis, the capital of Illyria.

"Over by the hedge," said Telesnikov. The skiff glided to the bushes. Twelve eyes surveyed the surroundings. No eyes looked back. The hatch flowed open—the only way Susan could tell was by the air on her face—and the two humans jumped out. By the time they'd walked a dozen steps the skiff was nothing but an unease-inspiring shimmer in the air.

Their clothes would pass as Illyrian, though plain. Short hair was not so uncommon as to be noticed. Their pockets were stuffed with Multiplier-copied Illyrian money. Each of them had a legal weapon—in the Duchy, wearing a knife was practically compulsory—and a small radio, of local manufacture but with Multiplier enhancements in its innards, most significantly an emergency alarm to call for a skiff and a tracking device to tell the skiff where to go.

They found a tram stop after walking a few hundred meters through the waking suburb—dogs barking, children running for buses—and rode into town accompanied by sleepy commuters.

Several people left newspapers on their seats; Telesnikov and Susan each casually picked one up.

Their reading did not stay casual for long. The front pages of both papers—the sensational *New Morning* and the sober *The Day* alike—showed a clear photograph of a daylight disk over Junopolis. The captions agreed on the date and time of the sighting—the middle of the afternoon of the previous day. *The Day*'s headline was "Mystery Skiff Evades Fighters." The *New Morning*'s was "SPIDER SKIFF STUNS CITY!"

Susan turned over the rest of the pages. The sighting over Junopolis was only the biggest of many similar stories. Editorials screamed for action; when she silently swapped papers with Telesnikov, she read that the country's elected representatives were doing the same. Buried in the longer articles were references to earlier official denials of various odd events of the past fortnight, at some of which she had been present herself. The independent confirmation of the "Lucifer Probe anomaly" had resulted in a particularly embarrassing climb-down, it seemed.

Susan folded the paper glumly and looked out the windows. The day was heating up. Fall in this hemisphere, spring at the base in Sauria—the contrast was fierce. Junopolis looked like a town well adapted to seasonal change. From the depth of the recesses of windows she could see that most walls were thick, at least on the older buildings. Garish color washes were the fashion, or tradition—it was hard to say, because compared with her hometown even the new buildings looked old-fashioned, solid and ornate. Clothes were colorful, hair and beards generally long, with a sprinkling of clean-shaven cropheads who also tended to wear duller clothes.

At the tram's terminal in the center of town Susan bought copies of every paper on sale—all of which led with the same photo—and she and Telesnikov made their way to a big low-ceilinged café with lots of marble and mirrors and took their coffeepot and cups to the most isolated table they could find. They puzzled over the papers for a while.

"Is it possible," Susan asked, in careful Trade Latin, "that one of our teams made a big mistake yesterday?"

Telesnikov shook his head, almost angrily. "We're the first team into Junopolis," he said. "Last night I checked every report, every image brought back. There is no question about it—whatever this was, it wasn't us."

"Is it even thinkable that the . . . that our friends are lying to us? That they did this without our knowing?"

"I suppose it's thinkable," said Telesnikov. "But that way madness lies. If we can't trust them we should abandon the operation right now."

"If we don't know what's real and what's—" She stopped. "This is what Matt said would happen!"

" 'Guerrilla ontology,' " Telesnikov said heavily. " 'Make people question their concept of reality.' The trouble is, it's happening to *us*."

Susan sat back and watched the surrounding salarymen and women scoffing their breakfasts, reading the papers with expressions she could not read, talking animatedly in a dialect she could not quite follow at that volume and speed. She had missed crowds, she realized, and new faces.

"I'm not so worried about us," she said. "I saw something myself that we couldn't explain, and Salasso saw a light, and Matt saw the prints. Whatever it was it didn't seem hostile. But whatever is going on here seems hostile to them."

"To the people here? Yeah, you could say that. And no doubt to the security apparatuses as well. But what's even more worrying is how this appears to people in New Babylon, and *their* security apparatuses. This is much more blatant than anything we've done."

"So who's doing it?"

Telesnikov shrugged. "Relict saurs? Other Multipliers we don't know about? The—uh, our own folk? Arrived here without our knowing? Or even a local power that has developed or gotten hold of skiff technology? Or something altogether unknown?

You can bet all of these possibilities are exercising some very bright minds right now."

"And the minds of very frightened people."

"Hell," said Telesnikov, "*I'm* very bright, and I'm very frightened." He swept his hand over the pile of newspapers. "What do you say we just head back?"

"No," said Susan. "I don't think the newspapers are enough. We have to talk to people."

"But how do we do that?"

"It's easy," Susan said. "I'm a journalist."

And with that she stood up and and wandered over to the other tables and started talking to people. It was easy. She was a journalist.

"Good morning," she said to a fat, anxious-looking middle-aged man with bags under his eyes and a cigarette between his knuckles, ash drifting on to a greasy plate. His greying hair was tied back in a ponytail and his coat and weskit were rumpled. "Mind if sit down?"

"Go ahead."

"Thanks. My name's Susan, I'm a journalist, from the—"

He held up his hand. "Don't tell me. The Dorian *Daily News*, right?"

"Yes," she said. Doria was one of the smallest and most remote of the lesser republics of the Genean League. It seemed a safe enough cover. "How did you guess?"

The fat man wagged a finger. "Your accent, young lady. Can't hide it. And I doubt if Doria can support more than one paper."

"True enough," she said, sounding regretful. She smiled brightly. "And your name, sir?"

"Horace Kamehan," he said, sticking out a hand. "And what can I do for you?"

She waved a battered black notebook. "I'd like to, uh, wire back a few comments from Junopolitans about the latest events."

Kamehan pushed his empty plate away and sipped his coffee. "Oh, right," he said. "Well, I don't think you'll find much disagreement. We should hit the bastards with everything we've got."

"How can we be certain that they *are* bastards?"

He blinked and frowned. "Maybe it's easy to be all even-handed if you're sitting out there on your rocks in Doria, but from where I'm sitting it's not. It's quite clear who's making the threats, and frankly I don't think our government should stand for it. Which I don't think we will, I hasten to add. The Duke's got a bit of spine, thank the gods."

Susan struggled to hide her confusion by nodding, smiling, and scribbling a note of what the man had said.

"And if it comes to it," Kamehan went on, "I'm not too old to bloody sign up myself."

"Sign up?"

He gave her another puzzled look. "For the army—maybe you don't have that expression in Doria? Not surprising."

"But Mr. Kamehan," she said, "how do you expect to fight aliens?"

"Aliens?" He stared at her as though she'd just come from outer space. "Aliens? The Spiders? Who believes in this palpable nonsense? Not even you lot, I hope."

"But the papers—"

"The papers? Don't you listen to the bloody radio?"

"Of course, of course," said Susan desperately. "It's all very disturbing." She stood up. "Well, thank you, Mr. Kamehan, for your comments. All the best."

"Gods look after you," Kamehan said. "Because gods know, you need them to." He muttered something under his breath about fishermen and foreign correspondents.

"Thank you," she said, and retreated as fast as she could to the table where Telesnikov sat mulling over the papers. On her way she noticed something that the fashion for long hair had concealed—almost everyone was wearing earphones. She sat down, nodded to Mikhail, and worried her own earpieces in. She set the little radio on the table in front of her and thumbed the dial slowly. The fingers on a wall clock were climbing to third before noon—the café was not emptying, although it seemed a likely time for office hours to begin, and people were looking at the clock or at their watches, listening intently. Susan kept tuning, trying to identify the sound of a program coming to an end, or some hint that an hourly news bulletin was about to—ah, there it was.

She turned the radio toward Telesnikov and pointed to the spot on the dial, and to her ear. He took the hint.

There was a sound like a series of splashes, which puzzled Susan until she realized that it was the station's signature, intended to represent an archaic water clock. The announcer's voice was grave, his Trade Latin more formal than the spoken dialect or the fretful rancorous rant of the press.

"Junopolis Calls, third hour before noon, eleventh day of Frugora, Anno Civitas ten thousand three hundred and forty nine. Reports are coming in of serious damage and an unknown number of deaths and injuries in the coastal town of Palmir. Witnesses have described a 'bolt from the sky' followed by fires and explosions. The Duke's Minister of Defense has just stated that emergency assistance is being rushed to the stricken town. An urgent investigation is to begin immediately. He refused to comment when asked whether the disaster is linked to the warning issued earlier this morning by New Babylon. More information will be available from Palmira shortly.

"Meanwhile, in a further deterioration of relations with our southern neighbor, the Ducal Palace has made public a note delivered to the Consul of New Babylon. Junopolis Calls is authorized to read the note in its entirety:

"Your Exellency: The warning issued by the Senate of New Babylon, and reported on your country's radio stations at six before noon today, is viewed with great concern by Us, Our Ministers, and Our People's Representatives. We reject, in the strongest terms, any suggestion that hostile forces are operating in or above Our nation's territory, and will

regard any action taken by your esteemed and respected country's forces on, around, or above that territory as an attack upon Our sovereignty and upon the sacred and inviolable territory of the Free Duchy of Illyria. In the presence of the indifferent gods and in the shadow of Our ancestors, We remain, your Excellency's humble correspondent, Duke Leonid the Second."

The roar that followed from the customers in the café—and the passengers in the terminal—drowned out whatever was said next.

VEE—DOO! VEE—DOO!

"What are they shouting?"

"Long live the Duke, I think," said Telesnikov. "Doesn't matter. Whatever it is, it means war. Let's get out."

They gathered their armful of now-outdated but possibly still-useful papers and made their way through the standing, chanting crowd. Their path to the door was suddenly blocked by Kamehan. Two younger men stood shoulder to shoulder with him.

"Where do you think you're going?" Kamehan demanded.

"Excuse me," said Susan. "We have a story to file."

"I'll bet you do," said Kamehan. "With the Dorian *Daily News*, huh?"

"Yes," said Susan.

"Now ain't that odd?" said the young man at Kamehan's right. " 'Cause I'm the *News*'s Junopolis correspondent. Maybe you'd do better filing your story with my friend Mr. Kamehan, of the Junopolis—"

Telesnikov slugged him in the stomach, punched Kamehan in the face and shoved both of them hard against the third.

"Run!" he shouted.

Susan pushed through a sudden domino-effect of people flailing and stumbling and ran out the door onto the concourse. Telesnikov caught up with her a moment later. He had dropped the papers and was clutching his radio.

"Nearest open space," he gasped, and sprinted for the tramline marshalling yard, which opened onto the two open sides of the terminal. Susan followed. Behind her she heard someone yelling "Spies!" and the cry being taken up. Diagonally across from her she saw a man in uniform running to head them off. Telesnikov saw him too and swerved. Susan took the opposite direction and the man dithered and lunged ineffectually. Then they were past him and in an area of metal grooves and overhead sparks and quietly gliding death that could come from any direction.

A tram loomed in front her, blue paint and polished brass, the startled face of a driver. She leapt across the parallel tracks and spun around on her next step, then grabbed a stanchion and swung onto the running board. The driver had just released the brake and hadn't seen anything beyond the fact that he hadn't run her down. She glanced back along the track. Telesnikov, with the uniformed man a few meters behind in hot pursuit, raced behind the tram and with a surge of speed caught up with it and jumped onto the rear platform.

The driver heard the thump and glanced in his mirror. The brakes squealed again. Susan felt a terrific wrench in her shoulders. She clung on, to see Telesnikov tumbling past as he was sent sprawling down the vehicle's aisle. As the tram slowed the policeman caught up and jumped aboard at the back. He ran forward just as Susan came through the open central door. She had time to see that he was not stopping—the deceleration pulled him forward—just before she ducked across his path. He tried to jump over her and succeeded only in kicking her in the ribs as he tripped over her back.

Telesnikov scrambled to his feet at the same moment as she did. The driver, almost thrown against the front of the cab, turned around and grabbed for him. Telesnikov caught his arm and slammed it on the half-door at the side of the driver's seat, then jumped down out of the door at the front, Susan following via the one she'd just come in by.

They both barely avoided stepping in front of another tram. When it had passed they saw they were outside the back of the terminal on a wide-open space of tarmac. Gleaming lines snaked to low sheds between rusty mounted wheels with coils of metal cable, like fishing reels for Leviathan, paired bare levers, buffered barriers. Telesnikov rounded the obstacles to the least-cluttered area, waving his arms above his head. Susan ran behind him, glanced back over her shoulder and saw the persistent policeman being helped to his feet by the driver. A few more uniforms ran in from various directions.

She turned her head forward again. Telesnikov had disappeared. Then she saw him, uncannily suspended a meter up in the air right in front of her, and Mr. Blue behind him. He was crouched down and reaching out. She jumped, they caught each other's forearms, and he hauled her into the skiff. They ended up sitting on the bench with their backs to the engine fairing. The sounds from outside abruptly ceased. The pursuers had stopped, and were looking at each other and at where they were. From the side of a wall about twenty meters away an old man in a bundle of rags staggered forward, pointing and shouting.

The scene changed to sky and the blue and white levels of air.

Telesnikov laughed harshly. "I'd like to see how they report *that* in tomorrow's papers."

Matt was indulging in one of his rants. For the Multipliers, he said at some length, speech was a distinctly secondary mode of communication. They shared knowledge through their fingertips. They tended to assume, he suggested, that more had been shared than had actually been said. As for the saurs, they volunteered so little about themselves that getting information out of them was like getting blood from a fucking stone.

The humans in the crew listened with embarrassment. The Multipliers formed a big circle and quivered and fingered each other. The two saurs stood together and shuffled occasionally. The day's missions had been hastily recalled. The sun was high and the hangar's interior was all in shadow. In the background a radio prattled away. Skiffs were still being sighted all over the place, and here and there were being chased by New Babylonian jet fighters or zapped by New Babylonian space-based plasma cannon, to the evident annoyance of every other power from Illyria to Doria. More details were coming through of extensive destruction in Palmir, apparently from a plasma-cannon bolt.

"So," said Matt in a chillingly reasonable voice, "do any of you have anything to tell us that you might not have thought worth mentioning?"

Salasso stepped forward and turned to face the others.

"There is something," he said, "which I hesitate to mention, but it may be relevant. Some of the very old legends of my people say that when they first came to the worlds of the Second Sphere, they met saurs who were *already here*. Saurs who flew in skiffs and behaved in . . . an enigmatic fashion, both intrusive and elusive. The rational explanation, which is usually given to the young of the species when they are told of these legends, is that different parties of saurs arrived on the various planets at different times, perhaps separated by centuries or millennia, and their first encounters were confusing on both sides. But I must admit that these stories . . . came to my mind when Susan described her encounter."

"Very good," said Matt. He laid a hand on Salasso's shoulder and looked down at the saur with a sort of troubled affection. "So you guys have Greys and flying saucers too, huh? Well, there's something nobody told me before. And, ah, just in case you've missed something out—have such stories been told about more recent events?"

"No," said Salasso. "These legends are of a time tens of millions of years ago. No such stories are of more recent date." He paused. "Other than literary pastiches, of course."

"Of course," said Matt. "Literature too, huh? We're advancing by leaps and bounds here."

"That is all I have to suggest," said Salasso.

"Thank you," said Matt. "Anyone else?"

Mr. Orange detached himself from a busy tangle of limbs and scuttled over.

"We do not understand and are distressed by the anger of the Matt Cairns. The invasion is proceeding according to plan. The mind of the world New Earth is responding as we expected it to. The humans of the world New Earth are misdirecting their defenses and in conflict with each other. Soon it will be possible to—"

"Excuse me," said Matt, waving a spread hand up and down. It was a way of getting the Multipliers' attention that often worked. "What was that about the mind of the world?"

II

Lithomancer

I N THE OLD days, the scientists of the Academy used to demonstrate the spontaneous generation of life: flies from rotting meat, mice from stored grain. What Gaius was seeing looked very like that: a tiny red spider forming out of a drop of blood. What shocked him was that Lydia snatched it up and swallowed it.

He grimaced. "Good trick," he said. "How did you do it?"

She picked up the knife and did it again. This time, she placed the spider—it was a different color, green—on his palm, and handed him a folding lens.

"Look at it carefully."

He peered through the magnifier. It wasn't a spider. *"That's a—"*

"Don't shout."

"Gods above." He held out his hand. It trembled a little. The minute Multiplier was turning around, as though looking for somewhere to run. He pushed his sleeve back from his wrist.

"Take it," he said. "Eat it, if you must."

"Swallow it yourself," said Lydia, daring him. Her eyes were bright. "Why don't you? It'll make you young forever, or so I was told. It's worked for me, so far."

He could believe her. "Take it," he pleaded.

She caught his bared wrist and kissed the bad thing away. "There," she said. "Well, not many people even have the chance to pass up a chance like that."

Gaius wiped his hands on his knees. "Is that how it works? How the Bright Star Cultures spread?"

"Yes," she said. "I suppose I'm a Bright Star Culture person, come to think of it."

"You haven't—?"

"Proselytized?" She leaned back and smiled. "I wouldn't tell you if I had, but . . . no."

"Why are you telling me this? Why did you show me that?"

"Because you needed evidence. These things, they live in my blood, small as cells. When it spills there's a sort of dog-eat-dog situation."

He nodded, understanding what he'd just seen, and why she'd told him. Telling him was no risk to her—he could not denounce her to the New Babylonian apparatus without giving them an intelligence coup that would strengthen them against his own country; her secret was now his, and, if she was thinking ahead as fast as he was, Illyria's. He had to get her out.

"Anyway," she went on, "they pass on bits and pieces of memories. All sorts of memories, of their progenitors and of the organisms they've been in. That's how I know that Multiplier navigation is precise enough to jump straight to a planet's surface."

"Why didn't they do that back in the first invasion?"

"Oh, I don't suppose they were expecting to be attacked. If it really is the Bright Star Cultures that are here now, they'll be expecting trouble." She smiled as if to herself. "The folks back on Mingulay and Croatan knew Volkov of old, and they knew he was coming here. They'll know what to expect."

"But what can they do?"

"With skiffs that can set up lightspeed jumps with an accuracy of a few meters? I can think of quite a lot they could do."

"When you put it that way," Gaius said, "so can I."

And all of them would tip the military balance against New Babylon. Whatever happened—and he was finding his assumptions about the long-feared arrival of the Bright Star Cultures shaken by Lydia's words and actions—it was surely better that

Illyria should face it in a position of strength. If New Babylon's space defenses were knocked out, and the Regime itself tottering, the opportunities would be huge. He had to return to Junopolis, and take Lydia with him if he could. He was just turning this over in his mind when Lydia reached out and caught his arm.

"Don't move," she said. She was looking past his face. "A couple of cops just came into the bar. They're looking for somebody. Probably after one of the local loan sharks. Play it cool."

A moment later two men in dark suits came over. Gaius looked up at them with what he hoped was an expression of surprised but not alarmed query.

"Lydia de Tenebre?" one of them said. "We'd like you to accompany us to—"

Gaius didn't so much see as later reconstruct what happened next. Lydia heaved her end of the table upward, crouched down and grabbed the middle of both sides, and threw it straight at them. They both stumbled back and then fell over backwards as the table, which Lydia leaped on like a flying cat as it hit, crashed down on top of them. Arms and legs projected from beneath it. Broken glass slithered across the floor.

Gaius was still sitting on the bench, a glass halfway between his mouth and where the table had been.

Lydia turned on the upsided table like a dancer on a low stage, and reached out a hand. "I think we should leave," she said.

They ran to the door, past people who were carefully not stopping them—whether out of hostility to the police, or to maintain their cover, or fear of Lydia's suddenly revealed fighting prowess. Lydia looked both ways before going out.

"They'll have backup," she said.

A car parked a hundred meters down the road revved its engine and headed straight at them. Lydia led the way in a dash across the street. Gaius distinctly saw the car's fender a couple of meters away as he followed. Lydia vaulted the wall. Brakes squealed. Gaius hesitated at a drop of three meters onto slippery boulders, heard running footsteps, rolled onto the wall, swung

227

down, clung and dropped. Lydia was already on her feet and steadied him as he landed and slipped.

The tide was out. The shore smelled like bad breath. Lydia ran alongside the bottom of the wall, surefooted. Gaius stumbled after her. He glanced up and saw two heads bobbing along above the top of the wall, keeping pace easily. This was hopeless. When he looked ahead again Lydia had vanished. A few steps more took him to the mouth of the tunnel she'd vanished into. He saw her face, pale in the light from the harbor. He ducked in after her. The tunnel's roof was low and its floor was a phosphorescent green stream. He tried not to stand in it.

"Industrial effluent," said Lydia. "You can walk in it. Just don't drink it. Come on."

Behind him, he heard a couple of crunching thuds, followed by yelled curses, then footsteps. He ran.

She had a pocket torch, and the faint glow from the effluent provided a path. It didn't last long. A few tens of meters in, Lydia turned off into a side tunnel just as voices echoed along from the entrance to the main one. There were other tunnels branching off, and Lydia led him through a maze of them. The voices and splashes of the pursuit faded after a couple more turns. Ten minutes later they reached a ladder up to a manhole and emerged in an alleyway off the lower end of Astronaut Avenue. Lydia rolled the heavy lid back into place, brushed her hands, and stood up.

"How the hells did you do that?"

"I'm not sure," said Lydia. "I may have seen the drainage system map in the Library."

"That's not an explanation."

"No," she said.

She strolled to a standpipe—it was not obvious, but she moved like she knew where to find it—and ran the tap over her boots. Gaius looked down at his shoes and trouser cuffs and decided to do the same. Better to be wet with water than with that gunk. It looked vaguely acidic and its smell, as it weakened in the open air, was becoming more nauseating, like cheap gin on the sinuses. He took off his shoes and rinsed them, then his socks and feet. Even wrung out, his socks felt horrible.

"Where now?"

"First thing I'm going to do," said Lydia, "is go to the nearest public phone booth and call home. See if the cops have come for them, too."

There was a phone around the corner. Lydia put down the receiver after trying a dozen numbers.

"Nobody home. Not good."

They walked on up Astronaut Avenue, pending some decision on what to do next. The streets were a bit livelier now, though not by the standards of Junopolis at this time of a fine night. No shops open, and few beer parlors or places of amusement. Three armored personnel carriers crossed a junction a few hundred meters ahead. Gaius desperately wanted to get off the street.

"Why did they come after you?"

"For the same reason as you did, I guess."

Gaius thought about that. "Let's get off the street," he said. He stopped outside a beer parlor. "In here."

"That's a bureaucrats' watering hole. One of the bugged bars I told you about."

"All the better," said Gaius. "We don't need to worry about that anymore. We need to worry about being bundled into a van."

The place was full of men and women in suits. Gaius was cynically unsurprised that nobody stirred. He bought a brace of drastically overpriced stiff drinks and sat down with Lydia in an alcove. There was a menu on the table.

"Suddenly hungry?" said Gaius. Lydia nodded. They ordered grilled patties of minced beef, the main item.

"The seafood used to be wonderful," Lydia sighed. The waiter went away.

"What do you want to do?" Gaius asked.

"Walls have ears," said Lydia.

Gaius leaned back and sighed. "I know about surveillance here," he said. "Believe it or not, I know more than you do. It's

229

used for evidence-gathering, not rapid response. Think about it. Unless there's a general alert out for us, or for you, all that's happening is that we're being taped, and sometime in the next few days some bored policeman is going to listen to us. And then only if they have reason to think this place's tapes are worth checking. Maybe a description of us has gone out to police patrol vehicles, but that's to cars, not bars. Besides, dragging people out of places like this is not their style. It tends to upset the lower middle cadre. So relax."

"All right," she said. "What I want to do is find out what's happened to my family."

"Have you ever been pulled in before?"

She shook her head. "They interrogate all the humans coming off Trader ships, release them, keep an eye on us but that's it."

"Any others like you?"

"Maybe one or two," she said, sounding evasive. She nibbled her lip. "I've checked this, I've asked around discreetly. The former Traders do sort of hang together, help each other out. It's only because of that that we haven't all ended up in a heap at the bottom."

"That's still a lot of people to check."

"It was," she said dryly. "But remember, most of the ships that come back haven't been in the Bright Star Culture's expanding sphere, and of those that have, very few have directly encountered the Mingulayans or the Spiders. We were one of the first to meet them, on Novakkad. Things were at a pretty early stage there. Mostly the krakens or the saurs pick up that something's going on within minutes of coming out of the jump, and they don't even land—they jump straight back. It's like a squid reflex."

Gaius was still smiling at this image when the waiter returned with two plates of food and three men with guns. Two of them looked bruised, and familiar. The third was a bit taller, older, and heavier, and acted like he'd had to take charge.

Lydia swallowed her drink and stood up. There could be no surprising them this time.

"Looks like there was a general alert out for me after all."

"It was the remark about the seafood," said the waiter.

Gaius held his hands out and stood up, sidling from the alcove.

"This lady is under the protection of the Free Duchy of Illyria," he said. "She has just asked me for asylum. I demand you let us go to the Consulate."

"The Consulate is closed," said the largest of the three men. "She's coming with us. And you, Mr. Gonatus, are *persona non* fucking *grata*. The only place *you*'re going is the train back to Illyria."

"I have an airline ticket—"

"The airport is closed."

"—and there are no trains back to Illyria."

"Oh yes, there are," said the big police agent. "Only they don't go quite all the way. Just to the foot of the mountains." He glanced at his watch and grinned nastily. "Consider yourself lucky. In a few hours you wouldn't be expelled for activities incompatible. You'd be fucking shot. So move it."

Gaius looked at Lydia. She was giving such a good impression of being unafraid that for a moment he wondered if she hadn't been setting him up. He dismissed it. She was brave and stoical, that was all. And probably difficult to kill or permanently damage. That must help.

"I'm sorry," he said.

"There's nothing more you can do," she said. She was shrugging into her jacket, which one of the men had returned to her after searching it. "Just go."

He thought about what the policeman had implied, and wondered if Lydia had picked up on it.

"See you after the war," he said.

The train left an hour before midnight. The one thing for which Gaius felt thankful was that his clothes had been left undamaged in his ransacked hotel room. He might not have his samples, but at least he had dry socks. He had filled the empty sample case with bottles of water and as much food as he could carry, bought in a hurry from the station's stalls and turning stale within hours. In every other respect he felt deeply ungrateful. The train was packed. He almost envied the people squeezed together on the wooden seats or sitting on the floor. The northwest train out of New Babylon was officially for latifundia peasants on their way to and from the official markets; and indeed there were quite a lot of peasants, mostly very old women, or men with faces red from sun and drink, snoring in cheap flashy suits. But unofficially, and blatantly, it was for emigrants. Tonight it carried far more than usual—refugees, he suspected, from the now widely rumored war. The cloud people carried more baggage than the peasants, and had better clothes, and before the week was out most of the baggage would be strewn along the passes, the clothes would be in rags, and some of the emigrants would be dead. Statistically, Gaius knew, he was looking at dead people, as surely as if he was riding a troop train heading for the front. Statistically, he also knew, he might be looking at a dead man reflected in the dark window.

The train rattled across the plain, labored up the long gradual slope, thundered across the Massif. Gaius, jammed upright by the press of bodies around him, jostled by the train's rhythm and the more annoying, random jolts as people made their way to and from the inadequate and increasingly foul-smelling toilets, dozed fitfully, now and again woken by a sudden shift in the balance of forces or by his forehead hitting the window. The train stopped every hour or so. At each stop some peasants got off and Gaius hoped the pressure would ease; but always, even more people got on. Mostly young men—draft dodgers, Gaius guessed and, patriotically, hoped. They drank a lot, smoked regardless of protests and talked loudly in a thick dialect. Gaius couldn't make out enough to gather any intelligence from them.

About three after midnight everyone on the train woke at once, as a shock and shouting ran through the packed carriages and all heads turned to the windows. Gaius found himself looking out through the yellow reflections then, as he managed to cup his hands between the glass and his face, directly, at a dozen slowly moving lights that suddenly changed color, loomed, flashed, and danced away. Minutes later, something fell from the sky and like lightning lit the rough land from horizon to horizon. Nobody slept much after that.

Dawn came up at five and a half after midnight. An hour later, the train halted at some crummy town: a water tower, a lithomancy pylon, a tractor depot, a straggle of houses. More peasants got off here, and mercifully few new passengers got on. Kids hawked papers along the platform: The morning edition of the Regime's official and only newspaper, wired from the capital and printed locally, with a local name. Gaius tugged the window down and exchanged a handful of Volkovs for the *Pergam Truth*. Lots of other hands stretched out to do the same. Gaius found a space to sit down and read it.

ILLYRIA MUST ACT, SENATE WARNS

In an emergency all-night session, the Senate of the Democratic Republic of New Babylon warned that the Illyrian aristocracy's criminal passivity in the face of recent incursions by Spider skiffs (see page 2) is a threat to the entire planet. The Defense Forces of the Republic stand ready to aid the Duchy's small military establishment at a moment's notice, but reserve the right to act unilaterally in defense of all the peoples of New Earth. Any rejection of this fraternal invitation to stand shoulder to shoulder against the alien menace will be regarded, by all reasonable people, as treachery to the species and collaboration with the enemy. The Senate strongly urged patriotic Illyrians, and in particular its brave though ill-equipped armed forces, to consider where their true loyalties lie.

A threat of war, and an incitement to treason. Gaius gritted his teeth and turned to page two, which gave—for the first time, as far as he knew—a quite sober account of the sightings and other strange events reported in his own country's litter press. A few incidents were recounted from within the Republic, all of them—unlike those reported from Illyria—described as having been swiftly countered by air or space forces. The implication here too was that Illyria was implicated in the Spider incursion—there were a lot of heavy hints about decadent aristocrats selling out to the enemy, though quite what they were selling and what they were getting in return was not stated.

Gaius turned over more pages as the train pulled out. Editorials, interviews, maps bristling with menacing arrows, vox-pop rants . . . the hostility to Illyria was so venomous that he felt very glad he wasn't instantly identifiable as Illyrian. Like most republicans in the Duchy, he followed the ancient fashion of short hair, and his clothes were by now as shoddy-looking as the locals'. One thing he'd expected to see in the paper, and that wasn't there, was any reference to enemies within—no incitement to spy mania, no warnings about foreigners or Traders. They seemed an obvious scapegoat. He doubted that the Regime was simply missing a trick. It didn't seem the sort of trick they would miss.

He opened his case, drank some tepid water and took out a curling sandwich. The very old woman sitting opposite him looked at it far more hungrily than he felt. He passed it over to her. She thanked him with a gap-toothed smile and munched it in a minute, wiped her hands on her already greasy black dress, and fiddled with something in her ear. Gaius noticed the wire that snaked to her clutched leather bag.

"You have a radio?" he asked. "Any further news?"

"Lithos is troubled," she said. "Lithos is afraid."

Gaius forced himself not to show his disdain. The old woman wasn't listening to the news, she was listening to the meaningless babble from the lithomancy pylons. The cult was seductive to the old, and to the bereaved who heard their loved ones' voices.

"She hears rumors of war, she sends her engines of light to meet the Spiders. She weeps at the lost blood filled with Spiders, the blood of life. The Spiders are close, they crawl over us, they hang in the spaces between the stars."

Gaius felt his skin go cold and his hair prickle. The old woman didn't notice his response. The lithomantic trance glazed her eyes, and the rest of what she said was gibberish, vocalized no doubt from the atmospheric howls and mutterings of the lithosphere. Then she fell asleep, drooling slightly. The man sitting beside her, an emigrant in a smart and sweaty shirt, shifted uncomfortably and gave Gaius an embarrassed look.

"The peasants go in for that sort of thing," he said. "Can't say I blame them, with the President setting such a bad example."

The man had recognized him as a foreigner, Gaius realized, hence the defensiveness. He smiled reassuringly and waved a hand, though his brain was buzzing so much that he could have done without a conversation.

"Oh, don't worry about it," he said. "Our own farmers are a lot of old pagans too, I must admit. They sacrifice mice to the new moons."

The man chuckled. "You're from—?" He nodded backwards, in the direction of travel.

"Yes," said Gaius. "Just had to cut short a business visit."

"You shouldn't have," the man said, defensive again. "You wouldn't have had anything to worry about."

"Hmm," said Gaius, raising his eyebrows.

The man sighed, and sat back and lit a cigarette, without apology, not that it made much difference by this stage in the journey.

"Yes, I'm a fine one to talk," he said. "I'm as patriotic as the next man, you understand, but when the Society's goons turned up last night and told me my workshop had just become part of the national defense, I thought, to the hells with them." He glanced affectionately at a woman and two teenage boys slumped in sleep on the adjacent seat. "And the lads, well, they're both conscription age . . ."

"I don't think," said Gaius gently, "that the passes are much safer. Or Illyria, for that matter."

The emigrant looked gloomy. "You may be right," he said. "But we've talked about it, and we'd rather die on the slopes than in this futile fratricide."

Gaius resisted the temptation to point out that these possibilities were not mutually exclusive. "What about the Spiders?" he said.

The man snorted. "I don't bloody believe it. If the Spiders were coming, do you think the Illyrians wouldn't join with us at once? Or that our government wouldn't ask them nicely? No, it's just an excuse."

"But last night we saw—"

"Some funny lights. Yes indeed. Let me tell you, my friend, funny lights over the Massif are not as uncommon as you may think. And in any case, who's to say these skiffs people claim to have seen aren't from Sauria—I'm sure there are a few saurs hanging on over there—or from a ship?"

"You may have a point there," said Gaius. He wondered how widespread this skepticism was, and decided to change the subject. "Ah, what was it you said about the President?"

The emigrant smiled and stubbed out his cigarette on the side of the seat. "It's a scandal, you know," he said, leaning forward and speaking in a low voice. "Madame President is kept alive with wires and transfusions and gods know what, all because of that leprous camarilla around her which fears more than anything else what happens when she dies. The poor old woman is capable of little more than clacking her false teeth and listening to that lithomancy gibberish. In her lucid moments she makes decisions. It's pathetic, it's shameful, to tell you the truth."

"How do you happen to know this?" asked Gaius. He thought himself well-informed on the Modern Regime's crepuscular politics—the tensions between the Society, internal security, and the Defense Forces were well known, and avidly followed by Illyrian intelligence—but this was news to him.

"Rumor," said the emigrant. He looked over his shoulder, then smiled as though at himself. "Malcontent scandal sheets circulate, you know."

"So I'm told," said Gaius, more dryly than he'd intended. Many of these sheets were, to his certain knowledge, drafted in Junopolis by the Department. Quite possibly this particular rumor had come from there in the first place. "Can't say I've come across them myself. Interesting."

"Yes," said the emigrant. "I say, my friend, you've gone rather pale. Are you unwell?"

Gaius forced a smile and stood up. "I think I need to stretch my legs and stick my head out of a window for a bit. Uh . . . would you mind keeping my place?"

"Not at all," said the emigrant, and put his feet up on Gaius's vacated seat. "Take your time."

Gaius made his way to the space at the end of the carriage by the door and wound the window down. He really did need fresh air. The lumpy landscape of the Massif crawled past, irrigated fields between outcrops and escarpments crested with olive groves and lemon trees, gnarled pines, windmill generators and lithomancy poles. What was really making his head swim was not the rocking motion and the smoky, fetid air of the carriage—though now that he thought about it, he wished he hadn't—but the connections he'd made. Lithomancy, Spiders, blood of life, transfusions . . . the rounding up of Lydia and her family, and the absence of any sign of a round-up of anyone else, even the mistrusted Traders. Thinking about what the old lithomancer had said still gave him chills. *The lost blood filled with Spiders, the blood of life*—where in the hells had that come from? And what if the other old woman, the one in the top of the tower of the Ninth, had picked up the same electric rumor?

He was torn between the desperate fantasy of going back to New Babylon and (somehow) rescuing Lydia, a more sober assessment that she'd likely just end up on a train after having had a blood sample taken (and the desperate fantasy of waiting for her at the end of the line) and the urgent and practical need to get back to Junopolis. If Madame President had let herself be infiltrated, literally, by the enemy in her frantic clinging to life and hope of rejuvenation, then the opportunities for Ilyrian active measures were enticing indeed.

He wondered if there was a telephone still working at the station at the end of the line, and if he dared send his message through in clear.

Gaius wondered if the air was already noticeably thinner at this altitude. He stopped, leaned forward with his hands on his knees, and panted for a minute. Looking back, he could see the long straggle of emigrants behind him like a line of ants on the slope. Far below was the rail terminus and the cluster of houses around it, where a friendly peasant had taken his last money (real money) for enough water to fill his bottles and enough cheese and some kind of dubious-looking and worse-smelling wind-dried meat to fill his case, as well as (for a handful of Volkovs) the couple of meters of rope with which the unwieldy item of luggage was now lashed uncomfortably to his back. He had debated with himself whether to stick with the family he'd met on the train, and had decided against it—not that they seemed inviting. He had lost them while he'd been waiting in the queue for the telephone.

At this time of year the journey through the mountain pass was supposed to take two days, for a fit man, with only half of the second day above the snowline. For a fit man. Most of the emigrants he'd seen were, in one way or another, not fit men. They could count on three days, and a whole day going through last winter's snow. Or this autumn's, if the weather turned bad.

A pair of jet fighters from the southwest streaked across the Massif at five hundred meters, well below his vantage, flipped up and kept the same height as their bellies flashed by above him. They'd be over the mountains in seconds, above Junopolis in minutes. On the other hand, they might not come back.

A little while later the rough path took him along the bottom of a deep cleft, with a sharp upward slope. As he toiled up the slithering scree, he was aware, from the cliffs at either hand, of an inescapable sense of presence that made him look around, again and again, to see whether he was being followed, or watched. He was alone, and knew he was alone. There was no sound but the drip of water, no smell but the metallic scent of wet algae, no presence but the countless trillions of microorganisms and nanobacteria in all the crevices of the rockface; no communication but the radiation of their minute electrical potentials, and from the piezoelectric noise of the stresses in the rock itself. It was a natural and spontaneous lithomancy, and it carried no rumors to him.

12

Rocket Science

"THE MIND OF the world is a consciousness which emerges from the interactions of the biosphere and the lithosphere of life-bearing terrestrial-type planets such as this one. It is similar to that of the smaller celestial bodies, the minds which some of you call the gods. Unlike them it is incoherent. Unlike them it is capable of manipulating very large energies, and of forming real images from plasma generated by atmospheric or tectonic polarities and hallucinatory virtual images from the effects of these electrical potentials on the nervous systems of animals. Its response to the intrusion of new and unfamiliar intelligent species, especially those using quantum manifold devices, is to generate real and virtual images of them. It is excitable, unpredictable, playful, and violent. Its communications are confusing and in part subjective on the part of the percipient. It is what produces phenomena such as the 'saurs who were here already,' of which the Salasso saur spoke, and it is producing such phenomena now in response to the skiffs of our expedition. We thought you knew," said Mr. Orange.

"We didn't," said Matt. "None of us did." His glare focused on the saurs. "Am I right?"

"We did not know that there was a god in the world," said Salasso. "And we did not know what it was capable of."

"All right," said Matt. He turned again to the Multiplier. "What I thought we were doing was surveying the planet and simultaneously generating a degree of paranoia and mass hysteria which would at least weaken the credibility and unity of the New Babylon regime, and thus give us more possible points of contact and support. What did you think we were doing?"

"Very much the same," said Mr. Orange. "With the addition that we knew that the mind of the world New Earth would generate many real and virtual images which would be quite unpredictable and uncontrollable and which could result in much military and political instability such as coups and wars and so forth, thus degrading the system's defenses to a point which would enable an easy assault by your and our main forces."

"*That* was your idea of an elegant invasion plan?"

"Yes," said the Multiplier. "It would have led to large numbers of deaths on the opposing side without great risk to our forces."

"We were kind of hoping," said Matt, "to accomplish our objectives without large numbers of deaths on any side."

"Ah," sighed Mr. Orange. "That makes a difference."

He scurried back to the other aliens and rapidly conferred by touch, then rotated to face the humans and saurs again.

"Death is different for us because our memories are distributed. It is not easy for us to bear in mind at all times that this is not so for you."

"Oh yes," said Ramona. "You'll have noticed how careful humans are to avoid killing each other in large numbers. Just out of idle curiosity—I had the impression you had picked up from Matt's memories some idea of something similar that happened on Earth—all kinds of strange phenomena that taunted and baffled the military forces and excited the populace. How did that not lead to wars and coups and so forth?"

"Did it not?" said Mr. Orange. "We had not formed from the Matt Cairns' memories an impression that the twentieth century was a period of political and military stability. However, as you have been told, the past is not of great interest to us. We may have misunderstood the probable causes of events."

A babble of speculative conversation ensued. Mikhail Telesnikov stood up and raised his fists to his forehead.

"Friends," he said, "let's agree with the Multipliers that the past is not a priority. The only history I'm interested in right now is the history that is happening right now, and that we can do something about." He waved a hand at the radio. "Armed clashes are beginning already. New Babylon and its neighbors could be at war within minutes or hours. We have to intervene right now to calm things down."

"Yes!" shouted Ramona. "Tell us a way to intervene that won't make things worse, why don't you!"

"I have an idea," said Susan. "We could just land somewhere real public, and tell them the truth. By the time the rest of the Bright Star Cultures arrive, we might well have convinced them it wasn't a threat."

"In principle that's a good idea," said Telesnikov, surprising her. "Unfortunately I don't see any of the major powers giving us mass media access to put our case, or even access to the political leaderships. We'd more likely just disappear instantly into the maw of the security apparatuses."

Matt slapped Mikhail's shoulder. "Brilliant!" he said. "That's exactly what we have to do."

"What?" asked Mikhail, voicing the general feeling.

" 'Disappear instantly into the maw of the security apparatuses,' " said Matt. "Now *that*'s a way of getting their undivided attention."

"It's not one I care to try," said Telesnikov. "We need to think this through very carefully. These plasma-cannon bolts are obviously—or at least ostensibly—aimed at what seem to be skiffs. Now there is no way I can think of that the forts in New Earth geostationary orbit—there are three, as far as I know—can be spotting them directly. They must be responding to information relayed from ground observation, probably radar. If we could take out these radar stations, we could blind the forts to anything happening in the atmosphere or on the surface. That's one vulnerability. Second, New Babylon has a launch facility on the coast of Genea, at the equator. If it's put out of action the orbital forts will eventually run out of supplies, and the farthest away—the ones out on the moons and asteroids—are likely to run out fastest."

"Other way round," said Matt. "They're likely to be more self-sufficient. Also, they'll have local resources, maybe even water ice."

The three Cosmonauts went into a brief technical bicker.

"All right," said Telesnikov, "we don't know. My point stands—the launch facility is a choke point. We should consider ways of taking it out."

"Before we do that, assuming we can," said Ramona dryly, "we'd do well to think through the politics. New Babylon's Space Defense may be aiming at skiffs, or what it thinks are skiffs, but it's actually hitting towns and villages and bits of random countryside in Illyria. It's risking war with Illyria. That strikes me as one hell of a big step to take in response to a few UFO phenomena, especially as Illyria seems quite ready to pick up the gauntlet."

Susan and Telesnikov nodded.

"They certainly are," Susan said. "And the guy I spoke to was pretty skeptical about the skiffs being from what they call the Spiders. I don't think he was in much of a minority. He sure didn't think he was."

"Okay," said Ramona. "So what else do we have to go on? New Babylon's Senate, no less, isn't afraid of antagonizing Illyria. That strongly suggests Illyria doesn't have nukes. But still, there's a sort of paranoid intensity about this reaction that strikes me as being about more than a few skiffs and so forth—ours or otherwise—seen over Illyria, and even over New Babylon's own territory. They're worried about something we don't—"

"Hey!" shouted Ann Derige, who was sitting closest to the radio, which had become unregarded background noise to everyone else. "Listen to this!"

She turned up the volume. It was the same news channel as Susan and Telesnikov had tuned into an hour or two earlier, in Junopolis.

"—Minister responded immediately to the news just in of a devastating explosion in downtown New Babylon with the following statement: 'We deplore the damage and loss of life in the capital of our neighbor and stand ready to offer all necessary humanitarian assistance on request. The present defensive mobilization of Illyrian armed forces is suspended by Ducal decree and with immediate effect. The Ministry of Defense strongly rebuts initial suggestions in New Babylonian reports that Illyrian forces are responsible for the explosion and repeats its longstanding categoric assurance that Illyria does not possess, and does not seek to acquire, nuclear weapons and supports the monopoly of such weapons by New Babylon's Space Defense Force. The Illyrian armed forces are hereby ordered to take no actions other than in immediate self-defense and to await further orders.' Now we go live to our correspondent in New Babylon, where—I'm sorry, the line appears to be down. Please stay tuned for further news flashes."

The voice was replaced by somber music.

"Fuck, fuck, fuck," said Matt. He looked utterly dismayed, his face pale and running with sweat.

Ann was already turning the dial.

"—small nuclear device aimed squarely between the HQ of the Ninth and the Space Authority building, both of which are now completely destroyed along with approximately two square kilometers of the eastern end of the island, which until half an hour ago was the administrative and business center of the entire Republic. So far, all known potential opponents have denied responsibility and—"

"—initial radioactivity readings confirm suspicions that—"

"—pointed out that the sole possessor of nuclear weapons is the Space Defense Force itself and strongly hinted that this may be related to an internal power struggle rather than current international tensions—"

"—possibility of a Spider attack has not been discounted, sources close to the Patriarch have averred—"

"—continuing emergency launches from the rocket base at Kairos—"

Telesnikov stalked over and turned the radio off. "Shut up, everyone!" he shouted above the chorus of protest. "We need a few minutes to think without all that speculation. Oh, all right, Ann—plug in your phones and tell us when any *news* comes in, okay?"

Ann glanced at Phil Johnson; the captain nodded.

"Suppose we believe the Illyrians," Telesnikov went on. "If it wasn't them, who was it? We can rule out the Lapithians and the lesser powers of the Genean League, they don't have the capability. I very much doubt that our own forces—unless the Bright Star Cultures have changed fundamentally in the past century—would do that even if they were here already, and I still think we would know if they were here already. They'd make some effort to contact us, and they could detect the presence of our skiffs. That leaves the only power we know for sure has nukes or equivalent—kinetic-energy weapons, heavy-duty plasma cannon or whatever—the New Babylon Space Defense Force itself. And there's only one reason I can see why they'd do something so drastic as to take out their own official headquarters—they believe that the enemy, the aliens, the Spiders—us—have somehow subverted it."

"There is another possibility," said Salasso. "You mentioned kinetic-energy weapons. It's possible that this was not a nuclear strike but a large meteor which was too fast for the orbital forts to stop, or too small for them to detect until it was too late."

"Yes," said Telesnikov heavily, "that's a possibility. But if it was a meteor strike the SDF would be saying so loud and clear. If they do, fine, in a sense. We can actually help if the gods are attacking, and it's help they'd be likely to accept. If it's the SDF itself that's attacking, we have to stop them before they do more damage, and stop them without destroying the orbital forts. That means jumping Illyrian troops into the forts."

"How do we let the Illyrians know about this offer?" Ramona asked.

"We do what Matt suggested," said Telesnikov. "We vanish into the maw of their security apparatus. Volunteers?"

Susan jumped up. "I'll go, in case they need convincing about the—about what happens when—"

Telesnikov nodded. "Understood. Matt? It was your idea."

Matt shook his head. "I'm sorry," he said. "I think this is all my fault, and I'm pretty useless for the moment."

"Okay," said Telesnikov. "Take it easy."

If Mikhail and Susan hadn't reported back by the end of the day, or if general war broke out, the others were to use their initiative; if all else failed, as Telesnikov pointed out, they could always navigate a jump to the nearest habitable system in the Bright Star Cultures' likely path, and warn them off. Some of the Multipliers took this as a hint to start constructing astronomical instruments from improbable materials.

Less than half an hour after the plan had been finalized, Susan found herself looking down at the garish rooftops of Junopolis.

"The building from which the greatest density of encrypted microwaves emanate is over here," said Mr. Blue, guiding the invisible machine toward a large yellow office block on whose roof—and, Susan guessed, unnoticeable from the street—dish antennae bristled.

"Are you sure it's not the television station?" she asked, half joking.

The Multiplier rattled some fingers like a bunch of twigs. "Television is not a major medium in Illyria. The population seem to have retained the traditional saur prejudice against it. In any case, the television tower is there."

She looked where it had pointed, to a tall building on whose roof meter-high neon letters spelled out "Television Tower."

"Oh, right," she said, somewhat abashed.

The rooftop stabilized a couple of meters below her feet. Her knees were knocking. She could see them. The plan was brutally simple. They were to gain access to the building from the top, find the most senior person they could, and tell him or her their story, producing their concealed weapons if necessary. They both had their tracking and comms devices rigged with hidden throat mikes, set up to maintain continuous contact on their own encrypted channel—if they called for help Mr. Blue would simply jump the skiff into the building right beside them. The skiff's emergence from a jump in a space occupied by other objects would damage the other objects, but not the skiff. It was, he assured them, something to do with the exclusion principle. Susan hoped he was as certain as he sounded, and also that any falling brickwork or whatever didn't fall on her skull, which as far as she knew, was not protected by the exclusion principle.

"Ready?" said Telesnikov.

They were both wearing the black suits—faked up from plant cellulose by the Multipliers—that they'd used earlier on what Matt had called MIB work. If they looked like intruders, at least they would look like respectable intruders, not Nova Babylonian commandos.

"Yes," said Susan, loosening her tie above the throat mike and patting her shoulder holster.

"Okay."

The hatch's opening was indicated by the inrush of hot city air. They jumped down. The skiff stayed where it was, like part of the mirage off the flat roof. Beneath it some gravel and grit on the tarpaper had been swirled into a complex circular pattern. Telesnikov cast about and led the way through the electronic shrubbery to a two-meter-high wooden box with a door in it.

"Not even locked," he said, and opened it. An alarm shrieked immediately.

"Dammit to hell!"

"Keep going," said Susan.

Telesnikov descended the ladder, looked around and beckoned. When she closed the door behind her, the alarm stopped.

"I don't think that's a good sign," said Telesnikov. "Shutting off when the intruders are inside strikes me as what Matt would call a *feature*."

They were in a corridor dimly lit with caged electric lights and a red light at a metal door at the end. The door was thick and it was locked from the other side.

"There's a CCTV camera up there," Susan pointed out.

"Oh yes," said Telesnikov. "Well, let's see if anyone's watching."

They both stepped back from the door and stood waving their hands above their heads. After a minute they heard a lot of heavy steps coming up stairs. Something clunked against the other side of the door.

"Step back and put your hands on your heads," a voice boomed, amplified by the door as well as by whatever was behind it.

They complied. After some grating and clicking the door banged open to reveal two men with black visors and protective gear and rifles. The rest of the squad were literally backing them up, muzzles poking over the top of the stairwell.

"Who are you and how did you get in?"

"Cosmonaut Mikhail Telesnikov of the Cairns Fleet, Mingulay," said Mikhail. "And Susan Harkness, mission recorder. We're part of the advance party of the Bright Star Cultures. There's a Spider skiff above your roof. If has unlimited stealth and jump capability. If I ask—or if its pilot hears any sounds of violence—it can jump into the exact space where you're standing now, about two meters in front of me. I suggest you lower your weapons and take us to the most senior available officer of the Illyrian Defense Department."

Five blank visors and five black rifle muzzles glared back at them.

"All right," said the squad leader. "We'll have to search you first."

"We both have pistols in shoulder holsters," said Telesnikov.

Two of the men stepped forward and frisked them while a third and fourth kept everyone covered. They took the pistols and then tugged off the mikes and the adapted radios.

"Hey!" said Susan as the radio was pulled from her inside jacket pocket. "That wasn't—"

"Shut the fuck up."

The squad leader and his mate tossed the devices, then the pistols, back to the others.

"*Now* we take you—"

Susan heard an enormous crash behind her and hit the deck. Telesnikov's reflexes were just as fast. A split second later, the rifles opened up. Susan clasped her arms over her head and waited for it to stop. After a few seconds and a yelled command, it did. An implacable grinding noise, accompanied by more crashing, continued. Susan raised her head slightly. The two men who'd searched them were crouched at the top of the stairwell; one of them had an arm raised. He motioned to Susan and Telesnikov to get up. As they scrambled to their feet they glanced back and saw the skiff advancing down the corridor toward them. It was a lot wider than the corridor and on both sides its forward edge was cutting through plaster and lath, concrete and steel, like a plowshare through black earth. Telesnikov faced it and waved his hands above his head. The skiff stopped.

Glass tinkled somewhere.

"*Now* you take us," said Telesnikov.

"You may go," the Director of Military Intelligence told the two visored guards who'd escorted Susan and Mikhail to his office.

"But sir—"

An upraised hand and a mild querying look sent the two guards out. The Director sat back down. The office was modest, its only distinguishing feature what was undoubtedly the best view over Junopolis that the building afforded. An uncluttered desk, a leather office chair, a couple of smaller chairs and a few bookcases and a filing cabinet. The Director, a man in his thirties, was likewise modest in a dark suit with a minimum of slashes and padding. Only his ringletted red hair and luxuriant but neatly trimmed beard made him look vain, almost foppish.

"Please, please," he said. "Take a seat." He flicked his fingertips as though shaking off water. "And your weapons and

250

radios." It was like he didn't want them spoiling the layout of his desk.

They sat down. "My name is Attulus," he said. "I have come here from a much busier and more crowded room, as you can imagine. So let's get down to business. The guard relayed what you claimed, and I'm willing to believe it. A Spider skiff on my top floor is . . . compelling. Tell me more. Fast."

He listened intently as they told him.

"This is fascinating," he said. "And your plan is feasible—if your alien allies can jump a skiff with this precision, they can jump right inside the orbital stations, whose location of course we know. But how can you ask us to trust you that"—he wiped a hand wearily across his face—"you're not as much of a menace to the rest of humanity as Volkov always warned?"

Susan stared at him with a feeling of angry helplessness, a sense that she had walked through a mirror into a world where truth was no argument. It was the world to which Matt had taken her, when they had walked through the door into the house of that frightened latifundia chairman and messed with the poor guy's head. He'd had a picture of Volkov among the family photographs on top of his television, and had squirmed when Matt had casually asked him about it. The older cadres were still loyal to the Engineer.

At that moment, Susan realized something that she wanted to blurt out right there, but it would have taken too long to explain her intuition and her reasoning. It would have to wait, and she had a more urgent point to make.

"We're not asking you to trust us," she said. "We're offering you a chance to get *your troops* inside the orbital forts. If by the time the Bright Star Cultures arrive we have not persuaded you, that's our problem. Besides, you must have information by now from Traders who have encountered the Bright Star Cultures."

Attulus gave her a very sharp look. "That's an interesting point," he said. He stroked his beard with thumb and forefinger. "Very interesting."

He reached for his telephone.

The Ducal Marines were a tough bunch. There was something almost comical about the looks on their faces when they climbed into the skiff and saw Mr. Blue, and about the way they relaxed in the few seconds it took for the Multiplier's pheromones to overcome the sweat of fear. Then it would all happen all over again when they tumbled out of the packed skiff and into the hangar and met the other Multipliers, and saw the *Investigator*, and saw the other skiffs arrive, disgorge their comrades and depart to repeat the operation within seconds—a continuous shimmering shuttle. Even the saurs were unfamiliar to most of them, almost legendary. The Marines looked at them as though they were elves.

The five hundred Marines were already geared up for action, having just been stood down after preparing for commando raids on the coast of the Half Moon Sea. Their new mission profile wasn't much different. Even their weapons—plasma carbines, submachine guns, and short swords—were preadapted for use inside the space stations. The decision to use the hangar in Sauria as the base had been taken hastily—despite the suspension of hostilities, nobody knew whether the orbital forts, or for that matter the New Babylon air force, would strike at Illyria. For the moment the whole military and administrative apparatus of New Babylon was not so much paralyzed as flailing about after the blow struck at its center.

There were nine orbital forts—three in geostationary orbit, two on the moons, one at the Trojan point that intercepted incoming merchant starships, and three in the inner reaches of the asteroid belt. Only the Trojan one was known to have a significant contingent of actual troops—in effect, space marines—and even they had mainly experienced nothing but decades of unopposed boardings. Nonetheless, the most effective way to take them on would have been to hit them all at the same moment, so that none would have any knowledge of what was happening to the others. This wasn't possible, because there were only six jump-capable ships available: the five Multiplier skiffs and the

Investigator. Of these, only the skiffs could emerge unscathed inside another object, destroying anything that happened to be in the same space more thoroughly than an explosion. The battle plan required a staggered departure of the skiffs and a careful calculation of the light-minutes and seconds that separated the targets, as well as of their military significance—the most distant, a fort that happened to be on the other side of the sun from New Earth, was about thirty light-minutes away, but it presented the least immediate threat.

The plan, then, was for the five skiffs to hit the five forts within easy reach first, and substitute force concentration for surprise in overwhelming the others—first the one in Trojan orbit, then the three in the asteroid belt. Only in these three would there be a need for microgravity tactics—the geostationary and the Trojan forts had centrifugal spin, the lunar ones had low gravity. The three Cosmonauts were hastily explaining microgravity movement and fighting to the troops, but there was no doubt that they would find it difficult.

The *Investigator* and its one onboard Mingulayan skiff, were assigned the role of recovery and backup. Its precision jumping would have to rely on a Multiplier navigator, Mr. Magenta, working together with Johnson and Derige. Its rocketeers and gunners would do whatever was necessary. Their missiles and plasma cannon didn't amount to much but they were better than nothing. In terms of weapons deployed outside the ship, nothing was what the Marines had.

Susan hopped out of the skiff after its first return journey and watched the preparations in the hangar's late-afternoon gloom, recording with her tiny Mingulayan camera gear and murmuring her own notes. She managed to corner Matt and Mikhail after they'd both stepped back from a conference of the Marine officers around a table spread with sheets of paper. Matt seemed to have recovered his morale.

"You're not coming," he said as soon as she faced him. "It's not a question of danger, it's just that it would leave room for one less Marine or Cosmonaut on—"

"Oh, shut up, Matt," she said. "I know that. History will have to make do with what I record here, and that'll be more than enough. No, it's about something you need to know. Both of you. And the troops."

Matt reached for a mug of coffee that Johnson handed him. "Okay."

"You too, Phil," said Susan, pulling in the captain before he could get away.

"So what is it?" asked Mikhail.

"Volkov is alive," she said.

"What?" they all said at once.

"How would you know?" Matt asked.

"I'm not saying I know," she said. "I'm saying it's very likely. Think about it. Who else could have ordered a missile strike on New Babylon, and been obeyed? Who is the one person who had more authority than the Senate and the President and all the rest of them put together?"

"Yes, informally, when he was alive, but—" said Matt.

"Come on Matt, Mikhail, you knew him, you've told me all about him. The consummate political Cosmonaut. He would never have fallen to a palace coup. Oh, the coup might have been carried out, the plotters might even have thought they'd succeeded, but Volkov would have been ahead of them. And I'll bet he's been up in one of these orbital forts for all the decades since. The SDF *must* have been Volkov's power base. So I think you and the brave lads there are going to face absolutely fanatical resistance in at least one of the forts."

"That or some very clever negotiation," said Mikhail, with a skeptical grin that partly humored her.

"You overestimate him," said Matt, half to Mikhail and half to Susan. "He had a way of setting things in motion that ran away from him. That's what happened with the Modern Regime, I don't doubt. But, yeah, I can see he could still be alive—hell, he still has supporters in the bureaucracy and the SDF, sure, if he was alive he could get them to do it if anyone could . . . but why should he attack New Babylon? Especially with a crisis like this. If he wanted to make his comeback he could do it without wiping out the people who ousted him. I mean, the old President was just about dead of—"

He stopped, and his hand jolted so hard he splashed hot coffee over it—Susan could just see the half-started gesture of slamming his fist on his palm.

"That's it!" he said. He was smiling for the first time in days, for the first time since it had all gone wrong, and now he was straightening up, a weight off his shoulders.

"Yes," said Susan. "I just thought of it when we were speaking to Attulus, and I mentioned the Traders who'd met our side already."

Mikhail and Phil frowned at them.

"You've lost us, you two," Phil said.

"Whoever hit New Babylon," she said, "wasn't just aiming to wipe out the central apparat. They were aiming to wipe out people in the apparat infected by the Multipliers. People right at the top."

She hardly had time to explain the rest—to the Marines as well as to her friends—before whistles sounded, and the run for the skiffs began.

Recording events from the hangar was a safe but uncanny and terrible way of being a war correspondent. The skiffs blurred into their jumps and returned for more troops about once every minute as they zipped back and forth at lightspeed between the geostationary and lunar forts, then in longer jumps as they took on the Trojan-orbit fort and, at even longer intervals, two of the three asteroid bases. It was from the Trojan fort that the first casualties from both sides came back, sliding in blood down from the skiffs' hatches. The dozen or so Multipliers who weren't piloting pounced on the wounded men and began repairing them without waiting for permission. Ramona and Susan rushed around explaining. All that the combat medics could do, and all they had to do, was hold down thrashing, screaming men while the Multipliers worked. After the first few terrifying miracles, soldiers who'd been mangled or dead minutes earlier could reassure the new arrivals that the Spiders were doing them good. Even some of these revenants were frightening—men with only a scaffolding of Multiplier offspring, a webwork of minute Spiders passing blood and bits along where parts of their bodies had been, visibly being repaired on the run. Some of the revived Marines went back into action, carried away by the fever of the benign infection, the ecstasy of the strange vision through their rebuilt eyes. There were still deaths—not even the Multipliers could do anything for a blasted-out brain. Corpses were laid out one by one, but they were not stacked up by the score, as without the Multipliers they certainly would have been.

After about half an hour of fighting, the first prisoners began to come back—initially the few armed men on the geostationary forts, then SDF cosmonauts and technicians, then a sudden flood from the Trojan fort and the two lunar stations. The space marines had fought hard, but the sheer surprise and the prisoners' shock as they arrived in the hangar after being thrown bodily aboard the skiffs made them compliant. As the nearer stations were secured forty-odd soldiers piled into four skiffs that were assigned to the first two asteroid forts, one only five light-minutes away, the other twenty-five. Matt traveled with one pair of skiffs, Telesnikov with the other. The departures were staggered by twenty minutes, so that they would hit each fort simultaneously.

A skiff from the first squad returned, with casualties and prisoners, after about half an hour. One of the prisoners, triumphantly collared by Matt, was Volkov.

The two Cosmonauts came off the skiff still screaming at each other. Blood ran from Volkov's mouth. Matt's pistol muzzle had been jammed against his upper lip, but despite that, he was still yelling. What they were saying was hard to make out but Matt's most oft-repeated epithet was "Murdering commie bastard" and Volkov's was "Spider-loving scumsucking traitor son of a bitch." Two Marines rushed up and parted them. Matt used his advantage as he was being dragged off to kick Volkov as hard as he could in the crotch. Volkov gasped and doubled up, almost wrenching himself away from the Marine, then shouted:

"You haven't won, you bastards! Give up while you still have a chance!"

"Jeez," said Matt, shrugging off his restraint, "I should kill him now."

"Do that if you want, you can't stop us!"

Then Volkov slumped, whether with delayed shock from the kick or in passive resistance it was hard to say, but at least he shut up. He was dragged off and snap-cuffed with the other prisoners.

"What happened?" Susan asked. One of the Marine officers rushed up.

"He got an appeal out before we got him," Matt said. "A call to the citizens and military of New Babylon to rise against the Spider-infiltrated remnants of the de Zama clique and resist their Illyrian pawns. Don't know how effective it'll be, but it may be taken up."

"Damn," said the officer. "Civil war and national resistance in the Republic is not what we need."

Matt jumped back on the skiff at the head of a fresh squad. Both skiffs returned shortly afterward, the station secure. The squad led by Telesnikov came back from the farther station in a bad way. They'd won, but they'd had a struggle getting back through howling, thinning air and then, briefly, vacuum as the defenders suited up and evacuated the air from the areas of fighting. The Multipliers had a lot of repairing and reviving to do.

"They got warnings off," said Telesnikov. "The third station will be ready for us, they'll have suited up and blown all the air out and they'll have armed men in every compartment."

"How many suits have you got?" the Marines' CO asked.

"Ten," said Johnson. "And our people aren't well-trained in them, let alone for fighting in them. Training up your guys would take too long."

"Could take the other sides' suits," said Susan, looking at

some prisoners being taken off the *Investigator*, to which they'd been shuttled by a skiff on site.

Matt and Telesnikov were shaking their heads.

"Same problems, plus sabotage and creative misunderstanding," said Matt.

"Do we need to take the third station right away?" Ramona asked. "It's not like it can hit New Earth from the other side of the sun."

Matt glared at her. "You *know* this? I don't. It has onboard nukes which I don't want to see coming our way, even in a couple of months. And it can zap the other stations with its plasma cannon. No way are we going to leave it a minute longer than we have to. We'll have to nuke it from the outside."

"We don't have—" began the Marine commander. Then he grinned. "We do now."

"You'll need someone to arm it," said Ramona.

Matt and Telesnikov stalked off among the prisoners. After a few minutes in a clamor of raised voices, the two returned, to everyone's surprise, with Volkov. His arms were in their grip and his wrists were cuffed at his back, there was blood on his chin and bruises were swelling on his face, but he still looked defiant and dangerous.

"He has something to tell us," said Matt. "The others bear him out, for what that's worth."

"You've got all this wrong," Volkov said. "The strike on New Babylon did not come from us, I swear. When you have time you can check the stations' computers, check their arsenals, and you can verify what I say. All the nuclear weapons are there and accounted for. And none of them are small tactical nukes. They're all multimegaton asteroid-busters. What hit New Babylon today was a large meteor traveling very fast, punching vertically through the atmosphere. Unless it was a quite extraordinary accident, it came from the gods. They are capable of that, we know they are, they can line up orbital instabilities over decades ready to strike at will. There could be more at any moment, or worse. You know they have been preparing something, you've seen the comets!"

"Why should they strike now?" Matt asked. "It seems another extraordinary coincidence that they should finally get around to hitting New Babylon decades after you started annoying them and just when we happen to be—"

He stopped. "Oh, shit."

"Oh shit indeed," snarled Volkov. "They know you're here, and they're fighting on *your side*." He glared around. "Or you're fighting on theirs—that's what all my men concluded when you attacked the only defenses we have!"

"The defenses didn't work today," Susan said.

Volkov looked at her curiously. "They're not much use against something that small and fast. They're very useful indeed against something bigger and slower. Salasso can tell you all about major impact events."

The saur responded with a thin smile.

"All right," said Matt, "but if it wasn't you and it wasn't a nuke, why the hell didn't you say so?"

"I have to admit that we were still considering whether we could wring some political advantage from the misconception," said Volkov.

Matt let go of Volkov's arm and stood back. "You know," he said, "I can believe that. You haven't changed."

Volkov nodded. "Be that as it may, I can help you now. If you take me to any of the captured stations, I can use its comms to tell the remaining orbital station what is actually going on, and order them to accept your boarders without resistance."

"They'll do that?" said Telesnikov.

"Oh yes," said Volkov. "One thing you got right, they'll do what I tell them."

"Even if it means handing over the station to the enemy?"

Volkov snorted. "New Babylon's decapitated and in convulsions. Illyria is now the only power that can take charge of space defense—it's *our side*, not the enemy."

"Who is the enemy?" Susan asked. Quick, to record this, to get the history. . . .

Volkov's eyes narrowed. "The Spiders—the Bright Star Cultures may be the enemy. We'll see how that works out, and I would strongly recommend that these gentlemen"—he nodded at the Illyrian officers—"bear that in mind, whatever the tactical alliances of the moment. But the enemy of the moment and for the future, our certain and eternal enemies, are the gods. And we have good reason to think the gods have more of these strikes lined up. We have to hit back at them immediately and terribly, to make them aware that they cannot hit us with impunity."

"How can we do that?" Matt asked.

Volkov grinned suddenly. "You were looking for someone who could arm a nuke."

"This time I'm coming along," Susan said.

Volkov had been to the nearest orbital station and back, and a positive reply to his message had come back after over an hour's inevitable delay. They had used this time to mount an asteroid-buster warhead to one of the *Investigator*'s ship-to-ship missiles, and to download the location of an asteroid that, according to Space Defense, had an indwelling god. The plan was for Mr. Orange to plot a jump to within a kilometer of the asteroid, fire off the missile with a hacked one-minute fuse, and jump back instantly to ten thousand kilometers, just ahead of the light.

"You're not coming," said Matt.

"It's not up to you," said Susan.

Phil Johnson, with some reluctance, was persuaded. Susan followed him, Ann, and Matt aboard. The rest of the crew consisted only of Salasso, Volkov, Mr. Orange, and Obadiah Hynde the rocketeer.

Crouched in the cockpit, videoing through the window, Susan fought the sense of panic and strangeness at jumping from the ground in a human-built ship. The scene in the hangar, with soldiers and revenants and prisoners milling about in the dusk and skiffs blurring in and out of jump, was bizarre enough to make her queasy even without this. The cabin lights were out, so that they could see the asteroid's night side.

"Coordinates set," said Mr. Orange.

"Coordinates entered and checked," said Matt.

"Missile primed and deployed," came Obadiah's voice on the speaker.

"Comms open and clear," said Salasso.

"Jump," said Phil.

The next thing that appeared in Susan's viewfinder was a dim-lit wall of rock. The impression that it was falling on them was overpowering.

"Fuse set to one minute and counting down," said Volkov.

"Release missile grapple," said Phil.

"Missile released," said Obadiah. "Holding fire."

Phil and Ann looked at each other. The first ten seconds of countdown ticked away.

"I can't make this decision," said Phil. "Handing over command to First Contact Convener."

"Nuke the fucker," said Matt.

"Mr. Hynde," said Salasso gently, "fire the missile on my responsibility, and on my mark. Is this entirely understood?"

"The missile trigger," said Obadiah shakily, "is the red-handled knife switch on the left of the control panel."

Susan was never able to tell from her recording whether it was Matt's hand, or Salasso's, or Volkov's, that reached the switch first.

13

Blood of Spiders

T HE MIST THINNED. Gaius Gonatus walked a few more steps down the rough trail and found that he was below the cloud, and looking over forested foothills to the moors of southeastern Illyria. The wire of the refugee camp glinted in the valley just a couple of kilometers below. It seemed farther away than the entire journey behind him. He wondered if the perception of distance to be traveled was logarithmic. He wondered if "logarithmic" was the appropriate analogy. Pondering this thought kept him going until he reached "asymptopic" and the gate.

The guard had the green helmet of the Civil Corps. He had watched Gaius's slow approach without moving to help.

"Welcome to Illyria," he said, without moving his eyes.

"Fuck you," said Gaius. "I'm Illyrian."

He lurched through the open gate and into the reception area. His feet had just been examined for frostbite and treated with disinfectant for blisters and cuts when the Department's man in the camp found him and loaded him onto a big military autogyro reeking of paraffin and full of North Genean mercenaries. He was back in New Babylon in two hours. The autogyro landed between craters at the main airport. The sound of distant small arms fire came from several directions. The mercenaries deployed to the perimeter. Gaius limped to the terminal building. Illyrian, Lapithian, and Genean League soldiers were everywhere. Attulus met him in the lounge. The window was broken but the bar was open.

"What the hells happened downtown?" asked Gaius, as soon as the first brandy was inside him and the next was in front of him.

"Tactical nuke," said Attulus. "Volkov is alive, apparently. He ordered the strike from orbit."

Gaius felt the back of his neck tighten, hunching his shoulders against a blow from above. He straightened up.

"It's all right," said Attulus. "Volkov's safe in our hands. So are the space stations."

"How?"

"Mingulayan advance guard. It was their skiffs we saw. They came in on our side. They and their furry alien friends."

Atullus scuttled his fingers across the tabletop. Gaius closed his eyes and opened them again.

"Why did Volkov nuke his own capital?"

"He made an impassioned television broadcast just before he was captured, calling on all good Volkovists to rise." Attulus waved at the window. "Which they have. He claimed that the central apparat was riddled with people who had sold out to the Spiders, starting at the top. The very top."

"Good gods above. Where did he get that idea from?"

"You should know, old chap," said Attulus.

Gaius took a gulp of brandy to stop the hot rise of his gorge. "They tapped my call?"

Attulus grinned thinly. "Nothing so melodramatic. As soon as we got your call we passed every juicy detail, garbled rumor, and reckless speculation to our contacts in the Volkovist old guard in the SDF. I must admit, we didn't expect to get quite so much detonation for a dinar, but there you go."

Gaius said nothing. His mouth had dried up completely. A burst of small arms fire echoed from beyond the perimeter.

"The same with Volkov's call to his supporters to attack the Regime's degenerate apparatus. Very convenient for us. That's exactly what we want them to do. With the Regime's air force in disarray and the space stations in our hands, we've been able to just walk in. Unopposed air and sea landings, mostly. Of course he also called on patriots to attack the aristocratic reactionary invaders, but our boys are giving them something of an education in confining their attention to easier targets. It's not just the old guard, of course. We've won, but there's no one left to surrender to us. Various units of the Regime's forces and local militias are running around shooting at each other for tediously obscure reasons. All sorts of scores are being settled out there. Lampposts and petrol, you know the sort of thing. Very messy. But it means we're the only force which can maintain order, so we'll end up on top of the heap."

"Some heap," said Gaius. "And what about the Bright Star Cultures?"

Attulus shrugged. "The Mingulayans and the Multipliers—I gather that's what the Spiders call themselves—are presently firmly under the guns of the Ducal Marines, though they may not realize it yet. They can't move against us, that's the main thing."

"I was thinking of their main force," said Gaius.

"Well," said Attulus, "they evidently thought New Babylon's Space Defense was a threat to that main force. It's now *Illyria*'s Space Defense—which rather suggests we can handle them when they do turn up."

"We're not going to *fight* them?"

"Not for me to say, old chap. Political decision. Point is, we have the option." Attulus frowned. "Same applies here, of course. Until we're quite certain that the Spiders aren't going to eat our brains and turn us into drooling zombies, we need to keep a very firm grip on people with baby Spiders swimming around in their blood. Without going quite as far as Volkov and his brave band of renegades, one can understand his concern about the ex-Traders and de Zama's camarilla. Potential enemy within, and all that."

"I don't know about the ex-Traders," said Gaius, "but surely de Zama and her lot are all dead under the rubble."

"I rather think not," said Attulus. "If they are, they'd be the first ruling clique in history to stay in their top-floor offices while expecting war within hours. We may hope so, of course, but it would be foolish to count on it." He smiled. "Which is where you come in, Gonatus. You know your way around the city—what's left of it. Find the de Tenebre woman and her sept. Find any Traders or senior Modern Society members that you can. Find them, and pull them in."

"I may possibly need a revolver," said Gaius. He looked at his feet. "A decent pair of boots would not go amiss."

Attulus snorted. "We're not asking you to do it on your own. We're rounding up both categories as part of the peacemaking operation—protective custody, detention centers, fair trials, health inspections—you know the score. All you have to do is winkle out the Spider people. Plenty of backup on call, and a couple of good assistants."

He stood up and beckoned. Gaius turned to see two junior officers of the Illyrian Army bestir themselves from a nearby table and head toward where he sat.

"John Terence and Matthew Scipion," said Attulus, introducing them. "Sound chaps. They'll look after you." He stuck out his hand. "Must be off. See you around."

The low-slung, open-topped Army vehicle careened down Astronaut Avenue, swerving in and out between abandoned cars and fallen masonry. After a certain point all the windows were shattered, their glass covering the street like ice on a refrozen lake, shards crunching under the thick tires. A few hundred meters further, and everything was covered with dust. There was black dust and there was white dust, and here and there a flash of color from something—the side of a car, a scrap of clothing, a sign—that had been momentarily sheltered from the monochrome hurricane. A little further on, the ruins started. All the buildings of the Volkov era and the Modern Regime had been blown away, leaving the granite and marble and sandstone blocks of the ancient city merely damaged.

Closer now, and everything was down. Rubble blocked the streets. People with and without equipment were already—or had been all night—hauling it off chunk by chunk, shovelful by shovelful. Black-furred flying squirrels pawed through it like demonic rescue workers. At the sound of the car, they glanced over their caped shoulders and resumed their sinister rummaging and occasional exultant caw.

Terence pulled up and turned off the engine. They got out. It was the first morning of Gaius's new job—he had collapsed with exhaustion the previous afternoon and slept all night—and he had felt obliged to see the destruction before he settled into any kind of routine. Terence and Scipion had not queried his motive.

They ascended the rubble barrier—it was like going up a very unreliable staircase—and paused at the top. The sun was in their eyes.

"Gods above," said Gaius.

For about a kilometer, there was not even rubble. The very stones had been pulverized to jagged lumps, fist-sized and smaller. Faint traces of radial lines indicated the direction of the blast, outward from a central crater several meters deep. A dozen or so yellow-painted ground vehicles and two green autogyros stood about at random points within the blast radius, as though they had miraculously survived it. Whatever initial impulse had taken them there had ebbed at the sight, leaving them stranded. There was simply no possibility of anything's being alive here. Not even the carrion-eating flying squirrels were looking into it.

Gaius crunched and slithered forward down the atomic scree, occasionally stopping to peer and poke at the ground. Terence and Scipion came after him.

"What are you looking for?" Terence asked.

Gaius straightened and put the heels of his hands on the small of his back. "Spiders."

There were no Spiders. The three men traversed the blast area in two directions and returned to the vehicle in a couple of hours. A stench had risen with the sun, but it didn't come from the blast area. It came from the wider area around it, the next circle of hell.

"Boss," said Scipion, after draining a water bottle, "shouldn't we get to work?"

"That was work," Gaius said. His back ached and his eyes stung. He was beginning to worry, belatedly, about radioactivity. He brushed his palms together briskly. "But you're right. Let's go and look for Spiders somewhere else."

What constituted a safe route through the streets changed by the minute. Scipion crouched on the back seat yelling instructions with a radio-telephone at his ear and a street map in front of him, penciling updated locations of allied occupation troops, Regime loyalists, Regime defectors, Volkovist partisan bands, and gangs of youths who had gone immediately and utterly feral.

For all that, the streets outside the bomb-damaged area and the immediate rescue or recovery operations were busy and, Gaius thought, livelier than they had been before the war. Stalls had sprung up everywhere, selling food, Illyrian goods, and loot. Most businesses were open. Above all people were talking to each other, in ones and twos or in larger groups, in a way he hadn't seen before. They talked to the troops and to the members of the less belligerent, or just temporarily inactive, militias on the corner. Every so often a flurry of shots would clear a street, and then the firefight would continue until superior forces arrived, or would die down of themselves, and people would drift back and resume their activities. Here and there Terence had to swerve or reverse rapidly out of such incidents, or away from scuffles as Illyrian soldiers broke up lynchings, or arrived too late to do more than cut down the bodies of the victims and shoot at the likely—because fleeing—perpetrators.

Eventually the car managed to fall in with a convoy of New Babylonian trucks driven by Illyrian troops and escorted by Lapithian motorcycle outriders and a clattering autogyro high overhead. The convoy took them to a newly built camp on the outskirts. Hundreds of meters square, it was surrounded by four-meter posts with barbed wire still being strung around the outside. Existing buildings had become part of the camp, and soldiers and prisoners were busy erecting prefabricated huts.

Gaius and his men showed their passes and drove in. They parked the car in a big pound and headed for the admin block. The Ducal raptor-claw crest on a sky-blue flag fluttered above it. There was a long list of names to look through, and it was extending with every courier who came in from the screening sheds. The clerks were far too busy to help, and the names they'd typed out had not gone into their long-term memories. They did not put it quite like that.

"Look for de Tenebre," Gaius said. "Any other Trader names you recognize, sure—Rodriguez, Delibes, Bronterre. But de Tenebre is the goods."

Scipion found a cluster of names within half an hour. "De Tenebre, P, F, C, and E," he announced.

Gaius hid his disappointment with a pleased smile.

A clerk was able to tell them, by a quick flip through a card index, that the three people mentioned had been screened and had not yet had their health check, so they were probably in the—

"Oh, and thank *you*, gentlemen," he said to the banging door.

A burly man with ginger hair and a stubborn scowl stood in front of a long table behind which sat medics in white coats.

"Why?" he was saying.

"There's a big demand for blood products," the technician said. "A lot of burns and lacerations and major trauma. Suspected radiation sickness. We need every contribution we can get."

"Ah, I understand that," the man said. "Unfortunately I can't help." He glanced around at three women on the front bench a few steps behind him. "Nor can my w . . . my wife and her friends. We're all Traders, and we've all picked up some nasty bugs on our travels. Always been told not to donate."

"I know that's been the policy," said the technician patiently.

She glanced at the impassive Illyrian military policeman at her shoulder. "Nevertheless. This is an emergency and frankly the people down at the hospitals are not worried about malaria or odd tropical diseases. They're *dying* down there for lack of plate-lets and plasma." She licked her lips. "Come on, this is just a test. If there's anything really nasty, we'll pick it up. Stick out your hand. It's just a prick in your finger."

The man folded his arms.

"No."

Gaius tapped his shoulder. "Esias de Tenebre?"

"Who the hells are you?"

"Gaius Gonatus, Allied Civil Assistance," Gaius improvised smoothly. "I believe I can help you to find Lydia."

De Tenebre's face convulsed with consternation and rage. "I *know* where Lydia is," he said. "She's in the hospital. Emergency Field Hospital Two, Ward Five. The serious burns unit." He looked away. "You can tell who she is by the name on the end of the bed."

Gaius met his eyes. They were distressed, but calmer than his voice had sounded. "You know she's going to be all right," Gaius said. "And I know that's why you don't want to cooperate here."

Esias tensed and looked around but it was too late. Five military policemen had already surrounded the three women, and Terence and Scipion were closing on his arms.

"Now please come with us," said Gaius. "There's nothing to be afraid of. Only a little prick in your finger."

The building to which Gaius took the four prisoners had been some kind of cattle shed. It stank of herbivore shit, and the electric lamps were few and dim. Gaius dismissed the military policemen with thanks and asked the prisoners to line up against a stack of bales of hay. Under the guns of Terence and Scipion they complied. Gaius shoved a barrel against the door with his foot and sat down on it, cradling a revolver. The polygamist and his three wives were, according to their particulars in the admin files, in their early fifties, but they looked a lot younger. Gaius was not surprised.

"I and these gentlemen," said Gaius, "have been asked by Illyrian Military Intelligence to detain people who are suspected of being infected by the Spiders. What I know, and what these gentlemen don't, is what Spider infection does to people. Citizen Esias de Tenebre, I am about to toss a small knife on the ground in front of you. I strongly urge you not to do anything foolish with it. Instead, I would like you to demonstrate to my colleagues some of the more, ah, spectacular effects of Spider infection."

"Sure," said Esias, picking up the knife. He opened it and tested the blade on his thumb. Then he held up his hand and made a quick, deep slash across the palm. The welling of blood was dark and clear in the yellow light. He clenched his fingers over it, laid the knife back on the trampled straw, and walked over to the two soldiers.

"Boo!" he said, opening his hand.

Childish though the gesture was, it made them jump.

"Five little Spiders," said Esias. He clapped his hand to his mouth, then held it out again, palm upward. "And then there were none."

"He never cut himself," said Terence.

"Good gods," said Gaius. "Please repeat the demonstration, slowly."

"Do I have to?" said Esias. "It bloody hurts."

"Your own fault for leaving open the possibility of a trick," said Gaius. "Do it again."

Esias retrieved the knife and did so, right in front of Scipion and Terence. This time he didn't close his hand.

"Satisfied?" said Gaius.

The soldiers nodded. Esias strolled back to his wives.

"How long have you had this infection?" asked Gaius.

"Ten years," said Esias. He glanced sidelong at his wives. "The ladies, a bit less."

"Now, if—purely hypothetically you understand—I and these gentlemen were to shoot you down where you stand, what would happen?"

Esias paled. "If you were to blow our brains out," he said, "we'd be dead. Otherwise, we'd, well, recover. Not that I would like to try it." His voice became more cheerful as he added, "Blood would get everywhere, you know."

"Oh, I know," said Gaius. "I've seen what happens when people are shot. Blood gets, as you say, everywhere. Especially when brains are, as you say, blown out. And we've seen what happens when your blood is spilt, and starts to dry. How easy would it be, do you reckon, to retrieve or confine or destroy the little Spiders that would swarm from your blood?"

"Not easy at all," said Esias. "They come in all sizes, down to the size of germs, and when they have to survive independently they can be very hard to deal with. You'd have to catch or kill every last one, and I don't know if even burning the barn around us would do the trick. You'd have to, I don't know—"

"Nuke the place," said Gaius. "I know."

He looked over at Terence and Scipion. "As we saw this morning, that seems to do the trick."

"What's all this in aid of?" said Scipion. "I mean, it's very interesting, but where's it getting us?"

"Ah," said Gaius. "In a moment, gentlemen."

He gestured to the de Tenebres. "Please, citizens. Haul yourselves down some bales to sit on, and heave a couple over for my friends here. This may take some time."

It took some time. At the end of it, Gaius and the soldiers returned with the de Tenebres to the medical shed. He led them over to the blood transfusion technicians.

"We've checked them over," he said. "Unfortunate misunderstanding earlier. There's nothing wrong with their blood. In fact, you can put them down as universal donors."

The technician looked at him suspiciously. "Are you certain of that?"

"Absolutely," said Gaius. "We've tested them thoroughly.

Take as much as they can spare out of each of them. There's no time to waste. People are dying as we speak. In fact, I can take their donations directly to the hospital—and any others you have ready, of course."

"That would be helpful. Thank you."

"You're welcome," said Gaius. "We're going there anyway."

He had thought the center of the nuclear blast was the most appalling place in the city, but the emergency field hospital was worse. It was a town of tents in a park, and it was full of people who had been pulled from the rubble or who had staggered in or been carried from the flash radius. The serious burns unit was the worst of all. Perhaps not quite. There was a closed ward beyond it, where great efforts had been made to maintain a sterile atmosphere, and to which there was no admittance. Gaius had a horrible suspicion that there was nothing much on offer there but palliative care and opiate euthanasia.

He and his two guardians were stopped by a teenage soldier at the positive-pressure plastic flap of the burns unit. Gaius showed him the chit from the transfusion service.

"Go ahead."

Gaius had three liters of the de Tenebres' blood in sterile plastic bags with valves at the top. The other two had larger quantities of other blood donations from the detainees. They walked over to the harried nurse at the admissions desk, averting their eyes from the scores of beds. The place smelled of disinfectant and of cooked meat. Gaius realized that transfusions would not do the job, would not begin to do the job. He felt sick and feverish, and a little light-headed. He smiled at the nurse and walked on past the desk and up the ward. He took out his knife and slit the bags one by one and squirted and sprayed blood over every patient he passed, aiming at what areas of exposed flesh were visible. He got all the way to the end of the ward before a man in a white coat rushed up.

"*What are you doing?*" he shouted.

"Excuse me," said Gaius, and straight-armed the medic hard

as he walked past him, faster now. There was a lot of screaming going on, not all of it from the patients.

"Soldier!" yelled the medic, staggering as he rebounded off the end of a bed. "Guard!"

The young soldier ducked through the flap.

"Stop that man!"

Gaius slashed the remaining bag and whirled it around as the soldier raised his rifle. Blood spattered everywhere, like in the ceremonies of a primitive cult. The bag was empty, and the room was still not bloody enough. He threw the bag against a wall.

"Careful, soldier," said the medic. "He's got a knife."

Terence and Scipion had slipped out. Good. They would do their bit too, in other wards.

"Drop that knife! Sir."

"Please don't shoot," said Gaius. "I'm about to drop the knife."

And he did, but not before he'd managed to slash his left forearm. Down, not across, wasn't that the way? The blood spurted with shocking speed and abundance. The knife clattered. Gaius clawed his arm, trying to keep the wound open as long as possible. There was a loud bang and something hit him very hard in the chest. The last thing he saw before the floor hit his face was a reddish mist.

Gaius awoke from strange dreams that, unlike most dreams, didn't fade from his mind. It hurt to breathe. His left arm throbbed dully. From the woolly feeling in his head he knew that he would be hurting a lot more if he weren't soused in opiates. His eyes opened stickily to focus on Attulus. He found himself suddenly and acutely aware of the man, of his uniqueness and of the universality of the divine spark that blazed behind his eyes, the consciousness that—

"Ah, there you are," said the Director, without enthusiasm.

"Where am I?"

"Illyrian military hospital," said Attulus. "You have been unconscious for two days, from the infection and from your bullet wound."

"Ah." A military hospital. That would explain the green walls and the scratchy sheets. "How much trouble am I in?"

"You really have been very foolish," said Attulus. "Because of your bizarre actions in the burns unit, seven of the patients there have died, in considerable pain. The fever of the infection raised their body temperature to the point where they went into hyperthermic shock. The other patients are making . . . remarkable progress. Similar outcomes are reported from the other major trauma units where Terence and Scipion made their own dramatic blood donations." He sighed. "I suppose it's my fault. I didn't realize you would consider yourself responsible for the New Babylon blast."

"If I hadn't—" Gaius began miserably.

Attulus raised his hand. "Your action was a link in a chain of causes. Even if it had led to the attack, that still would not make you morally responsible. As it happens, it didn't. There was no nuclear attack."

"What?"

"It was a meteor strike. Volkov has said so, and we've confirmed it. The raised levels of radioactivity in the immediate area and in the fallout plume came from pulverized granite. All that your action triggered off was Volkov's call for an uprising."

"Oh, gods," said Gaius. He felt immensely relieved, and at the same time guilty all over again.

"And don't start a whole new round of beating yourself up over the patients who died," said Attulus. "Those who wouldn't have died anyway would have wished they had. Well, perhaps not, if the Spiders' healing powers are as great as your friends claim. Still. You have other problems."

"What—"

"Oh, what you might expect. I'm spending a lot of political capital holding back people who regard you as a menace to the human race."

"To hell with the human race," said Gaius. He tried to raise himself on his elbows, failed and settled for raising his head off the pillow. "What has happened to Lydia de Tenebre?"

"She is one of those who are recovering. She already was, as I'm sure you know."

"I would like to see her."

"You would not," said Attulus. "Not for some time. I assure you of that."

"Where was she?"

"In de Zama's private clinic, somewhat to the west of the blast area. So was de Zama, who had decided, on the brink of death, to accept the Multiplier infection—which she already had heard rumors of, and which her agents were alert to evidence for. Evidence which, one way or another, you or your contact may have inadvertently provided."

Gaius winced, remembering how quickly the agents had come for Lydia after her demonstration of the infection. Or had it been lithomancy that had done it, after all? It no longer mattered. Attulus was still talking.

"Madame President poses something of a problem, as I'm sure you can imagine." Attulus smirked. "One solution that's being floated is to affect not to recognize her. Not diplomatically— physically, we would literally not recognize her when she completes her recovery. The healthy and younger woman who then claims to be de Zama is obviously deluded or an impostor."

Gaius laughed painfully. "It's too late for that."

Attulus fingered his beard. "You're right, of course. Rumors are spreading faster than the infection. People are actively *demanding* the infection, for themselves or for people who are seriously injured. Particularly in New Babylon, there is a huge wish to believe that the Bright Star Cultures are not a threat. In a sense they are throwing off the defensive part of Volkov's legacy, and embracing the part which he used to attract initial support—the quest for longevity and other benefits of biological engineering. One or two Traders who've escaped the dragnet have popped up with wild tales of what the Bright Star Cultures have achieved in symbiosis with the Multipliers—not just in biological matters, but in terms of wealth. I reserve judgment on that, but for the moment we have to accept that it is unstoppably becoming the popular view. Unfortunately it undermines the rationale for space defense, which we now need more urgently than ever."

"Ah, yes," said Gaius. "The meteor."

Attulus nodded. "Precisely. More where that came from, as they say." He twined a ringlet of hair around a finger. "And, ah, this may come as a shock. Volkov and the Mingulayans—with the cooperation of some officers in the Ducal Marines, I'm astonished to tell you—have already taken some preemptive action in that respect."

"They've stopped another meteor attack?"

"No," said Attulus uncomfortably. "They have destroyed a god."

Gaius fell back to the pillow and stared at the ceiling for a while. The knowledge that he, like every educated person, had in the back of his mind suddenly became vivid and visual. He could see, he could imagine, the ring of asteroids and outside it and the farthest planets, the light-year-wide sphere of cometary bodies around the sun. An unknown but large proportion of them, he knew, harbored the strange slow life of the extremophile nanobacteria, and the innumerable fast minds that that life sustained. Trillions of intelligent beings, megayears of civilization, lay within each one, and over all the sum of the minds of each a wider consciousness, a god. To strike at and destroy such a thing, even in self-defense, was blasphemous in its disproportionality, appalling in its hubris. To exterminate all life on a planet to avert a sting—even a fatal sting—from one of that planet's insects would be only the faintest analogy to the shocking scale of the offense.

His hands were clutching the sheets, regardless of the pain in his arm. He wanted to pull the sheets over his head.

"Gods above," he said. "Do the people know this?"

"Not yet," said Attulus.

"Good." Gaius was beginning to calm down, and beginning to think through the ramifications. "There's a serious danger of the returned Volkov—in our hands or otherwise—becoming a popular hero. From our point of view, he was the tyrant, and the Regime since his departure is an improvement. From the point of view of a lot of people in New Babylon, he's a much more ambiguous figure, to say the least. The camarilla and the bureaucracy are hated much more than his memory. The fact that Volkov can still raise a small army of insurgents while many people suspect his supporters in Space Defense of having struck at the heart—or the head—of New Babylon just shows how dangerous things are. The one thing that could shock people out of their deluded fascination with the Engineer is if we can nail the charge of theicide to his forehead." He lay back and thought some more. "The same applies, of course, to the Mingulayans and the Multipliers—also implicated, and also potential contenders for popular influence."

Attulus frowned. "Very astute, Gonatus. But I thought you were sympathetic to the Multipliers—given your propensity for spreading their infection about!"

"You misunderstand," said Gaius. "The Bright Star Cultures are founded on mutual adaptation between the Multipliers and the Mingulayans. There is no reason why there should not be a new culture, based on Multipliers adapting to us." He smiled. "The way the Multipliers reproduce, after all, is to *divide*."

"As I said, I'll reserve judgment on that. The question is, what do we do now?"

Gaius wasn't sure whether the Director really was asking him for advice, or brainstorming for ideas to which he would apply his own judgment. He decided not to flatter himself too much.

"What I would suggest," he said, trying to sit up again and succeeding in propping himself on his right elbow this time, "is that we return Julia de Zama to power as soon as she is fit to be seen in public. New Babylon is unlikely to accept Illyrian occupation for long, memory and gratitude being what they are. She is unpopular, but she is likely to be more popular than us, and an element of stability. And who knows, if she has visibly become rejuvenated she should make a very different impression than when she was a living corpse on a drip. Meanwhile, we make quite clear to her that she is in power on our sufferance, and get as many concessions as possible with regard to internal reforms, trade, and peace. We talk individually to the members of the Bright Star Culture expedition—not all of whom, I am sure, will have gone along with the theicide, and even fewer of whom will be willing to stand by it in the cold light of day. We isolate Volkov and his Mingulayan accomplices, and then we make the evidence of what they have done public. The resulting howl of execration should demoralize the Volkovists, including those in the Space Defense apparatus."

"Hmm," said Attulus, rising from his bedside seat. "This has been a very useful conversation, old chap. You have, as they say, given me something to lay before the Duke. There is one problem. If we expose Volkov and his accomplices as theicides, we shall have no choice but to shoot them."

"Is that a problem?"

Attulus chuckled darkly and went out.

14

The New Moon's Arms

"S O THIS IS how it ends," Matt said. "Up against a fucking wall."

He sat warming his feet in front of a fire in a hut in the detention camp on the island in the sound off New Babylon's harbor, smoking a cigarette and drinking whiskey. Susan had brought a good supply of both. Matt's fellow prisoners, Salasso and Volkov, sat with him and her around the fire, variously soothing their angst and ennui with hemp and whiskey. They both nodded philosophically. Their attitude annoyed Susan intensely.

"You shouldn't just give up," she said.

"I've had a long life," Matt said, "and I'm not too bothered by the prospect of not having more of it. I'm after immortality."

Volkov snorted. "Immortality doesn't last, my friend. I've outlived mine already. All it takes is a good hammer."

Salasso, who was evidently turning his last weeks or months to good account by testing the limits of his species' capacity to smoke hemp and stay conscious, turned a loll of the head into a nod. This irritated Susan even more.

"Your crewmates are doing everything they can for you. You could at least pretend you appreciate their efforts."

"We do," said Matt. "But we know they're not going to get anywhere. And so do you."

Susan nodded glumly. She had spoken often enough to Phil,

Ann, and the others, who had not been indicted and seemed to feel obscurely guilty about that. They had petitioned and agitated with a sort of Mingulayan Scoffer militancy and naivete, and had almost been lynched themselves. It was like defending child murderers.

"Your appeals might get through the Senate," she said. "And then there's the Assembly of Notables."

The two men guffawed. Salasso's shoulders shook a little. The winter wind rattled the windows; even now, in mid-morning, the place felt like night. Farther up the fuggy hut sat other men, Volkovist prisoners and a few criminals, around other fireplaces and around tables of dominoes and checkers. A few of them read. There was nothing much else to do. All of them kept a respectful distance from the dead men on leave, and had even refrained from overt primate displays when she had walked in. They knew who she was, and who she was with. It was far from her first visit.

She had arrived by a Prison Department launch across the choppy water of the sound, through rain and sleet. New Babylon's winters were cold and pervasively damp, the converse of its hot and pervasively humid summer. She had found a niche there—a politically savvy and, at the same time, inquisitive and naive journalist, especially one from off-world, was just what the newly liberated media wanted—but she hated the place. There was too much of the prehuman in New Babylon, and not only in its architecture. Something in the culture of the place looked back to an age of giants. Too much antiquity, too much continuity, had accumulated here for it to be a place where something new could begin. No wonder Volkov had failed; as, in a different way, de Zama was failing. Susan wanted to get away, to do things that had never been done before, to see new worlds like that of the selkies, outside the Second Sphere altogether and away. At the same time she wanted to stay here, to be with Matt and the others to the bitter end, or to help them avert that end. She wanted her experiences, her very self, to be multiple. She realized she was thinking like a Multiplier.

Matt wasn't, instead contemplating his end with a gloomy relish. He pointed out of the nearest window, which overlooked the sound and afforded through the rain and mist a view of the city's mutilated skyline.

"Look at that," he said. "No matter what the gods do that should make people angry, it only makes them more afraid. Cringing bastards. They're as bad as the fucking saurs, no offense, Salasso."

"No offense is taken," said Salasso. "I despise them myself. Even millions of years after something much worse than genocide was committed against my people, they still regard the gods as good and theicide as the ultimate sin."

"The Multis don't," said Susan. "They would be quite delighted to help you escape. To help *us*. The migration will continue after the Bright Star Cultures arrive, you know. There are people—humans and saurs—who are interested in going with it. Hundreds of light-years, thousands, right across to the next spiral arm. They could take you off the island at a word, and hide you in the forest until—"

"No," said Salasso.

"Not a chance," said Matt. "I'm not running away. I'm not giving these people the satisfaction. Fuck 'em. They either accept self-defense and retaliation as a justification for theicide, or not. If they don't, then nothing we've done means anything anyway. I don't want to live another few hundred years, or whatever I've got left, with the gods behind the back of my neck."

Susan wanted to shake him. "Look, when the Bright Star Cultures arrive, this'll all change. The Illyrians, the Postmodern Regime, whatever—they'll all be overwhelmed by people like us, people who have the Multiplier outlook, not just the infection but the attitudes. Besides, the Cairns Fleet sent us to do a job, and we did it. They can't let you be shot for doing what you had to do."

"Well, yes," said Matt, more cheerfully. "There is that."

·　　·　　·

They came in the spring, on the eighth day of the month Florida, A.C. 10,350. A swarm of ships like enormous flies—multilegged, wide-bellied, stubby-winged—appeared suddenly in the sky above New Babylon. Susan, walking down Astronaut Avenue in the green fresh post-rainshower morning to cover a story—for Junopolis Calls, ironically enough—about the rebuilding of the Ninth HQ, saw them and saw the city stop around her. She started running. The ships came down so fast they had disappeared behind buildings before she could see where they were landing, but she made a guess that they would head for parks, and so she turned at a corner and ran along a side street of apartment houses and there it was squatting on the grass among the trees like a piece of play equipment for giant children.

Around her other people approached more cautiously. Among them a couple of members of the militia, the Ninth, had unslung their plasma rifles and were talking fast into their radios as they jogged forward, bravely in the circumstances. Susan outran them all, vaulted a low fence and padded across damp trampled grass. The only children in the park this early were quite young. They bawled and clutched at their mothers or stared, thumb in mouth, at the ship. Flying squirrels fled to the trees and chattered abuse.

A curved segment of the side of the ship slid back and a ladder rattled down. Susan was by now close enough to see and hear it. The mechanism was reassuringly clunky and creaky, not like the seamless refinement of the Multiplier or even saur skiffs. It wanted oiling somewhere. A young man in loose green fatigues came down the ladder and stood at the foot of it, blinking in the sunlight and gazing at the buildings and the slowly gathering crowd. From the dark of the hatch at the top other faces, including children's, peered out. The man shaded his eyes with one hand and waved with the other.

"Trade Latin still spoken here?" he called out.

"Yes," said Susan, walking up to him and holding out a hand. She had the camera and the mike on the side of her head. "You should really try to say something more historic. Anyway, welcome to New Babylon."

"Thank you," said the man, shaking hands. "Are you a Mingulayan?"

"Yes," said Susan. "I came here with Matt Cairns."

"Oh my God," the man said, in English. "You're the one who's fucking historic." He waved vaguely in the direction of the harbor. "The First Navigator's ship is coming down over there. You should probably go and report to him."

"Yes," said Susan, stepping back to let the militiamen check the guy out. "I probably should."

The people from the neighborhood were still hanging back about fifty meters away, as if that would make them any safer. The arrival of the ships, and even their appearance, was not unexpected. But it was only when a purple and a red Multiplier descended the ladder, stepping down after a few more adults and children had emerged and stood around on the grass talking to the militiamen and a few other bold locals, that the crowd surged forward, children in the lead. The new arrivals were almost bowled over, and the Multipliers had to move their limbs smartly and skitter about in a slightly threatening manner to clear some space around themselves.

"Make things!" the children were shouting. "Make things for us! Please!"

In the past half-year, since the Crisis (as it was now called, or the Events) the Multipliers who had arrived with the *Investigator* had themselves multiplied by the thousands. They had begun to integrate and educate the numerous free-living small offspring that had resulted from the mass infections that had spread from the recovering casualties of the attack. They had taken up residence in old warehouses and under piers and bridges. They roamed the streets and conjured things out of air and grass and dirt. They talked on the radio and on television, wheezing and waving their limbs like mad old scientists. It was all strange and unsettling, but also in a way reassuring to the people of New Babylon. The whimsical frivolity of their conjurings—here a piece of jewelery, there a machine for making shoes—and their enthusiasm and curiosity as they scuttled around factories and fingered all the pages of all the volumes of the great libraries, all this could not help but charm. The decades of preparing to fight off the dreaded Spiders only increased the relief at the arrival of these engaging octopods. Eight-limbed fuzzy shapes of many different colors had become the most popular type of soft toy.

Susan made her way out of the park and back to the avenue, where she headed for the nearest underground station. Street-level traffic looked like it would remain snarled up for hours. The trains were unaffected. She emerged from the underground at Port Station One and immediately found another crowd surrounding several of the Bright Star Culture ships. Multipliers swarmed in the trees, displacing complaining flocks of flying squirrels. Multiplier skiffs flitted, autogyros hovered overhead, microphones and cameras dangling—she was not filing the story of the century, and she didn't care. The search took a while, during which she ruthlessly used her journalist's card and her elbows. Eventually she found the ship of the First Navigator, and her parents.

They were in a small inner ring of people: the President and her entourage and bodyguards, who had arrived, grandly enough, by skiff. Susan saw Elizabeth and Gregor through the surrounding heads and almost did not recognize them. She had thought of their parting as being over a century long, which of course was irrational—they had traveled the hundred-odd light-years in not much more time than she had, with stops of a few days or weeks while the next course was plotted and new ships were built. Somehow this brought home to her for the first time the sheer force of the Multiplier migration, its quality of being a cascading explosion of thistledown birling through and filling and abhorring the vacuum. Her parents had been changed in those months, perhaps more than she had; they looked younger, almost as young as herself. It was weirder than seeing Matt naked and remembering he was centuries old. She had a shocking premonition that a world in which the senior generation did not grow older would have its disadvantages that could only be overcome by endless expansion, if the hominidae were not to become a second version of the saurs. Almost she started her own trajectory in that expansion right then; almost, she fled. But Elizabeth saw her and smiled, and Susan pushed through and rushed forward. She hugged Elizabeth and Gregor, everyone babbled for a bit, and then became serious again. The conversation with the President resumed, slightly out of Susan's earshot.

Susan slid a finger under her hair and switched on her recording equipment. Her channel might as well get some benefit from her proximity. As Susan watched her parents talking to Julia de Zama and to the President's new security adviser, a memorably forgettable-looking man called Gaius Gonatus, she found herself standing beside another of the President's entourage, Lydia de Tenebre. She'd met the Trader woman at some diplomatic banquet whose afterglow had been open to the press, and had interviewed her briefly. Lydia was now some kind of high official in the Space Authority, and spent much of her time, as far as Susan could make out, trying to reassure the saurs and krakens on newly arrived Trader ships, without much success so far, other than to persuade one or two saurs to remain with their skiffs. Hence, no doubt, the President's prestige vehicle.

Susan smiled sideways at Lydia, who looked as though she too had been pushed to one side.

"It's like a conspiracy," Lydia said quietly. "A conspiracy of the old against the young. Except they now have the advantage of experience, and we don't have the advantage of vigor."

Susan nodded, craning to catch what was being said, upping the gain on her mike. The voices became clearer. As she leaned closer she suddenly realized they were talking about the theicides.

"No question," her mother was saying, "it's a hard one, but we can't intervene. It's a capital crime in our code too, one of the few—"

"No!" Susan's outcry was involuntary, turning heads, raising eyebrows. She broke into the charmed circle and confronted her mother.

"You can't let them carry out the executions!" she said. "You can't let them kill Salasso!"

Elizabeth looked at her sadly. "I can and will," she said. "Look, I'm sorry, Susan. I loved that saur, and Matt I liked and Volkov I could, well, I could stand, but it's out of my hands, it's out of the President's hands. We can't let theicide go unpunished. The precedent is too dangerous. There are some crimes that can't be forgiven. That's why we have the category of heinous crimes, and theicide is one of them—in the Bright Star Cultures too."

"But everything else is changing around us," Susan protested. "The Multipliers, they're changing everything, they're changing us. They've changed you. Why can't we change the law, or at least recognize that this time it was justified?"

"That's exactly why we can't change it," said Elizabeth. "It's very difficult to maintain our humanity. The Multiplier outlook literally infiltrates us. We have their worldview in our blood. There is a continuous option to simply dissolve into Spiders, if not physically then culturally. For that reason we maintain our own laws with scrupulous severity. And we are not going to interfere with New Babylon's."

Susan's vision of Elizabeth blurred. She felt as though she had been punched in the stomach by this stranger who could have been her sister. Her father's face was more concerned but, with its tracery of smoothed-out creases, too frighteningly reminiscent of Matt's to be of any comfort.

"*What* bloody humanity?" Susan shouted. "Just because *you're* the Science Officer doesn't make you—"

"Don't lose it with me," Elizabeth said, in a flat, calm voice. It was an order Susan had last heard at the age of nine. It infuriated her to hear it now, but it had its effect, a cold blade in the belly.

Susan blinked hard, clenching her fists at her sides. "You've lost it already," she said. "Your humanity."

She knew this was not true. It was a stone to hand, and she threw it, and she could see the hurt and she didn't care. She could see right through her mother to the omnipresent deity infinitely greater than the gods, and she could not see why Elizabeth couldn't see it too, in her and in the condemned. Or did she, she thought wildly, and did it make no difference?

Susan whirled on de Zama. The young-old President was a very strange-looking person, her smooth skin thin and shining, like the paper of a lantern over her bones.

"Can't you at least use your gods-damned prerogative, Madame? Can't you give clemency? Surely you still feel something for Volkov, he was your partner"—*in crime*, she almost said—"for fifty years or longer, and you have already killed him once! Isn't that enough?"

"For that very reason I cannot give clemency," said de Zama, quite unperturbed by Susan's flaming disrespect. "People would say it was personal. And I cannot give clemency to the other two without giving it to Grigory Andreievich. In any case, when the people have spoken, and the Senate has spoken, and all the world knows what the Notables will say, it would be a foolish President who cast the prerogative in their teeth. There would be a constitutional crisis, which with things as they are we cannot afford." She spread her hands. "With the best will in the world I could not do it."

And you do not have the best will in the world!

Susan turned and walked away, out through the inner circle and the growing crowd. She had just reached the area of devastation at the bottom of Astronaut Avenue when Lydia caught up with her.

"I can't stand it either," Lydia said. "Come on—we can't stand for this, we can do something."

She seemed furious and determined, standing there in the grey dust, incongruous in a fluttery, flower-printed silk trouser-suit and platform shoes.

"What *can* we do?" Susan asked.

"We have experienced the Multiplier enlightenment," said Lydia. "We can think of something."

"So have they!" said Susan. "Much good it does them!"

Lydia laid a hand on her arm. "That's no reason for us not to use our heads. Come on."

"Where? Where is there to go?"

Susan sniffed noisily and wiped her nose on her sleeve. She felt disgusted with herself. She switched the recording gear off. Lydia put an arm around her shoulders, and that made them start to shake. Susan willed their shaking to stop, but it didn't. Lydia said nothing for a while. When Susan opened her eyes again, Lydia was regarding her soberly. Susan blinked away the rainbow effects on her eyelashes, sniffled noisily again, smiled weakly.

"I don't know about me," said Lydia, "but you could use a drink."

Susan took a deep breath. "Oh, yes."

Lydia led Susan around a corner into one of the relatively undamaged shorefront streets, to a drinking den called The New Moon's Arms. The sign that swung above the door was a stylized orbital fort, petaled with solar power panels, bristling with weaponry.

"Old malcontent hangout," Lydia said as she held the door open. "I suppose it's still bugged." She laughed suddenly. "This time it'll be Gonatus who will be listening."

It was almost empty, and the barman was watching television, agog at the landings, begrudging the attention it took to pour them drinks. The pictures flickered silently; he was listening in with earphones.

"Amazing," he kept saying. "Amazing. A great day."

"A great day," Lydia agreed. She bought a clinking double handful of bottles. Susan turned away to sit down. Lydia caught her elbow.

"Outside," she said.

They returned to Astronaut Avenue and sat down with their

backs against one of the Volkov plinths. A selkie, walking past, glanced down at them from its swaying height, then strolled on, rubbernecking. Lydia wrenched the tops off two of the bottles. The drinks were sugarcane spirit diluted with a bittersweet juice. It tasted rough.

"What was that about Gonatus?" Susan asked. She had to talk about something else for a while. They would get back to what they had to talk about soon enough. From here, the prison island was visible on the horizon.

"I first met him last year," Lydia said, "about the time you people showed up. I took him to that bar back there for what I thought was a secure enough chat. I was a malcontent and he was an Illyrian spy. Still is, I suppose."

"Perhaps I should file that story with Junopolis Calls," said Susan, with a shaky laugh. "Give them one scoop at least, having missed today's big news."

"Oh, they'll know," said Lydia. "They'll spike it."

"You know my employers better than I do?"

"Yes," said Lydia, unabashed. "I've lived here longer than you have. A hell of a lot longer. It's not like good old free-wheeling, free-thinking Mingulay. They have security apparats here that go back to deep antiquity. And the Illyrian one, remember, is just a chunk of the old Nova Babylonian one that broke away."

"And Gonatus has just changed departments?"

Lydia smiled sourly. "Yes, you could see it like that. He's an interesting guy, in his way. Very intense, very sincere, strange though it is to say about a spy."

"What was his interest in you?"

"Well, I worked in the Space Authority, I had been in the Bright Star Cultures, and I had known Volkov."

They looked at each other. Susan put her drink down. The bottle drummed momentarily as it touched the pavement. "I think you have some explaining to do," she said.

After a while she interrupted and said: "You were once in love with Gregor? My *father*?"

"Yes," said Lydia. "Well, maybe, but . . . anyway, that's why it was so weird just now, seeing him just as he was when I knew him twelve years ago."

"Twelve—oh, right. I see. I think."

Susan pulled out a notebook—it was a local one, made from paper, which, as Matt had once said, sure cracked the screen-resolution problem—and started writing names and drawing lines.

"Fuck," she said. "It's lucky none of you had a sexually trans-missible disease."

Susan opened another bottle. The pain of her parents' refusal to intervene was still like a coiled snake in her belly. The alcohol was stunning it, but it would come back. She would vomit it out.

"So is this why you want to save them?"

"No," said Lydia, bleakly. "I want to save them because they were right. They don't deserve to end up against a wall."

"A wall is what all this feels like," said Susan. She knocked the back of her head on the plinth. It hurt a little. "And I'm bashing my head against it."

"Every wall has its weak points."

"The weakest point I can see," Susan said, "and the only one we can work on directly, is their bloody-minded refusal to es-cape." She clenched her fist in front of her. Her knuckles were grazed, she noticed from a distance. She looked out past the docks and the harbor to the island. "They could do it, you know. I could raise enough Multis to lift them off within minutes. But they'd have to be dragged, because they think they'd lose the argument by fleeing."

"Fuck them and their fucking arguments," said Lydia vehe-mently. "They'd rather die than lose, and they can't win. It's not a political argument, it's not even a cultural one, it's a . . . I don't know, a superstition. How is it that we can see past that, and the Multis can, and our friends themselves can, and most people can't? When did we lose our respect for the gods? How did we lose our fear?" She nibbled at her lower lip. "I don't remember, myself. I haven't feared the gods since I was a little girl. Not since after my first journey."

Susan frowned. "Space travel?" she said. "Lightspeed jumps? That's what we all have in common. Even the Marines who went along with our attack on the god."

Lydia shook her head. "Doesn't work. Your parents—"

"My parents don't fear the gods! They're just committed to the law taking its course for political reasons, cultural reasons. They think there's a line to hold—damn them."

"You're right," said Lydia. "And Esias and Faustina and all my family, even Voronar, an old saur who stuck around with us, they don't have that horror either, and they're pretty conservative. I mean, apart from Faustina"—she waved a finger at Susan's scribbled diagram—"they'd be happy to see Volkov shot, they detested what he did to this city, and Salasso and Matt mean nothing to them, but they don't *execrate* them like everyone seems to be assuming everyone does."

Susan thought over all the buzz and mutter she'd heard in the past months, weeks, hours. "Well, about everybody else, they're right."

"*Vox populi, vox Dei*, huh?" Lydia said bitterly.

The voice of the people is the voice of God. Which people, and which god?

"That's it," said Susan, with a cold feeling like water down her back. "That is it."

"What is?"

"The answer. It is space travel. I mean, I can see how it might be."

She felt a sudden surge of relief, perhaps no more than a rebound from her earlier dismay and despair, but it was something to feel hope again. She jumped up and drained her bottle and hurled it to crash on the rubble, and reached down to grab Lydia by the hand. "Come on, get up. We have to talk to some of the Bright Star Culture people. If I'm right, they'll feel the same as we do."

She fell over. Lydia helped her up and made to go back to the area around Port Station One.

"Not back there," Susan said. "One of the small parks."

Taking a complex route through side alleys to circle around the area of destruction and reconstruction, Lydia led the way unerringly to the nearest park. A Bright Star Culture ship squatted there, and around it stalls had been set up, by the humans and saurs and Multipliers on board and by those of the locals whose entrepreneurial talents had emerged from under the overturned bushel of the Modern Regime.

Lydia said: "This is just like something I saw before, on Novakkad. We're becoming a Bright Star Culture already."

"How long do you think trade will last, when the Multis can reproduce anything?"

Lydia looked at her sideways. "Good question. What the ships end up selling is space travel, and the access to space to gather the exotica to make more ships."

Susan grinned. "Good."

"Why?"

"I'll tell you later."

They walked over and started talking to the Traders. Almost every one of the new arrivals were shocked at what was being done to people whom they regarded—once the background had been quickly filled in—as heroes. Many of them hadn't even known about the advance expedition, and how it had saved them from being blasted from the skies as soon as they emerged from the jump. With the locals it was a different story entirely.

"These three?" The man they bought coffee from drew a finger across his throat. "They should have been shot months ago." He leaned closer. "You know, it's safe to say now, I always admired old Volkov, got that from my own old man, real old Modernist he was. But now, gods above—" He caught himself and chuckled nervously. "So to speak. Volkov and the others *killed a god*. The sooner they're rotting in Traitors' Pit, the better for all of us."

With that, quite unselfconsciously, he looked up and shivered.

"Hmm," said Susan. "Thanks for sharing your thoughts."

They wandered on. The coffee didn't really sober Susan, and she became less discreet in her questions. After one particularly awkward moment, the two women had to flee the park.

"Are we satisfied?" said Lydia, as they emerged halfway up Astronaut Avenue after running a kilometer through a warren of apartment blocks. Traffic was getting back to normal, but people were still hanging around and talking a lot. The early edition newspapers were being so eagerly snatched up that Susan felt vaguely in dereliction of duty.

Susan ducked her head around the corner. No signs of pursuit. "I don't know," she said, a little short of breath, heart pounding, "but I think we're safe."

"Good," said Lydia, putting her shoes back on as the cuts in her feet cleaned themselves. "Now, can you tell me what difference this is going to make?"

Susan told her. "It's Lithos," she said. "It's the god in the world, the god under our feet." She looked down and swayed. Lydia steadied her. "The gods in all the worlds. They fuck with our heads. It's only by space travel that we break the bond. You see?"

Lydia shook her head. "I don't see what difference it makes, except to make things worse. Nothing we do can make people who've never traveled through space change their minds about theicide."

Susan looked at her. Gods, the woman could be so stupid sometimes.

"Exactly," she said, straightening up and letting go of Lydia's arm and walking on very steadily. "So there's no need for our friends to die if it won't change anything."

"I think we can sell them that," Lydia said. "That one will fly." Her expression became distant, calculating. "Or if not that, something else. Do you have a phone number for any of the *Investigator* crew?"

"Oh, sure, I have them all."

Lydia jerked a thumb toward a newly repaired public phone stall. "Call them now."

"You aren't thinking of—"

"Maybe," said Lydia, "but the first thing we have to do is check this out with your friend Mr. Orange. Come to think of it," she added, "a lift to the island by skiff would not go amiss."

The Prison Department guards might have challenged and surrounded an autogyro, and impounded an unauthorized boat. They had a healthy respect for a Multiplier skiff. They let it land between the huts and didn't so much as give a dirty look to Susan, Lydia, and Mr. Orange. Matt, Volkov, and Salasso were easily enough spotted, strolling by the cliff at the far end of the small island.

Susan's heart sank a little at their eager expressions. They had affected fatalism, but they must have placed a lot of hope in the arrival of the Bright Star Cultures. She gave them the news of Elizabeth's unwavering decision.

"I'm sorry," she said.

"Bitch," said Matt.

"Bourgeois," said Volkov. He made it sound a nastier epithet than Matt's.

Salasso took it more stoically. "People change," he said.

"Let's find somewhere to sit down," Susan said. "Mr. Orange has something to tell you. There's a way out of this."

There was a windbreak shelter with benches and a table, built by prisoners, a hundred meters away. As they headed for it Matt rushed off to the hut. He came back with a pot of coffee and some mugs. The Multiplier draped itself across the supports like a gibbon and leaned down, its speaking mouth forward, and delivered its usual wheezy breathless ramble. People, saurs, everybody who lived on planets, it explained, were influenced by the minds in those planets and formed attachments to them. Only space travel could break those attachments. In the long run many more people would travel in space and would lose their fear of the gods. To die for the sake of not fearing the gods was both superfluous and futile.

"We thought you knew," said Mr. Orange.

The two men and the saur stared at Mr. Orange for a few moments.

"Fuck off," said Matt at last. "What difference does it make, if the space-going people have a rational attitude and the others don't? It's the others who have decided to kill us, and I am not going to let them off that hook. Let them see the consequences of their actions and their beliefs. That's what a public stoning is *for*! It's not to deter the wicked, it's to deter the righteous. You should know that, Susan. You were raised a gods-dammed Scoffer."

'Well, I was not!' said Lydia. She slammed a fist on the table. "I was raised a good Stoic, and I *became* a Volkovist. No thanks to you, Grigory, but behind all your Communist claptrap there was something great. And there is still something great there, in the Space Defense cadre who still look up to you. And in the new traders, the Bright Star people, and the Multipliers. Between them they have the power to rescue you, not to run away and hide but to defy the world and all the superstitious gods-fearing bastards that live on it like nits in its hair."

Volkov folded his arms. "And then what? Another revolution from above? I've lived through three already, two of them my fault. I'm not doing it again. Enough people have died here, and not only here. Enough."

"Adding three more deaths won't help," said Susan.

Volkov snorted. "It's not a question of what *helps*."

Susan turned to Salasso. "You can see it, can't you?" she pleaded. "You've tried to change minds, and now you know why you couldn't. It's not political, it's not cultural, it's a physical influence. You could—"

The saur's sneer was thinner than the men's, but no less scornful.

"Take my people on day trips to space?" His mouth stretched sideways a few millimeters. "Most of them are already in space, and no doubt on their way to fight the gods' battles somewhere else."

Susan felt herself shaking inside again, and tears escaping through that treacherous instability. She turned it to anger, and the anger away from herself.

"You can't just sit here and wait to die!" she said. "What honor or defiance is there in that? It's just the same wretched passivity you say you're fighting against. Go away—*come* away! Join the Multiplier migration, join *us*. There's no need to hide now, we're here, and we're going away."

She did not know if she meant that. She was too various. It was the small offspring within her talking, just as her mother had feared. It was what her mother was fighting. She could almost sympathize; or rather, she could, and she could not.

"You might have a point," said Matt, reluctantly. His voice sounded as if it was being dragged out with hooks. "I mean, why push it, if these people can't change no matter what—"

The skiff came out of nowhere—not out of a jump, but out of an aerial manouevre so fast that its hull glowed red as it halted right beside them. The shock wave was still rocking the gazebo as a dozen heavily-armed men jumped out and surrounded them, plasma rifles leveled.

One of the men removed his helmet to reveal a pair of earphones, which he likewise removed.

"You were right, Lydia," said Gaius Gonatus. "We're still listening."

The sun was in their eyes and they had disdained the offer of blindfolds. Susan was at the front of the crowd, with the other reporters. She could zoom her camera, zoom the mike, and watch and hear them all. It was only her concentration on this, her fierce determination that her draft of history would be the one to get through all the edits and be in all the books and tapes about the event, that kept her from weeping. That and the thought that weeping would be self-indulgent, because she was not mourning the two men and the saur. She would be weeping for the loss of her mother, who in clinging to her humanity had become inhumane.

The officer with three black cloths over his wrist was holding out two packets. "Hemp or tobacco?"

"I'll go for a joint," said Volkov.

"Let's share it and a cigarette," said Matt.

"All right."

"I think I wish to die consciously," said Salasso. "Hemp would tend to prevent that. Therefore, I will take a cigarette. I have on occasion wondered what their attraction is."

"They're bad for your health," said Matt, predictably.

They accepted the officer's offer of a light, and he returned to the squad. "You may address the public while you smoke," he said.

Volkov and Matt glanced at each other. Matt shrugged and waved his cigarette. They swapped their smokes around.

"I wish I respected you all enough to despise you," Volkov said to the outstretched microphones and to the world. "But you aren't worth it. You have chosen to become part of an alien culture. That is your choice. What will you do when the next alien culture comes along, one which may be less easily adapted to? You will have to fight, as I taught you to fight. I hope I taught you well."

He looked as though he was about to throw the diminished cigarette on the ground, but Matt reached out for it and passed him the hemp.

"Ah," said Matt, exhaling gratefully, "there's nothing like a butt for a roach. If you're looking for words of wisdom from me, you can fucking forget it. I've had a good run and I have no complaints. Volkov was defending the human race according to his lights, and so was I. Come on, man, give Salasso that roach."

"Thank you," said Salasso, taking it and sucking hard. "The small quantity remaining should not affect my lucidity. Tell Bishlayan I love her, and tell Delavar I quite liked him, on the whole. As for most of the rest of my species, they have feared the gods, they feared the hominidae, and now they fear the Multipliers. I have shown that I feared none of them. I have killed a god, I have had friends among the hominidae, including Matt and including Elizabeth and Gregor, and when my blood runs out it will be full of Spiders."

"Gods above, Salasso," said Matt, "you never told—"

The rifles, as ever, had the last word.

Coda: State of Play

T HERE IS NO meanwhile. But, across a hundred thousand
years and light-years, the events of A.C. 10,350 and the
Seasonally Adjusted Year of Our Lord 2360 were approximately
in step with the year A.D. 2362.

In the year A.D. 2357 the god in the asteroid 10049 Lora
made one of its regular close approaches to Earth; and, as had
become customary, a delegation from the Military Subcommittee
of the Executive Committee of the Solar Commonwealth came
out to visit and consult. Their skiffs hovered above its pitted
surface, gently docking with the vast web of the interface that
gave them access to the wealth of information in its many minds.

Greetings were exchanged, something that the humans managed through the combined actions of a myriad quantum computers and the god with the equivalent of the twitch of a toe.
With some slightly higher-level processing it conveyed its thanks
and congratulations on the defeat of the octopod invasion. The
humans acknowledged that the war against the Spiders had been
long and terrible, but that driving the alien invaders from the
Solar System had been worth the cost. They mentioned the cost
with a certain urgency. The long-term damage to Earth's atmosphere and biosphere, and the losses to the many habitats across
the system, had been substantial and painful.

The god thought they were taking a very short-term view,
given that habitats could be replaced within decades and the

atmosphere and biosphere restored to something like equilibrium within a million years. It did not, however, convey this thought to the delegation. Much as it appreciated their defense, and much as it appreciated their cooperation in maintaining a blessed radio silence throughout the system—their plethora of tight-band laser comms were only a minor annoyance—the billions of humans of the Commonwealth were, it well knew, touchy. Especially, for some reason, those who had lived in space habitats. It would be deeply unfortunate if more humans had to move off the damaged planetary surface and settle in space habitats. It would be even more unfortunate if their expanding, though cautious, skiff and lightspeeder operations were to encounter the saurs who remained in and around the Solar System. The humans' lightspeed expedition to Alpha Centauri had been a close call, it had been given to understand.

The god was beginning to experience a certain impatience. The universe was full of much more interesting phenomena than this multicellular infestation. Briefly, for a second or two, several of its inner civilizations devoted the equivalent of centuries of human effort to investigating the possibility of resetting the planet's evolution completely, and of arranging a simultaneous set of collisions between habitats and stray heavy-metal junk. On balance the decision was negative. Even for the gods, some exercises in celestial mechanics were just too complicated.

Even for the gods, some inspirations take time to emerge. When the box is large enough, even the greatest minds sometimes have difficulty in thinking outside it. But once it had succeeded in doing so, it took very little time for the god to communicate its inspiration to the delegation of the Military Subcommittee. They were greatly delighted with the description it gave them of hundreds of underpopulated habitable planets, and deeply grateful for the coordinates it provided to guide lightspeed jumps of a hundred thousand light-years.

They assured the god that building the ships to evacuate the entire human species would take them only about five years, and they promised to keep the noise down.

At the edge of New Babylon's old industrial zone, near where the coal wastes leached into ponds, was a deep hole known as the Traitors' Pit. Only the senior officers of the Ninth knew exactly where it was. The material consigned to it was always delivered at night, in an unmarked truck, and thrown in without ceremony or compunction. On this particular night two colonels, their uniforms concealed under rough overalls, heaved three bodies—two of them large, one small—over the side and waited only to hear the thuds before they drove away.

After a couple of days a Multiplier emerged from the shaft. It was not large, about the size of a cat, but it had assimilated, one way or another, many millions of its fellows. It had survived an intense process of natural selection. Its mind was limited and fragmentary, its obscure sense of self flagrantly contradicted by its disparate memories. It scuttled off across the waste ground with a sense of accomplishment, both from its long and perilous ascent and from the memories it had assimilated. It was eager to sort them and share them and acquire more.

It remembered having hands with four digits, only one of which was opposable, and with those hands controlling a skiff that skimmed across endless forests that looked strangely like the complex pipework it could see in the distance. It remembered swaying on two legs, through a city of lights, and shouting in a strange language while colorful explosions lit the sky overhead and a cold liquid in the mouth made the belly warm. It remembered different hands, with five digits this time, moving over an instrument covered with glyphs. It remembered looking out from behind a transparent curved pane at a red, hot surface, while the air hung heavy and still around it and the breath sounded loud in the ears. It remembered skin cool and yet warming, under hands, and hair long or short brushing the skin that felt that electric touch. It remembered looking at stars, and at the gardens of the gods.

What memories, it thought, for one so small to have. It turned two of its eyes upward, and watched as new lights appeared in the sky.

Overhead, quietly, without any fuss, the starships were coming in.